PALACES OF DESIRE

PALACES OF DESIRE

KAREN ALEXANDER

Coward, McCann & Geoghegan, Inc.
New York

Copyright © 1978 by Karen Alexander

All rights reserved. This book, or parts thereof, may not be reproduced in any form without permission in writing from the publisher. Published on the same day in Canada by Longman Canada Limited, Toronto.

Printed in the United States of America

HISTORICAL NOTE

A child presumed to be Louis XVII, the uncrowned, ten-year-old King of France and son of the guillotined Louis XVI, was pronounced dead of natural causes in a filthy, solitary cell in the Temple in Paris on the eighth of June, 1795.

The boy's grave may still be seen in the little cemetery of the church of Sainte-Marguerite, 36 rue Saint-Bernard, with its small stone cross engraved with a line from Lamentations, "Behold and see if there be any sorrow like unto my sorrow."

For many years stories persisted that the little king had escaped prison, and that another child had been substituted for him. At last in 1894 the body was exhumed before reliable witnesses. Medical experts all agreed that the bones they saw belonged to a boy between the ages of fifteen and eighteen, and could not possibly be those of the true King Louis XVII.

1

France in the Spring of 1789

Six paces across the room, ten along the outside wall with its long windows giving on the Parterres du Nord. Even in her mood of exasperation, Nicole hated to walk on the exquisite Aubusson carpet, and kept to the parquet floor, where she paused every few minutes and stared disbelievingly at the majestic gardens and imperial park. Then she would sigh again and resume her pacing. After five lonely days, she could not wait to escape from the imprisonment of this luxurious suite.

Was it only five days ago that, trembling with excitement, she had first set foot in the royal palace of Versailles, expecting to receive a warm welcome from the guardian she had never met, the clever, powerful man her father had picked to protect her after his death?

But the liveried servants of the Duke of Falkland, British Ambassador to France, had made one excuse after another: His Grace the Duke hunts with the king at Fontainebleau, His Grace must attend the queen at Petit Trianon, His Grace once again sends his regrets, but hopes to make the acquaintance of Mademoiselle de Clervaux upon his return from a journey of short duration.

She tried to press the British servants for more information, but they offered her stony indifference, or pretended to be unable to understand either her French or the slow, careful English she shyly ventured. Once, when she tried to stroll in the corridor, a footman blocked her way with a bow, and led her back to the duke's apartment. So she had little choice but to endure the frustrating delay with patience. Sometimes Nicole felt as if she had passed her whole life waiting. Alone or almost alone, waiting . . . waiting.

By choice her scholarly father, Robert de Clervaux, had lived the last years of his life in isolation, loving only his estate of sunny vineyards, his extensive library, and his beautiful daughter. Once, in better health, he had traveled widely and written books that gave him a distinguished reputation as a military historian. But always he had shunned the other Bordelais gentry as hopeless philistines, and had left the motherless Nicole alone to grow up a quiet child who read too many books, and found her pleasure in daydreams of adventure and romance. Because of her father's influence, she believed herself somehow superior to her neighbors, and came to have expectations of marvelous, if undefined, privileges and pleasures.

All during his final illness, she had nursed Robert and suffered with him, wondering if the pain would ever end. But now he was mercifully dead, and she had been summoned to live in the household of the Duke of Falkland—and to enter the glittering world of the royal court at Versailles.

What a miraculous change it would be from her lonely world, where, even though she was eighteen years old, she had never had a single suitor. Now her future husband would inevitably be chosen from the wealthy and sophisticated nobles at court, barons, counts, princes, even handsome young members of the royal family itself. Nicole was agog with the romantic future she envisioned for herself: fêtes, balls, admirers, courtships —perhaps more than one! she dreamed, with rather guilty pleasure—and finally a brilliant marriage to a man she truly loved.

But what if she were not really a beautiful girl after all! Sheltered as she had been, she had no real evidence that her appearance would please a man, only the loving assurance of an indulgent father and a few overheard whispers by servant girls. Her own belief that she was unusually attractive could well be a lonely, wishful delusion. Once again she examined her face in the cheval mirror in her room. Staring back at her were large, serious brown eyes set in long black lashes under arching brows. Her dark eyes made a dramatic contrast with her fair skin and thick ash-blond hair, which fell in silky waves on her shoulders. Her nose was small and delicate, her lips full and red.

After carefully locking her door, she removed all her clothes and stood before the mirror to decide with complete honesty her worth to a husband. Someday a man would look at her in this state—but no, she did not want to think about that now. She studied her high, full breasts, her slender waist, and the hips and bottom that were as prettily rounded as statues of marble nymphs she had seen. In spite of her puritanism, Nicole had to approve the graceful nude figure in the looking glass.

Here she was in the heart of the court, so close to pleasures and triumphs, yet so tantalizingly far! All she could do was peek out the double doors of the duke's suite at the passing nobles—usually in a little procession led by a pair of footmen and followed by a flock of attendants in clothing of varying degrees of importance—or servants bearing trays of food and wine; valets with armloads of clothes, hats, or wigs; and maids scurrying as fast as their feet could carry them.

Finally Nicole could stand her confinement no longer and slipped out, darting down the corridor as though the palace guard were after her. Memorizing landmarks—a statue of ancient lovers, a mirror larger than any she had ever seen before, a huge crystal chandelier in a vestibule of pink marble—she at last found an outside door, tugged it open herself, and ran across the terrace.

How marvelous it was to fill her lungs with cool, fresh air! Exhilarated, she backed away from the palace recklessly, and almost fell down an unexpected flight of stairs. How enormously wide the palace was, the largest building Nicole had ever seen. The size of everything was overwhelming —palace, gardens, lakes, and forests, even the vast blue sky itself, unblemished by a single cloud. What a joyous day it was! What an incredibly lucky girl she was to live at Versailles!

Strolling groups of noblemen and women in rich attire enjoyed the gardens, sometimes stopping to greet one of the horsemen. An occasional carriage traveled the *allées* lined with statuary and elms or ash trees. Fortunately, no one seemed to notice the lone girl in her modest country clothing. Encouraged, Nicole wandered among the flower beds enclosed by precisely clipped hedges, and paused to dip her hand in a fountain with a bronze sea serpent spouting water fifty feet in the air.

Suddenly a man's voice behind her made her jump a foot and almost fall into the fountain. "Are you looking for someone, mademoiselle? For me, perhaps?"

"No, no! I'm only—I'm merely enjoying—" she stammered, and stumbled away from him. His eyes under elevated brows bore into her, as though to convey some unspoken message. Then she saw another man, companion to the first, wearing the same leering smirk.

Nicole did not try to disguise her fear and ran toward the palace without looking behind her. Even with her sheltered background, she knew they meant to use her in some dreadful way. *Yes,* she told herself, she understood what they wanted, and trembled with disgust. *How dare they think she could possibly consent to—*! Finally turning around, she decided she had lost them. But her enthusiasm had been replaced by discouragement, and she reluctantly entered the palace and searched out the duke's apartment.

Falkland's majordomo, usually imperturbable, betrayed annoyance at her excursion, and announced her name with a certain emphasis to the nobleman and woman who were obviously waiting for her in the duke's salon. The rotund, elderly gentleman, dressed in a stylish tailcoat, embroidered waistcoat with conspicuous jeweled watch, culottes, and even a sword, lumbered to his feet and kissed her hand.

Surely this could not be the duke! Nicole tried to conceal her shock and disappointment, then realized with surprise how much she had wanted him to be young and handsome, not old, stout, and grandfatherly like this man. But Falkland *was* young! She knew his age, about thirty-four, some twenty years younger than her father, younger even than her mother would have been. Quickly she composed her thoughts. This man could not possibly be her guardian.

It was the woman who took command of the interview. She was years younger than the gentleman, though her true age could hardly be discerned beneath the careful makeup; and she was elegantly clothed in a gown of striped silk offering a generous display of bosom, and wore a high coiffure fantastically decorated with artificial flowers, berries, and even a small bird. She said they were the Marquis and Marquise de Vaucroze, and begged Nicole to do her the honor of addressing her by her given name, Sybille. "We are going to be very great friends. The Duke of Falkland has asked us to see to your every need, provide you with companionship, and spare you the sort of boredom that drove you to commit such an—ah, indiscretion as wandering alone in the palace gardens. Fortunately, you encountered no one of importance. Dear child, perhaps you thought your simple clothes gave you a protective anonymity or conveyed the impression that you were only a servant; but in reality, even servants at Versailles dress with more—shall we say—style. As you found out to your own dismay, you were taken to be a little trollop from the town, come to ply her trade on the palace grounds."

Though Nicole recoiled with shame, the marquise ignored her reaction. "Doubtless you did not realize that until you can be presented to Queen Marie Antoinette, you are simply not here; you must be invisible; you absolutely must not venture forth from the confines of this apartment. Now you will immediately ask when you can undergo the honor of presentation, and I can only tell you that proper application has already been made. And for now we have our hands full! First of all, I must obtain for you some experienced maids. None of your country girls will do—" The marquise held up her hand to silence Nicole's protest. "And a coiffeuse and a couturière—my own, perhaps, if she can find the time, though, greedy woman, she has lately increased her charges to unbelievable heights. Fortunately, we can ask the duke to make you a very generous allowance."

Nicole could control her mounting irritation no longer. "*Madame la marquise*, I beg to inform you that I am not poor. I have no need of charity from the duke, as he must be aware—"

"Oh, my dear! Forgive me! Of course I meant a dispersal of your own funds. I am well aware of the large size of your inheritance: fifty thousand hectares of highly productive land in the Haut-Médoc; a dozen farms —or *châteaux*, as you call them—one of which is your own home, Beaux-Clervaux, a beautiful old stone house; wineries at each farm save two, bottling some very distinguished red wines and a few lesser whites; and all operations netting as much as one hundred thousand livres after a good harvest. You see I am well informed about you after all!"

Nicole was shocked and suspicious. "Why in the world would my guardian disclose information to you that I hardly know myself?" Who was this annoying woman with her superior airs? What kind of man was Falkland that he would gossip loosely with this frivolous woman?

"Do not be alarmed, dear Nicole. It is entirely necessary for me to possess such information if I am"—the marquise paused for dramatic effect—"to arrange your marriage." She laughed merrily at the sudden change in Nicole's expression. "There! How relieved you are. Naturally, you could not know. Of course, Falkland would do nothing unethical, and he has no intention of neglecting your future, so he has very wisely delegated this task to me."

Nicole asked anxiously if the marquise had already taken any steps, but was assured that she had been waiting to meet her, and intended to consider Nicole's wishes in every possible way. "We will work together to find just the right sort of young man!" the marquise gushed, with an excess of zeal Nicole instinctively distrusted.

Changing her tone, the older woman asked, almost coyly, "You have never met the duke, have you?"

"No, madame."

The marquise smiled to herself as she subjected Nicole to a leisurely examination. "And he has never seen you." Then she gave a rueful little laugh. "What a lucky man Falkland always is!"

Suddenly, she leaned forward intensely. "May I be frank with you? I find complete honesty so much the better policy, don't you agree? I am relieved to meet you, for I had feared that you were the natural daughter of the duke." Nicole could only stare at her with astonishment. "I dreaded the job of arranging such a marriage. It is one thing to find a husband for a little heiress from Bordeaux, and another to provide appropriately for the bastard child of a British duke who carries the blood of the ancient kings of Scotland in his veins."

Nicole jumped to her feet, abandoning any pretense of courtesy. "I won't allow you to utter such an insult to my mother! What you are accusing her of is impossible! My mother was a virtuous young woman of twenty. The duke was only sixteen. A boy of sixteen! How can you think she would prefer him to my father, who was so kind, so adoring—"

"But you confirm by your unreasonable anger that you too suspect she was in love with Falkland."

"No, never! She worshiped my father!"

"How can you know that when she died the day you were born? What you really mean is, *you* worshiped your father."

"How unfair, how cruel you are!" Then Nicole paused, and anguishing a moment, reluctantly asked, "Has the duke said . . . anything . . . to make you believe . . . ?"

"No, my dear, he has said nothing—though of course he would not. I had only my own suspicions, based on a long acquaintance with Falkland. . . ." She glanced briefly at her husband, whose slumped posture made it difficult to tell if he were awake or asleep. "I have watched dozens of women make fools of themselves over the duke."

"I assure you my mother was not one of them!" Nicole exclaimed, with fierce pride. "Many years ago, the duke passed a year at Beaux-Clervaux to study military history with my father. In the summer of the same year, Lucienne, a young Norman girl, who was betrothed to my father, came with her chaperons to spend some months with her future husband. Servants have told me that Falkland fell madly in love with her. He made no effort to conceal his intense ardor; but everyone, including Lucienne, regarded it as amusing adolescent foolishness. Apparently, he had convinced himself she would actually marry him. On the day the banns of her marriage to my father were read, Falkland made a melodramatic scene, then departed for England, never to return to Beaux-Clervaux. He and Lucienne never saw each other again.

"In a few weeks my parents were married, on Christmas Eve of that year. It was exactly one year later that I was born. My mother died the same night. She died on Christmas Eve, the first anniversary of their marriage." Even the supercilious marquise had visibly softened at this story. "So you see, it is absolutely impossible for Falkland to have been my father!"

"But I already knew that as soon as I saw how blond and petite you are. Falkland is unusually tall and has hair as black as a Saracen's." As Nicole began to relax, the marquise laughed to herself at some secret joke, then added teasingly, "I am sure you will think he looks more like a pirate than a courtier and diplomat," and narrowed her eyes to study Nicole's face for signs of awakening interest.

Who was this woman who had Falkland's close confidence, yet was so callous as to sully her mother's memory, and now vulgar enough to try to pique Nicole's romantic interest in a man she had only thought of as a substitute father? What kind of relationship did the marquise have with the duke? Surely she was older than he was, even though Nicole had to admit grudgingly that she was still beautiful. One thing was certain—Nicole did not like or trust the Marquise de Vaucroze, and shuddered at the realization that her own future marriage was in her hands.

Despite such misgivings, Nicole had little choice but to submit to the marquise's domination, and cooperate with the new servants who took over her life. After a maid had patronizingly surveyed Nicole's few dresses, the marquise issued orders to her couturière for elaborate court gowns of silk and velvet, less formal dresses of fine linen and India cotton, riding habits, pelisses edged with fur, flounced petticoats, robes de chambre, nightgowns, and undergarments of the finest muslin. A modiste would deliver frilly caps, and huge, high-crowned hats wrapped in yards of gauze or wide, ruched ribbons. Then the marquise bought an endless list of accessories without any apparent consideration of cost: slippers of silk, brocade, velvet, and kid; hose with embroidered clocks, bouffant kerchiefs to cover the shoulders; fob watches; and fans, gloves, drawstring purses, muffs, and parasols of every material.

Nicole was barely consulted for her opinion—"Do you prefer blue? No, I think not; green is your color"—and required to stand half of every day in tedious fittings. Yet by the end of a fortnight she could not help but be thrilled by the elegant clothes already collecting in her armoire, and grateful to Sybille, from whom these riches seemed to flow.

Nicole had grown accustomed to running in and out of the suite of rooms assigned to the Marquis and Marquise de Vaucroze, since she had been directed to obtain the marquise's approval after every fitting. One morning, wearing a half-finished satin ball gown held together by pins, Nicole tapped on the outer door of their apartment. She had just seen one of their footmen hurrying away on some errand, and was not surprised when the door pushed open on an empty salon. Shivering in the low-cut dress and pricked by pins in her waist, she decided not to wait for a servant, and knocked on the door of the marquise's bedchamber. A muffled voice inside seemed to call to her, and she turned the knob.

A canopied bed with its draperies fully closed stood against the far wall of the large room. In the foreground was a breakfast table set with porcelain and silver, and attended by several waiters. Seated at one end, wearing an elaborately ruffled peignoir, was the marquise, her fork arrested in midair by the shock of Nicole's entry.

At the opposite end, a tall, ruggedly muscular man, his black hair tied at the back of his neck with a velvet bow, put down his cup with icy control, then dabbed at his lips with a napkin. He arose slowly, silently, all eyes riveted on him. He was wearing a collarless white shirt, dark breeches, silk hose, and buckled shoes, but no coat, waistcoat, stock, or cravat. Without once looking directly at Nicole, he crossed the room to a distant door.

As soon as it closed behind him, Sybille exhaled a great sigh and rolled her eyes heavenward. "My dear child! Whatever do they do in the Bordelais for a moment of privacy! Were you never taught at home to have yourself announced before you barge in on heaven knows what intimate scene?"

"But there were no servants in sight and I knocked on both doors. I was sure—"

"*Mon Dieu,* have you been here all these weeks and not learned that at Versailles we do not knock, we *scratch* on the door—unobtrusively, discreetly, inoffensively. At court we do not pound like carpenters!"

Nicole's eyes began to fill with tears and her voice quavered as she began, "I cannot tell you, madame, how dreadfully sorry I am—"

"Then calm yourself, you silly girl," the marquise said sourly.

"But who was that? Was it, was he—?"

"You know perfectly well it was the Duke of Falkland."

"But he did not speak to me—or even look at me!"

"Dear heaven, how could he in such a circumstance!"

"Perhaps he did not know who I was—" Nicole began hopefully.

"Of course he knew who you were!" the marquise snapped. "Who else could be so gauche?"

2

"Mademoiselle, wake up! You must hurry!" Someone was shaking her. With great difficulty Nicole roused herself from a gloomy dreamland and fought to remember where she was. A servant was impatiently trying to lift her into a sitting position. "Here, drink this; it will wake you," the woman said, and thrust a hot cup of chocolate into her hands.

Nicole blinked at the still-shuttered windows and saw that dawn had barely begun to break. The early hour and the brisk, almost rude treatment by the servant could only mean that she was being sent home to Beaux-Clervaux!

All day long after she had blundered into the marquise's chamber, Nicole had hung about the duke's apartment waiting for the inevitable interview when he would chastise her for her stupidity. Suspense built as the morning passed with no sign of him. Both her luncheon and her dinner were served in the usual elaborate style at a table set for one. It was only after she had spent an unpleasant hour trying to force herself to eat the evening meal that she saw a tray being carried out of his *cabinet* or office. So the duke intended to avoid her! Somehow she hated that more than receiving his rebuke.

Tossing on her rumpled bed that night, believing sleep would never come, her mind raced with almost hysterical fears. How long would Falkland shun her? Clearly he could not avoid her forever, unless—unless he might actually intend to send her home! But surely he could not be so cruel! On the other hand, he obviously had no place in his life for a young female charge. For a month he had been too busy or too indifferent even to receive her. And now! Now that she had invaded his privacy, had actually burst into a bedchamber where he had probably just finished making love to a woman who was not his wife!

Nicole cringed as she relived the terrible moment when he had coldly refused to look at her. How icily contemptuous he had been! How cruel his dark handsome face, how scornful his black eyes—were they really black, or perhaps dark gray like slate? She had never dreamed he would be so handsome, so young and tall and strong. Of course the marquise had tried to tell her, had even teased her about him. . . .

The marquise! The thought of Sybille made her seethe. Somehow everything was the fault of the marquise. If only Sybille did not exist, the duke would have to tend to Nicole himself, would become her friend, would not have palmed her off on that dreadful woman. That woman who was his mistress! At last Nicole now understood the shameful source of Sybille's influence and power.

How could her father's trusted friend be so immoral, so sinful? How could he have an adulterous relationship with a woman right under her husband's nose? Nicole could not help picturing the guilty lovers: Sybille in one of her absurd negligées on the lacy pillows from which she had often lectured Nicole; and Falkland—a heavy dark lock perhaps falling across his brow—embracing her passionately, kissing her with burning lips.

Nicole shuddered and shook her head to dislodge such thoughts. She sat up, lit a candle, and tried to read. But her thoughts would not be tamed. She could not help wondering how he could let himself make love to this older woman, who was surely far less attractive than Nicole herself!

What would it feel like if he took her in his arms and crushed his angry mouth on her lips—what would it feel like to lie in his powerful arms in some lacy bed . . . ?

But she must stop! How wicked! How could such an impossible fantasy ever occur to her? Aching with fatigue and a strange diffuse yearning, she almost hoped he would send her home and she would never see him again.

Nicole could hardly sip the steaming chocolate the maid had given her, and set it on her bedside commode with a trembling hand. The woman was already rummaging in her wardrobe among the court dresses Nicole had never used. What irony that she would wear one of the new gowns on the long, dusty ride home to Beaux-Clervaux!

Then, in rapid succession, two extra maids, a dressmaker, and the marquise's own coiffeuse bustled into Nicole's chamber. Dear heaven! She would surely not be given a special hairstyle for her coach ride into exile! Then the first maid, whom she had thought so brusque, said with a friendly twinkle in her eye, "Hurry yourself, mademoiselle, we have little time. It will take us two hours to prepare you for your presentation at the queen's levée!" Nicole uttered a cry of delight and jumped out of bed.

They offered her the best new chemise and drawers, trimmed with Alençon lace, then laced her stays tighter than ever before. After several soft cotton petticoats, they covered her with a commodious garment, unfamiliar to her, which they called a combing jacket.

One maid unlocked a cupboard in a corner of her room, revealing a small empty closet. Nicole was placed on a stool before the door, which was open at such a level that she could bend her head forward, her neck on a padded support, and let her long hair fall into the enclosure. Then the coiffeuse poured scoops of white flour over her hair and worked it in carefully with her hands. Several times Nicole was ordered to shake her head vigorously, and the hairdresser increased her speed as the dust billowed into the room. Just when they all began to choke and cough, Nicole was assisted from her stool, the powder vigorously fanned back into the closet, and the cupboard door banged shut.

She winced as she looked in the mirror at the unruly mass of dusty hair. To her surprise her hair looked more gray than white, but the coiffeuse explained that the current style, set as always by Marie Antoinette, called for a fairly light powdering. While the woman brushed her hair, Nicole wrinkled her nose in distaste. Her young face was surrounded by the hair of a fifty-year-old. Why in the world would women deliberately try to age themselves in this way?

But as the coiffeuse's expert hands stiffened her hair with pastes and pomades, then piled it high on rats made of horsehair, Nicole was amazed to see herself transformed into a woman of dignity and importance. She looked as proud, regal, and stately as she imagined the queen herself. The hairdresser finished her creation by pinning a festoon of pearls just above each temple. Finally she placed at the highest point, more than a foot above the hairline, three white ostrich plumes, which, she told Nicole, were required for all court appearances.

As soon as Nicole stood up, a strange basket-like framework of wicker, extending far out over each hip, was fastened to her waist. With these *paniers* she would be an unbelievable four feet across, albeit a far less cumbersome width, the servants assured her, than a six-foot set Marie Antoinette occasionally wore. Over the framework, a maid dropped a rose and white striped silk petticoat—stripes were the current rage, Nicole had learned—then a gown of heavy rose satin, cut like a full-length coat open in the front to reveal the petticoat. Nicole was relieved when the deep neckline was partly covered by a white gauze fichu.

As the seamstress fussed interminably over the gown, Nicole stared at herself in the cheval mirror. Certainly the apparition was a very grand court lady, but it was nobody she had ever seen before. Only one more Comtesse de so-and-so, one more of the nearly indistinguishable noblewomen at court. Nicole shrugged a little. Her own natural beauty and individuality had been completely disguised.

At last the marquise arrived and exclaimed admiringly, then, before Nicole knew what she was doing, fastened two strands of pearls around her neck. Nicole quickly protested, "I have my own jewels, my mother's jewels. I would much prefer—!"

"No doubt you would, but I have no time to pick over your mother's things, and these pearls are the required size and length for a girl of your position. What, my dear! Have you never had your ears pierced! Dear child, how old *are* you? Then you will simply have to go without earrings," the marquise announced, with a grimace. "Now pay attention! I am going to have my hands full teaching you to curtsy." Nicole was forced to practice dipping straight down to the floor without bending her back, until she thought her legs would break.

Then came a scratch at the door, and she was hurried down one corridor after another, only to be kept waiting in some antechamber where she had to perch on a stool, her *paniers* preventing her from fitting in any armchair. Her only companions were the wife of an ambassador and her two daughters, none of whom spoke French.

At last the four women were called into a chamber so crowded with standing courtiers that it was impossible even to guess the size and importance of the room. Nicole could only look straight up. The high ceiling had an elaborate painting of statuesque goddesses and fat cupids cavorting in the clouds.

The entrance of another party forced her flat against the brocade wall. Over the crowd noises of whispering and coughing, she could hear a man's voice calling out a series of names. Soon an usher grasped her elbow, and she squeezed forward with great difficulty, brushing so tightly against several courtiers that her *paniers* and dress were twisted. She finally reached a circle of settees on which a privileged half dozen men and women and even some small children were seated. In the center of the circle, before an ornate dressing table, surrounded by noble attendants including the Marquise de Vaucroze, sat Marie Antoinette.

The small, delicate queen, charged with nervous energy, was twisting in her chair to the consternation of her hairdresser, gesturing with little bird-like movements, and exclaiming with girlish excitement at the array of bonnets, lengths of fabric, and pieces of jewelry presented for her approval. She loved them all and bought them all. Her enthusiasm was contagious. The whole crowd strained to hear every word, and laughed and exulted with her.

Marie Antoinette was dressed in a robin's-egg gown of moiré taffeta, cascades of lace ruffles at her wrists and bodice, and a wide striped bow between her breasts. Though her hair had been dulled by powder, it was obviously auburn. Her huge blue eyes were playful, beguiling, shameless. The only imperfect detail was the famous prominent lower lip, the hallmark of the Austrian House of Hapsburg. But the dominant feature was her white, glowing, transparent skin, amply displayed by the low cut of her gown. Every woman at court drenched herself with rice powder to imitate the milky perfection of the queen's complexion.

The usher announced in a clear voice, "Mademoiselle de Clervaux"—nothing more. Nicole remembered to make her curtsy, unfortunately somewhat stiff and shallow, as the queen glanced briefly in her direction, looking more at Nicole's dress than her face. Almost imperceptibly, the queen nodded her head. It was the crucial sign of royal acceptance.

As Nicole regained her balance, the queen turned halfway around to scan the room, then spotting someone, bent the upper half of her body forward in a showy gesture meant to convey much honor. A man was returning the bow. Nicole recognized with a start the Duke of Falkland, whom she had not noticed before.

He vanished as suddenly as he had appeared, and Nicole was soon led out of the queen's salon by the same usher and deposited in the antechamber. When she finally gathered that she had been dismissed, she returned to the obscurity of her own room. After more than two hours of preparation, she had stood less than a minute in the presence of the queen, who had not deigned to speak to her.

But Marie Antoinette's lack of attention was a small matter. Nicole was thrilled that Falkland had not abandoned her after all, but had graciously functioned as her sponsor, as he naturally would be expected to do. In fact, the suddenness of her presentation might be due to his intervention. How could she ever have been silly enough to doubt him? Apparently, her loneliness, fear of the court, and dislike of the marquise had taxed her nerves almost to the breaking point. After a maid helped her out of the dress and *paniers* and unlaced her stays, she dismissed the girl, then sat on her bed gazing dreamily out the window and hugging her knees with anticipation. Now her new life would really begin.

"At last here comes Falkland to greet you!" the marquise whispered urgently in Nicole's ear. "Curtsy to him, silly girl; he is a duke, not a wine waiter!"

Nicole had not had long to enjoy her daydreams. Sybille had begun a stream of instructions, which kept her changing from outfit to outfit for the rest of the day. By ten o'clock she was nearly exhausted, and longed to shed the painful stays and pinching slippers. But the nightly reception for the whole court had only just commenced in the Galerie des Glaces.

The incomparable hall glittered with the reflection of heavy chandeliers in the seventeen tall mirrors that reached from the floor to the wide gilded cornice and the vaulted ceiling covered with paintings. Now the crowd of courtiers had begun to pour in the double, mirrored doors.

As Falkland approached, Nicole dropped into a painfully deep curtsy, then tottered as her leg muscles cramped. Gallantly, the duke caught her and assisted her to her feet with one hand behind her waist. Like a disappointed schoolmistress, the marquise admonished her for her clumsiness and urged her to practice. Falkland suavely assured Nicole that such difficulties were entirely normal. But Nicole could only stare at him, her poise shattered and the carefully worded greeting she had dreamed of making him completely forgotten.

She found herself looking into his dusky, deep-set eyes—yes, they were gray, not black or brown, gray like the lochs of Scotland—and felt terribly flustered. He was not at all what she had imagined, not stern or haughty or contemptuous, any more than he was the kindly father figure she had believed in for years.

His eyes twinkled with a kind of idle amusement, as though he was laughing at her a little under his smooth veneer. His words and manners were perfect; but something about him—perhaps it was the fleeting vacant look in his eyes or his lazy, careless smile or the way he let his hand linger at her waist, then as absently removed it—suggested that he was jaded and world-weary, that nothing had any great meaning for him anymore.

As he made a charming but not very sincere-sounding apology for his long absence, she began to regain her composure, and soon became confident, optimistic, almost euphoric. She even liked the marquise—or at least, disliked her less—as the older woman stood watching them knowingly.

What could Sybille be thinking? Even if she could read Nicole's mind, she would discover only gratitude and polite respect for the duke, Nicole told herself. And, in truth, a certain thrill of pleasure just to be standing near him. Her flesh still tingled where his hands had touched her. But Sybille could not know that.

Falkland was expressing formal words of condolence about the death of her father. "How unfortunate that official duties prevented me from visiting him after he became seriously ill. There was no man I counted a better friend, nor admired more, despite the difference in our ages. We became well acquainted a decade ago—though I had known him as a boy when I spent a year at Beaux-Clervaux—after he wrote me and requested permission to be the biographer of my father, Duke Andrew. Many years of research were required in papers at Langmuir Castle, and we often worked together. I greatly admired your father's industry. He actually retraced every step of the duke's victorious campaigns on the Continent. How fortunate that Robert finished writing before he died. The six volumes make a fitting memorial to your father—and mine!"

Nicole murmured her appreciation, and he continued, almost subdued. "When last we met in London, some three years ago, Robert disclosed his plan to name me your guardian in case of his death. He had no male relatives, he said. I consented without giving the matter serious thought, for he was at that time in excellent health. No doubt I should have informed him that my situation in life allowed me little opportunity to care properly for a young girl." Then he flashed a disarming smile. "Nevertheless, we will do our best to provide for your—er, happiness." Was there a flirtatious light in his gray eyes?

The duke turned toward Sybille as though he intended to take her arm, but looked back briefly at Nicole with an unmistakable expression of pain. "May I tell you how much you resemble your mother?" he asked, in a low, confidential voice; then seizing the marquise, quickly disappeared into the crowd of nobles.

Nicole's heart sank. Just as she had begun to relax with him, he was gone. Fortunately, she was not alone, but stood in a group of young unmarried girls, mostly daughters of ambassadors. With a forced smile, she tried to make conversation as they all gazed wide-eyed at the elegant men and women gathering around tables in the long, narrow hall. Finally, from the peculiar chorus of cheers and groans, Nicole realized that bets were being wagered.

Suddenly a mysterious hush fell over the throng. Nicole saw, on her right, men bowing and women sinking in curtsies. She winced, then glancing at one of her companions read the same reaction on her face, and they both laughed. It was as painful for the other new girls as for herself. Nicole dipped again, wobbling only a little this time, as, a few feet before her, passed King Louis XVI and Queen Marie Antoinette.

The king was tall and hulking, somehow awkward, his gait almost shambling. Obviously uncomfortable, he bore a look of great effort and concentration. On his extended arm rested the hand of the queen, who, in contrast to her husband, was radiant and self-assured—as gaily enthusiastic as he was reluctant.

As she passed, there were whispers at the novelty of her costume. She had evolved the new style of the "chemise" dress to a shocking degree of form-fitting softness. For the first time she seemed to be wearing no crinoline at all and hardly more than three petticoats. All the world was free to stare at the natural curves of her hips as outlined by the swing of her skirts.

When Nicole inched forward to peek at the crowded gaming table where the queen seated herself, she gradually became aware that someone —a young man—was watching her as he moved in a parallel course. At first refusing to meet her eyes, he finally found a little courage and smiled shyly at her.

He was very young, not more than twenty, and charmingly unsure of himself. *How unlike the suave poise of the Duke of Falkland,* she thought. And he was handsome too, not with the dark sensuality of the duke, but blue-eyed and freckled, with unruly blond hair.

"Would you like to play faro—I mean if I can get us a place? It's so terribly crowded, of course. My name is Philippe Rohan. I haven't seen you here before. I'd remember if I had."

She told him her name and explained that she knew nothing at all about faro. He seemed almost relieved and began giving her detailed instructions, which she could hardly follow. At last forcing their way to the table, he leaned forward between two seated noblewomen to buy chips and place a bet. "Name your card," he directed Nicole, but she told him to choose for her.

She was actually more interested in peeking over Philippe's shoulder for a glimpse of the queen than she was in the play. "I picked kings for you. If one of the four kings is drawn, you will win," he explained. Nicole nodded politely, then shifted her position until she had a good view of Marie Antoinette, who was gossiping with a group around her and not watching the table.

The dealer pulled three cards from the ebony box holding the deck, and placed one face up on the green felt table cover. "You win!" Philippe cried. "It's the king of spades! You must have beginner's luck. Shall I leave the whole pile of chips on the king?"

"Oh, no, I'd rather wait. Perhaps later. . . ." Nicole prudently collected the little stack of ivory chips in her hand.

The young man laughed at her caution, so seldom seen at court, and played several rounds himself, winning handsomely each time. "You bring me luck, mademoiselle! I have not had a winner for a week, and now three in a row! Surely it is an omen—" he began, and then grew embarrassed at his own boldness.

At just that moment, a strange silence fell over the table, and the dealer discreetly signaled a suspension of betting. There would be a private round. A man standing directly behind Marie Antoinette bent forward to place a triple stack of chips on the sector marked Queen. Marie Antoinette arched her elegant white neck to whisper some joking remark in his ear, then blew a kiss in the direction of the deck of cards. The dark, handsome man laughed dutifully. It was the Duke of Falkland.

The dealer drew a card from the box and placed it smartly on the table. It was the queen of diamonds. A loud cry of wicked pleasure went up from the spectators. The symbolism was clear to everyone. Falkland had won the red queen—at least at cards.

The crowd grew rapidly around the table. As Falkland reached down to scoop up his huge pile of chips, the queen placed her gloved hand on his. White glove on white glove, lingering a moment too long. She was ordering him to let his money ride. The crowd exclaimed, thrilled by her daring.

The alabaster skin of the queen flushed with enjoyment. She intended to give them something to gossip about tonight. In turn, they responded with vulgar chuckles and knowing winks betraying no great surprise— quite the opposite. Nicole could not believe her eyes and ears. Here she was in Versailles in the bosom of the royal family, and the queen and nobles and her own guardian were amusing themselves in this scandalous manner.

There was a gasp when the queen picked up the ebony card box herself and held it dramatically in her two hands. Slowly, savoring the suspense, she drew a card from the top and turned it over on the table. Nicole guessed from the raucous burst of cheering what the result was before she could see the card. It was the queen of hearts.

But she was preoccupied by quite another matter the next morning when she hurried to Sybille's chamber, and, carefully requesting permission to enter, was admitted without a wait.

"Some brilliant insight told you I might be alone this morning. Clever girl!" the marquise muttered sarcastically.

It took Nicole a moment to realize what she was talking about, then she blushed. "Oh, madame! I had no intention—I mean, I never thought—"

"Of course, my dear, you never do! But I would have believed even you might have noticed the outrageous public display by Falkland and the queen last night."

"Oh, yes, of course, and I was dreadfully shocked, but I decided it couldn't be as bad as it seemed, and just tried to put it out of my mind.

Besides, I was very excited about meeting a young man who is terribly nice, and that's why I wanted to hurry here. . . ."

The marquise was in no mood to concentrate on Nicole's chatter. "Your childish naïveté is neither becoming to you, nor does it bode well for your success at court. You must learn to be more realistic. Things can be, and usually are—to use your words—as bad as they seem. Like most other women at court, the queen takes lovers from time to time. Her most recent choice was made public last night."

She stared at Sybille in disbelief. To possess the queen was to betray the king, to betray France itself! If Falkland must be ruled by lust, let his mistress be the unblushing marquise—not their precious queen, whose honor was France's own. But surely Sybille was exaggerating, probably to excuse her own adulterous affair. Finally Nicole blurted out, "I don't believe you!"

"I'll forgive your rudeness because you are obviously very upset. No doubt it was inevitable you should fall in love with Falkland."

"On the contrary, madame, I came here today to tell you that I met someone last night whom I like extremely well, and I believe he is very attracted to me." Sybille yawned and said nothing, adding to Nicole's exasperation. "You wanted to know my choice of husband," she insisted, "and I'm sure this young man is a very good possibility. He was wearing some kind of uniform with several medals on his chest, so he must have a fine career already, even though he is only a little older than I am." Nicole's eyes pleaded for her serious attention.

The marquise stretched lazily and finally asked, "What name did he give?"

"Philippe Rohan."

"Philippe Rohan!" The marquise sat up with a start. "*Mon Dieu*, Nicole, he is the young Prince of Soubise! My dear child, you can't marry into the House of Rohan! They are one of the great noble families of France."

"But why not? I don't understand. My father left me with a fortune; our estates dominate half a province."

"How can I explain it to you?" The marquise sounded almost sympathetic. "The Rohans have always been one of the most powerful houses of France, and actually ruled, hundreds of years ago, as kings in Brittany. Perhaps you will understand if I compare their importance to that of the Dukes of Falkland in Great Britain. Your family, on the other hand, has no claim to nobility in any degree, and while rich, amassed its fortune in the wine trade. *In trade*, my dear—can you understand what that means?"

"But my mother was the only child of a Norman nobleman."

"What was his title?" the marquise asked doubtfully.

"Baron de Saint-Mathiez."

"I do not know the name," she answered, dismissing the family with the rise and fall of her eyebrows.

"But Philippe—Philippe might want to marry me."

"He might, indeed. But his family would never approve. That is certain. And I am not foolish enough to approach them with such a plan. Don't cry, silly girl. You hardly know him, and there are men more handsome." Her heart softened a little at the dejected look on Nicole's face. "No doubt he *is* nice. I'm not surprised. I knew his father—er, quite well. Even though you can never be Philippe's wife, you can certainly become his mistress. Of course—why not? He is young and has not yet acquired a mistress at court. He would adore you, a beautiful young virgin. There! Does that solve it? And we can find you a husband too. Someone with a future in the king's household, so you can stay at court near Rohan."

3

Never, never would she consent to become any man's mistress! Nicole beat her wet pillow with her fist. *Not good enough to marry Philippe Rohan! Thank God her father was not alive to hear such an insult.* Whatever could he have been thinking of to send her to this wretched palace of sin and corruption, this wicked court that had apparently ruined the young man, Falkland, he had admired and trusted so much.

For the next few evenings Nicole successfully avoided Rohan. But one afternoon as she stood waiting for the doors of the palace opera house to open, she saw him walking eagerly toward her. With a sad heart she forced herself to speak to him coldly, rudely, then turn to a stranger near her and take his arm. To add to her pain, she had to sit beside the dull, unattractive stranger, who was much intrigued by her boldness, through the long opera by Gluck, and only got rid of him afterward with great difficulty.

She deliberately put Rohan out of her mind, and tried to concentrate on learning the intricate procedures at court and enjoying the countless entertainments and receptions, which already seemed more like work than play. *But if not Philippe, who in the world was she going to marry?* Reckoning the social status of every man she met turned out to be a hopeless task. With stubborn pride, she resolved never to bring up the subject with the marquise again. And Sybille, for her part, chattered only of clothes and hairstyles, or chided Nicole for some minor infraction of court etiquette.

Nor would Falkland be any more help. But why did her hopes constantly return to him, why did she dream he would take her part against the marquise? She laughed at the idea, and told herself sternly that he was nothing more than a vain, arrogant courtier, a male counterpart of the marquise who cared about little more than preening his own feathers and seducing elegant ladies.

In spite of these warnings, Nicole kept up a tireless vigil for him in their apartment, even though she rarely found any clue to his presence. He never took his meals with her, nor anywhere in the suite as far as she could tell, and she had no idea if he slept there. In fact, she did not even know which room was his bedchamber.

One afternoon, curiosity drove her to explore, and she was able to identify his room by the ceremonial sword, required for all formal court appearances, resting on a marble-topped bureau. The chamber was smaller than her own and decorated in a less ornate style than any other room she had seen at Versailles. At least he had been kind enough to give her the grander bedchamber. Very few personal possessions were visible, except a faïence tobacco jar, a leather case that usually held one or two miniature portraits, and a small pile of rather worn books. All were in English except one entitled *Duc de Falkland*, which she recognized as a volume of her father's work. She instinctively reached out to pick it up, but a sound outside the room frightened her, and she hurried to escape before she was discovered.

Soon after, as midnight struck one night, Nicole stood undressing in her chamber with the help of a maid, donned a new white lawn nightdress; then instead of slipping directly into bed, impulsively reached out for the beautiful robe de chambre that had come from the dressmaker only that day. It was a silk velvet of the apple-green color especially identified with Madame de Pompadour, the celebrated mistress of the previous king. Nicole put it on, fastened its satin frogs, then spun around before her mirror, thinking how particularly becoming it was as her golden hair tumbled over her shoulders. She wondered idly if Pompadour had had her same coloring, and laughed to herself at the danger of asking Sybille such a question. The marquise would probably devise a plot to make her the mistress of Louis XVI!

Just at that moment a maid opened her door, carrying the tray of wine and cakes that was always offered at bedtime and which she usually left untouched. With a little start, she saw the face of the duke peering into her room over the shoulder of the serving girl.

"How fortunate to find you still awake! If you will do me the honor of joining me for this little repast—" He took the silver tray from the maid and beckoned to Nicole to follow him into a nearby sitting room. She hesitated only a second, then padded along on bare feet. Surely it could not be improper to sit and chat with her own guardian, even though she was wearing only a nightgown and robe. After all, he had given her no chance to refuse. She tucked her feet under the ample folds of velvet and hoped he had not noticed them.

Sprawling amiably in a soft chair, sipping a little cognac, he studied her with unabashed curiosity, enjoying the fluster he created. Boldly, he examined her face, her hair, her beautiful robe—how lucky she was wearing something so flattering—and even glanced at her feet, which she shuffled nervously. Had he spotted a bare toe? Though his eyes were not unkind, she found she could not meet them. He seemed to be subtly offering her some sort of challenge to make herself entertaining, to help him wile away the hours. She shifted uncomfortably in her chair. Whatever could she say to break the silence? What would the marquise chatter about to amuse him?

He yawned lazily, and drawled a few questions about her daily activities. Had she been riding yet? Any girl raised at Beaux-Clervaux must be a fine horsewoman. Did she prefer the court ballets or operas? Had she seen the queen perform in a play? Had she been into Paris yet?

She thought she could detect his effort not to condescend to her, not to treat her like a child. No doubt he would find it taxing soon enough. As he said, "Then I may assure myself that you are agreeably settled, and adjusting well to the rigors of life at court?" she told herself he was getting ready to dismiss her.

But when he saw the brief look of unhappiness she could not suppress, he said, "Such a lovely face to be marred by discontent," and raised his eyebrows quizzically.

What did she dare answer him? She could hardly tell him that she was shocked by the low moral tone of the court, and his own scandalous behavior in particular; or that she despised his mistress, deeply resented the power Sybille had over her, and was, in fact, jealous of her intimacy with him. Tentatively, she began, "I never realized it would be so difficult to arrange a—to find a proper husband—"

His laughter stopped her. "Oh, you poor child, so solemn and earnest, so innocent. Why can't you relax and enjoy life? Sybille has told me how charming you are, how *serieuse*. Such a refreshing change in this jaded court. So you would like a 'proper husband,' would you? Then we must find you one! But whatever do you mean by 'proper'? Rich, handsome, virile—?" He watched her closely at this suggestive word, but when her expression remained blank, he cleared his throat and continued, "No doubt we should choose someone as young, earnest, and *serieux* as you are yourself. A boy with a fine future in the King's Life Guard or the army—" He paused for a slow sip of cognac. "Alas, no, not the army at this time." His voice took on a hollow tone. "Perhaps the military is not a wise choice, nor the king's household. You will be far safer to go abroad for a few years."

"I'm afraid I don't take your meaning."

"Already the streets and quays of Paris are torn by rioting. The lower classes believe aristocrats are hoarding grain to raise the price of bread. Last night the shops of several gunsmiths were looted. The king has seen fit to surround the city with regiments of troops, including foreign mercenaries who are bitterly resented. And you must have heard that the Estates-General has assembled here in Versailles with angry demands King Louis has no intention of meeting."

"Oh, yes," she murmured, relieved he had meant no reference to her personally.

He laughed a little. "Then you *have* heard," he said, mocking her. "But the subject does not interest you nearly as much as selecting your future husband. Therefore, we must concentrate on the truly important things at hand and make a choice for you from the young men at court—the white hope of the aristocracy, the scions of a great civilization, the flower of France! Oh, my dear! Things are not what they seem. The king, the whole nation is bankrupt, sinking ever deeper into the clutches of moneylenders. This foolish court is a house of cards, soon to collapse on its debauched courtiers, who are deaf to the cries of the suffering peasants."

Whatever could he be talking about? Nicole was shocked and dismayed. The king was certainly not bankrupt! Never in her life had she seen such a display of wealth as was paraded here daily at Versailles. The peasants she knew in the Bordelais were not suffering; and as for debauched courtiers, she would agree with that description readily enough, but surely the duke himself would be first among them!

She did not notice the light scratching on the door until the duke called out for the servant to enter. A footman brought in a silver tray holding a small envelope. The duke broke its seal and read the brief message with no change of expression, then stuffed it inside his waistcoat. He simply nodded to the footman, who withdrew.

Falkland warmed his brandy snifter over a small candle in a silver holder. He seemed to have lost the thread of his words, and when he resumed, it was in a light, bantering vein. For several minutes he continued, but Nicole sensed he was disturbed and distracted. Perhaps the arrival of the note had annoyed him in some way. But of course, she reflected, he was a professional diplomat who must often conceal his true feelings; and, for the first time, she suspected that he was very skillful at his trade.

Rather abruptly he arose, expressed his regrets, and withdrew. Caught off guard, Nicole stared emptily around the room, then happened to glance into the antechamber through the door that was still ajar. She saw the duke speak to a servant, who proceeded out of the suite. The duke waited a minute or two, then followed him at a discreet distance. The servant was attired in the white and gold livery of the queen.

Sybille's tone made it entirely clear that an adequate expression of gratitude was due her. By unexplained clever strategems, she had obtained for Nicole an invitation to the evening's exclusive Fête Champêtre or Shepherd's Ball to be given by Marie Antoinette at Petit Trianon.

Everyone must dress in a rustic style, the men as shepherds or cowherds or foresters, the women as shepherdesses or goose girls. The marquise described some possible costumes, gave Nicole scarcely a moment to comment, then settled on a simple milkmaid outfit—lemon-yellow organza with a white apron—that could be ready for a fitting late in the afternoon.

Just as Nicole was leaving, Sybille remembered to add that she had arranged an escort for her to the fête. Breezily, she said his name was Simon de Brizac, and most women found him irresistible. "I have no doubt you'll fall madly in love with him."

"But—what about his family—how will they—?" Nicole asked anxiously.

"His family? Don't be such a little snob! What do you care about his family?"

"I mean," she tried to explain, "will his family find me—acceptable?"

"Oh, dear, are you forever planning your future? Someday you'll learn that you don't have to marry every man you fall in love with. Though, I dare say, his old father, Comte de Brizac, would be tremendously relieved to lay his hands on your fortune. I hear there are gaping holes in the roof of their château in Provence. But Falkland would never approve such a marriage. No, no, my dear; Simon de Brizac is just for fun."

Nicole felt no enthusiasm as she endured the elaborate toilette. Gloomily, she decided that Sybille had not been able to find anyone more appropriate who was willing to spend an evening with her. Certainly Nicole had no desire to dally romantically with an unmarriageable man. She would have to tolerate him tonight, then avoid him in the future, just as she did Rohan.

But only minutes after Simon first kissed her hand, she was chatting gaily and laughing with him until her stays cut into her sides. He was swarthily handsome with deep dimples in each cheek, and never stopped joking, poking fun at himself and everyone else in sight, and whispering outrageous gossip about all their fellow guests. Apparently there was nothing he did not know—or pretend to know—about Versailles and its inhabitants.

As they dined at a banquet table in a huge tent decorated with orange trees in silver tubs, she delighted in his exposés of the nobles seated near them. For the first time, the court did not frighten her. When the Marquise de Vaucroze took a seat at a nearby table, Nicole felt a guilty thrill of anticipation at Simon's inevitably wicked comments.

With relish he confided that Sybille had had more illustrious lovers than any other woman at court. She had been a great beauty and was well preserved for her age, which, Simon had learned from an unimpeachable source, was forty-five, although she told Falkland and everyone at court that she was only thirty-eight.

"What in the world does he see in her, a woman more than ten years older than he is?" Nicole could not help blurting out.

"But she's the cleverest woman at court! There is no end to her ambitious schemes. Not only does he value her advancement of his career—"

"Oh, I won't believe that! Whatever else Falkland may do, he would not advance himself by a woman's wiles."

"You little innocent! The handsome, spoiled Falkland presently uses the queen herself to advance his career! Marie Antoinette sings his praises to the king, and now My Lord Duke is regularly invited to join the royal hunt, and even assists the king with his eccentric hobby of locksmithing. Just the other morning at his Grande Levée, Louis ordered Falkland to take a seat, thereby forcing a Prince of the Blood to remain standing. Don't underestimate your duke. After all, diplomats are professional plotters and schemers."

"I won't listen to any slander of my guardian," Nicole said rather weakly.

But Simon was not deterred. "The marquise has finally won her lifelong ambition of becoming lady-in-waiting to the queen—as payment for graciously sharing Falkland's favors with Marie Antoinette. I hear there will soon be a fat sinecure for her husband, the old marquis. Very likely, dear Sybille herself put the idea of seducing the queen in Falkland's head." When Nicole attempted to protest again, Simon scoffed, "You owe your invitation to this very party to one of Sybille's schemes."

"What do you mean?"

"She finally realized—a little tardily, I thought—that you were just too tempting a morsel. It wouldn't do at all for Falkland to lose interest in the queen before a few more plums have been plucked. Only last night he invited you for a midnight tête-à-tête. You were clad, albeit modestly, in a nightgown and robe." Simon laughed at Nicole's amazed expression.

"There *are* no secrets at Versailles!" Then he said conspiratorially, "I am supposed to engage your highly susceptible emotions and involve you in a little love affair to take your mind off Falkland. Sybille believes I am a past master with pretty young girls!" His self-mockery was so disarming Nicole could not help laughing along with him.

At the end of the third course of rich food, Simon led Nicole to the dance floor, and then invited her on a tour of the gardens. He said they could return to their table later. The meal would run a dozen courses and last throughout the evening.

The wooded park at Petit Trianon, designed in the new natural, English style, was lighted everywhere by bonfires on which attendants threw chemicals to produce surprising colors. Simon and Nicole skirted the beautiful small palace, then followed a man-made stream past the classical Temple of Love. He placed his arm around her waist, and she found his closeness very pleasant. What if he did tell her tales she did not want to believe? His exaggerations were simply part of his comic style and not to be taken too seriously.

Beyond an alpine landscape made of artificial rocks, they found a small prominence, which he told her was called Snail's Mountain. Knowledgeably, he led her down a secret path into the mouth of a cave. Inside, he gently slipped his arms around her. "Would you like a kiss from the past master?" he whispered, and she laughed nervously in his embrace. His lips touched hers lightly, then pressed firmly. Her fear vanished as she felt the warm, protective comfort of his circling arms.

With seeming restraint, he broke their embrace and took her hand in his, swinging it a little as though they were two children. Climbing out of the grotto, they saw by the light of the bonfires some apparently rustic buildings surrounding a little lake. It was the famous Hamlet, built by the queen at great expense in painstaking imitation of a humble farm village. Simon pointed out a mill, dairy, piggery, rabbit warren, aviary, dovecot, hen house, and several farmer's cottages. Beyond a cabbage patch, he led her into a tiny thatched house. Nicole could see that cracks had been carefully painted on its stucco walls.

Inside there was a dim light from glowing coals in the big fireplace. She sniffed the faint odor of food, and as Simon closed the door behind them, protested that someone must live there.

"No, no. The attendants have gone for the night. It looks like a real home, but it is only a playhouse for the queen and her ladies, and is kept in constant readiness in case she wants to bake bread or make cheese or simply take tea."

As their eyes grew accustomed to the faint light, they discovered a spinning wheel, a blue and white porcelain churn bearing the queen's monogram, and a long rough-hewn table set with pewter and monogrammed porcelain that matched the churn.

Confidently, Simon pulled her to him and kissed her long and deeply. Nicole shivered with sudden pleasure. She instinctively pressed against his body and tried to answer his increasingly insistent lips. Then suddenly aware of her own boldness, she shrank back and turned her face away.

"Be natural with me, Nicole. Don't be afraid. I won't dishonor you," he said, his face touching her neck. The little electric shock of the word *dishonor* went through her, a strangely delicious thrill. But there was no real danger. She knew from his tender hands and mouth that she could trust him. He nuzzled her neck, then his lips traveled to the little hollow at the base of her throat. She pulled away modestly, murmuring a protest.

He politely released her, and appeared to concentrate on exploring the room. But suddenly he embraced her again. "You are just too beautiful, too warm and soft and exciting! How can I stop?" So the fault was hers for being too attractive! She laughed at this logic, but was in fact extremely pleased by his compliments. How comforting, how soothing, after the long weeks of loneliness, disappointment, and disillusion.

Sensing her pleasure and trust, he kissed her still more passionately, until they both gasped for breath. *Surely there was no sin in kissing*, Nicole tried to tell herself. How good it felt when his arms tightened around her, how good to press hard against his strong, muscular body. But, of course, she was behaving unwisely. Just as she resolutely pushed him away, he slipped his hand inside her bodice and cupped a naked breast. Frantically, she backed off. "Oh, no! You must not!"

He apologized smoothly, saying he was grossly inept. Would she be able to forgive him? "The marquise told me you were still a virgin, and I would have to proceed slowly—"

"Proceed slowly!" Nicole echoed with alarm. As his real intention—and the marquise's—dawned on her, she demanded sarcastically, "Did she tell you precisely how and where to seduce me! Did she tell you to bring me here to this isolated cottage!"

Roused to anger, he grabbed her roughly and pinned one arm behind her back. "She neglected to tell me you were a teasing hot wench who would press her burning mouth on mine, thrust her hips against my swollen groin, and then pretend outrage when I started to do what is necessary to satisfy us both!"

As though altered by a magic spell, Simon's carefree, comic personality had become demanding and cruel. Nicole could hardly believe the deep sneering lines that marked his face. How could she have been so wrong about him? What a fool she had been to lower her guard and let him lure her to this secluded spot!

Before she knew what he was doing, he pulled the cord of a set of draperies that appeared to cover a window, but instead parted to reveal a narrow alcove bed. In her confusion, he was able to topple her onto the deep feather tick, then throw himself on top of her body. She began to hit and kick frantically, but he subdued her by cuffing her once or twice on the head and straddling her legs with his own.

"Struggling with a girl only excites me more; but perhaps a tease like you is well aware what a little flailing and thrashing can do for a man!"

He took her momentary inaction for compliance and tried to unpin her fichu with one hand, but she surprised him with a violent twist of her body. In answer he tore open the bodice of her dress, completely ripping off the fichu and tossing it away. Her breasts glowed luminous in the dim light. To control her feverish writhing, Simon grasped both her arms, then greedily kissed first one erect nipple and then the other.

Suddenly Nicole and Simon froze with terror. The door of the cottage swung open, as two men carrying lighted candelabra entered noisily. Simon immediately clapped his hand over her mouth, but she was too startled and too intimidated by her shameful nudity to know what to do.

In a moment other servants bustled in, bearing trays of covered dishes and decanters of wine. One man poked up the coals on the hearth and threw on some wood, as the others prepared to serve a meal. None of the servants had yet noticed the couple cowering in the shadowed bed.

Nicole tried to summon up her courage to call for help. If only her dress were not so badly damaged! She had heard buttons fly off and seams rip when Simon tore it, and was afraid she would not be able to cover herself decently.

Then someone held the door open and bowed low. The queen herself, dressed as a shepherdess and carrying a crook decorated with ribbons and flowers, glided in, exclaimed enthusiastically over the rustic setting, and took a seat at the long table. She was followed by four or five ladies and gentlemen, whom Nicole could not identify.

The small room was now crowded, and inevitably someone would soon see the couple in the bed. But Nicole's desire for help had vanished the instant she saw Marie Antoinette. Sybille had taught her that royalty would tolerate no invasion of their privacy or tranquillity. Only public mortification would follow her discovery, no matter how innocent she might protest herself to be.

Equally desperate, Simon began to pull at the drapery cord with tiny, almost imperceptible movements. Nicole prayed that his efforts would be successful, for now she feared Simon less than she did the queen. At first the drapery traveled smoothly, but then the cord stuck on some impediment, and one tug too many brought the metal rod crashing to the floor.

In the tumult that followed, a muscular footman hauled Simon out of the bed. Nicole sat up, frantically trying to cover her breasts with whatever pieces of fabric she could grasp. Someone thrust a sputtering candelabrum near her face, and she blinked at the man who gripped her roughly by her arms and pulled her to her feet. Was it a servant? He had turned his head away to avoid the sight of her bare breasts. His face was only inches from hers when she finally recognized the Duke of Falkland.

Someone behind her, a servant perhaps, placed a cloak around her shoulders, and Falkland released his grip to wrap her in it. Only then did he look her in the face. Never before had she seen such cold contempt.

During their coach ride back to Versailles, Falkland sat beside her in crushing silence. At the door of the palace, he let her stumble down from the carriage by herself. In a cruelly brief farewell, he ordered her to prepare to return to Beaux-Clervaux the next day.

4

Would nobody come? But of course not! Half out of her wits with despair, Nicole could not take her eyes from the tall door of the palace opening here on the Cour de la Chapelle. She could hardly believe that some messenger from the duke or even the marquise would not rush out with her reprieve to end this nightmare. But the door did not open, the courtyard was empty, as the lone footman loaded her luggage into the coach. Only the marble audience of plumed warriors and pagan gods and the Sun King himself staring down from the upper levels of the facade would bid her farewell.

Then finally extinguishing his lantern as the dawn sky lightened, the footman stepped ahead to watch for the unlocking of the gates, as was done at half after five every morning to admit the public to the grounds and even the palace itself. At last came his signal, and the coach lurched forward to begin the lonely journey home to Beaux-Clervaux.

As they passed out of the wide gilded gates and through the little town, Nicole was overcome by another bout of weeping. Thank heaven she was alone in the carriage, for she doubted she would ever gain control of herself. She had cried all night long while she tried to pack or tossed on the bed for the brief hour before a maid entered to help her dress. Her eyes were painfully swollen, and seemingly dry of tears, yet when some new wave of recollection would sweep over her she would break down again.

If only she did not feel Falkland's eyes burn into her and read the contempt on his face. If only she did not hear Simon's insulting names for her, see the sneer on his face, feel his hand clamped over her mouth as they cowered in the alcove bed. Worse yet, she could still feel the sting of his caresses on her shoulders and back—and on her breasts! Somehow she must put that sickening memory out of her mind! Then for the first time she noticed reddish bruises on her arms and wrists. Of course, Simon had wrestled with her painfully. But wait, these had not been made by Simon!

Nicole shuddered as she realized that Falkland's hands had left their mark when he had pulled her upward, toward him, averting his head from her naked breasts.

But she would go crazy if she didn't stop. She must fix her mind on something pleasant, something she loved, imagine herself on Jupiter riding down the poplar-lined lane to the old stone *chaix* and the cool *caves* underneath where Maître Poujade would brag about the latest vintage and give her a sip from his *tastevin*, the flat silver cup that always hung from a chain around his neck, and then offer her a hunk of bread still warm from his wife's oven. Or picture the little woods beyond the hill where she had often discovered nests of woodcocks and partridges. Or Clémence's kitchen or the cool courtyard with its tinkling fountain where she could read for hours or. . . .

Perhaps the rocking of the carriage and a soft rain were soothing, for she dozed a little and awoke beside a field of nodding wheat. In the far distance, across the broad plain of the Beauce, rose Chartres Cathedral, its unmatched towers highlighted by a ray of light breaking through the clouds in a scene of mystical beauty. And in the days that followed, Nicole's mood gradually improved until she could delight in the fairy-tale châteaux of the Loire Valley, where the Kings of France had once held court—first Chambord; then Blois, with its famous spiral tower; and Amboise, where Leonardo da Vinci lay entombed; then Chenonceaux, built on pillars above the rushing Cher; and finally Azay-le-Rideau, the exquisite château that rose out of a placid pool of the Indre, where she was fortunate enough to spend a night in a country inn.

The hills to the south gradually grew brown and rugged, the towns sleepy and sunbaked. In Angoulême and Poitiers, the mellow Romanesque churches looked back seven hundred years. After she took time to see an ancient Roman ruin, she realized how much she was enjoying this chance to explore the world a little. Her father had been a tireless traveler, she reminded herself. Perhaps she too could fill an empty life with journeys to Rome and Vienna, Egypt and Turkey, even China. Yes, why not? Of course she would need some companion or other, some chaperon. But who? Perhaps that maiden aunt at one of her tenant châteaux—what was her name, Tante somebody-or-other? Nicole cringed. No, better to go alone, with only a maid or two, even if she had to defy convention. Soon enough she would turn into a dried-up, dreary spinster herself!

To Nicole the truth seemed glaring—she had little chance of marrying now. At home she would seldom if ever meet anyone of the proper social class. Half the gentry in the district were her own tenants, and the few other landowning families would not be likely to forgive her father's undisguised snobbery. Only one or two had bothered to make formal calls of condolence at the time of his death. And who else was there? The wine merchants who called regularly at the château? Some old widower? Her father had had a friend, a distinguished *jurat* of Bordeaux, who was well over fifty! She shook her head sadly, then began to cry again.

Nicole spent one of the last nights of the journey in the little village of Cognac, where she sampled the local brandies with a highly competitive spirit. Beaux-Clervaux made its own brandy, and she was far from ready to admit the superiority of some other region's. Even the Grande Champagnes presented by the innkeeper failed to win any concession from her.

As the coach lumbered at last out of the brown hills, she saw spread before her the undulating green slopes of the Bordeaux region, the largest and most productive wine district in all France. Graceful as the curves of a woman's body, the hills were wound by endless rows of grape vines now in full leaf. She felt a great surge of love for this land, and a thrill of anticipation of the glorious summer, the harvest, and the exciting festivals in the fall.

The coach reached the wide estuary of the Gironde, and took a slow ferry to the opposite shore, the area called Haut-Médoc, home of the most celebrated red wines. Nicole watched closely now for the boundary of her own estates, and sighed deeply as soon as she saw a small stone farmhouse and waved to her tenants. Within an hour, the coach climbed a long slope, rounded a hill, and beheld the imposing château of Beaux-Clervaux, manor house and principal winery of the whole region.

But despite a turret or two, her ancestral home was less a castle than a gracious country house. A pair of old, squat towers dated back hundreds of years, but the two mansarded wings coming forward to make an entrance courtyard spoke of more modern prosperity. The afternoon sun beat hard on the stone walls with their tall narrow windows through which could be glimpsed the cool, dark refuge inside. Just in front of the east wing was a patch of grass where sheep grazed, but almost the entire château was surrounded by the rows of vines, reaching even to the walls, boldly climbing the towers themselves.

No sooner had the coach stopped than Nicole jumped out, ran across the grass, and entered not the heavy, creaking main door, which she never used, but a small rear entrance leading to the cellar. Abandoning any pretense of dignity, she jumped down two steps at a time and rushed into the giant kitchen, calling a greeting to the servants at work there, and throwing her arms around Clémence, the cook. "I've come home where I belong, and will not leave soon again!" Nicole exclaimed tearfully, as the sturdy peasant woman stroked her head gently.

Clémence cooked a feast of capon in aspic, lobster, venison pâté, pheasant, duck, lamb, jam tarts, cream flans, and a bombe of fresh fruits that evening, and supper was served at the long trestle table in the basement dining hall meant for servants. To honor Nicole's arrival, Poujade, the *maître de chaix*, or master of the winery, accompanied by his large family, came to dine, bringing as he always did a wide assortment of wines of various ages. If a bottle did not please him after a sip or two, he refused to serve it and consigned it to the kitchen for a sauce or soup.

For the next week Nicole indulged herself almost every day in a *grasse matinée*, a lazy morning in bed, followed by a breakfast in the kitchen of chocolate and croissants piping hot from the oven, while the servants young and old exclaimed over her descriptions of Versailles. Then she would ride Jupiter across the fields to visit peasant families, especially the Gaillards. Mère Gaillard had taken Nicole to nurse on the day her mother died, and Nicole had believed for the first years of her life that the Gaillard children were her own brothers and sisters. Now she would race Quentin or Gabriel or Marc, or the girls, Jeanne or Noémie, as they rode their old nag, Dauphin, across the meadow to the pond. Of course Jupiter always won, unless Nicole had allowed two or three small peasant children to climb up beside her on his back.

Soon she settled into a routine modeled on her father's. Early in the day she would handle the estate business, going over accounts with the *maître*, and perhaps writing a tenant or wine broker about some overdue payment. Then she granted interviews to her peasants, who expected to be able to receive advice and protection from their *châtelaine*. She managed to find a nurse for an invalid tenant, accepted the older children of a widow into service, and wrote a letter to the *maître* of a château across the Gironde that one of his men had got with child a young peasant girl at Beaux-Clervaux. Maître Mérillon would handle the matter with dispatch, Nicole knew, and the girl could begin to sew her wedding dress.

After the heavy midday meal and a pleasant nap, Nicole would work in her father's library, sorting his papers or cataloging one of his many collections: ancient coins or pistols or engravings or books. She loved to sit in the cool, dark room with its north view of the blue haze that was the Gironde. She had not lost her childhood fascination with the full suit of armor complete with dusty ostrich plumes on the helmet, or her pride in the coat of arms of the Clervaux family carved on the walnut boiserie above the mantel: a stylized grape vine within a bordured shield, supported by a panther passant dexter breathing fire, and a beautiful swan sinister. Underneath was carved the family motto, *J'ai du coeur*, I am courageous.

There were two miniatures of her mother on the mantel and a framed charcoal sketch drawn by her father himself. He had caught young Lucienne laughing gaily, the breeze tossing locks of her long blond hair. Nicole was said to bear a striking resemblance to the young girl, her father having called the similarity a true miracle. But Nicole doubted, in her present subdued mood, that she herself could ever again laugh with such spontaneity and joy.

At night she retreated gratefully to her high-ceilinged bedchamber, and sank deep into the goose-down tick that Clémence had had freshly filled. Kept closed all day against the July heat, the room was blessedly cool at night, and Nicole would order the shutters left open just enough to admit rays of moonlight and the song of the *rossignol*, the nightingale that lived in the linden tree just outside her window. Once again she told herself that she was—would be—content in this, her permanent life. She was at last grown-up, and mature enough to accept her fate. She would never marry. She had to face the truth. She would fill her life with conscientious administration of the estate, charitable acts toward her peasants, and someday perhaps long journeys to exotic regions of the world.

But to be honest, she had to admit how disappointed she was. Bitterly disappointed. No, not bitterly. It was too strong a word, she thought stubbornly. But in truth her future had been destroyed in the cottage at Petit Trianon. She would lead a lonely life without a family, without children. Without a husband, without his love, without the powerfully exciting caresses Simon had begun to teach her. . . . But she must not think of that. She had sternly forbade herself to remember that last night at Versailles.

The nightingale finished its midnight song, and Nicole tried to fall asleep in the silent house. How quiet Beaux-Clervaux seemed after Versailles. She had grown accustomed to the ceaseless activity of the great palace. Suddenly she sat bolt upright, her eyes wide open. She heard footsteps in the corridor. A door clicked shut. The duke had returned to the apartment, home late as usual. She had been listening for him. Where had he been tonight? With what woman? Surely not the queen again!

Then she knew she had been dreaming. She was here at Beaux-Clervaux. There was no duke—no duke here. Had there really been steps in the hall, a door closing? Of course it was only her maid Julie, stealing in again after a night with that good-for-nothing Pascal. Nicole must put a stop to the affair tomorrow. Pascal must declare himself to Julie or stay away from the château.

Even Julie had a lover. But Nicole might never again see the duke, never again drop in her awkward curtsy to him, never again feel his hand at her waist or elbow as he lifted her to her feet. Tossing in her bed, she relived his gracious greeting in the Galerie des Glaces, and their midnight conversation in his sitting room. Had he really seen her bare feet? She giggled a little at the possibility. She recalled his teasing smile, his gently mocking laugh, his manner always so suave and confident. No wonder women found him irresistible.

Too many women. Sybille. The thought of Falkland in bed with Sybille! Or Falkland in bed with Marie Antoinette! How well she remembered that shocking night when she had seen him walk off down the corridor behind the queen's footman.

Why couldn't Nicole succeed in turning her thoughts from him? Would he always be there to haunt her, more upsetting than any ghost? How she wished she had never met him! He was surely a wicked man—immoral, insincere, self-absorbed!

As though in contradiction, she suddenly saw the flicker of pain pass across his face when he had mentioned her mother that night in the Galerie des Glaces. Falkland had deeply loved Lucienne—Nicole believed it. And what had her mother felt for him? Surely not love! Had he touched her, kissed her, caressed her! Dear God, had she let him? So soon before her wedding? She was betrothed to Robert de Clervaux, living here in the château. Where was her room then? And where was Falkland's? Did they lie in bed locked in each other's arms, pressing their lips together until they gasped for breath—!

Nicole jumped out of bed almost hysterical and groped for a candlestick. Pulling on a cotton wrapper, she hurried downstairs and opened the door of the morning room, which they called the Petit Salon. It was entirely filled with her mother's dowry furniture brought from Normandy, except for a large oil painting hanging above the fireplace. A month after their wedding, Robert had called down from Paris a famous artist who had painted his bride's portrait in her heavy green velvet gown that cold January. Newly married, she was self-consciously dignified, leagues removed from the uninhibited, flirtatious girl of the charcoal drawing. But despite her stiff posture and the self-assured tilt of her head, her eyes were soft, her expression gentle.

As Nicole held the candle up toward the painting, she sighed and frowned. She could never be so beautiful or so dignified or sensitive or kind or loving. She could never compete with the superbly lovely dead mother, whom she had always adored with the most idealized love. But now Falkland had forced her to look at her with jealous eyes, had reduced her to the ignoble hope that he might love her because of her resemblance to Lucienne, if for no other reason.

Even though she tried to cure herself of her obsession with Falkland, Nicole still met every *courrier*, half believing that some message would come from Versailles. Even if he ignored his responsibilities as her guardian, he remained the trustee of her father's estate and would expect some kind of an accounting of the income from Beaux-Clervaux. But there was no communication at all until one day a rickety *voiture des postes* climbed the hill of the château and unloaded three large, handsome trunks Nicole had never seen before. The address tags told her nothing about the sender. When she questioned the driver he knew only that their point of origin was the Royal Palace of Versailles.

Too impatient to wait, Nicole unbuckled the straps and raised each lid in the courtyard. With a shock she discovered all three were filled with the wardrobe made for her at court. Proudly, defiantly, she had left behind every stitch, every parasol, and pair of shoes ordered by the marquise, and packed only the country clothes she had brought with her. Now she knelt on the gravel and rummaged with distaste in the silks and satins for any kind of letter or card or message. But there was no evidence at all of the identity of the sender.

After two footmen had carried them upstairs to her chamber, she dismissed Julie and removed the gowns by herself, still hoping to discover some clue. Had not Falkland himself ordered her things packed up and sent to her as a gesture of friendship—or even of forgiveness? When she finally convinced herself there was no card or even return address, she seized rather desperately on the hope the trunks might be English. Possibly he had sent off her things in some of his own luggage, perhaps intending to pick it up himself someday at Beaux-Clervaux. Indeed the trunks were beautifully made and expensive, but at last she found that each was marked near a hinge with the small gold imprint LACROIX—PARIS.

Disappointed, she began to lay the gowns in her armoire. At each familiar sight her depression deepened. There was her elaborate presentation dress of rose satin, the blue ball gown she had been wearing in its half-finished state when she had burst into Sybille's bedroom, and the lovely apple-green robe. She found at least a dozen dresses she had never worn, and some she had no recollection of whatsoever. How beautiful they all were, how superbly well made! As she picked up a *mousseline* petticoat, she noticed that all its seams were bound with a silk ribbon. The very linings of the dresses and capes were more expensive fabrics than any she had ever owned before.

But what would she do with all this finery here in the country? How foolish she was to fill up the chests in her room. She should have ordered the trunks carried directly to the attic. She would never wear any of the gowns, and even their sight brought tears to her eyes. Whoever had sent them to her might have realized that they could only cause unhappiness.

As Nicole bent to remove the last dress in one trunk, she stiffened with horror. It was the yellow organza she had worn at Petit Trianon, the milkmaid costume Simon had torn open revealing her breasts for all the world to see. With shaking hands she examined it. Three long tears had been meticulously mended, every button replaced, even one buttonhole reembroidered. Then she spotted the single remaining piece of cloth in the trunk. It was the white fichu for the dress, which Nicole well remembered had been thrown on the floor beside the alcove bed. She had not carried it back to Versailles. She had been covered only by the cloak that Falkland wrapped around her.

Who in the world would believe that she could stand to look at this garment, let alone endure wearing it! Had some servant of the duke's innocently mended it? But Nicole knew no one in his household could execute this delicate stitch. Who would know that the fichu abandoned in the cottage belonged with the lemon yellow dress? Who else but the marquise! Who else could want to taunt her with the humiliation? Who else was capable of such petty hostility? The Marquise de Vaucroze had sent the trunks as a malicious farewell.

Then by some miracle, Nicole had an invitation to accept and an opportunity to dress for an afternoon at the home of strangers, or virtual strangers. A landowning family—thank heaven they were not just tenants—living in a small château on the west boundary of her lands had graciously asked her to come for dinner. Years ago, her father had had a dispute with the Coppins, and had refused even to salute them from a passing carriage, but now they were apparently willing to forgive and forget. Nicole was delighted and thought what fine, generous people they must be after all. And, if her memory served, they had an unusual number of sons, most of whom were older than she was.

But her first impressions inside the Château Rigaud-Coppin were surprise at the modest, almost humble furnishings of their reception room—it *must* be the salon, although the large fieldstone fireplace had a beehive oven and one hanging iron pot—and shock at the large size of the family gathered to meet her. Apparently most of the sons were married, for the room swarmed with small children. Some infants were being rocked in cradles beside their mothers' chairs.

After awkward attempts by several of the Coppins at conversation with her, an elderly gentleman called from across the room, "Kindly tell us, mademoiselle, what wine King Louis prefers at table."

"I regret I cannot say, monsieur." Nicole had no knowledge whatsoever of the king's taste in wine, for she had never even dined in the same room with him, and had only once been present in the back row of the hall, crowded among a hundred courtiers, while the king and queen ate together.

"But surely you can tell us if he prefers Bordeaux to Burgundy!" Some of the ire always aroused by thought of the competitive Burgundian wines crept into the old gentleman's voice.

She had to protest her ignorance again, and Madame Coppin, hoping to bridge a painful moment, quickly asked for a description of the royal children.

"But I never saw them, madame. I believe the dauphin is about ten and in rather poor health. His little brother—Louis Charles, I believe—is perhaps four. Madame Royal, as she is called, is the eldest. She must be eleven or a little more."

When her hostess pressed her for information about the dauphin's illness, Nicole said she knew nothing more and sensed that the family was embarrassed for her. She knew what they were thinking, that she was guilty of great exaggeration about her visit to Versailles. Probably she had stayed in the town of Versailles, not at the palace, and had been taken on no more than a brief tour inside the grounds. No one in the room had any conception of the size of the palace, the vast number of nobles living there, or their many gradations of rank. Nicole guessed none of the Coppins had ever visited Paris and Versailles, and had likely never been out of the province of Guyenne.

She was relieved when the group moved, without any apparent announcement by a *maître d'hôtel* or other servant, into the dining room and took chairs at the long table. Surprisingly the table was bare of linen, the settings were only earthenware and pewter, and food was brought from the kitchen in wooden bowls. Most astonishing of all was the presence at one end of the room of a large canopied bed. A bed in the *salle à manger!* Of course Nicole had visited peasants' homes where a dozen souls cooked, ate, and slept in no more than two rooms, but this family was regarded as gentlefolk. No doubt they believed themselves every bit as good as the Clervaux, yet their château was little more than a farmhouse.

Every head turned when one of the sons spoke to Nicole directly, and listened intently as he began about the weather—that perpetual obsession of *vignerons*—then talked for an interminable quarter-hour about horses he had owned or admired. Allowing her no more than a polite nod, he finally turned away and spoke again with the men. Family members smiled meaningfully at each other, and resumed their usual topics.

So *that* was the plan! Nicole had been selected to marry this son—what was his name, Arnaud? And apparently they had all found her acceptable, despite her Versailles misadventure, since Madame Coppin was now nodding and beaming toothily in her direction.

And well they might, with their homemade furniture, animal skins nailed on the walls, and dogs stealing food from every plate! Whatever would her father say about such effrontery? Seated between two docile daughters-in-law as pregnant as brood mares, Nicole wanted to jump up and run from the house.

But instead she sighed and kept her seat. Dear heaven, what a dreadful snob she had become! Was she going to let Versailles ruin her for the rest of her life? Were her father's ways likely to bring her happiness? Forcing a smile, she accepted one of the damp babies, and without protection for her embroidered linen gown made from Marie Antoinette's own pattern, she began to feed him a dish of pudding.

The post next morning brought a letter from a firm of London solicitors, Botwhistle, Feather, and Armacost, who had the honor, they reported, to represent the Duke of Falkland. Would Mademoiselle de Clervaux be so kind as to transmit on each quarter day a summary of all financial transactions direct to their address in Lincoln's Inn. Hopefully, before the end of the year, one of their partners would have journeyed to Bordeaux to make her acquaintance and conduct the annual audit of her accounts. In the interim, and at all future times, they would welcome her inquiries about her father's will, trusts, and investments. Desirous of earning her friendship and esteem, they, the undersigned, begged her to consider them her most obliged and most humble servants, etc., etc.

The letter indicated clearly that Falkland had rid himself of all burdensome responsibilities as her trustee.

5

Nicole tossed away the leghorn hat because its broad brim obstructed her view of the sky. A few gray clouds hung in the west above the ocean, threatening the *vendange*, or harvest, of the grapes. Rain would wash from the surface of the grapes the *moût*, or whitish coat of must, the natural yeast that brought about proper fermentation.

She loved the ink-blue Cabernet Sauvignon grapes hanging on the gnarled vines. Two days ago, Maître Poujade had pronounced the fruit fully mature and the *moût* stationary. Menacing weather dictated that all hands work in the vineyards, and each day Nicole had labored beside her peasant friends until the sun sank in the Atlantic.

Despite their back-breaking work, Nicole and the Gaillard girls were able to laugh and gossip. Yesterday Nicole had greatly amused everyone when she hid from Arnaud Coppin by running into one of the *caves*, or cellars. For a month now, she had succeeded in avoiding him whenever he came to call on her. Of course she would not be lucky forever. Someday no doubt she would have to serve him tea or go riding with him, and she wrinkled her nose at the thought. It was not that he was exactly ugly, but he did have an unusually low forehead and a ragged thatch of light brown hair that looked as though it had been trimmed with a penknife.

"There he is again, mademoiselle!" Jeanne cried out, and Noémie shook with laughter.

Nicole glanced up at the horse and rider silhouetted on the horizon. "It is only the *maître*," she answered patiently. No doubt the girls would want to tease her this way all day long, just as they had yesterday.

Nicole carefully laid several more blue bunches in her wide, shallow wicker basket, and once again glanced at the clouds. They were no darker, and had perhaps drifted a little out to sea. Until now, the summer had seen excellent weather. With a little more luck the château could press a superb wine this fall. Already, she had learned the financial difference between a good vintage and a great one, and could not help but desire the extra profits.

Perhaps she would become in her mature years one of those shrewd Frenchwomen who handle numbers better than any man. In her imagination she pictured herself on a high stool, quill pen in hand, deriving great satisfaction from the sums she was adding. And no doubt she would be far too attentive to her vineyards and wineries to take the foreign journeys she had dreamed of when young.

"Mademoiselle Nicolette, run and hide! The rider is coming this way!" Jeanne was joking no longer. Nicole stood up with annoyance, wondering if she still had time to flee. Arnaud was not yet close enough to recognize her, dressed as she was in a gingham frock like any peasant. But was it really Arnaud? Wasn't this man larger? Wasn't his hair dark and neatly tied behind his neck as Arnaud's never was? Hardly believing her eyes, she started toward him, weaving between the vines, hastily smoothing her hair. Unless she had taken leave of her senses, it was the Duke of Falkland.

He reined in his horse before her and obviously enjoyed watching the amazement on her face. She tried to utter some greeting, "Oh, *monsieur le duc*—" then could only stare up at him. How frightening were his dark eyes boring into her; how bronzed was his skin. Had he sat on the box during his journey south? He had no coat or cravat; his full white shirt was tied by a drawstring at the throat. She had never seen him mounted on a horse before. His fashionable buckskin breeches stretched tightly over the muscles of his thighs and were tucked into expensive black leather boots.

When she bobbed a little curtsy rather too late, he laughed and said gallantly, "The *châtelaine* of Beaux-Clervaux need not pay homage to some foreign wanderer who trespasses on her land to beg for hospitality."

As she tried to excuse her appearance and explain the urgency of the harvest, he listened politely, but soon requested that she change her plans and lead him on a tour of the wineries. He had already taken the liberty, he said, of borrowing from her stable and ordering that her own horse— was his name Jupiter?—be readied for her. When she asked for a chance to change her dress, he refused, replying that he would find it particularly diverting to pass the afternoon with a lovely peasant girl.

Walking beside him toward the stables, she pointed at the western sky. "We are all praying that the rain clouds will spare the grapes."

"Then I will ask my Scots god to help you, though he was little enough success at home."

"*Ecossais?*" she asked in her nervousness, though she was well aware of the complicated family history of the Fraser family and the Dukes of Falkland.

"My forebears are more Scots than English. You should read your own father's volume someday about the ancestors of the Duke of Falkland." He was trying to goad her. When she remained silent, he added, "The book has been published in French also," and cocked an eyebrow at her.

Surely he would only laugh at some lame effort to excuse her thoughtless remark. Of course she had read all her father's books, transcribed them even, and he must know she could read English perfectly well. What in the world did he expect her to say? She was far too frightened of him for repartee.

Maître Poujade, who said he remembered the Duke of Falkland from his days at Beaux-Clervaux as a boy, joined them in a *cave* as they watched the peasants crushing grapes. Six men were stamping in a circle in a wide vat, singing or counting together to maintain a steady pace. The swirling, bubbling, blue-purple liquid reached high on the bare legs of the men, who had rolled up their trousers as far as possible.

Poujade explained that both pulp and juice would be fermented in a large oak vat. There were no inferior stone or brick *cuves* at Beaux-Clervaux, he said proudly. Of course fermentation was entirely unassisted, entirely natural. No additives were ever used. His wines were the finest in the world. In truth he sold leavens to other vintners, who were eager to imitate the flavor, however feebly, of the great Beaux-Clervaux reds.

The *cuvaison* would be terminated by transferring the wine to barrels after only ten days. Too much time in the vat produced an acidic flavor and too dark a color. Perfect timing is the secret of great winemaking, the secret of his own genius, Poujade, the least modest of men, declared. By his order, the wine remained in the barrels for four long years to produce its unsurpassed flavor and bouquet.

Now as soon as a cool, dry wind blew from the north, bottling of the excellent vintage of '85 would begin. Each barrel of the long-awaited year was ready, having been clarified a month ago by the addition of four egg whites, which when accompanied by vigorous banging on the outside of the barrel, caused all solids to precipitate to the bottom.

Poujade called for glasses and served Falkland, Nicole, and himself samples of the latest *soutirage*, or drawing off, of the '85. He held the ruby liquid before a candle flame. All Bordeaux reds—but his wines above all— were famous for their clarity. The English nation had in fact named them "clarets," and believed that they, because of their purity, were the only red wines that did not cause the dread disease of gout. The French went further, and made extensive claims for their power to restore health and promote long life.

The duke and Nicole drank samples of several *soutirages*, but Poujade spit his wine into a bowl after each tasting. The *maître* was required to judge too many samples in the course of a working day. Two bottles of wine a day was enough for any man, and he preferred to enjoy his with meals. Bidding Poujade farewell, Falkland asked Nicole to guide him to some of her tenant *chaix*, where once again they tasted vintages that were always presented with pride and often a little bragging and bluster.

All afternoon Falkland was as urbane as if he were riding with her in the park at Versailles. She could not begin to guess why he had traveled more than a hundred leagues south to see her. Certainly he did not intend to chastise her today for her behavior at Petit Trianon. But how could he have been so scornful, so merciless that last night at Versailles, and so blandly unperturbed here at Beaux-Clervaux? His smooth manner gave little indication of any serious purpose, but she knew he valued his own time too much to waste it with her without good reason. She had only one idea. Though he need not oversee her finances, he still had the responsibility of marrying her off. As she followed his horse on a narrow path back to the château, she decided she had guessed correctly. Falkland would only have come down to tell her that he—or, more accurately, the marquise—had arranged for her to marry, and the thought gave her an unpleasant feeling in the pit of her stomach.

At the top of the path, he turned his horse sharply left to a small *pavillon* hidden by a copse of trees. She joined him and they dismounted to walk on the little terrace of this summerhouse, which she had hardly visited since she was a child. Going directly to the north side, he enjoyed the excellent view of the Gironde Valley, then with hardly a glance into the single, pretty room all surrounded with glass, he motioned her back to her horse. Obviously, Falkland had been here before. The *pavillon* was not visible from the path. So his recollections of Beaux-Clervaux were still clear. Several times that afternoon she had had the impression he was letting her tell him things he already knew.

As the delectable odors of Clémence's cooking floated up from the kitchen, Nicole hurried to dress herself with some elegance for her first dinner with the duke. Heaven knows, her maid Julie had no ability to handle an elaborate toilette. The poor girl could hardly press a garment without scorching it, and knew nothing at all about stylish coiffures.

Nicole was not foolish enough to attempt to powder her own hair, but she worked pomades into locks on each side of her head, then piled her hair high on the rats used by the coiffeuse at Versailles.

Trying on a cream satin court dress she had never worn before, she decided it was far too pretentious, and changed it for a soft lime-green silk with a black ribbon around the waist. In her mother's jewel box, she happily found a necklace and earrings of peridots, which matched almost exactly the shade of the dress. Examining herself critically in the mirror, she concluded that her hairdo, while a bit unnatural here in the country, gave her some much-needed sophistication.

At least Julie was able to watch for the duke's appearance in the *salle à manger*, and tell her that she must hurry down to the great echoing dining hall. Running through the corridor on her little Pompadour heels, Nicole thought for a terrible moment that she was going to be sick. How frightened she was of Falkland! Oh, why had he ever come! She could not believe she would be able to get through the long dinner.

Since her father had become ill, Nicole had not dined in this room, which had been in the Middle Ages the great hall of the castle from which the Clervaux had ruled a manor. There had been an opening in the center of the ceiling, and cooking had taken place on the stone floor for the dozens of relatives, retainers, travelers, children, and dogs who must have eaten here every night. Now a huge brass chandelier hung from the center of the room, and the score of burning candles only poorly illuminated the lofty reaches of the raftered ceiling.

Falkland kissed her hand, then his eye moved to her hair, and she thought she could detect surprise and even distaste for the new style. Of course he would say nothing uncomplimentary, but she felt crushed and the sick feeling seemed to grow worse.

Somehow she must manage to eat the sumptuous meal Clémence had prepared. As a first course, they were served caviar from the Gironde with a bottle of Sauterne made on the estate, then quail with truffled sausages, pâté of duck, beef roasted over cuttings from the vines and dressed with the local sauce of shallots and red wine called *bordelaise* by the rest of the world, white asparagus, the local mushrooms called *cèpes*, pastries, cheeses, and finally a crystal bowl of *fraises des bois* or tiny wild strawberries.

Gaspard, the *maître d'hôtel*, would show the bottle to the duke before serving each wine, even though it had been decanted a few hours before. Falkland exclaimed with increasing excitement at the sight of each label. "Fifty-year-old claret from the house cellar itself! Dear mademoiselle, these bottles are priceless. I shall be forever in your debt!" he said and made a little bow in her direction. "The King of France himself does not have such wines on his table."

Nicole merely smiled and nodded. She had not selected the wines herself, and knew there were older, more valuable bottles in the cellar. Then she took one more glass herself. How many had she had today? Too many, she was sure; but at last she felt better. Probably the food had relaxed her. That was it, she had simply been suffering from an empty stomach.

Accepting a glass of cognac, the duke launched into an account of the political turmoil—nay, true civil war—that had spread throughout the nation. On the fourteenth of July, an angry mob had stormed the prison of the Bastille in Paris. Now, after a hot summer, every aristocrat or large landowner in France was in danger, and many had already fled the country. "As ambassador, I have been recalled to England by my king, who has graciously given me permission to determine first the safety of my ward. As soon as I can leave you, I will sail from Bordeaux for London."

Glass once again in hand, Nicole was thrilled by this speech. How she enjoyed the sound of "my ward" and the thought that he would vigilantly protect her. Of course it was nonsense to believe there was any danger here in the Bordelais, but she was not going to tell him that. How marvelous that he cared so much about her safety. He hadn't arranged some dreary marriage after all. He had simply come because of an imaginary threat of revolt.

Tipsy on the wine and enormously cheered by his attitude, she was finally emboldened to broach the subject of her disgrace. Certainly she would never find him in such a receptive mood again. She thought of taking one more glass of wine, but knew it would only twist her tongue. "*Monsieur le duc*, please forgive me. . . . I mean to say, forgive me for introducing this painful subject, but I will have no peace of mind until I offer my explanation of the—er, unpleasantness in the queen's Hamlet."

Nicole almost lost her nerve when she saw the surprise that registered on the duke's face. His dark eyes bore into her from under raised eyebrows. Fumbling for words, she told him that the marquise had arranged for Simon de Brizac to take her to the Fête Champêtre, that she had found him very charming and extremely amusing—no, better not have said that; she must keep to the essential facts—and his behavior completely proper until she was foolish enough to enter the cottage alone with him.

Staring down at the twisted napkin in her lap, she stammered that she did not know quite why things had gone wrong. "Perhaps it was my own fault, perhaps I tried to be too polite—" She sat silent for a few moments. She could almost feel Simon's passionate embrace and her own excited response. "But of course I—" When she glanced at Falkland, she thought his face unusually flushed with wine. He was listening to her raptly.

But she could not bear to relive the experience. Surely the duke would understand what she was trying to say without any embarrassing details. In a rush of words, she concluded, "He forced himself on me. Of course I tried to fight him off as best I could—!" Then she turned her face away and pretended to examine a dim family portrait on the wall.

The silence hung heavily. Finally Falkland stirred and coughed a little. He seemed to be having some difficulty in clearing his throat, and then Nicole realized to her horror that he was shaking with laughter. After a glance at her face, he struggled to control himself, and held his napkin before his mouth. "So the marquise decided to get rid of you! No doubt even she was surprised when she succeeded on the first attempt. Brizac, of course, is notorious. Her plan was very shrewd. Any acquaintance with him would sooner or later have compromised you." He smiled suavely at her, as though she must appreciate the marquise's skill, as well as the humor of the situation.

Nicole's response was icy. Indeed he deserved one of his own haughty rebukes. Not that he would even notice her reproof. Falkland had little interest in reading her expressions. She was appalled at his cynical indifference to her humiliation, and had little doubt that he would enjoy another good laugh when next he saw the marquise.

Nicole awoke with a groan each morning, dreading the prospect of providing Falkland with entertainment and hospitality all day long. What in the world would she do with him? He had already declined to review the accounts of the *chaix*. Perhaps she could send him to her father's library. She had recently found some files in English, and wondered if they ought to be returned to Langmuir Castle.

But Falkland showed no interest in old papers. Instead he always requested—at first in the stilted manner of the courtier, later with more sign of sincerity—that she spend the day riding with him about the countryside. Why did he insist that she accompany him? She warned herself they were worlds apart in taste, position, even nationality, and certainly in moral standards. Some men, she had read somewhere, required a woman on their arms as an adornment, nothing more than a kind of feather in their caps.

One day he led her, guided entirely from his own recollections, hushing her when she tried to refresh his memory, over the hills to the mouth of an abandoned *chaix* boarded up a hundred years before after a tragic cave-in. Searching in the underbrush he found a second hidden gate, which he succeeded in forcing open.

"We dare not enter these tunnels!" Nicole protested. "The earth is too soft here. That's why the spot was given up and the new *chaix* constructed."

Ignoring her warnings, he pulled her along the narrow passageway into what was apparently a large chamber. As their eyes became accustomed to the dim light, they saw a few broken barrels scattered on the floor and a mound of earth and rock that must mark the site of the collapse.

"Go back, it's terribly dangerous!" Frantically, she tugged at his arm. "Six people were killed in this room. There have been many little cave-ins since then. Nobody ever ventures down here!" Her father had always sternly warned against any foolhardy exploring.

"But there are still bottles stacked in the *cave*. Don't you want to sample your oldest vintages?"

As he laughed at her cowardice, she managed to pull him out before he risked his life poking through the debris. Angrily, she asked, "You came here with my mother, didn't you?" She was certain that her cautious, sensible father would never have condoned a visit.

"Of course. She was not such a frightened rabbit as you!"

Another day they wandered by chance, or so it seemed, onto the ruins of a small chapel. Little remained but the foundations after some long-ago fire. When the peasants of the region had been accommodated at services in the then-new chapel of the château, the little structure was not rebuilt. But a peaceful graveyard, outlined by poplars, adjoined the ruin and was still in use by local families.

Nicole pointed out some of the oldest gravestones, covered with moss, barely decipherable, some without surnames: one simply, NICODÈME, 1507, and another, with a primitive engraving of a skull and crossbones, CRESPIN, 1523-1543.

Wandering about for a few minutes to observe the diligence of the *sacristain* in caring for the graves, she prepared to remount Jupiter. But the duke remained in the cemetery, slowly walking down each row. He was reading the name on each marker, oblivious of Nicole. In her growing impatience, she suddenly realized that he was searching for her mother's grave.

Let him think his own thoughts of Lucienne. It was none of her business. But Nicole was wounded by the idea of the love she imagined he had felt—still felt—for her mother and the resulting disrespect toward her father. She found she avoided the sight of her mother's portraits and tried never to enter the Petit Salon. The château seemed to be filled, as never before, with her mother's spirit—a different spirit now, one laughing gaily and frolicking mischievously with the young duke under the disapproving eyes of her future husband.

Yet at the same time, paradoxically, Nicole felt a growing familiarity with Falkland. Even as she grew more certain of his love for her mother, she became at ease with him and more indulgent of his aloof and sometimes condescending manner. While it was untrue to say that he no longer frightened her, she had learned to accept casually his hands while dismounting or climbing up a slope, and learned not to be surprised if he hurried her with a familiar tug on the sleeve. *Yes, she was used to him*, she told herself. Her flesh no longer tingled for long minutes with the memory of his touch.

One October morning, as Nicole breakfasted in her room, Julie brought the message, transmitted by the duke's manservant, Timothy, in heavily accented French, that His Grace desired a picnic lunch packed in hampers for a midday ride.

As their horses cantered along a westerly road they had not taken before, Nicole prayed that they were not heading on one more pilgrimage to shrines of Lucienne. They rode past peasant cottages and a tenant château, seemingly choosing lanes at random. Finally, the duke asked Nicole if they were approaching the ocean, and she replied that she thought they were.

They could hear the surf before they saw it, but were nonetheless startled by a sudden view of the vast ocean. After both mounts had carefully descended a rocky track, Falkland galloped ahead, riding exuberantly through the spray, and Jupiter gave chase eagerly. The horses raced on the wet, hard-packed sand, until Jupiter finally showed his superiority and overtook the duke's mount.

Reining in his horse, the duke gestured enthusiastically at ships visible offshore. Perhaps they were headed for England, he said, and added with evident pleasure that he must go home soon. Nicole glanced at him with sad eyes, but said nothing, and he seemed unaware of her silence.

The sea air was too brisk for a picnic on the beach, so they climbed to the top of the cliff, and sought a sheltered dell they had seen along the way. At last they dismounted, and pointed down at some flat rocks beside a little brook just below the hill where they were standing. As they wove their way through a patch of wild blackberries, the duke jumped down to a safe level, and turned to hold out both hands for Nicole. Springing after him eagerly, she caught her skirt on the brambles halfway down the hill. In her fear of falling—or was it excitement at his nearness?—she laughed nervously, then slipped a little and almost lost her footing. Her dress began to tear on a bramble, and she grabbed for another thorny branch that cut her hand. The duke laughed at her plight, and wrapping one arm around her waist, worked to free her dress. She had no choice but to place an arm around his shoulders and let him support her weight. To shrink from the contact would be awkward and foolish. She might cause him to lose his balance as well.

At last he could help her down. As she found a secure footing in the thick grass beside the brook, he did not immediately release her. How pleasant was the pressure of his arm around her waist, how lovely the feel of his muscular body through his linen shirt. His face was only inches from hers. When their eyes met, his expression was guarded, his deep-set eyes remote. His free hand clasped her injured one. Was there an unusual tension in his grip? Instinctively, she felt surprise and alarm. Without the flicker of an eyelid, he gracefully relaxed his embrace, and slid his arm from her waist. In a second she was free. Later, glancing at his impassive face, she could not be sure he had intended to kiss her, that the idea had ever crossed his mind.

But for the rest of the day, she felt a joyful contentment. They talked easily, laughed spontaneously, and exchanged more natural glances than ever before. After lunch, he lounged beside the brook, while a few feet away she sat and watched him, her knees tucked up under her chin, her skirts wrapped modestly around her legs, reaching even to the toes of her boots. When he rolled on his back and stared silently at the clouds, she thought he might fall asleep; but instead he began to talk at random about his childhood at Langmuir Castle, the few memories he had of his mother and father, a serious fall from a horse he had suffered when he was only ten, and the first time he was presented at the English court. Then he encouraged Nicole to tell him about her life at Beaux-Clervaux with her father. The duke asked many questions about Robert's later years, and she had the impression that he almost envied the freedom and independence the scholar had enjoyed.

Not once did he refer to her mother, nor did Nicole. Lucienne had faded and almost vanished from her mind. Would her ghost finally leave them in peace? Nicole even abandoned the resolution she had made to ask Falkland, before the day was over, if he had ever come here to the beach and this little dell with Lucienne.

When the light dimmed a little, she looked up expecting to find the sun obstructed by a cloud, but suddenly realized that the hour had grown late. The duke rose reluctantly and packed up their hampers, while she hurried to help him.

"We'll be very late for supper," she said. "Clémence and Gaspard will be worried about us."

"Will they be scandalized?" he asked with a light laugh.

"No, they will only fear that Jupiter has broken a leg."

They skirted the blackberries without incident, and regaining the road, looked back fondly at the little dell. Once mounted again on their horses, they could smile unrestrained at each other. The duke said, "I hate to go back. I hate to see this peaceful interlude ever come to an end."

Nicole dared not speak a word. She could not bear the thought that their delicate balance of happiness might be disturbed.

Now she could rest no longer, and jumping up, donned a dress and shawl. For once, Nicole had awakened with the first light of dawn. Tossing in bed would be no help. She longed to breathe the fresh air of the new day and see the brilliant sunrise.

Running across the farmyard in the half-light, she heard a single rooster crow. Too impatient to saddle Jupiter, she grabbed his mane and swung herself onto his bare back. Tearing off across the meadow, she enjoyed the slap of the wind on her face and the feel of her long hair flying free.

She had to escape from the château to think about Falkland. How could she know what she felt—ought to feel—with him lying in bed not three chambers from her own? Yesterday had surprised and upset her. How happy they had been together. And he had actually told her that he never wanted the afternoon to end. Could his pleasure in the day possibly mean that he loved her? Loved her as she loved him?

Then angrily, Nicole dug her knees into Jupiter and sent him jumping over a series of stoned fences. The horse sensed her tension and increased his speed and daring, flying across a broad field. But suddenly she knew this wild ride was insane. She could not risk her precious Jupiter on the high wall around the Gaillards' pasture. Urgently, she pulled on the horse's mane until he came to a reluctant halt.

Of course a few, rather ambiguous words did not make a declaration of love. The duke had merely been expressing some fleeting impulse, or perhaps he had meant that his "peaceful interlude" here at Beaux-Clervaux would soon be followed by civil unrest in the whole country. She must never forget the Falkland of the marquise's breakfast table, the Falkland flirting with the queen before the whole court, the cruel Falkland of Petit Trianon. Nicole had let her painful yearning for him impair her judgment. If only she could discipline her own thoughts, if only she could control her own dangerously enflamed emotions!

One windy morning the duke did not send Timothy to invite her to ride. No doubt the weather offered little inducement, she reassured herself. Finishing her breakfast tray, she dressed leisurely and went downstairs, expecting to find the duke in the library or Grand Salon. When he was not visible, she descended the narrow, winding staircase that led to the wine cellar, where she knew he often selected wines with Gaspard. Failing to find him there, she took the long underground passage to the kitchen and asked the maids for information. But no one could help her. Climbing upstairs again rather puzzled and anxious, she finally noticed that the door to her mother's little salon was ajar.

Nicole's heart began to pound, for she knew that she would at last confront him with his love for Lucienne. Only for a moment did she consider—and reject—leaving him in peace with the memory of her mother. She opened the door almost silently, but a floorboard creaked as she stepped in, and she knew he knew she was there. The duke did not turn around. He continued to stand a few feet in front of the fireplace, in which a fire was burning, with his hands clasped behind his back, his head turned upward at the portrait hanging high above the mantel. In the poor light, the slight young girl in her heavy gown looked somber, discontent, despairing.

"But you can't see her at all!" Nicole said crossly, and threw open the shutters, admitting the clear morning light. Immediately Lucienne changed into the poised and cheerful girl who was proud of being the wife of Robert de Clervaux. Nicole felt a little victory. Falkland blinked his eyes in the new light, then scowled at her for her invasion of the privacy.

Nicole hovered a few feet away, but he suddenly turned and pulled her by the arm until she stood before him, just below her mother's picture. Still holding her forearm, he studied her face as though he had never seen it before, then raised his head to examine Lucienne. Hating the comparison, Nicole struggled to pull away, and finally squirmed out of his grasp.

Coolly he began, "The resemblance is very great, the eyes, hair, and figure; and yet there is something so different—" He squinted at Nicole with a frown, and then at the portrait again. "She had a gentle light in her eyes, a kindness to her expression—yes, there at the mouth and chin," he said, pointing at the picture. "But your expression is willful, your jaw stubborn, your mouth self-indulgent!"

Shocked and wounded, Nicole blurted, "I beg you to leave this room, to leave my mother in peace! How can you flaunt your love for her in the house of the man who paid you only honor and respect!"

With merely an impatient glance in Nicole's direction, Falkland crossed to a table between the pair of tall windows and picked up a small, carved *coffret*, or chest, that had always stood, in Nicole's memory, in that location. First he raised the lid, but finding only a dried flower and a single glove, he turned the chest upside down, and twisted one of the wooden legs until the bottom of the box sprang open. As Nicole stood speechless, he removed two letters from the secret chamber, glanced through their pages quickly, then tore them twice across and threw them into the fire.

"How dare you!" Nicole cried, as she jumped forward to try to grab the fragments out of the flames. "They belonged to my mother! You have no right to destroy my mother's things! We have little enough left that was hers." With a poker she knocked one fragment to the hearth, and rushed to stamp out its burning margin. But Falkland paid little attention. He was watching with satisfaction as the other sheets turned to ash.

Nicole lifted the half-burned page and realized immediately that it was in Falkland's distinctive script. She had seen his handwriting when he had written, also in French, a formal letter of sympathy after her father's death. There was no mistaking the bold spikes and scrolls of his hand despite the blackened state of the paper. On one side of the sheet she read, "I waited in the *pavillon* till after the moon set and then . . . I . . . with heavy heart. . . ." Slowly she raised her head and looked at Falkland. He was staring absently into the flames, reliving some long-dead moment. She saw a look of helplessness and resignation so foreign to his usual proud pose that she could not help but feel a stab of sympathy for him.

Automatically she turned the page over, and soon realized that he was using the familiar form of *you* reserved in French for God, children, and lovers. She could only decipher fragments of sentences: "One night in . . ."; "I cannot permit you to . . ."; ". . . force you to admit. . . ." Some instinct told her she should not trespass farther. She glanced again at his face, as though for permission. But he was watching her indifferently, and she ventured on and read, "I merely kiss your throat and breasts"— here the paper had crumbled away; was there some word missing, *until* perhaps?—"I lie all night beside your naked form."

Dazed with embarrassment, Nicole stepped forward to return the letter to the flames, then hesitated, wheeled toward him, then stopped abruptly to avoid his eyes. Acknowledging he had some kind of right of ownership, she pushed the letter at him. She knew he knew what she had found, what kind of words.

As he read it for himself, Nicole stood by rigidly. He was taking his time over the salacious words, she thought with irritation. Why had she not instantly burned such a vile indictment of her mother's virtue? But surely Lucienne had done nothing wrong. The sinful ideas came only from his brain. Her mother had not met him in the *pavillon,* the letter clearly said that. As Nicole regained her composure, her anger against Falkland mounted. He was the would-be seducer of her mother, the wrecker of her father's home. But perhaps not *would-be!* Perhaps he *had* succeeded in stealing her mother's virginity. Nicole wanted to scream the accusation at him.

At last, with his face turned away from her, he knelt on the hearth and laid the paper in the center of the flames, where after once flickering out, it finally caught fire. Still kneeling, he watched its disintegration. To Nicole's angry eyes, the scene was all too similar to some kind of a ritual sacrifice on a pagan altar.

"Come then!" she cried at him. "I'll take you to see what you've been searching for all the while you've been at Beaux-Clervaux!" Only once turning back to see if he was following her, she ran out of the Petit Salon, across the vestibule, through a picture gallery, and along the peristyle of an inner courtyard. Pulling at a heavy oak door, which she managed to open before he could reach it, she led him into the dark, narrow, high-ceilinged room that was the family chapel. Near the door flickered a few votive candles in their little red glasses. The only other light came from small stained clerestory windows, piercing the gloom with ruby and amber beams. There was a faint odor of incense mixed with the burning candle wax.

Nicole genuflected hastily, then taking a fresh taper, lighted it from one of the votive candles, and hurried down the aisle to the altar rail. Turning to wait for Falkland to join her, she looked directly at him and told herself with satisfaction that he seemed uncomfortable in this holy place.

With anger flashing in her eyes, she gestured at the long brass plaque imbedded in the stone floor. Just where Lucienne had stood in the marriage ceremony, her father had once told her. And now Robert lay beside her, on her right, the brass fresh and shiny on his tomb. Bouquets of flowers —now *anémones*—were placed daily by the servants on each marker.

With a defiant voice, Nicole read aloud the engraving on her mother's plaque. "*Ci-gît Lucienne, née Saint-Mathiez, femme bien-aimée de Robert de Clervaux*—1749-1770." Then placing the candleholder on the floor just at the head of her mother's grave and leaving Falkland alone with his memories, she ran out of the chapel, letting the heavy door crash behind her.

6

His brusque manner suddenly softened at Nicole's impulsive exclamation. "Oh, can you be certain you'll return by Saint Martin's Day? Surely you don't want to miss the *Gerbaude!* It's our most important festival of the year."

For two days they had barely spoken to each other after the episode of the letters. Nicole had spent her waking hours in the Gaillards' cottage, where Falkland could hardly have joined her even if he wanted. How the duke had passed his time she had no idea, had not asked the maids because she feared her questions would be repeated to Timothy, who was already a favorite with the female servants at Beaux-Clervaux.

At last Falkland and Nicole had taken dinner together in the *salle à manger*. In crisp tones he had informed her that he must ride into Bordeaux, where he would probably spend a day or two. No reason for his trip was forthcoming. She no longer felt any ease of communication with him, and could only guess that one of his regular messengers from Paris had brought him diplomatic business that must be dispatched by a fast boat to England.

But to risk missing the harvest festival! During the month or more that Falkland had been at Beaux-Clervaux, Nicole had looked forward eagerly to the night of feasting and carnival gaiety, the night when the duke and she would dance together under the stars. Seeing that he was pleased by her urging, she took the opportunity to end the siege between them, and not only coaxed from him a promise that he would return by sundown of Saint Martin's Day, but also offered him Jupiter for the journey.

While he was gone, she indulged herself in hours of planning her clothes for the festival. After endless trials of the Versailles gowns, she settled on a white India cotton frock meant for mornings at court, which she had Julie decorate with velvet ribbons of forest green. Nicole had chosen the dress for its simplicity, since the other participants at the *Gerbaude* would be her own peasants and servants, and for its light weight, because the weather had turned surprisingly warm, a true Saint Martin's Summer. The sleeves were short, shirred just above the elbow, and the neckline wide, curving from the tips of her shoulders well down into the V between her breasts. Was it too immodest? Not by Versailles standards, though Nicole herself had never before worn such a daring décolletage. She planned to let her hair hang loose, as she had deduced Falkland liked it, though he never expressed his opinion in words. Only a single dark green ribbon would control the heavy blond cascade down her back.

She posted one maid or another all afternoon to watch for the duke's return. An hour before sunset, Nicole herself took a seat in an upstairs window, slowly brushing her hair as she peered anxiously for some sign of Jupiter and the duke. When at last the light began to fail, she knew a crowd would soon be gathering in the meadow by the pond. Sending off Julie and the other girls, she lingered, hoping against hope for the sound of Jupiter's hooves. The sky was blue-black now, and she could see the glow from the colored lanterns hanging above the outdoor tables and hear the tuning of the violins. Reluctantly she slipped on her dress, brushed her hair one last time, and started out alone.

But as soon as she reached the crowded meadow her spirits rose. The merrymakers were gathered near a vine-covered arbor that contained a huge rack of bottles and rows of barrels; and from the rowdy laughter, Nicole knew many of the peasants were already feeling their wine. As she was greeted jovially, someone ran up to her with the ornamental silver flagon reserved for the *châtelaine*. According to custom, the owner of the estate must down the whole pitcher on one breath. Nicole groaned as soon as she took the heavy flagon in her hand, but the spectators chanted, "Drink, drink!" She took a few mouthfuls, and the wine from the brimming container began to spill down her face. The chanting growing insistent, she forced herself to swallow, but she could already feel a burning in her veins. After another few gulps, she gasped and gave up, thrusting the flagon at the nearest man to finish. The crowd pretended to moan with disappointment, and then broke into applause at her valiant effort.

Some of her maids helped sponge her face and hands, examined her dress for drops of wine, then arranged the white shawl across her shoulders, for the night air was already growing cool. Soon Maître Poujade, official host for the evening, rang a large gong and started the rush for the tables. Nicole knew places of honor were set for herself and the duke. Searching hopefully through the crowd for him, she sighed with disappointment, then catching a small peasant boy as he ran by, asked him to go to the château to see if the duke had finally arrived. Until Falkland came, she wanted to avoid the throne-like seat of honor, and squeezed in between Jeanne and Marc Gaillard on the half-log that served as a bench.

The procession of lavish dishes seemed endless, and Nicole soon forgot her resolution to eat lightly. She had two bowls of wine-red soup, then servings of oysters, hare, lamb, beef, and wild boar. Tray after tray of cheeses, fresh fruits, and cakes came down the table. But the focus of attention was the wines—countless bottles of varying age and importance. Every new wine was proclaimed a masterpiece by the crowd, and a hundred toasts were shouted and drunk. Each additional glass was downed with more abandon. What if a bottle was spilled, a neighbor fell asleep, a normally sedate wife danced the *gigue* while the crowd clapped her on?

But Nicole carefully limited her own intake of wine. She wanted to be in possession of her senses when Falkland arrived, as she still trusted he would do. When the peasant boy came back to tell her that he could not find the duke in the château, she began to feel some alarm. Fortifying herself with another apricot tart, she decided to check on the stables. With no servants to help, Falkland would have to tend to Jupiter himself. But Jupiter's stall was empty. Had there been a terrible accident? Were both horse and rider lying helpless on some deserted road? She controlled her anxiety by reminding herself that Falkland was probably still angry with her, and was just as pleased to disappoint her tonight.

The little band—actually a few violins, a *musette, tambourins*, and old Colombian's booming *hélicon*, or tuba—struck up a lively tune. Before she knew it, Nicole was pulled onto the field reserved for dancing by Maître Poujade himself, then was claimed by the Gaillard boys and a dozen other servants and peasants.

After almost tripping and falling to the ground, she fended off a new partner and seated herself on a bale of hay. Her satin slippers were impossible on the soft earth. Already their slender heels were caked with mud. She took them off, and when no one was looking, pulled down her white silk stockings and stuffed them in the shoes. Julie could retrieve them all for her tomorrow, though no doubt the shoes were already beyond repair.

Because the night was brisk, the *maître* ordered a large bonfire built nearby, which soon filled the air with the unique aroma of burning grape cuttings. As Nicole danced a vigorous chaconne with a tall cowherd, she began to feel the heat from the fire. Certainly it had been lit too close to the dance area, but then perhaps the exercise and her consumption of wine were telling. She tossed away her shawl, and squared off for a quadrille with Marc Gaillard as her partner.

She had always liked good-natured Marc the best of the Gaillard boys, and now, at twenty, he had turned out to be impressively tall and as powerful as a bull. And when Julie ran to tell her that Arnaud Coppin was searching for her, Marc and Nicole and Julie all doubled up with laughter, and Nicole made Marc promise not to leave her side for a minute, to keep Arnaud at bay.

As he swung her around the field, Nicole noticed how effortlessly Marc lifted her off the ground, what an excellent, even exuberant, dancer he had become. Perhaps he was flattered that she had asked him to attend her for the whole of the evening, and no doubt she had been a little rash. But Marc had always been like a brother. She would never believe he could lose his head over her.

Just as she spun a little recklessly and fell heavily against his chest, Nicole spotted a face in the crowd of spectators standing near the fire. The tall, dark man scowling at her looked for all the world like Falkland. Then she felt a twinge of guilt. For a few minutes at least, she had forgotten all about searching for the duke.

She pulled Marc out of the dance, and told him she must go to find Falkland. Although she did not invite him, Marc followed her as she circled the field twice and looked carefully at every man, then decided sadly that she had only imagined she saw his face.

Instead of the duke, she had managed to discover Arnaud, who was now hurrying toward her. Laughing, she ducked out of sight into a circle of haystacks where tired dancers were resting and heavy drinkers were sleeping off their wine. Marc still followed her, and together they collapsed against a rick. Her shoulder was touching Marc's, her arm resting on his. She was too tired to move. He passed her a communal bottle of wine, and she took a long draft. It felt so good to rest. She thought she might fall asleep for a moment or two, as her head rested on Marc's comfortable shoulder.

The *musette*, or bagpipe, played its reedy, plaintive melody, and the light from the bonfire died down a little. Then suddenly, sitting up with a start, she realized that, standing very near her bare feet and exposed ankles, Falkland was staring down at her. In the heavy shadows, she thought she saw intense anger on his face. Or were the firelight and the eerie music only playing tricks on her?

Immediately, the duke turned and disappeared beyond the haystacks. Nicole struggled to her feet, noticed Marc was asleep—had she too been asleep when Falkland found her?—and tried to follow him. She could hardly distinguish faces in the crowd, and must watch for some man taller than the others. But the duke was not to be found near the dancers or the dinner tables or the wine barrels. Somehow he had eluded her and completely vanished from the *Gerbaude.*

Barefooted, shivering in her low-cut gown, she ran desperately toward the château. Why had Falkland glowered at her? What in the world was going through his mind? Why hadn't he called to her, awakened her, pulled her to her feet and joined in the festivities, as he must know she had longed all evening for him to do?

She searched high and low in the empty château, calling out his name, until she finally saw a light under the door of the little sitting room outside his bedchamber. Only after she had knocked and called for several minutes, did he finally admit her. From the dying fire, the strong smell of brandy, and the half-empty bottle, she guessed he had been sitting there drinking for hours before his visit to the *Gerbaude.*

She entered the room warily, and seated herself on a footstool. For a long time he only stared into the fire, and she was forced to sit humbly by until he was ready to talk. Finally he began to recount how three days before he had received word that the king and queen had been driven from Versailles by a mob and taken to Paris as prisoners behind pikesmen bearing the severed heads of the queen's own guards. Marie Antoinette herself had barely escaped from assassins inside the palace by running through a secret passageway from her apartment to the king's. The château of Versailles had been thrown open to the populace, and all the fabulous contents carted off by thieves.

The whole of France was in turmoil. Falkland's visit to Bordeaux had merely confirmed his suspicions that rabble-rousers were urging peasant revolts against all large landowners. The duke himself had heard the Clervaux name uttered more than once. He had no choice but to order Nicole to pack her valuables and sail with him to England by the next packet boat out of Bordeaux.

Her first instinct was to cry with relief. At last she could understand his black mood and the attempt to lose himself in drink. Of course she was distressed to hear about the peril to the royal family and the plunder of Versailles. As for her own safety, flight to England was ridiculous. Never had it been more clear than tonight that the peasants at Beaux-Clervaux were her devoted friends. But when she tried to argue with Falkland, she decided his stubborn resistance came from too much brandy. She would have to wait until tomorrow to reason with him.

But the duke seemed to want to belabor the subject. Suddenly rising, he approached her stool, and said, "No doubt England will be little to your taste, for you will seldom have an opportunity to carouse with menials, prance in the fields with bare legs flashing, and loll in the hay with drunken peasants!" Nicole cried out in protest, but he continued caustically, "Imagine my distress when my ward won for herself the label of trollop in a lewd display at Versailles before the queen herself; and now, when I hurry back from a mission of some risk, I find that she is sleeping in the arms of a peasant in a hayfield before the eyes of all her retainers!"

"You must be drunk! How dare you utter such distortions!" she shouted, jumping to her feet.

He grabbed her by the shoulders, whirled her around, pulled a handful of straw from the long hair hanging down her back, and held it up triumphantly. "Can there be any doubt you granted your strapping peasant the same favors that you gave Brizac?"

She struck at Falkland's face with all her strength, but he seized her arm before she hit him, and twisting it brutally, pulled her toward him and gave her mouth a burning kiss.

She tried to pound him with her free hand, but he succeeded in pinning both arms to her sides with an iron grip. Of course the kiss was demeaning, she told herself, his salute to a trollop—the word was still ringing in her ears. His lips seemed to bruise hers, and she returned the fire of his kiss. She longed to express the anger, exasperation, and anxiety of all these weeks. And the hopes and desires! How she had dreamed that someday he would press his mouth on hers! Gradually, Nicole began to feel a strange excitement well up somewhere in the center of her body.

Almost unconsciously, her mouth softened under his and finally yielded to his thrusting tongue. When she opened her eyes for a second, she was surprised at the intensity on his face. A moment ago he had vilified her. Where had the hatred gone? Now he seemed like a man possessed by an incredible greed. She was frightened by his passion, and as though asking for a little mercy, grew limp in his hands.

Suddenly he released his painful grip, and in her surprise she imagined he was done kissing her. On instinct, she turned her mouth toward his searchingly, and he understood her thought and laughed a little. Then he embraced her tenderly and buried his face in her neck. She was thrilled and amazed at his sudden transformation. Could it be that he really loved her? Impulsively, she threw her arms around his neck.

Falkland groaned with pleasure and began to press his lips on her neck and bosom. To prevent him from touching her breasts, she took his face in her hands and raised it again to her lips. He returned her lingering kiss, then gently pushed her hands away, and pulled her dress off one shoulder, nearly baring her breasts. She whispered a protest as he buried his face in the deep cleavage. Dear heaven, she must make him stop! What if she couldn't control him? She trembled a little with pleasure as he touched his lips on the fabric just above her nipples.

Suddenly a shoulder seam pulled loose, and he grasped one of her naked breasts, cupping it with his hand. "Oh, you must stop. I can't let you!" she cried. But he ignored her words, and adroitly controlling her hands, continued to stroke the satiny skin of the breast. Raising his head to watch her face for signs of pleasure, he teased the nipple with his fingertips. Ashamed of her excitement, she tried to turn away, then allowed herself to experience the sensation and gave an involuntary little moan. He smiled with satisfaction and brushed her lips with a kiss, before he bent down again to take the nipple in his mouth. "Oh, don't, please," she cried weakly. Her hands caressed his head as he worked the nipple with his lips. Finally, a belated attack of guilt gave her the strength to push him away and cover the breast with one hand.

"*Mon Dieu,* don't thwart me! I saw your naked breasts when you lay sprawled beneath Brizac! He possessed your body, while I have had to torture myself all these months—"

"But Brizac did not possess me!" Nicole exclaimed with indignation, retreating a step.

Falkland peered at her a little groggily, but then she saw his face fall. Her denial had had the ring of truth. "Then Brizac did not manage to—did not complete the act of love?"

"No! I told you I fought him off, and then the footmen entered—"

With a groan, he hugged her to him and stroked her hair. "God help me, I almost stole your maidenhead! Your father would have sent a thunderbolt down from heaven to strike me dead," he said with a rueful laugh.

A little dizzy from shock, she finally realized that she still held her hand over her naked breast and hurried to arrange her dress properly. Could he really mean to halt his frenzied lovemaking? Then she felt a wave of shame. Of course he was right. She shuddered at the prospect of losing her virginity, but somehow the thought heightened the excitement she still felt burning through her. But of course she must deny him. Of course she must tread the path of virtue.

What she hated was the show of almost fatherly good sense he was affecting. He was petting her like a child and offering her something that sounded like sympathy. "Poor Nicole, you have made yourself miserable all these weeks by allowing your imagination to construct an elaborate affair between your mother and me. All those years ago! And yet you've let yourself become obsessed with it!"

She wanted to cry out that she had not imagined his erotic sentences in the burnt letter, but instead she stared at him rather sullenly. All at once she felt extremely tired and only wanted to flee from the room.

But just as she started to leave, he reached forward to touch her bodice. A split second too late she realized he had only intended to arrange her dress modestly, but first she jumped with alarm and struck out violently at his hand.

In one swift motion of amazing strength, he swung her off her feet and high into his arms, then strode across the room to his bedchamber. Smiling wickedly, he told her, "It's too late, *ma chérie!* My enflamed desires cannot be denied. I'll leave sainthood to men more inclined by nature, though even saints, I dare say, could not resist the lure of your charms. Too late for you too, I'll warrant, from the petulant look on your face. Of course virginal girls are not believed to experience passion. If you truly are a virgin, that is! I can recall no other innocent girls with your, shall we say, sensuous proclivities. Perhaps they are merely natural appetites, *ma petite*. But we'll know that soon enough!"

He had tossed her in the center of his bed. Rolling her half over, he deftly unhooked her bodice and untied her stays. Her mind raced as she tried to decide how to escape him. "My Lord Duke, you will commit the greatest possible sin against me—" Trying to sit up, she beseeched him in a ringing tone.

"I doubt that, my dear. I truly do. I can conceive of far greater sins. Someday we must talk theology. But at the present moment, I beg you to cease your protests. The hour is late and my temper is short." To prove it he pushed her roughly back on the bed. "I will allow you no escape."

She did not resist as he pulled her dress off over her head and tossed it to the floor. He removed her stays and chemise impatiently, then sat back on his haunches triumphantly and examined her naked breasts in the moonlight. "I will not be robbed of the pleasure of seeing your beauty," he said and rose to light a candle from the coals in the fireplace. "Don't move, Nicole. Don't try to cover yourself. You should walk naked at all times. Your breasts are far too lovely to be concealed." He lightly brushed each erect nipple with his lips.

Then as she turned her face away with shame, he untied the drawstring of her drawers and slowly pulled them down her belly to reveal her mound of dark blond hair. He seemed to shudder with pleasure at the sight, and then pulled the garment off and threw it aside.

Without taking his gaze off of her body, he stood up and removed his shirt and hose and shoes, but left on his breeches as a gesture of consideration for her virginal state. Nicole could not help but notice the swollen bulge in the tight pants, then looked away quickly.

He lay down beside her and gently encircled her with his arms. She hugged him tightly to her almost with relief; at least so close he could not stare at her naked body. He kissed her forehead and cheeks gently and whispered something soothing in her ear. He would give her time to gain a little trust in him.

As she grew comfortable in his arms, she became bold enough to look deep into his eyes, which appeared black in the shadows of the bed draperies. For once his face was open, unguarded, without some fixed expression of haughty pride or ironic humor. His eyes seemed honest, trusting, gentle, even kind. What a confusing man he was! She could almost believe she saw a trace of love for her.

But then there was a flicker of impatience, and he turned to caress her body, first nuzzling her earlobe and shoulder and the hollow of her throat, and then covering each breast with tiny kisses. He sucked vigorously on one nipple, as he stroked her other breast until she sighed. Nicole felt a rush of the excitement she thought had left her in her fear and embarrassment. She could not help but caress his face and shoulders and chest tenderly, curiously, and when he leaned close, she clutched him to her without reserve.

The duke rose up on one elbow and began to brush his hand lightly over the skin of her belly. He traced a circular pattern, but when she shivered and cried out a little he leaned down to kiss her mouth passionately. She responded without restraint, answered his tongue with her own. Now she burned with the need for his mouth and caressing hands, feared ever to let him stop. The excitement she felt was more intoxicating than that of wine.

But she jumped with surprise when he touched the inside of her thighs, stroking gently, rhythmically, as he watched her face for her reactions. Gently he began to explore the folds between her legs. When she twisted and writhed with desire, he lowered his head and kissed her where his fingers probed.

Nicole jumped up and tried to push his head away, crying out in protest. But he pushed her down rather roughly and continued his prolonged kiss, then grabbed her hand and held it on the swollen front of his breeches.

"Unbutton it and touch me, Nicole! Caress me, love me!" he cried, as though in pain. He held her hand until she obeyed him, and she finally began to open the dozen buttons, then pushed her hand inside and closed her fingers around him. He gasped with pleasure and moved her hand a little with his own. Nicole was shocked and frightened by the size and implied power of this part of his body that she could feel but not see.

Quickly stripping off his breeches, he used both hands to force her thighs apart as she tried to fight him off. "We can't stop now. Neither of us," he said softly, and kissed her again between her legs until at last she moaned with desire and spread her thighs wide apart. Unable to control himself any longer, he gripped her hips with each hand and began to push into her. Nicole was not fully aware of what he meant to do until it was too late. She uttered a cry of pain and tried to shove him away. Remorseful for a brief moment, he stopped and clasped her in his arms. "Oh, chérie, I almost didn't believe you were a virgin. But it's over now . . . it's over now." He kissed her eyes, tasting the salty tears. "If you can only relax. . . ." But before he could finish, he had begun selfishly thrusting into her, deeper and deeper with each movement, deaf to her repeated moans.

To Nicole's surprise the pain quickly diminished, then mysteriously vanished even as the speed of his strokes increased. Her body caught the rhythm from his, and soon they moved in perfect unison. The pain forgotten, she was lunging with him with a frenzied necessity. How long she had dreamed that he would love, conquer, complete her! Now in frightening reality they were rushing together, united in some kind of a frantic race to reach a goal, to satisfy a need so instinctive, so animal that it did not even have a name. He had long since ceased to be the highly controlled man she knew, and had become raw and impassioned—even crying out now, crying out like a dying man with her name as his last word.

Collapsed together, they lay damp with sweat, calm at last in each other's arms. Finally he had the strength to give her a gentle kiss, the sweetest one of all—how different from the devouring kisses of a few minutes before. She knew it sealed her fate. She knew she could never love any other man as she loved this man tonight.

He snuggled against her and fell asleep without a word, and she felt almost a little maternal toward him. Perhaps she was asleep herself when she realized from his stirrings that he had begun to want her again. As his mouth fell greedily on her breast and his fingers pushed between her thighs, she felt her fatigue slip away and her desire for him leap again.

Dawn had begun to break when they finally rolled apart, and Nicole sank face down on the rumpled sheet—too tired to move or even whisper another word, sore and aching in every part of her body, sprawled as lifeless as though she had fallen from a great height—and quickly dropped into a deep, dreamless sleep.

7

Nicole watched the lantern hanging in the center of her cabin swing back and forth with an ever-greater arc, but she felt little doubt about her ability to endure rough seas. Her father had often boasted that he had never suffered a moment of seasickness. Very likely she had inherited his excellent balance. Lying here in the comfortable berth, she decided she had never felt better in her life. Although she had slept only five or six hours since boarding the ship in Bordeaux at midnight last night, she was totally revived after the strenuous day of packing at Beaux-Clervaux—and the unforgettable night before.

Unbelievably, only twenty-four hours had passed since she had awakened alone in Falkland's bed. Nervously slipping on her dress and rolling her undergarments into a ball (she had needed a minute or two to remember that she had been wearing no shoes), she had hurried down the corridor to her own chamber, unseen by any servant. Within an hour, she was receiving urgent orders relayed by Timothy to pack her most precious possessions and prepare to leave by coach at nightfall to catch the ship for England. Distressed to hear from her servants accounts of brewing revolts on other estates, and unable to speak with Falkland, who was closeted with couriers bearing more bad news, she finally consented to depart and began the task of packing her trunks.

At no time during the frenzied day did she see Falkland alone. Her meals had to be served on trays while she worked, and the day flew by as she searched cupboards, sorted papers, reviewed accounts, and issued a hundred orders to Clémence and Poujade for the care of the house and estates. She sadly bid farewell to a stream of friends who came to the château, and hugged Jupiter tearfully. In her fatigue at the end of the day she was relieved that Falkland had to hurry ahead to Bordeaux with his messengers, and only met her on board the English ship with a formal bow, whereupon, in view of the late hour, she was escorted directly to her cabin by a ship's officer.

Now she pulled the thick blanket up to her chin, and wondered when her breakfast tray would arrive. Without a maidservant on board—she had had to leave Julie behind, planning as the girl was to marry Pascal in a fortnight; and not a moment too soon, Nicole suspected, from the recent alteration in Julie's waistline—she feared she might have to breakfast in the lounge, where she would likely encounter Falkland.

Her brain still throbbed with memories of their unbelievable night. How would she ever understand that strange mixture of humiliation, violence, pleasure, and climactic joy? And how would she ever sort out the good and evil of what they had done? She had not wanted to sin—but surely that was hypocrisy! In spite of everything, all her instincts—her body itself—told her their lovemaking had been beautiful and good.

Yet when she dared to think about the future, she could only feel shame and dread and even panic. Of course she must face the duke soon again. Alone, without escape. On this very ship, even in this cabin. Somehow she must find the strength to convince him that she would not allow him to possess her again.

A great ordeal lay ahead of her, she knew. Even if she could avoid him tonight, she would soon be living in his own household in London, where he would have a thousand opportunities to break down her resistance. How much temptation would she be able to withstand? Especially when she had to admit her own undeniable desire for him and her inner conviction that she now belonged to him.

A valise slid across the deck of the cabin, then back again to its original spot. With one plunging wave, the porcelain pitcher and basin flew off the commode and shattered on the deck. Perhaps she would feel better if she closed her eyes. Now the timbers of the ship were creaking and groaning so loudly that she feared the vessel would surely break apart with the next crashing wave. Suddenly breakfast was unthinkable. Nicole could not imagine that she would ever want to eat again.

On the fourth morning she managed to keep down a little thin porridge. The steward tried to cheer her with the announcement that they would shortly enter the estuary of the Thames and find quiet water at last. Tonight she would be in London. Would it be her first visit? She nodded feebly and lay down again. Somehow she was going to have to find her clothes and comb her hair and prepare herself to meet Falkland on deck before the day was out.

But when the ship finally dropped anchor at a wharf beside a stone bridge in what was apparently the heart of London, Nicole had to inquire after the duke. She had already been standing on deck for an hour enjoying the passage up the Thames, feeling well at last and confident of her appearance in a blue velvet cape and plumed hat from Versailles.

The captain registered surprise at her question. "But surely you saw the man-of-war *Redoubtable* hove to off Gravesend at the mouth of the Thames, waiting only for the Duke of Falkland. The royal standard was flying from the mainmast, and when Falkland climbed aboard from the ship's boat, King George himself came forward to greet him. A fine spectacle it was, mademoiselle, and a pity for you to miss it. It's not every day one has a chance to see the king."

Though she was flattered to be met by the duke's luxurious carriage—a new four-horse berlin bearing the ducal coronet in gold—she lamented his absence. What a pleasure it would have been to hear his comments on every sight as they drove through the fascinating city.

"Of course you've guessed this is London Bridge, mademoiselle," Timothy offered, considerately speaking to her in French. In his kind way he had sensed her disappointment. "And there is the new bridge called Blackfriars just upriver. And to our right is, as you surely know, the Tower of London, where Anne Boleyn and many other fine folks have lost their heads."

"Oh, Timothy, climb in the cab with me, and tell me all these interesting things as we ride along."

"No, mademoiselle, I couldn't do that. Not in England. But I will jump down from the box and call to you through the window each time we pass a famous place."

In their slow ride through the busy, narrow streets, he pointed out a tall fluted column on Fish Street Hill that commemorated the Great Fire of 1666; and St. Paul's Cathedral, whose great dome she had seen from the river, but now so close beside it here in the Churchyard, could only sense its massive size from the shadows it cast; and the Temple Bar, the boundary of the City of London, an elaborate archway over the street with iron spikes on top where the heads of executed men were exhibited. And on into the City of Westminster with its handsome parks, squares, and mansions, until at last they entered the district called Mayfair, that Timothy told her was considered the most elegant of all. In a while he called down to say they had reached Berkeley Square. Three sides of a lovely park were lined with stylish attached houses, but the fourth side was entirely devoted to the grounds of a stately mansion of recent style. "And here at last is Falkland House!" he announced proudly.

The horses turned into the gate and wound up the broad carriageway, stopping before a perfect Greek temple of white marble columns rising to elaborate capitals and a frieze of ancient warriors. On either side of this amazing portico swept two brick wings made the more imposing by great pedimented windows and heavy granite quoins. As several footmen escorted her into an echoing rotunda lined with marble statues of Roman emperors, Nicole was stunned by the grandeur and pretentiousness of the house and grounds, surely one of the most lavish properties in all of London. Somehow, it had never occurred to her that Falkland was very rich. She had known him as one tenant among hundreds at Versailles, and then simply as her own guest at Beaux-Clervaux. Of course she knew he had inherited a large stone castle in the north of England. But somehow she had not expected him to live in princely elegance in the most fashionable part of London. And she felt a little disturbed and disappointed.

It was not until late the next day that Nicole heard the duke arrive home. Entering the rotunda, he seemed to be speaking in unusually cheerful tones. Forgetting to be shy, wanting only to express her delight at seeing him again, she ran to descend the staircase, then stopped abruptly halfway down. He was not alone. Two—no, three gentlemen had entered with him. Then she saw that one man was escorting a lady into the drawing room. Nicole could only glimpse the back of her skirt of rich taffeta.

As Nicole gripped the balustrade uncertainly, Falkland chanced to look up toward her. Although there was little light on the staircase, she was certain he knew she was standing on the landing watching him; and she believed she could discern his surprise and annoyance at seeing her, as though he had forgotten her presence altogether. Without a single word or gesture to her, he turned away and directed his attentions to a lady who had stood concealed behind him. As he offered her his arm and led her into the drawing room, Nicole could see that she was elegant and beautiful.

Nicole was appalled by this apparent rudeness. Was there some possibility he had not seen her after all? But he had looked directly at her. Could he possibly have mistaken her for some servant lurking in the shadows? No, she could not believe it. He had simply not wanted to include her in his party. But why not? Who in the world were these visitors that she could not even be introduced to them? Were her manners so crude that she must not meet his aristocratic friends? Could he actually imagine she would disgrace herself once again as she had done at Versailles?

When she encountered the duke the next morning at the abundant buffet in the breakfast parlor—what a strange practice it was to eat a huge meal so early in the day! however did the English ladies keep their figures?—he was distant and formal. After murmuring only a few words, he ate hastily and pretended to have to hurry away.

But then at last the summons came, and she could not help but heave a sigh of relief. His Grace requested her presence in the library, and Nicole knew from the servant's manner that she was to go now, immediately, without changing her dress or even pausing to brush her hair.

The duke was standing at a window and staring pensively at the cold, misting day, but he turned to bow when she entered. How different was this stiff reception from the greeting she had both longed for and dreaded! Had she ever really believed that he would besiege her with kisses and caresses when they next met alone?

The duke was so altered from the man she had grown to know and love at Beaux-Clervaux as to seem a total stranger. Without doubt, the pompous grandeur of this mansion, the formality of English manners, and even the frigid November weather worked the change. Versailles had been luxurious and elegant in the extreme, but was always lightened by the bustle of the crowded palace and the nobles' carefree, even frivolous, pursuit of pleasure. But apparently the English aristocrat was only concerned with making solemn proof of the importance of himself and his nation.

When he did not speak for a few moments, she nervously pretended to look at an enormous painting of some stern-faced nobleman. "Gainsborough," the duke murmured. She nodded, not knowing whether he meant the artist or the subject. "The portrait is of course my father, the eighth duke," he added condescendingly. At least he could still read her mind. But there was no hint of teasing in his voice today.

As he watched her silently, she surveyed the imposing room with its heavy columns of rose marble supporting the high, coffered ceiling. Hardly less grand than the royal apartments at Versailles, she thought. However did their English king live, if this man was only a duke? She looked at the endless rows of matched books recessed between the pillars, and a dozen paintings, mostly Dutch landscapes, and large statues of men in Roman togas, whom she thought rather grim. Why was it the English had such a fondness for the ancient Romans? At last she found a Gobelin tapestry and exclaimed with relief at the familiar sight.

"You must force yourself to speak English, Nicole," he advised. "You may remain in this country for many months or even years."

The command left her wordless, but he had little interest in hearing her reaction. Having girded himself for an unpleasant task, he continued gravely, "I have invited you to join me for this interview in order to express my deep regret for my drunken excesses at Beaux-Clervaux, of which you were the innocent victim. I am guilty, not only of committing a craven and dishonorable act, but of violating the memory of . . . of your mother and father. . . ." He had turned his face toward the window, but she could still read his expression. ". . . a memory that I happen to revere." She was amazed to see real distress on his face. Had he allowed himself to become open and sincere at last?

How could she express her jumbled thoughts in English! After a brief attempt, she lapsed into French to try to tell him that the surprising alteration in his mood was very distressing to her. But he silenced her with an impatient gesture. "There is no occasion for debate, Nicole. Only one thing remains to be said. I want to swear to you that I will never require you to submit to me again." Whether from embarrassment, fear of forgetting his resolution, or simply impatience to be free of her, he immediately turned on his heel and marched out of the room.

That same night when Nicole was wandering aimlessly through the reception rooms, believing the duke had safely gone out for the evening, she shrank back in surprise as a strange gentleman entered from the garden through a french window.

He shook the rain off his fashionable redingote and stamped his muddy boots without regard for the carpet, then cried, "Hullo! What have we here!" After examining her from head to toe through narrowed eyes, as though passing judgment on a horse offered to him for purchase, he exclaimed to Falkland, who had followed him inside, "You lucky devil, you have one waiting up for you. Living right here, is she? And why not! These are modern times. And, I must say, your taste is vastly improved!"

Icily, Falkland introduced her as his ward, Mademoiselle de Clervaux, orphaned daughter of the distinguished scholar Robert de Clervaux. Without bothering to present the man, who was still regarding her with a skeptical smirk, Falkland led him directly into the library and slammed the door.

It was at breakfast next morning that he declared, "Such an insult to you was inevitable. I have foreseen scandal ever since your arrival here. A young girl cannot live in the home of a bachelor, especially one it— ah, pleases the popular fancy to believe given to amorous conquest. Once again, I offer you my most profound apologies." In consequence, the duke explained, she must leave London and travel to his seat at Langmuir Castle. There she could lead a wholesome life without social constraint, and benefit from the invigorating country air. Happily, she would be able to practice her equestrian skills. He would send orders for her to be allowed to select her own mount from his stables. And also she could enjoy . . . er . . . well, no doubt she would find a dozen other diversions about the historic castle. In any case, the matter was settled. She would leave immediately for Northumberland.

If only she could see more than five feet out the coach window, perhaps she would find something to occupy her mind and prevent her from brooding one more whole day about the duke's cruel treatment. But rain was falling in sheets once again. Yesterday the coachman had begged permission to wait out the dangerous weather at their inn, where Nicole had chosen to escape the reek of that vile beverage called beer or stout or ale by sitting all day in the women's bedchamber. How dreary this journey had proved to be. And at their present rate it would surely take a month to cover the hundred leagues. Already twice today the coach had had to be dug out of the mud. How many more nights could she endure the strong mutton fit only for dogs, and boiled potatoes without a drop of butter or grain of salt that every country inn apparently served.

And then she felt the stabbing pain of rejection once again. Perhaps she had disappointed him in bed. Yes, that must be it. Why hadn't she thought of it before? Inexperienced, always stupidly awkward, she must have failed to delight, to satisfy him. But surely that was ridiculous! Heaven knows, the man had seemed satisfied! Then what could it be? What had she done wrong?

Or did he have another woman whom he desired so ardently as to have no further interest in Nicole? Perhaps it was the lovely creature she had seen on his arm in Falkland House. But surely the duke must learn to love quickly, for he had hardly been back in England four days when he sent Nicole away. Then was the lady an old love, newly revived? But could even Falkland be so changeable, so fickle?

In her reveries, when she had finally relaxed and become cozy on the leather seat, Nicole imagined that he had really sent her away because he wanted her too much. It made no sense, of course, because if he had wanted her he would undoubtedly have seized her once again. She could not believe his claim to honor. The man who had admitted he did not seek sainthood was the real Falkland—and far from befuddled by drink. But she could not resist the fantasy that he would come north soon to Langmuir Castle and call her to his bed. And how would she endeavor to fight him off? Oh, but that was another matter, and one that called for a further hour of absorbing daydreams about her pleas and struggles until he finally forced her—yes, gave her no choice at all—to open her thighs and admit him once again.

The rains gradually slackened in the next few days; but as the skies lightened, the temperature fell, until Nicole had to wrap herself with every shawl and cloak she possessed. Soon she no longer could generate even the briefest daydream. As she sat and shivered, she could only condemn Falkland as her enemy and despoiler, the nemesis of her whole family, seducer of herself, false friend to her father, ravager of her virgin mother.

Dear heaven, what had really been Falkland's relationship with her mother? Nicole had hardly let herself consider it since the burning of the letters and her own vindictive, almost sacrilegious foray into the chapel. Her father had always described a blissful year of marriage when Nicole would beg him for stories of her mother. Had he been fooled, duped, or had he excused and forgiven Lucienne's sexual submission to another man just prior to their marriage? And under his own roof? But her voluntary bedding with Falkland was ridiculous! He was a mere boy and younger than she! Had he raped her, as he had forced himself on Nicole, told her ruthlessly that "I will allow you no escape"?

But of course the burnt fragment gave evidence of her mother's innocence. He had waited for her in the *pavillon,* but she had not come. At least not that night. But others? If only her mother had not saved his letters in the secret compartment! And he had known she had. He knew where she had hidden them and how to open the *coffret.* There had been a little conspiracy between them, a little *affaire* of secret messages and summerhouses and stolen caresses. But not consummation? Was that why he had desired Nicole so fiercely? Had his conquest of the daughter finally exorcised the ghost of Lucienne from his mind and body? And had it relieved him of further yearning even for Nicole herself?

Would Nicole ever learn the truth from Falkland's lips? Would he ever even come to visit her at Langmuir Castle? But even then, it would not be the same as the beautiful afternoons at Beaux-Clervaux. How she longed for sunny Beaux-Clervaux! When would he ever allow her to return? The question filled her with painful homesickness in her icy confinement in the carriage.

Just as she closed her eyes to try to sleep, the air cracked with a blast of the postilion's horn. Was there another flock of sheep obstructing the road? Anxious for any diversion, she craned her neck out the window and saw before her a massive, ancient fortress that seemed to grow out of a jagged granite ridge beyond the moor. From the vantage point of a small hill, she realized that the castle stood beside the ocean, the incredibly bleak

North Sea. Cut into the contorted, sea-worn rock foundation of the fortress was a small harbor of fishing boats surrounded by a little town, which climbed toward the overhanging castle as though seeking protection. The sky, the sea, the rocks, the moors, even the slate-roofed houses, were shades of gray. Nicole marveled that all the world at Langmuir Castle looked joyless and godforsaken.

8

But Nicole's first days in the castle surpassed even her most gloomy presentiments. *Godforsaken* was too mild a word. Surely the place was inhabited by mocking devils or some great Celtic spirit of vengeance.

As though the visual impression of the rugged walls, treeless enceinte, and battlemented towers from which weapons seemed to be trained on her was not bad enough, Nicole found that she could understand scarcely a word of the dialect of the servants who unsmilingly received her. Nor could they understand her painfully precise English. Not that they seemed to worry! She was silently led up flights and down corridors to a cold, dark bedchamber and abandoned. No servant brought her luggage or delivered any water, hot or cold, for her preparation for supper. Apparently she would have been allowed to starve to death if she had not finally retraced her route all the way to the drawbridge before she found a servant.

The lonely dinner was served in the largest room she had ever seen, where she was placed at a small table beside an enormous empty fireplace in which the wind was howling. She shivered and pulled her cloak tightly around her. Should she ask the old man serving her to light a fire? But he had disappeared completely this time, leaving her with the inevitable plate of mutton.

The ancient hall must rise four stories to its rafters. She noticed there were only a few high windows of leaded panes, which now revealed that night had fallen. Hardly a stick of furniture could be seen, except a few great leather armchairs along one wall, and there was no carpet on the dusty stone floor. The high, smoke-stained walls were decorated by antlers, armor, and crossed swords. A broadax, blade downward, was poised almost directly above Nicole's head.

She shivered once again, finished her meat with a wince, and reached for the pewter goblet to wash the taste out of her mouth. But instead of the wine she instinctively expected, a malty fermentation, warm as the stew she had just finished, poured down her throat and made her cough violently. It was all she could do to keep from spitting up the beer and mutton. Not that these heathens didn't deserve such a comment on their culinary art!

Would the serving man come back so that she could beg a glass of wine? To think of the bottles she had opened for Falkland! And surely some kind of sweet must follow this incredible offering. Nicole had developed a fondness for English puddings. But there was no sign of the old man. As she listened carefully for the sound of his footsteps, she began to detect faint squeaks like those made by mice. Of course! This old dungeon would be filled with rodents. She picked up her feet and wondered if it would be safe to run across the shadowed floor.

Then in a new current of air she caught a glimpse of a small swooping creature in flight above her head. *Mon Dieu*, the room was full of bats! Just as one seemed to dive for her hair, Nicole screamed and waving her arms frantically ran from the hall.

Taking refuge in her bedchamber, she wanted only to crawl into bed and find oblivion in sleep. No servant had bothered to bring her luggage, deliver a lighted candle, build a fire, or even turn down her covers, and she stamped her foot in annoyance, then resolved to sleep in her dress and hose for warmth. Under the thin blanket, she discovered a straw mattress. Had the servants, or Falkland, intended to insult her with this damp, freezing, uninhabitable room? Or were his servants only slovenly?

Even curled into a ball she could not stop shaking. She reached up suspiciously to touch the cold stone wall and felt moisture. And there was a heavy musty odor, which was gradually sickening her. She must have a fire. She would catch her death if she lay here all night in this seeping cell.

Was there a bellpull somewhere on the wall? She had not noticed one, but had seen a tinderbox beside the fireplace. Groping in the dark, she laboriously lit a fire, which finally flamed up brightly despite her fear that the kindling would be as damp as the walls. But in a moment a cloud of smoke had billowed out of the fireplace into the room itself. Dear heaven, the flue was not drawing at all! The room was filling rapidly with smoke, and Nicole, coughing violently, grappled with the window, which she finally decided was not meant to open. But as she fled through the door, the smoke followed her out into the hall. Obviously, she must seek help. In the bright firelight she could make out a bellpull across the room, and covering her face with her skirt ran back in to pull it.

She had to retreat to the end of the corridor before a stout serving woman, carrying a candle, waddled toward her. Fortunately no words were necessary to describe Nicole's plight. To her surprise, the servant showed little concern, and pushed open the window in her chamber without difficulty.

"Them flues be stopped up i' this auld place. Daid birds and anm'ls, it is. Dinna ye ken? I no hae 'nother bed for ye; a' the others is mouldered. Auld feathers do, ye ken. Excepting, then, His Grace's own bed, and so it'll hae to be, tonight."

With no qualms as to the propriety of the solution, the woman led her along to a wide, nail-studded door, and ushered her into an enormous chamber containing a great gilded, heavily draped bed surmounted by a crown, and nearly as tall as the room itself.

"Kings hae slept i' it, mistress, and all the dukes born thair," the woman said as she saw Nicole's startled reaction to the bed. After lighting a fire and several candles, she turned to go, gave a shrug when she failed to comprehend Nicole's request for her "valises" and departed without a pang of conscience.

The new, conspicuously honorable Falkland would disapprove of her presence, Nicole thought with mischievous satisfaction. Thrilled to be transferred to this room that was both comfortable and fascinating, she could not restrain herself from exploring a little in his wardrobes and chests. She found few personal possessions except a cupboard of boots and a press filled with clean linen. Why not borrow a nightshirt? What could be more appropriate than sleeping the night in linen belonging to her lover? Or more exciting! Nicole quickly pulled off her clothes and slipped the cool stiff garment over her bare body. How wonderful it felt. She hugged herself with pleasure. How exciting it was to sleep in his clothes and in his bed! Suddenly she had a premonition this would not be the last time she would remove her garments in this room. Of course he would be along in a month or two, and—and the rest was inevitable.

But the next time she was here she would have no chance to search the old oak scrutoire. A key was sticking out of the carved door of the desk, so her intrusion would hardly be a sin. Perhaps she could find some clue to the mystery of his enigmatic personality. Perhaps she would even find letters written not *to* but *from* her mother. The prospect was irresistible.

But as she turned the old key in the lock, its shaft twisted with the slight force she used. Desperately hoping to bend it back, she reversed her direction, but the soft metal suddenly snapped in her fingers. Panic-stricken, she thought of hiding the key, but found she could not remove the stub from the lock. She wanted only to flee—Falkland was certain to find her out. Or, worse, he might believe a servant had tried to force the desk, and punish the man or woman in some way. But the duke must know these old servants well. Of course he would guess that Nicole had been trying to poke through his most private papers.

When she picked her way down tortuous steps that led from the fortress to Langmuir Haven and wandered its narrow streets, she found that the fair, ruddy-cheeked inhabitants, who looked as though they ought to be amiable and jolly, merely watched her with unfriendly eyes. How different from the hospitable reception a stranger would receive in a French country town, she thought chauvinistically. How cold these English were! But then perhaps they were only children of their climate and studied the chill of the moors and the bite of the sea wind.

For days the weather had been too foul to consider a ride on the moors, but at last she found her way to the stables and asked a boy to prepare her a mount—preferably an Arabian, she added politely. But he only scratched the dirt with his toe, then called an older man, who surveyed her silently and took his time bringing the head groom.

"No Ae-rabs here, missy. And no nags for ye at a', today. I'll no risk my gude hunters under a lass on these soaking hills."

Implore him as she would, the groom stubbornly denied her a saddle horse. He had no orders from the duke, he said, and conveyed his belief that he never would. Then as she turned away with disappointment, he seemed to soften a little. "I'll give ye a cuddy, mistress."

"A cuddy?" She despaired of this dialect.

"A donkey, a bonny donkey. Maggie is her name."

But Nicole did not know the English word either. With a sigh for the hopeless ignorance of foreigners, the groom led her to the small gray beast.

"*Un âne!*" she exclaimed indignantly. With fiery cheeks, she marched out of the paddock. She had enough sense to know when she was the butt of a joke.

Eagerly she ran to meet her caller, apparently some clergyman, who was awaiting her in what the servant had called the Armory. She was delighted to have any caller at all. Surely he came on a friendly mission. But then, she thought with a cringe, perhaps this parson only wished to warn her in dour northern terms of her prospects for eternal damnation.

She was relieved to find the Armory a small comfortable parlor, though it was decorated with rather gruesome pictures of stag-hunting. And she was immediately charmed by the Reverend Doctor Littleton, who spoke English she could understand, and who genially extended to her a sort of official welcome. Alas, he had been three days in bed with the gout or he would have come before.

The rector was a short, portly gentleman who wore an old-fashioned wig and long clerical bands of white lawn at his neck. When he told her he had received a letter concerning her from Duke William, as he called him, she felt a thrill of anticipation. Littleton said the duke was anxious that his ward should occupy her time at Langmuir Castle profitably, and suggested she continue her studies in the grammar and literature of the English language.

Nicole almost snorted with annoyance, then checked herself out of consideration for her kindly visitor. Her father had schooled her carefully in English grammar and literature! Besides she would be nineteen years old in less than a month. Her days in the schoolroom were long past. How irritating to have the duke treat her like a child! Still, any employment would be a relief from this grim prison, so when the rector handed her a volume of Milton and arranged to quiz her on it Tuesday next, she assented meekly.

"You speak English with precision, mademoiselle. But I am not surprised, for I have spent many hours in the stimulating company of your scholarly father during his frequent visits to Langmuir Castle." He expressed his condolences on her bereavement and related a few memories of Robert. "No doubt he also gave you an excellent education in your native tongue?" When she confirmed it, he said, "Then may I extend to you an invitation to join us in our little school as the French mistress. True, we have never had one, but this opportunity cannot be ignored. We have many bright children, some of gentle birth who go on to one of the public schools, though most are only the sons of yeomen and fishermen. We teach girls too—a little reading, handwriting, ciphering, and the practical arts of sewing and embroidery. No doubt you can help us with needlework. The girls are preparing a new altar cloth for our church." Then after considering a moment, he added, "But perhaps you would object to serving an alien religion. Forgive me for an indelicate suggestion."

Nicole hastily assured him that she knew no reason to despise the English church, but regretted that she had no knowledge of embroidery. However, she could tat a little lace, as Clémence, her cook at home, had taught her. He expressed approval and arranged for her to start her classes the next day.

What could be easier than teaching a few sentences of your native tongue, especially to young children? Nicole felt no anxiety whatsoever about her new job until the moment she entered the classroom and found two dozen boys of assorted ages sitting ramrod straight and regarding her warily. Suddenly terrified, she had to force a cheerful greeting, then quickly gave instructions to them to repeat each French word or phrase just as she said it. "*Le garçon,*" she began hopefully, but only silence followed. "*Répétez, s'il vous plaît.* Please repeat, if you will be so kind, each word or phrase just as I say it." But they remained silent once again, and began to twist in their chairs. Then it dawned on her that they could not understand a word she was saying. Wringing her hands desperately, she wondered if she should attempt to imitate the local burr.

Suddenly a boy cried helpfully, "She wants us to echo her words!"

Nicole sighed with relief, and managed to endure the painful hour only with constant "translation" by the kind boy. Not only was their dialect impossible, but she doubted they would remember a single word of the French she had tried to teach them. She had written each word on her slate, and then repeated it over and over as they laboriously copied it on their slates, mumbled it once or twice in their hopeless accents, and then rubbed it out and no doubt forgot it forever. She must be sure to ask the rector for some pens and sheets of foolscap.

Dabbing at her brow with her kerchief and trying to compose herself, she thanked the helpful boy when he came down the aisle. Not only was he thoughtful and alert, she said, but he had shown a real talent for French, pronouncing the words more carefully than any other child.

"I cannot tell a lie, mistress. I ken some French already, because my father speaks it varry well indeed, and has taught me how to count and say all the names of animals and many other things, and even sing songs."

She studied the bright, courteous boy, who was about ten years old and tall for his age, with a mop of thick brown hair. Of course he must be the son of some gentleman in the district. She was not surprised that Englishmen with some position in life should choose to learn her native tongue. In parting, she asked the boy to tell her his name.

"Robbie Maclure, mistress. I think ye must know my father, living as ye do in Duke William's household—"

Whatever did he mean? "I know no one, Robbie. . . ."

"He's Timothy, mistress; and I know he was at yer place in France. He sent us a letter from there, telling how pretty it was. Timothy Maclure, the duke's manservant."

Nicole exclaimed with pleasure. Of course, kind, considerate Timothy would have a son with such a fine way about him. Naturally genteel, they both were. The boy did not look much like him, but perhaps Timothy had simply put on weight with the years. What was most surprising was the boy's natural poise and leadership. She would never have taken him to be lowly born, though her own father had often observed that high intelligence and excellent character had been equally distributed among all classes. Not to disparage Timothy's abilities, but Nicole made up her mind that Robbie's mother must be a woman of superior wit and virtue.

"Then you live with your mother here at Langmuir?"

"Nay, we cannot live with her, for she is varry ill. All six of us live in the Manse, and Mistress Kate takes care of us."

"And who is Mistress Kate?"

"She serves Dr. Littleton, mum, and she has instructed me to beg you come home and take tea."

The Manse of St. Cuthbert's would have been as grim and somber as the other dwellings of the town if not for the fine old evergreens that relieved the stark lines of the stone house. The other trees in the churchyard, huge oaks, had already shed their leaves for winter. No blossoms remained in the little border, though the privet and holly beside the gate were flourishing. Ducks and geese scurried away as Robbie led Nicole up the path to the front door with its lion's head knocker and handsome fanlight window.

Kate Dalrymple suffered only a moment of shyness, then received Nicole as though she belonged in the comfortable house. The five younger children—Eliza, Jane, Davy, Gabriel, and the baby, Toby—soon swarmed over Nicole, begging her to examine their toys or to eat a sweet or tell them how it feels to be a schoolmistress. Nicole could not restrain herself from laughing at the sandy, freckled children, each one a quaint copy of Timothy.

Kate, plump and red-cheeked in a white mobcap and apron, beamed at the children's pleasure in their guest, and Nicole was gratified by the sight of an English face at last wreathed in friendly smiles. Before she had had a chance to drink her tea or try the stotty cake, Kate wrapped a pinafore around her, and handed her a bowl of gooseberries to pick over.

"Ye don't mind, do ye, miss?"

"Oh, no, I'd love to help, I'd. . . ."

"I thought ye might, thought ye might be gude and ready for a little family life after a few days in that great old pile of rocks. And before that was not so bright, I'll be bound. Losing your pa, I mean, and then finding yerself on His Grace's doorstep. I can well imagine—I can well imagine what ye have been through!" The woman clucked her tongue a few times to make it clear she was saying less than she might.

From that day forward, Nicole spent every spare minute in the Manse, only returning to the castle to sleep. When she was not teaching her classes, tutoring with the rector, or completing the studies he assigned her, she helped Kate with the cooking and the care of the children.

As the rector smoked his pipe drowsily beside the fire one night, and Kate sitting nearby was cracking a bowl of nuts, Nicole asked about the children's mother, whose name she had learned was Annie. Where did Annie live? What disease was she suffering from? Was she expected to get well soon? The children had all gone to bed. Nicole had always refrained from asking about her in front of them, sensing her condition was grave.

Kate sighed a little. "She lives right here in Langmuir Haven. I thought ye knew that, thought maybe one of the bairn had told ye. Annie Maclure lives at the bottom of High Street in the stone house next to the miller, where a country woman takes care of her. Do ye ken the house?" Nicole shook her head. "Handsome it is. Two stories and a stoop with ten steps." Kate cracked a walnut with unusual force.

"Then Annie's people were someone of substance? I thought perhaps they might have been—"

"Why did ye think that, pray tell?" Kate asked with irritation.

"Because Robbie takes after her, and he is the smartest boy in my classes, and so I thought—"

"Ye thought wrong. Annie Plummer was no more than a shepherdess who slept nights on the moors with her flock, when she was lucky enough to marry Timothy Maclure."

Dr. Littleton stretched, then tapped out the bowl of his pipe on the fender. "I remember Annie as the most beautiful girl ever to wander the hills of Northumberland," he said rather lyrically.

Kate snorted a little. "And her beauty was no unmixed blessing, ye can be sure!" she said with a trace of jealousy or other malice in her tone. Repenting, she hurried to add, "But the poor soul has suffered more than her or any other mortal deserves, and she ain't daid yet."

"Then her condition is very serious?"

"Aye," said Kate. " 'Tis her lungs. She cannot live many months."

"And when she dies, it will be a tragic loss for all," the rector said rather sharply, glancing in Kate's direction. "Every medical effort has been made. His Grace has even given Timothy leave to take her to a warm climate, but she cannot bear to part from the children. We hope Timothy will be home at Christmastide, if the duke can spare him. His Grace has always been very generous with Timothy, what with the fine stone house and a good education for all the children." Nicole had already noticed that the rector never missed an opportunity to praise the duke.

"And in turn Timothy would give his life for His Grace!" Kate declared with fervor.

"Nay, lass! Never stir the cake backwards, for it lets the devil in. Always stir the way of the clock, or it will never rise a tittle!"

"Oh, Kate," Nicole laughed, setting down the wooden bowl. "I never heard such a thing before, and I've always helped Clémence in the kitchen. It must be one of your local superstitions."

"Superstitions? I have no superstitions."

"Nay?" Nicole said, mocking her. "Only yesterday you told me it was bad luck to mend my hem while wearing the dress, and that a yew tree growing in a churchyard must never be cut down."

"Ye mean like the rule always to shod yer right foot before yer left?" Kate asked with a chuckle. " 'Tis only wisdom handed down from generation to generation." Kate was silent for a minute, then said rather slyly, "If bees nest on a roof, the daughter of the house will never marry." She waited a moment, but Nicole made no response. "Well, did bees ever nest on yer house at Bo-clair-vo?"

Nicole grinned and answered, "No, no, never!"

"I thought perhaps they might of. Since yer getting no younger."

"How cruel!" she laughed.

"Thair ain't nobody for ye to marry in this town, missy."

"Then you wish me away?" Nicole asked, without much apprehension.

"Nay, ye know I don't. I'm only thinkin' serious about yer future happiness."

"Someday I'll go home and marry—uh, perhaps the son of one of the neighboring *châtelains* in my district," she said, with a detectable wince as she remembered Arnaud Coppin.

"I can see that ye pine for him," Kate said drily.

"Oh, Kate, I really believe—" She hesitated, fearing to betray her secret dreams to the canny woman. "I really expect the duke will arrange a marriage for me. It's his responsibility as my guardian."

"I was afraid ye was placing yer hopes in the duke," she said slowly.

"Only to find me a husband—"

"Only to find ye a husband?" Kate stared at her profoundly.

"Yes," Nicole murmured.

" 'Tis double-talk, missy. 'Tis no arranged marriage yer meaning. Ye been placing yer hopes that Duke William will claim ye as—"

"No, Kate! You must not speak those words!"

"—will claim ye as his own bride!" she finished stubbornly, hoping to shock Nicole to her senses.

"It's not true! I have never expected—nor hoped—nor even dared to dream that he would ever marry me! Never!" Nicole began to sob as though her heart would break, and Kate put her arm around her, shaking her head with pity.

With occasional help from Eliza and Jane, who stood on stools to reach the kitchen table, Kate and Nicole baked for two weeks to be ready for the festivities that would extend from Christmas Eve to Twelfth Night. All of the parishioners would call at the Manse, and Timothy was expected home with the usual treasure trove of presents for everyone.

On the morning of Christmas Eve, the duke's coach, arriving at last from London, came to a halt on the frozen cobblestones before the gate of the Manse, and the five older children ran squealing down the path before Kate had a chance to wrap them warmly.

As Nicole stood in the door of the house with Toby in her arms, she knew from the sudden cessation of the children's merry sounds that something was wrong. Slowly the five came back up the walk, their faces drained of all happiness. Robbie listlessly handed her a packet of letters, and she directed him to read aloud the one addressed, in the poorly formed hand that was apparently Timothy's, to the children.

Their father deeply regretted that he would not be coming home at all this Yuletide because he must accompany Duke William on a foreign mission of great importance. Timothy begged them to forgive him and to convey his great love to their dear mother, who had suffered so much. He prayed that the packages he had sent would ease their disappointment and help him to retain his place in their hearts.

Nicole gave a letter in Timothy's handwriting to Kate, and sent Robbie around to his mother's house with the one for her. The last letter bore the bold script of Falkland's hand and was addressed to Dr. Littleton. She could not help feeling a pang that the duke had had no wish to communicate with her.

Especially when it was her birthday. Modestly, Nicole had declined to tell anyone that she would be nineteen years old that day. Perhaps she had made a mistake, for the children might have enjoyed making a fuss over her, but she had been in a gloomy mood for days. This anniversary only reminded her of all the distressing events of the past year. Last Christmas Eve she had celebrated at her father's bedside, and remembered that he had enjoyed a day surprisingly free of pain. They had both taken heart, and dared to express their hopes that he could still recover—that the year ahead could well be far brighter. But instead—! No, she must not count her misfortunes today. She would devote all her energies to the children and their preparations for Christmas.

As Kate put finishing touches on a Christmas cake filled with marzipan, iced with a fluffy white frosting, and decorated with red berries and sprigs of holly, Nicole must help the children rehearse their pantomime for Christmas Day. The girls sewed on the costumes and the boys made paper hats, and all contrived to learn their parts. In the traditional play, Robbie was the Lord of Misrule and Eliza the Jester. Davy got to wear a paper coronet and carry a wooden sword as Duke Andrew just returned from the wars. Nicole noted with interest that there would be no impersonation of Duke William, and could not resist asking Kate if it meant he was not well liked.

"On the contrary, he's liked too well, miss. 'Twould not be respectful to play his part."

"But Davy is playing Duke Andrew, his father."

"Oh, Duke Andrew is a legend, so thair can be no disrespect. But Duke William is very much alive and is our lord and better than us all! Which some among us would like and try to forget!"

Hurrying against nightfall, the rector and Nicole, with the help of the older children, hung evergreen boughs and holly from the beams of the parlor and laid it across the mantel. Just as they stepped back to admire their work, a pounding on the door signaled the arrival of the long-awaited yule log, an enormous section of oak thick as a man across and a full yard wide. Two of the duke's foresters dragged in the massive block, which they had cut on a distant fell on the manor.

"Gone are the days when the Great Hall of Langmuir Castle rang with the songs of Christmas minstrels, and a log seven feet long burned on the hearth," the rector said nostalgically. "I well remember the court kept by Duke Andrew. Not only did he observe all the English festivals, but the Scottish ones as well in special honor of his wife, the Duchess Isabella, come as she was from Highland nobility. On Hogmanay, or New Year's Eve, as the pipers skirled, she boldly slit the haggis—that's a sheep's stomach, Miss Nicole, stuffed with a pudding of oatmeal and onions—with her hereditary *skean dhu,* or black knife. And the whisky flowed for all the court, you may be sure! Whisky's a part of every Hogmanay."

Nicole had just started to ask if Duke William ever observed these traditions at Langmuir Castle, when she realized the eyes of everyone in the room had turned toward the door. Leaning on the arm of an old woman was a small, extremely thin creature whose white face, half hidden in the hood of a cloak, gave the momentary impression of a death's-head. The rector rushed forward to take her other arm, and the children gathered around her, clutching at her cloak.

"Dear Lord, Annie, out in this freezing night and with yer fever raging!" Kate exclaimed.

Sinking gratefully onto a divan, the sick woman embraced her children, and then told Kate almost apologetically that she could not rest until she had tried to make up to them for Timothy's absence. When the rector called Nicole forward, Annie tried to make a little bow from her reclining position, but Nicole quickly grasped her hand instead. At close range, Nicole could see that Annie's large eyes, though sunken, were still beautiful, and that her thin, graying hair, pulled back tightly into a bun, had once been a rich auburn. No doubt the strong, regular bones of her face, now so distressingly prominent, had once given her a lovely symmetry of feature.

In the excitement wrought by Annie's valiant presence, Kate could not refrain from producing many of the dishes she had meant to accompany tomorrow's feast of roast goose and plum pudding. For tonight she had planned a simple spiced beef with roast potatoes and pease pudding, and perhaps a ham or pork pie or two, followed by a dessert of parkin, a spicy oatmeal cake. Nothing more. But gradually during the meal, finding their way from the kitchen on one pretext or another—"I must test a little of this" or "How hungry we all are!"—came leek soup, sausages, herring baked in rolls, standing pie (a mixture of mutton, apples, and raisins), cheeses, gingerbread, fig pie, muscat raisins, nuts, and homemade ginger wine.

When during the long meal the children became restless, Nicole noticed whispered exchanges and furtive nods and signals. For a while she sensed she was the target of some plot or other, but finally the rector announced in an indulgent tone that he could no longer resist their desire to open their presents from London, and added that no doubt Timothy himself would understand and approve.

Then for an hour ribbons and papers flew about the room amid cries of delight. Not only had Timothy supplied each child with a horde of toys and clothing, but the duke had sent expensive gifts to all six, including a handsome leather writing case for Robbie.

Feeling suddenly lonely and perhaps a little jealous, Nicole became aware of tears welling in her eyes, and she began to lecture herself sternly. Surely she was no longer a child, and ought not to react like one. She knew perfectly well the children would give her their handmade presents tomorrow, and no doubt Kate and the rector had something for her, as she did for them. Certainly it was more blessed to give than receive. What could be wrong with her tonight?

Suddenly she felt little hands covering her eyes. "Guess who?" sang Eliza's voice in her ear. While her eyes were covered, another child deposited a paper construction of some sort on her head. She caught his hand before he escaped, and pulled him around in front of her. It was Davy, six years old, and she made him give her a hug before she let him go.

"What have you done to me?" she asked, putting on a gruff voice, and poking the unseen hat with a suspicious finger.

"I can't tell ye, missy!" Davy shrieked.

"It's yer special crown for tonight!" little Jane whispered, for fear of bursting with the secret.

"But why?" Nicole asked.

"We can't tell ye!" a chorus squealed.

As every eye in the room watched Nicole's face, Robbie came forward ceremoniously, and placed a small gift box in her hand. In unison, the whole group cried, "Happy Birthday!"

Clearing his throat, Robbie said formally, "We didn't know, Mistress Nicole—I mean, we didn't know in time to make ye nice birthday presents. We only found out today, so we merely have the paper crown—"

"But this lovely box—?" she protested.

"Oh, I wish it was from us," the boy said. "It came from London on the coach this morning."

"From—?" Nicole caught her breath.

"Why, from Duke William, of course!" explained the boy with surprise at her dismay.

She hoped that her spectators could not see her hands shake as she removed the ribbon and wrapping paper. Inside was a beautiful black silk box, the like of which she had never seen before. At first she could not raise the lid, but finally found that she must push the jet pin on the front to make it spring up. On a bed of white satin lay a fiery golden topaz the size of a bird's egg. It was set in gold and attached to a heavy braided chain. Tucked in the lid of the box was a visiting card engraved simply, His Grace the Duke of Falkland. There was no handwritten message on the card.

Holding up the pendant, Nicole could not suppress a little gasp of pleasure. When one of the children ran up with a looking glass, she tried the jewel around her neck. She was wearing a demure, practical dress—gray faille with a white fichu—that Kate had insisted on making for her, her first English dress. On the long chain of rich gold, the topaz fell to the very point of her neckline. She could feel the cold metal touch the sensitive skin of her bosom. Yes, it was a beautiful sight in the mirror, glowing harmoniously with her golden hair, a flashing accent with her dark-eyed, tawny beauty.

But she was embarrassed to have the whole room witness her vanity, and put down the mirror hastily. Graciously, the rector uttered a few compliments about her beauty and the duke's excellent taste in the choice of the gem, and each child came forward to rub a finger over its faceted face. Nicole smiled a little when she caught Kate's look of disapproval of the gift.

She knew what Kate was thinking, that Falkland was preparing to conquer the lovelorn girl and would meet with little resistance, or that he was perhaps paying tribute to the charms he had already enjoyed. Other less worldly observers like the rector would see the topaz only as an appropriate gift from a wealthy man to his ward, as the duke had perhaps intended by his choice of a semiprecious stone. No doubt he gave the marquise emeralds. There should be nothing scandalous about a topaz.

Everyone cheered when Kate carried in the steaming wassail bowl, on which roasted apples floated. When the rector told Nicole that the hot punch was made of her despised ale flavored with spices and a little sherry wine, she made a face, then had to admit, after a drink or two, that she enjoyed the curious blend. All the adults grew merry as the evening wore on, Annie seeming to relax and grow comfortable at last, and Dr. Littleton remembering old stories which he told at unprecedented length. Finally Kate touched his elbow with a gentle warning. He must be sure to have a clear voice for tomorrow's sermon.

As Nicole prepared to depart for her bed at the castle, she held up the topaz fondly one more time. What had the duke meant by this thrilling gift? That he desired her as fervently as the fire burned in the wild eye of the gem? She shivered a little with the pleasure of such an idea, however improbable. Then she realized that someone was watching her. Nicole raised her head and met Annie's gaze. The sick woman was staring at her with a bitter, envious expression, but as soon as Nicole looked at her, turned away and sank back into the dull trance in which she had been lying. Astonished, Nicole searched her mind for any reason she might have aroused the poor woman's jealousy. But perhaps Annie had only realized, at the sight of a young and healthy girl, that she herself now had only suffering and death before her.

In his book-lined study, Nicole and the rector passed many winter afternoons. Often the elderly man digressed from their reading of Spenser or

Shakespeare or Dryden to tell her anecdotes about Duke William and tales of his ancestors. Soon she gathered that Dr. Littleton was sincerely fond of the duke, even rather fatherly toward him. Littleton saw fit to affirm that His Grace was beloved by the whole region, always being fair in his administration of justice and generous to those in need.

"My loyalty to Duke William requires me to paint him as he really is," the rector said. "I have sensed your, shall we say, anxieties about the kind of life he has led. Very often, those of us in that great God-fearing class that is neither high nor low but noted for its solid and respectable virtues —and may I take the liberty of counting you among us?—have great difficulty in understanding the aristocracy. Different moral standards, seemingly wicked, prevail in the highest classes of society. What looks to us like debauchery passes unnoticed in many noble circles and even royal courts, though not, heaven be thanked, in our own English royal family, for King George cherishes the sanctity of the home.

"After a long life," the rector continued, "I have finally learned to judge sinners with charity. The high-born live in another world. We can hardly understand their values and traditions. Consider the *Droit du Seigneur* or *Jus Primae Noctis*, the right of the feudal lord to require every bride on his domain to—er, grant her favors to him the first night of her marriage, before going to lie with her husband. This dreadful pagan custom may still exist in remote regions of this kingdom, but was long ago abandoned—er, completely—yes, I can say completely abandoned by the Dukes of Falkland, and commuted to a payment of a few coins, no more than a fee for a marriage license. Still, consider the lingering influence of such a tradition, the inevitable belief that noble lords are entitled to live by standards far different from our own."

When he began to question her about her impressions of the French court, he obviously intended to allow her to unburden herself of anxieties and even guilt, if she chose. But she was far too embarrassed to speak freely about herself. Nor did she want to carry tales about Falkland's affairs with the Marquise de Vaucroze and the queen herself. Nicole merely stated rather lamely that she had been dismayed by the license she had seen.

"My dear child, I will distress you with no personal questions. But it is impossible not to suspect, knowing Duke William as I do, and observing your own great beauty and innocence, that he has not hesitated to arouse emotions that are naturally very susceptible in a sheltered young girl. You must feel no shame, for I suspect you are entirely blameless. I have only pursued this difficult subject today to warn you to beware of further heartbreak. Alas, my dear child, Duke William will never marry you!"

Nicole flinched as though he had struck her a blow. The fateful words had been delivered in such a solemn voice, a voice she could not disassociate from the pulpit itself. There could be no doubt that truth had been pronounced.

"But why not?" she asked despairingly.

"He *cannot* marry you! He cannot marry any woman of his own choosing because King George, who dotes on him, insists that he marry one of his six daughters, presumably the eldest, the Princess Royal. Yes, Nicole, the fact is well known in court circles. Duke William must—whatever his own desires may be—marry into the royal family."

9

The poor woman was seized by a paroxysm of coughing and spat blood into a handkerchief. Nicole supported her shoulders as she lay down against the pillows. How sharp her bones felt through the cotton gown! What could be the meaning of life, if this gentle creature must suffer like some lost soul in the seventh circle of hell?

As Annie drifted into a restless sleep, Nicole picked up her book and tried to concentrate on the poetry of Herrick. "Fair daffodils, we weep to see you haste away so soon." Dear Lord, she would surely burst into tears and wake Annie! She must tell the rector that she could not work her way through this poignant verse today.

Nicole had been locked in a depression ever since Dr. Littleton's revelation. She had tried to convince herself that he could not possibly be informed about court affairs from so far away. Or had the duke confided in him? If the princess and the duke were to marry, why did they wait? But perhaps the princess was still too young, or the situation in France considered too unsettled.

No matter how hard she tried to wish the words away, they still rang in her ears: The duke must marry into the royal family whatever his own wishes may be . . . whatever his own wishes may be. But what were his own wishes? He would never tell her, and she had no faith at all in her own intuitions.

Then a distressing vision of the future flashed before her eyes. There was a pale, fat princess—Nicole remembered seeing in Falkland House a most unflattering portrait of the King of England. What would her name be, perhaps Georgiana after her father? Then there was the suave, debonair Falkland, a dutiful husband by all appearances, who undoubtedly enjoyed his royal rank, and would never lose sight of the true values in life. But in the shadows lurked the lovely Nicole—she was beginning to hate her own beauty—well known to be the duke's mistress, but forced to hide herself away for fear of public embarrassment to the royal family. She had been married off to some palace equerry or other so as to be available for Falkland's pleasure at all times—*mon Dieu*, it was beginning to sound like a tale spun by the Marquise de Vaucroze!

Never would Nicole sink to such a role! Little better than a prostitute she would be, a painted woman fearful of losing her looks, peering anxiously into every mirror, because when Falkland tired of her, she would have nothing; a woman whom the ambitious sought with ostentatious courtesies, then sneered at after she had passed; and whom the proudest and most virtuous would not acknowledge at all. As though she were invisible—that's how she would be treated by the best people! And then the pain she would cause the Princess Georgiana and her children, not to mention the suffering of any children Nicole might have by Falkland. Oh, what a shameful nightmare!

But even as she declared her abhorrence of such a life, she wondered at her own powers to resist Falkland. What kind of magic potion had suffused through her brain and held her thoughts and feelings in bondage to this man? If only she could set her mind and body free by some charm or amulet. No wonder some people still believed in witchcraft.

But, of course, she assured herself, this new obsession that she had to write a letter to the duke was not bewitched. Common decency required an expression of gratitude for the beautiful pendant. During the week after Christmas she had thought about nothing else but the composition of the letter. Finally after a dozen false starts, she penned a few stiff, timid words of thanks, then went on to describe with greater ease her pleasure in teaching and her enjoyment of life in the Manse with the Maclures, Kate, and the rector. She asked the duke to send her any news of Beaux-Clervaux and France, for surprisingly she had heard nothing from home. In closing she said artlessly, "Just as the children eagerly await their father, we all look forward to a visit by Your Grace."

Was the letter too formal, too awkward, or was it presumptuous to compare the importance of his visit with that of a mere servant? Presumptuous to suppose he might be interested in her daily life in classroom and kitchen? Or, on the other hand, had she missed an opportunity to tell her true response to the topaz? She rewrote the letter a hundred times in her mind after it had been sent.

The winter passed without any answer from the duke, without any word at all from London. Finally in March a letter arrived from Timothy for all to share. The duke and he had been away these months, were back but briefly, and would soon leave again. Regrettably he could not tell their destination or the duration of the trip.

But Nicole's doubts and disappointments paled to insignificance beside Annie's suffering, as the disease progressed. At last at the end of March, Dr. Littleton decided that Timothy must be called home. Annie would not linger many days.

But the duke and Timothy had not returned to Falkland House, the majordomo, Pickering, replied with haste. He would make every possible effort to contact them, and himself begged the liberty to express his own deep regret at Annie's grave condition.

Her pathetic calls for Timothy could only be answered with white lies. "He is on his way. It can't be long now. Please wait for him, dear Annie. . . ." For the first time, Nicole heard the rector express anger at the duke. Why had His Grace not anticipated this inevitable turn of events? He had thoughtlessly kept Timothy away from her for months, caring only for his own selfish needs. And now they were off again on another jaunt, no doubt for the most trivial purposes.

But of course! Nicole suddenly saw the light. While she had assumed that Falkland occupied himself with diplomatic affairs, the rector had known perfectly well all along that he was pursuing affairs of a very different kind—hunting, gambling, adultery, debauchery! No doubt he had kept Timothy from them at Christmas only so that he could be valeted at some house party. And now Annie would die without seeing her husband! How naïve Nicole always was! How right the marquise had been, and now the rector had said the same thing: She would never understand a man like Falkland.

The spring was late, but finally a few sunny days brought out the flowers, and Nicole managed to slip away for a walk on the hills, or fells, as she had learned to call them. The heather was just forming its small rose-pink blossoms, which from a distance gave the moors a purplish hue. She picked spring gentians of the brightest blue, fairy primroses, and wild pansies to take back to the sickroom, and aromatic mint and thyme in the bed of a stream for Kate's kitchen. There were newborn lambs in the flocks she passed, and she caught a glimpse of a herd of wild goats. She must remember everything to tell to Annie.

But when Nicole returned, the dying woman had sunk into a deep sleep from which she could not be roused. The doctor was called, and a frantic message dispatched to London. Annie could not last more than a few days or even hours. To be certain they saw her alive one more time, the children were brought to her bedside that night for a final kiss.

To spell Kate and the regular nurse, Nicole offered to spend the night at the silent bedside. There was little chance Annie would wake again. Nicole prepared a trundle bed for herself before the fireplace in the sickroom and soon fell asleep. She had no idea what time it was when some noise awakened her. Then she saw by the glow from the coals that Annie was sitting bolt upright, her eyes wide open. As Nicole hurried to light a candle, the sick woman was shaken by a dreadful convulsion that flung her to the bed.

Surely this must be death itself! Nicole had heard incredible, though no doubt exaggerated, accounts of final agonies, but she had never witnessed a death, her own father having died peacefully in his sleep. Having no experience, she was terrified to be alone with Annie, but there was no chance to call for assistance, to call for someone of age and wisdom who might help the poor woman cross the river of death.

Annie was groping for her hand and called weakly, "Mistress Nicole . . . Mistress Nicole. . . ."

"Yes, Annie? Please save your strength. If you want, I'll run to get someone. We can be back in three minutes—"

"Nay . . . nay. . . ." She was sucking greedily for air, as though she had just come up from a deep dive. "Robbie!" she gasped, and then fell back.

"Robbie? Do you want Robbie?"

She could shake her head, but she could not talk. Heaving her chest violently, she managed to hiss a few words, "Ye must tell . . . Robbie! He doesn't know. . . ."

Then there was only silence; no more writhing and gasping, no more movement at all. Only silence and a blessed peace.

Nicole was dreaming that the church bells were tolling. The bells of St. Cuthbert's. Yes, they were ringing faintly, very faintly. Suddenly she realized it was morning and she was back in her own bed in the castle, where she would hardly be able to hear the bells so far below.

But throwing open the casement, she recognized the tones of leaden Tom and silvery Peter carried aloft by favorable sea winds. They were solemnly, patiently, tolling a death and calling the mourners to church. Could Annie's funeral be held so soon? Dr. Littleton had announced late last night, after Kate and Nicole had laid out the body, that he would hold back the service three days or even four on the chance Timothy might arrive.

Donning her only black frock, Nicole flew down to the Manse. Kate, dressing the tearful children, was almost too busy to talk. Yes, Timothy had arrived in the middle of the night and desired a prompt funeral. The children surely could endure little more. Yes, he was distraught with grief, but had at least been able to give Annie's lips a final kiss.

When the assembled family—Robbie as a dignified leader, tear-stained Timothy holding the hands of Eliza and Jane, Kate following with Davy and Gabriel, and Nicole bringing up the rear with the baby in her arms—crossed the churchyard, Nicole had a clear view of the castle barbican high above their heads and noticed a strange banner flying from its battlements. Surely the bold flag, bearing some coat of arms, could have nothing to do with the funeral of a poor peasant woman.

Nicole pulled on Kate's sleeve and gestured toward the banner, and Kate replied, "Aye, *he* has come back too. The duke, lass. They came together, whence I do not know. Now here, he'll make his annual visit, I gather. Hush, now, 'tis no time—"

"The duke! In the castle now!" In a moment, she whispered again, "Will he come to the funeral then?"

"Ha, lass, be silent! Have ye no sense!"

Nicole hardly heard a word of the service, occupied as she was with comforting the children and craning her neck to see if the duke had entered. The nave was filled with townspeople, but Nicole could not locate his dark head. Was there some special pew or gallery where the lord of the manor was privileged to sit? Finally, Kate glowered at her, for she was twisting too much in her seat.

"I will lift up mine eyes unto the hills, from whence cometh my help," the rector intoned. Yes, that was appropriate. Nicole liked to think of Annie in the hills, a young shepherdess of rare beauty tending her flocks on the moors Nicole had come to love. Then, "The Lord is my shepherd, I shall not want . . ." and finally, "I am the resurrection and the life, saith the Lord. . . ."

Annie's grave had a handsome setting, in front of the church and near a great gnarled oak now in full leaf. There were no other graves close by. Annie must have no local family. Or were they buried in some less pretentious site? A large sector had been allotted to Annie, Timothy, and their descendants. Who had made such a decision? Of course the rector had a soft heart. But still, to grant the family of a servant the best plots in the cemetery. . . .

Nicole searched the little group of graveside mourners. For some reason Falkland had chosen not to come at all. At Beaux-Clervaux Nicole attended even the lowliest funeral. But this was not Beaux-Clervaux, and many English customs and attitudes still remained incomprehensible to her.

". . . Unto Almighty God we commend the soul of our sister departed, and we commit her body to the ground; earth to earth, ashes to ashes, dust to dust. . . ."

Nicole pressed Timothy's hand tenderly, led the children back to the Manse, and helped serve the platters of food brought by kind parishioners. As soon as she could decently depart, she slipped out a rear door and scurried up the lanes and stairways leading to the castle.

Once across the drawbridge, she found that many servants had suddenly materialized whom she had never seen before, though they were apparently local. When she asked for His Grace, some new servingman pointed toward the massive donjon in the center of the castle.

She ran across the cobblestone enceinte between the outer walls and the bailey, passed through its narrow mouth to the inner bailey, now relieved with green lawn reaching to the fosse or ditch around the donjon, that oldest and strongest tower of the castle. Crossing a fixed drawbridge she entered the great, silent tower that she had never explored before. How long ago had these granite blocks been cut and set? A thousand years? The doorways of the cell-like rooms were so low she feared to hit her own head on them. There were no amenities like fireplaces or glass in the small barred windows or even doors to give privacy to these rooms. Though the bleak pile seemed unfit for human habitation, she knew the family of the lord, Falkland's ancestors, must have dwelled here for centuries.

At last she heard voices, and just around a turn found a knot of local citizens peering into some large chamber. As she approached they made way for her, and she found herself standing in the door of a kind of courtroom crowded with spectators. Facing her on an ancient dais, the Duke of Falkland presided as the judge.

Dressed in a rather old-fashioned suit of the local tweed fabric and looking brown and relaxed, Falkland held up his hand to interrupt the speaker. "If we may have a moment, bailiff, to welcome our esteemed schoolmistress. Pray do us the honor, mademoiselle, of taking a seat so that this session of our Court-Leet may proceed." Then he smiled mischievously, and added, "We must inquire with trepidation if you have come as another plaintiff in the present case." The spectators burst into peals of laughter.

"No, Your Grace, I don't even know what it is," she answered in dismay.

"We are enormously relieved to hear it," he said and there was more hearty laughter from the crowd, several men actually slapping their knees with delight.

Pleased at his own wit, the duke directed her to a bench. Nicole was so embarrassed she could only grope clumsily for a seat, knowing every eye was upon her. As the testimony continued, she gradually discovered that a tinker named Bartholomew, a short, scrawny fellow who traveled from town to town with his wares, was claimed as legal husband by two buxom wives, one a Langmuir woman with six children and another in a distant town with five. At each new revelation in the case, Nicole laughed a little as she knew she was expected to do from the merry nudges given by her neighbors. Apparently, one was obliged to marvel at all the duke's jokes, even if they were made at one's own expense.

Falkland and the spectators found the tinker's story highly entertaining; and only reluctantly, when there was no additional testimony to be had, did the duke announce the verdict: The first marriage was the legal one, but the tinker must support the second family and visit his children. Of course he would have to forego conjugal relations with their mother. When the duke's inflections indicated his belief that such abstinence was hardly likely, the room laughed once again and applauded a verdict they approved.

With equal gusto, Falkland heard a case about pig stealing (the culprit got a year in jail); another on breach of promise ("No real harm done," Falkland opined and dismissed the young man, to another round of applause); and several cases of public drunkenness, for which the guilty were sentenced to serve time repairing the town almshouse.

Nicole feared the session would never end, but she was now far too wary of Falkland's high spirits to risk attracting his attention with an early departure. She could not bear to be the object of more laughter. But then the duke yawned and stretched, and his steward, sheriff, and a dozen spectators followed his example. What indelicate manners he affected here in the country, Nicole noted with a little amusement.

At last he arose, announced he was hungry to a chorus of "Hear! Hear!" and said court was risen for the day. There was much curtsying, bowing, hulloing, and even back-slapping as he marched down the aisle.

Calling for Nicole to wait, when she had walked out ahead of him, he declared loudly, as though pleased to have his friends gather around and listen to him, "You ran in eagerly enough, mademoiselle, but now I can see that your nose is out of joint!"

Fortunately she had learned the English expression and did not have to stare at him stupidly. "Not at all, Your Grace. I only grow a little shy when I am teased."

"Ho, ho!" he cried with delight. "How will I ever be able to resist teasing you when I find that you have managed to learn English with the local burr! What a quick student you must be, my dear. How long have you been here now? Alas, you must not say 'Yer Grace.' The word is 'Yoor.' What would you say to a child you found lost in a lane?"

"Why, I would say, 'Where is your home?'"

"Aha! My dear child, the word is home, not hy-am! It is the acid test for a Northumbrian. Now repeat after me a dozen times, home, home, home. . . ."

When he invited her to take the midday meal with him, she quickly accepted, then hesitated, doubt written on her face. "Then I hae distressed ye, lass!" he said, enjoying his linguistic games.

"No, Your Grace, but I know there are—the truth is there are bats in the Great Hall!"

He laughed heartily. "No doubt there are—no doubt there are! But the dogs will keep them away. Had you no dogs when you ate there? A pity! No wonder you have eschewed our hospitality for the rector's all these months."

The floor had been swept in the Great Hall, a pleasant peat fire burned in the grate, and half a dozen field dogs milled about, as Nicole dined with the duke at a long, heavy oak table that had appeared from nowhere. The food was improved, though she was served a stoop of ale and some curious pink fish called salmon, which the duke praised excessively. He seemed willing enough to listen to her account of her activities, but he was interrupted every few minutes by some retainer or other with a pressing problem, and several times he invited his interlocutors to pull up a chair and join the meal.

When the dinner was finished and the men seemed likely to sit forever and talk business, Nicole rose to excuse herself. Falkland, pretending regret at his neglect of her, made an ostentatious effort to praise her accomplishments at the school. His tone was not only a little condescending in his old style, but worse yet, downright fatherly. How pleased he was she had made a success of her French classes. No doubt she had had a difficult time at first, what with the dialect to learn. But she had triumphed over all obstacles, just as he had trusted she would do. Was the duke actually planning to take credit for her job when the idea had clearly been the rector's? Nicole hoped his new irritating pose was only designed to convince the townspeople there was nothing unseemly between them. Anxious to escape, she extended a casual invitation to visit her classes at the school, bobbed a curtsy, and ran out.

She was not invited to dine with him again for several days, and glimpsed him only in the company of his steward or some importuning tenant. Then early one morning another schoolmistress rushed into her classroom. Duke William had come to the school wanting to inspect every room, and intended to start by hearing recitations from Nicole's pupils.

In mere seconds, or so it seemed, he was pacing before her class, his hands clasped behind his back as he delivered a pompous speech about the value of the French language to a man pursuing a life of culture or a career in foreign trade or politics. Nicole laughed a little to herself, expecting that the only use many of her students would ever have for French would be to call to some fishing boat invading their home waters. Attending Falkland were, in addition to the rector and several masters, a train of functionaries she did not know, apparently stewards, secretaries, and the like. Timothy stood in a corner, come along to observe his own children.

With a silent prayer that her boys would be able to remember at least a few fragments from their lessons, Nicole called upon the oldest student to lead off, but the duke interrupted her. "Let Robbie Maclure recite first," he decreed, and Nicole noticed that every adult eye in the room glanced at him with something like surprise, then hastily looked away.

As Robbie stood up, she could see the boy's knees were shaking, but after a terrified start, he succeeded in presenting the entire fable of the wolf and the lamb by La Fontaine without a single mistake.

Though Timothy was beaming, Duke William refused to soften his stern expression. "Well done, Master Robbie, but I would enjoy another, longer selection, perhaps something more taxing to yourself."

At first Robbie seemed paralyzed with fear, but then the color came back to his face. Holding his head erect, he accepted the duke's challenge and recited the long dramatic speech by the Cid from the play by Corneille ending with the famous line, "And the war ceased for want of warriors."

As everyone exclaimed, the duke, breaking at last into a wide smile, pumped Robbie's hand and tousled his hair, after which Timothy embraced the boy. Pausing only long enough to hear short selections by two or three other students and to bow stiffly to Nicole, Falkland departed with his entourage.

Long ago finished with her dinner, Nicole could only stare at Falkland, her chin propped in her hand. Completely indifferent to her, he sat at the end of the long table attacking a slab of beef. How handsome he was in the candlelight, which made him seem even more remote and mysterious. Had he perhaps lost a little weight? Was his skin newly browned, browner in fact than yesterday? She was certain it was. Then he had gone riding again, once more without inviting her along.

But why, why? Why did he never touch her, never speak words of any intimacy whatsoever, never even try to spend an hour alone with her?

Was there another woman, even here in the country? But who? Nicole knew everyone now, at least by sight. Yesterday she had noticed a pretty blond chambermaid who had tucked a flower in the ribbon of her cap. Was this the girl? Nicole was beginning to look at every woman with suspicion.

Once again, the duke was conversing with some assistant and jotting notes. In the brief intervals between callers to the table, he always read *cahiers* and letters, and often penned an answer on the dining table beside his trencher. From time to time he remembered to make a polite remark in Nicole's direction. Though he hardly listened to any of her comments or questions, he became annoyed and refused to let her go when she tried to excuse herself and run away.

Days ago, she had managed to interrupt him long enough to thank him personally for the topaz, at which he hardly even nodded; and another time to ask him to give her news of France. He had answered that the king had been forced to accept a constitution officially abolishing the nobility, all titles, and even coats of arms. Those few nobles left in France must hide themselves away. Desperate to raise money, the new government had seized all church lands, and was issuing paper money called *assignats*, which had already produced a dangerous inflation. Then he had added that he had not been able to make contact with the Bordeaux region for some time, and could tell her nothing about Beaux-Clervaux. Surprised at her own boldness, Nicole had asked if he had had any news of the Marquise de Vaucroze. Without looking up from his writing, he answered tersely that he had heard nothing at all and did not know where she was.

Each night Nicole tried to devise a new cure for the boredom of these long suppers. She had failed to make friends with the dogs, who snarled if she held out a friendly hand and only came near her to snag a scrap of meat from her plate. When she had tried to tat some lace she found the light too poor, and no doubt she would have the same experience tonight with her book. With a sigh she drank the last of the ale she had learned to tolerate, and once again rehearsed a little speech requesting wine tomorrow night—yes, tomorrow night for certain.

When Falkland suddenly called her name, she jumped in her chair. Without looking up from his writing he complained, "Why is it you never wear the topaz pendant I gave you? Run now and put it on. And don some soft, colorful dress. My tired eyes long to see a pretty sight. Must you wear the same dreary frock every day?"

"But I don't! Kate has made me several dresses of different shades of gray and brown and blue. Perhaps they all look—" But he waved her away impatiently, rudely. Frightened and offended, she hurried to her chamber. Why did he suddenly care how she was dressed? Especially when he rarely even bothered to look at her. She stood numbly before her wardrobe. What colors would harmonize with the topaz? She tried it against a brown velvet dress and nodded with satisfaction, then scowled and abandoned the dress when she remembered he had specifically requested something "colorful."

She could not avoid the suspicion Falkland intended to do more than look at her tonight. Why else the order to change clothes? He had sent her to her room to make herself attractive enough to arouse his desires, which judging by his distant, irritable mood must be somewhat flagging. Obviously passion was the farthest thing from his mind as he toiled over letter after letter. Evidently tiring of his work, he had hailed her with little more than a snap of the fingers and ordered her to make herself ready, just as he would any bought woman.

Of course she could flee from the castle down to the Manse and Kate's comforting arms. But surely that would be ridiculous, even hysterical. After all, what was wrong with her guardian asking to see the gift he had given her? Whatever the rational arguments were, she realized she had little inclination to disobey his commands. Somewhere deep inside her was a desperate longing that only he could satisfy.

When she returned to the Great Hall in a low-cut silk gown of the lightest aqua, he bestirred himself to rise and kiss her hand. After a few compliments, he studied her hair and face and bosom with obvious pleasure. *What an alteration in his mood*, she thought with relief, and felt a surge of pride in her own beauty.

"May I?" he murmured, and reached out to touch the heavy gem. Lifting it, his fingertips grazed the skin of each breast. Of course the little caress was no accident. Had he noticed the involuntary flicker of her eyelids? She found his face quite expressionless.

"How I have neglected you, my dear, all these nights," he said lazily. "How patient you have been, when you might have passed your time in . . . far more interesting pursuits. . . ." She felt herself stiffen. There was an unmistakable note of irony in his voice. "To make it up to you, I have another little gift, not as lovely as the first, but perhaps . . . more instructive. . . ." His words were heavy with sexual innuendo. "But you will have to come to my chamber to receive it. . . ."

"No!" she cried, jumping away from his encircling arm. To think she had yearned to love and be loved by this man! How could she stand still and listen to his insults?

"But I really can give you no choice; you will see why soon enough.

And if you fear for your"—he let his eyes linger on her breasts—"virtue, we can leave the door ajar."

"Ajar?" she asked in surprise, then realized he had succeeded in making her sound naïve and clumsy once again. What was he up to? Was it simply more of his teasing? Or a crueler kind of mockery? With a shiver, she sensed he was playing some devious game.

"Of course," he grinned wickedly. "Did you forget I made you a solemn promise in London? How strange it would slip your mind." Taking her arm firmly, he led her along to his room.

A fire burned on the hearth, and several candles had been recently lit. Nicole noticed nervously that the counterpane was turned down on the great ornate bed. Then she jumped back a little as he allowed the door to click shut behind them.

"Of course you will admire our State Bed. It was built to accommodate my cousin, King James of Scotland, on his progress south to ascend the throne of England. King James slept here. And so did little Nicole! I am told you slipped between my cold sheets one winter night. Unfortunately I was not here to warm them for you."

What in the world was he planning? Would he tease her forever? She wished he would remove his painful grip from her arm. But instead, he took her face in one hand, positioned it as though for a kiss, studied it with heavy, sensual eyes, and dragged his thumbnail along her lips roughly, forcing them slightly apart.

"Stop," she protested weakly. Indifferent to her response, he patted his waistcoat as though he had forgotten the pocket, and then pulled out a small package.

"No fancy wrapping, I'm afraid," he said. She received it with curiosity, then reproached herself for her apparent eagerness. Of course it was nothing more than a bribe to submit to him once again. She untied the string and unrolled a piece of brown paper to reveal a large brass key. It was obviously new, but she recognized instantly by its distinctive loop that it was a replacement for the one she had broken.

Dear heaven, how could she have forgotten the incident of the key! Not once since the duke's arrival had it crossed her mind. At first she had been too excited just to see him; then his apparent indifference no doubt lulled her into complacency. Even now when she had re-entered the scene of her little crime, she could think only about the threat of seduction.

"You can see why I had to bring you here—to satisfy your curiosity about my most personal papers. Even though we had to remove the broken pin and web from the lock in order to cast the new key, you need not take my word that the writing cabinet has not been opened since your attempt. Examine the key carefully," he directed, taking it from her and holding it near a candle. "Here now—" When she lagged behind, still staring speechlessly at him, he jerked her forward roughly with barely suppressed fury. "Here now, you can see that the shiny brass has absolutely no scratches on it. Please examine both sides. You will have to admit that it has never been used, that it is, in fact—quite virgin!" He drawled the word sneeringly.

Nicole shrank from him and lowered her eyes, but he pressed on sarcastically. "Dear child, please pay attention. I have gone to considerable trouble to satisfy your curiosity about the contents of this old desk. Now I ask you to insert the new key—here, take it!" he snarled, forcing it into her hand. "Now turn the lock!"

She did as he ordered, and the lid dropped forward to disclose dozens of old scrolls. "No doubt you will find our ancient vellum Hundred Rolls extremely interesting. Here, let us see what we can find." He untied and unrolled one fragile scroll. "What luck! This one goes back to the twelfth century. Do you read Latin, *ma chérie?*" When she made no response, he shook her and demanded, "Do you?"

"Only a little," she whispered.

"Like Shakespeare, you have small Latin and less Greek. Then perhaps you find these historic records tiresome after all. What a pity that there are no smoldering love letters from a dozen fascinating women, including perhaps your own lovely mother? Or shredded, tear-stained attempts in my own hand to declare my soul to you! Is that what you thought you were going to find?" he demanded fiercely. "How romantic your teeming brain must be, a whole theater in itself!"

Seizing her roughly and drawing her so close that her face brushed his shoulder, he said, "What you need is a good thrashing!" Terrified, she struggled free of him. But as she took a dozen little backward steps, she found he was making no effort to stop her, that she was perfectly free to run from the room.

Then a wide mocking grin spread across his face. He had never intended to spank her. He had never meant to touch her at all, never meant to spend a passionate night in the great bed. It had all been a joke. Once more she had completely failed to understand him. All her anxieties had been for naught, and his knowing leer told her he imagined she had enjoyed all her little sexual terrors.

"Go then," he laughed. "We have no other business tonight. Did you believe we had?"

10

The liveried page, a boy of twelve or so, stood by as Nicole twisted nervously in her chair in the rector's study. "Tell His Grace," she finally decided, "that I must attend Dr. Littleton this afternoon. We have only just begun my lesson, and after that—"

"Nonsense, my dear. I can easily dispense with your company, delightful though it may be," the rector hastened to assure her. "Indeed, you should not reject your guardian's kind invitation. A ride in the country will do you a world of good. How thoughtful Duke William is to suggest it!"

Nicole followed the page back to the castle with resignation. For several days, ever since the humiliating episode in his bedchamber, she had succeeded in avoiding Falkland, spending most of her time in the Manse until the canny Kate had seen fit to observe drily, "So ye finally decided a little distance would make the heart grow fonder."

Putting on a black riding habit with starched blouse and catching her blond hair behind her neck in a silk ribbon, she paused briefly to look in the mirror, pronounced herself in fine form, and set off for the stables with a quick step. Undeniably, it was a glorious summer day. She admitted to herself that she would enjoy the excursion. If she treated the duke with perfect courtesy no matter what he said or did, perhaps they could get through the afternoon without another contretemps. But heaven knows she would never feel at ease with him again.

At the paddock she realized instantly that he was in a jaunty mood. "Will you ride this stout fellow, Miss Nicole?" he called as soon as he saw her, indicating the largest horse Nicole had ever seen. Falkland, discoursing genially, told her this black Shire was descended from the English Great Horse, which had been bred in olden times to carry the enormous weight of the fully armored knight. "My forebears rode into glorious battle on the backs of the ancestors of this beast. He and I are the last of our noble lines," he said, patting the animal affectionately. "But today he only draws a wagon and dreams his dim dreams of ancient honors. *Sic transit gloria mundi!*"

The head groom, without any sign of recognition of Nicole, led out two new hunters for Falkland's approval, and announced their names when asked. "Not Lancelot and Guinevere!" the duke laughed. "What a bad example you set us, with a pair of illicit lovers! Do you also have Tristram and Iseult, Héloïse and Abélard, Paolo and Francesca? But then perhaps it is a good moral lesson for us all to think on the painful fates they suffered!" he declared loudly, while Nicole paled with embarrassment.

But soon she was breathing easier as they trotted along a deserted road. The duke also seemed to relax in the peace and beauty of the countryside. For an hour they rode with little conversation, though occasionally he would wave a greeting to a shepherd or point out a pretty sight, a little *lough*, or lake, or a glimpse of rare wild white cattle.

Almost as though it had taken him a while to work up his courage, he finally drew alongside her horse and asked, "Have you forgiven me for my little joke the other night?" His eyes were piercing yet guarded, as always.

She mumbled a few words, nodding her head shyly. Of course she must lie and say she had.

Soon he told her they were approaching the ruins of the Roman Wall, built more than sixteen hundred years before by the Emperor Hadrian across the width of England to contain the warlike Celts—his own ancestors, he did not mind pointing out—whom the Romans had found impossible to subdue. The wall had once been almost ten feet thick and too high for one man, standing on the shoulders of another, to scale. But now its scattered stones were overgrown by plants or missing altogether for long stretches.

Dismounting, the duke and Nicole followed the ruin on foot along a spine of small hills. He explained that for centuries the stones had been removed in order to build cottages and roads and the endless drystone walls that crawled across the moors and even the ramparts of Langmuir Castle itself.

"Your ancestors destroyed the Roman Wall to build their castle!" she exclaimed indignantly.

He laughed at her reaction. "Sins of the fathers! But it was no sin then. Once, our fortress protected the lives of hundreds of vassals and serfs, while this poor relic seemed utterly useless. No doubt you think I should arrange to replace the purloined stones, even at the cost of tearing down drafty old Langmuir!"

At the remains of a watchtower, one of a series that had studded the wall, she stroked the ancient stones with awe. Gently he told her that she put him in mind of her father. "Sometimes you have the same earnest look in your eyes. You have his eyes, you know; not hers. Did anyone ever tell you that? Her eyes were green, not brown. Green flecked with brown. But yours are a true brown and warm and soft as velvet. They are. . . ." He checked himself, and quickly returned to the earlier thought. "I brought Robert to this very spot. It is the finest existing tower. He was fascinated and stayed behind to make notes and sketches for hours."

As she listened to this memory of her father, her eyes began to fill with tears, and he turned away to spare her embarrassment. "Perhaps I have told you something you did not know. Perhaps I have been of some small service after all."

When they returned to the horses, they both noticed that Guinevere was limping badly, apparently having turned her leg during their absence. She could not be ridden, Falkland announced, and Nicole readily agreed. Mounting Lancelot, the duke pulled Nicole up to join him, perching her in front of himself and holding her tightly around the waist with his left arm.

She trembled at the first sensation of Falkland's hard-muscled chest against her back, and prayed that he could not feel her shake. But he seemed to settle her against him as though their closeness was a wholly natural thing. Gradually she relaxed, only uttering an involuntary sigh from time to time. During the long ride, necessarily slow because they must not tax Guinevere, conversation lapsed and was replaced by the suffusing pleasure of their embrace. Indeed it was an embrace. Falkland was holding her closer, tighter than he needed, cradling her until she rested her head against his neck and shoulder.

Then by some trick of memory she was back at Beaux-Clervaux lying in his arms. How natural it all was! Why had she ever had to suffer anxiety and doubt and guilt? And he must know they belonged to each other. Surely he must know it, just as she did. All through the long ride, she could feel his breath on her neck or ear or even her cheek. How close his lips were, almost as though he was about to kiss her. If only she dared to turn her face, if only he would turn it for her. If only he would raise his left hand to stroke her breasts. Dear heaven, she never wanted this ride to end!

The sky was dark when they finally saw the silhouette of the stables and heard the distant voices of the grooms. Before dismounting, Falkland kissed her gently on her neck below her ear. As she jumped down, she reached out for him and dropped naturally into his arms. But he held her only a minute, then firmly planted her a step away from him. With a little groan, he said, "If only you could learn to trust me. Perhaps you never will."

"Trust you? Of course I trust you."

"Nay, you do not. Not as needed. At this moment, you trust me to please your senses. But I mean something far different. You must trust me to make a painful decision of great importance. Despite your low opinion of my character, I feel a responsibility to discover some brighter future for you than a term as my mistress." Then with a rueful laugh, he added, "God knows it is a tragic loss! Perhaps you will take some comfort from the knowledge that I too burn for what I cannot have!"

It had been a rare, happy day like the afternoon in the blackberry brambles at Beaux-Clervaux. How seldom he would let himself become tender and affectionate. Unconsciously, Nicole touched her finger to the spot where he had kissed her neck.

But then had come the blunt announcement that he would never take her as his mistress. Not that he had been cruel. He had made no slur upon her beauty or desirability. She was not unworthy. Rather, he cared too much—no, not true! He had never said he "cared" or "loved"! To be precise, he had said he felt a responsibility. Dreary word. And then he had merely laughed with a little shrug at the sacrifice of her sexual charms.

But of course his decision was right. She knew it. She had no wish for the ignoble role of mistress to another woman's husband. But when would she ever find any pleasure and peace in her own life? How would she ever satisfy her consuming desires?

Nicole had no trouble putting these thoughts quickly aside when she saw Falkland the next morning. With a smile of greeting, he took her hand and led her across the cobblestones of the enceinte. His manner was easy, kind, but perhaps a little subdued. They talked about the excellent weather, a sky as clear as she would ever see it in this northern world. He led her into the donjon. "Come, I want to show you our superlative view!"

They climbed a steep spiral staircase, lighted only by narrow slits for bowmen, and Nicole grew a little dizzy before they finally stepped out on the roof of the tower, the highest in the castle. Slowly she followed him toward the battlements, not certain that she would want to look down from such a height. The wind was fierce, tearing at her summer dress. He stood framed by a crenel like a bowman of old and beckoned her forth, but when she reached his side, she jumped back with fear. There were slits in the floor as well as the wall—machicolations, he told her, to allow arrows to be shot down at attackers or burning coals dropped, and he pointed to several blackened firepits on the roof.

But they could hardly hear each other in the whistling wind, and he had to pull her close beside him. As he pointed in the direction of Norway and Sweden and Denmark, Nicole fancied she could make out their coastlines behind a narrow bank of haze on the horizon. "And there is Holland," he said. Another imaginary coastline. "And France there to the south, beyond that piece of Norfolk." She stared at the distant English coast, trying to pierce through to her own land.

The sky, cloudless except for a few high fragile plumes, was the same gray-blue as the wide sea. Though she might seldom see the vibrant blues she knew from the south, nevertheless here on the North Sea she could feel a unique excitement, a sense of strength and fortitude that she had never experienced in her sunny homeland.

Perhaps it was only Falkland's nearness. Or the biting, relentless wind. Or the ghosts of bygone warriors, who had defended this tower how many times. She could almost see the heraldic pennants flying from the towers and hear the clarions sounding as bowmen leaned from each crenel to shoot their deadly arrows at some medieval army. She knew the same strength and bravery they had known. How thrilling to stand where heroic warriors had fought and died. How thrilling to look down on the sprawling, powerful fortress that had once ruled the North. She too would learn to endure and prevail. Was not courage the motto of her own ancient family?

Then she saw he was staring at her sadly. Pointing to a small frigate lying off the shore, he said, "I brought you up here to say farewell!"

She jumped a little at the shock, and grabbed his arm. "You leave by sea?" she asked with alarm. "But where are you bound? Not to London. . . ." And from the somber look in his eyes, she knew the answer, and whispered with a shudder, "To France!"

The wind tore at her light dress, and he took off his coat and put it around her. Holding her by her shoulders, he studied her face tenderly for a long time. His eyes were soft and yearning. The wind had pulled loose a strand of his black hair from its ribbon. He brushed it aside futilely, then tried to control her own billowing hair. At last, impetuously, he crushed her to his chest.

She tried to wrap the coat around his body, too, and they stood huddled together, attacked by the flailing wind. He kissed her cold cheeks, and at first his own face felt like ice. But when his mouth fell on hers, it was as frenzied as the wind.

No words passed between them. They kissed with insatiable need, until

Falkland, as though fearful he would lose the will to depart, suddenly broke away and ran down the stairs. Nicole, clutching his abandoned coat around herself, stood watching for an hour until she saw him board his ship. Even in the punishing wind, she was oblivious to discomfort. She only felt the touch of his mouth and arms, and the revelation of his love for her.

She would no longer doubt. Words meant nothing, after all. It was the passion in his face, the urgency of his mouth and arms, that told her he loved her. And her alone. There were no other women to reckon with. No noblewomen or princesses or Queens of France or even the implacable ghost of a long-dead girl. He loved only herself. She was sure.

Months passed without any word of the duke. Her twentieth birthday came and went with no gift from him this year. But she cared nothing for finery or jewels, only desiring that he should survive his dangerous journey. Every day she begged the rector for news of the civil war in France, and the likelihood of war between France and England. He could tell her only that France was still torn by fighting, and that even her own district, renamed the Department of the Gironde, had become a center of revolutionary activity. But Nicole could bear any news as long as she did not read in the rector's eyes the anguish that would tell her the duke was dead.

What was Falkland really doing in France? Dr. Littleton refused to join her in speculation, nor could she pry out of him any confidences imparted by the duke. But Robbie, as concerned about Timothy's safety as she was about Falkland's, had managed to learn from his father that the duke and he had made other dangerous missions into France since the fall of the Bastille, rescuing nobles, carrying gold to battalions loyal to the crown, and even replenishing the coffers of the royal family itself.

Of course Falkland had behaved heroically, Nicole suddenly realized. How could she ever have doubted his honor? Had not Dr. Littleton tried to persuade her from the earliest days that he was a man of sterling worth? How foolish she had been to confuse his fondness for amorous adventure at Versailles with a basic weakness of character!

When news came from London about an attempt by the French royal family to flee their confinement and their subsequent capture at Varennes, Nicole and Robbie wondered what role the duke and Timothy had played. A rash of conflicting reports, some of bloodshed by the king's supporters, had caused much agonizing in the Manse. *Mon Dieu,* how would she ever be able to endure it, until Duke William returned to England alive and well? Until she could hold him in her arms again?

Carriages plied between Falkland House and Langmuir Castle at monthly intervals, transferring supplies, servants, messages, and funds. Whenever Nicole spotted a newly arrived coach in the enceinte, she looked first for any sign of mourning on the part of the coachmen or other servants, then hastened to question Dr. Littleton to find out what news he had learned.

But today, even though she knew the coach had brought the formidable London majordomo, Pickering, home on holiday, and that he had already called on the rector, she could get nothing out of Littleton when she ran to see him after classes. She sensed he was concealing something when he begged that he be allowed to defer till later the pleasure of chatting with her.

Still standing thoughtfully just outside the door of his study, she heard Kate call kindly to her, "Come and take yer tea. I made ye a singing hinny."

The hinny, a scone-like cake, earned its name by whistling a little as it cooked on the griddle. Kate fussed over its preparation so unnaturally that Nicole finally exclaimed, "Oh, please, I can stand little more. What is it you're afraid to tell me?"

"Don't get excited, missy. 'Tis nothing tragic. Quite the opposite, I'm sure."

"Then what?"

"Duke William is back. In London, I mean."

"Back from France? Is he wounded—or ill?"

"Nay, missy; he's quite fit. But . . . he's been back a good while, a month or more."

"More than a month? But why have I—we had no letters? Is there some message for me on today's coach?"

"Nay, missy. Only presents from Timothy for the children."

"But perhaps Duke William is coming north soon—"

"Nay, I think not. Oh, dear child, the rector don't want me to tell ye—"

"What?" Nicole whispered, cold with fear.

"The duke dinna return from France alone. There is someone—in fact, a whole family with him. French nobles, escaped at great risk. Shot at, they all was, as they slipped across the border into Spain."

"But, of course! We knew he was involved in something very dangerous—"

"The duke brought them all to Falkland House, the elderly husband, his wife, and several grown children. They are penniless now, of course;

so Duke William has generously bought them a house, a very fashionable and expensive house. It faces right on Berkeley Square itself, only a stone's throw from his own gate."

"What is the name of this family?" Nicole asked, although she already knew the answer.

"They are the Marquis and Marquise de Vaucroze."

11

So he was as cynical and cruel as she had always believed! For a bit of diversion on the battlements, he had made her pay with bitter disillusionment from which she would never recover. The duke had always been able to read her mind. He knew she would interpret his tender looks and caresses as evidence of love. Frenzied passion might be explained away as man's animal nature, but tender acts, which Falkland guarded against so vigilantly, could only mean sincere love. Right or wrong, she would reason thus and think he loved her—and he had known it.

He was not a man of honor, she decided with finality. Whether stealing a woman's virginity or breaking her heart, he paid little heed. But Nicole had to admit the duke had never spoken a single promise of love. In fact he had warned her they had no future together. What did a single embrace mean to a man of his habits! Oh, what a romantic fool she had been!

Wanting to detest the duke, Nicole found it easier to hate the marquise and blame her evil influence. How uncannily similar to the vision Nicole had had was their pretty arrangement in London. At last the beautiful mistress was installed in a townhouse so very convenient to his own. Only she was not young, awkward, naïve, and emotionally demanding. How much easier that she was experienced, skillful, happily a little world-weary; a haven not a tempest, when he could steal time from his rigorous schedule to visit her bed. She was in every way superior to young Nicole—provided Falkland did not mind a few wrinkles and sagging contours! *Grand Dieu*, what strange tastes the man must have! But she, Nicole, had no intention of standing in line until he should decide to put Sybille out to pasture.

Of course the duke was now finally ready for marriage. How unseemly to have to scout for a mistress after the wedding, how much more delicate to have her hidden away well in advance. Now at last he could consent to be married to H.R.H. Charlotte Augusta Matilda—Nicole had found out her name in some book about the king. She was twenty-five years of age already, and would not want to lose another day. Clearly, the announcement of the engagement would come at any time.

Mon Dieu, the sighs of sympathy Nicole could expect from Kate and the rector! It was an ordeal Nicole intended to avoid at all costs. She had made up her mind to run away from Langmuir as soon as she could find some means of transportation. Since he used her so cynically—she was no more than a toy to be teased and titillated on infrequent occasions—her pride would no longer allow her to live as the duke's dependent. She would use the gold louis she had scooped from her father's bureau that last frantic day at Beaux-Clervaux to buy her passage home to France. Lord knows her father would have had her flee from Falkland's guardianship before now.

Surely the dangers at home were greatly exaggerated. Nicole was not a member of the nobility. Her lesser status had been made crystal clear to her at Versailles. As for some sort of hazard at Beaux-Clervaux, she would never believe that any of the peasants on her estates could attack her. They were like members of her own family. No doubt she had received no answers to her letters home because Clémence and the others were so unpracticed in the art of penmanship or because the postal service had become completely unreliable.

Nicole considered every possible means of escape. To take the post chaise to London or Edinburgh would be to invite interception before she even reached her destination. To hire her own vehicle would be comfortable if expensive, but she knew no hostler in Langmuir would assist the ward of the duke in running away. Nor likewise would any of the fishing captains who called this their home port.

But the harbor was constantly visited by foreign boats put in for supplies or repairs. Nicole had heard their foreign tongues in the market, where they often disposed of aging cargoes, and once she had been called to translate for an ailing French fisherman. Norwegian, Dutch, French, even Spanish boats put in frequently. She prayed she would find some honest French captain to take her home.

Leaving the Manse after dark one night supposedly to go back to the castle to bed, she covered her head with a generous cloak, and climbed down to the water's edge. Finding the docks deserted, she decided to hide herself in the shadows outside a public house frequented by fishermen, and listen for the sound of French.

Growing stiff and cold in her uncomfortable perch, and hearing only English voices for more than an hour, she finally convinced herself to give up and go home. But she had hardly gone five steps when out of nowhere a strong arm grabbed her from behind and a foul-smelling hand was clapped over her mouth.

"Would ye believe what I caught myself!" the man whooped drunkenly. "It fights like a bag o' wildcats, but I feel there's something jolly inside this cloak. I feel me a pair of boobies, that's what I do!" he bellowed with pleasure. Nicole was thrashing frantically and trying to kick backwards.

The shadow cast by a second man fell across Nicole's face. "Let her go, ye fool! This wench's no for ye. Let her go, 'or it's too late!" he shouted with alarm.

"What the deevil," the first fisherman exclaimed thickly, and twisted Nicole's neck until he could see her face. "Gawblimy, it's the duke's own piece, the chit in the castle, what's-her-name! So if it's his goose—then why not mine!"

"Stop it, fool. He don't wish to follow ye. Let her go and hie yerself away!"

Nicole learned her lesson from this narrow escape and ventured henceforth to the waterfront only in broad daylight. She found her best disguise was an apron and market basket, and simply pretended to be shopping for fish. After three or four visits, she had bought herself passage. Unfortunately the boat was not French, but Portuguese, though the captain had an obliging and honest manner. The boat, newly repaired, would sail tomorrow night on the tide.

All the next day she worked alone in her room in the castle to pack the two small valises she had decided to take with her. Even fully loaded they would be light enough that she could travel by foot if necessary. But she was distressed to find she must leave so many things behind. God knows she never expected nor wanted to see Langmuir Castle again. Perhaps someday she would be able to write and ask Kate to forward everything, but with the unpredictable post, and possible angry prohibitions by the duke, she knew she must be prepared to kiss good-bye whatever she could not pack.

She had already left her heavy things behind in London—and they too might be gone for good. On that last heady day at Beaux-Clervaux, she had packed too much. Reposing in the cellars of Falkland House were trunks containing most of her Versailles finery, her father's manuscripts, his most valuable collections of coins and artifacts, boxes of ledgers and records of the estate, and several crates of silver.

To Langmuir she had brought only a half dozen of the simpler Versailles frocks, undergarments, toiletries, a few mementoes of her father, and most important of all—her mother's lovely small case of rosewood inlaid with ivory that held the jewels passed down through generations of the Saint-Mathiez family.

Here in her castle chamber, Nicole had no trouble parting with the remaining Versailles gowns. The great royal château itself was just an empty shell. How appropriate then to abandon the last of these dresses, which had never brought her anything but bad luck! Surely the whole wicked court had been cursed! The last dress she had worn was the aqua silk, on that humiliating night the duke had presented her with the key to the scrutoire. Oh, *mon Dieu*, she could not live another minute under his roof!

She quickly selected three somber dresses of Kate's creation, a summer-weight cloak and a heavier one, an adequate supply of undergarments, and three pair of sturdy shoes. All other clothing would be left behind. But she could not bear to part with a handsome watch of her father's or a leather-bound copy of a book he had written about Julius Caesar or his large album filled with sketches of her mother and herself as an infant or child. It was easy enough to pack the watch and the book, but the album was too large for either of her satchels. She had no choice but to leave it, and hated the thought that it would fall into Falkland's hands. But perhaps it was right after all that he should see this evidence of the love her father had had for Lucienne.

There remained only the problem of her mother's jewels. She could not stand to leave them for Falkland, but was well aware of the risks she would be taking. On this Portuguese vessel itself and a dozen other places, she might be prey to dishonest as well as lascivious men. The incident with the drunken fisherman had made that terrifyingly clear.

Some of the jewels had great value. There were several diamond rings including her mother's beautiful wedding ring with a large central emerald, an old-fashioned ruby necklace that would have been worthy of Marie Antoinette herself if it were restyled, and some heavy pearl necklaces. The other pieces were merely old gold or semiprecious stones of sentimental more than monetary value.

After an hour of fretting, Nicole concluded that she must try to conceal each piece of valuable jewelry, as well as the gold louis she would be carrying, in the waistbands, seams, and linings of her garments. Leaving out only the five louis she had promised to pay the Portuguese captain, she labored for hours until she had successfully hidden them all. The heavy ruby necklace went under the stiff collar of her cloak, the diamond rings in seams and hems, and the coins were glued inside the spine of her father's book. The less valuable jewelry she left in the pretty rosewood box and packed it in one of the valises.

When at last she could finally sit back and congratulate herself on her ingenious work, she suddenly spotted the angry eye of the topaz pendant in the back of a drawer. Her first instinct was to hurl it across the room, then considered leaving it behind as a defiant gesture in the duke's own chamber, perhaps inside the famous desk itself. But after calming herself, Nicole knew such vindictiveness was against her nature. Besides, its fiery beauty possessed an almost hypnotic power over her. Staring at it, remembering the thrill she had felt at the first sight of it, she realized she longed to take it with her; and to soothe her pride, promised herself she would sell it first if she had need of money.

As she crept out of the castle with her valises that night, she stopped halfway down the steps to the town, and leaning against the balustrade, turned and looked back. The great black hulk of the fortress nearly obscured the starry sky. There were only two lighted windows in a barbican tower, where she knew lived the elderly seneschal and his wife. No longer overwhelmed by the castle, Nicole felt a surprising fondness for the ancient ramparts and even sadness at its decrepitude. But no doubt the Princess Charlotte would soon transform it into an efficiently run royal retreat.

She had to slip into a shop doorway to hide from passersby on High Street, then ran through the gate of the churchyard. Just beyond St. Cuthbert's itself was the stone school building where she had spent so many happy hours. And over there beside the oak was Annie's grave. Dear heaven, she could not allow herself to linger here for she must have no tears in her eyes when she said good-bye to the dear occupants of the Manse.

Hurrying against the certainty that she would soon break down, Nicole hid her valises in the privet, then entered the front door and deposited a package behind a curtain. It contained her lacework for Eliza and her father's volumes about Duke Andrew for Robbie. Nicole was certain she would never want to read about the Dukes of Falkland again. Then she searched out the rector, and without saying a word gave him a kiss on the forehead. As she had known he would, he grunted affectionately without looking up from his work. Unobserved, she placed a snuffbox of her father's on his desk. Perhaps tomorrow he would realize whence it came.

Forcing a playful manner, she ran about the parlor kissing all six children as though it were some kind of game. Only Kate she could not face. The shrewd woman would know immediately from any show of sadness or sentimentality what Nicole was planning.

But when Nicole peeked into the dining room, she saw that the housekeeper was starting to cut another dress for her from a fine length of navy blue wool. "Oh, Kate," she exclaimed. "Don't cut it yet! Pray wait until I consult with you."

"Then yer tired of my styling already?" Kate replied, with ruffled feelings.

"Oh, no! It's only that I've—er, lost weight—yes, several pounds, and you must take my measurements afresh!" she improvised, then added, "Promise you'll wait!" and ran out before she began to sob.

She would never see Langmuir Castle or the little town again, Nicole told herself as the fishing boat sailed out of the harbor. The Manse, with its generous, loving occupants, had been her home for just under two years—truly her second home—and now she would never see it again.

Nicole gave herself up to uncontrolled crying as she tried to fall asleep on a pile of salt bags below deck. Not only did she hate to leave Langmuir and England far more than she had expected, but she was already distrustful of her Portuguese hosts. The captain had demanded payment as soon as he weighed anchor, and offered no reproof when his crew made insulting gestures and remarks in her direction. Fortunately she could understand nothing they said, but the meaning of the gestures was all too clear. That night below deck she made her bed as far as possible from the forecastle where the crew's hammocks hung.

The next day offered clear weather and a light sea, for which she was very grateful; but by afternoon she realized they were moving north along the British coast, evidently searching for fish. When she repeated the single word *Francia*, Spanish for France, to the captain, he only smiled and laughed. Perhaps he had never understood her destination at all. Perhaps the Portuguese word for France was something far different. In any case he had no intention of taking her there today, or apparently any day until he caught a load of fish.

Cries of *"Arenque!"* awoke her the next morning, and she watched the sailors haul in a dozen full seines and dump them into the hold of the boat. As some of the small fish expired at her feet, she recognized them as herring, which she had come to enjoy at Langmuir as bloaters or kippers; but she had great difficulty that night in choking down the fried fish dinner she was served.

Even though the crew poured salt into the hold, the stench from the catch below deck was soon overwhelming. When a storm blew up during the third night, Nicole became violently ill. The bags having been emptied, she had to lie on the bare deck with one of her satchels as a headrest, but the frenzied pitching of the boat made her more sick than she had ever felt in her life. Surely her little indisposition on the voyage from Bordeaux to London was nothing compared to this. Never again would she eat another fish as long as she lived. Never, never would she set foot on another boat.

As one seizure of vomiting followed another, she knew she could not recover until she escaped the choking fumes of the cargo. Finally dragging herself up to the open deck, she found rain was pounding, but only wrapped her cloak tighter and lay down on the streaming planks. What did it matter if she froze or drowned when at last she could fill her lungs with clean air? Little caring whether she lived or died, she placed her head on a coil of rope and fell asleep.

She was dreaming that she was wrestling with some demon, an epic struggle between Virtue and Vice like a passage from a moralistic English writer—except that Virtue, Nicole herself, seemed to be losing. When a ravenous mouth fell upon her own, she roused instantly from her deep sleep. A great reeking sailor lay on top of her, pinning her arms down on each side of her and wetting her lips with hideous kisses.

At the first taste of him Nicole began to gag, and reflexively pushed at his shoulders and chest with all her strength. But even as she choked and shoved, he tore at the bodice of her dress and dug his knee between her legs to force them apart. Managing to pull her face away from his, she yelled at the top of her lungs, calling for help in French and English. She hardly knew ten words of Spanish, less of Portuguese. *"Capitán, capitán!"* she screamed, and then *"Muerte!"* death! But the wind was far more shrill than her voice. There was little chance the lookout would be able to hear.

As the man's hand pushed high between her legs, kneading her flesh clumsily in some kind of vile effort to arouse her, then tugged on her drawers until he broke the drawstring, she fought with desperate strength. *Grand Dieu*, he could not win! At the realization of her near fate, she began to retch violently, pouring vomit over the man as well as herself. Crying out some Portuguese oath, he jumped up slapping at his face and chest to clean them, and gagging, ran away.

The storm lasted throughout the next day, and Nicole knew she could endure little more. Not only had her sickness worsened as she grew weaker, but she knew one more night on the open deck would likely bring another rape attempt. More than an attempt—she might not be so lucky next time. Frantically she implored the captain once more. Perhaps his full hold, perhaps his awareness of her desperation caused him to consent —provided, he said in fluent French, she supply a few additional gold coins. In the end she had to pay him double their original bargain to set her down on a rocky beach in the middle of the night.

Nicole waded through the icy surf until she felt dry land beneath her feet, then allowing her valises to drop from her hands, collapsed full length on the sand. She had heard of people kissing the ground beneath their feet after some hard-fought journey. She had the will but not the strength, and besides, was by no means certain she was really home in France. The captain could have dropped her anywhere from Norway to Spain. She had long ago lost her sense of direction.

The moon shone only briefly through heavy clouds, but she made out a high cliff immediately in front of her. Perhaps she would be better off to follow the beach. But after stumbling in each direction for a few yards, she found the shingle was limited on all sides by large boulders. She had no choice but to climb the cliff.

For an hour she groped in the dark, tripping over her muddy cloak, skinning her legs and slipping dangerously in the renewed rain until at last she reached a level field. With a cry of success she felt the furrows made by a plow; she knew she had reached a cultivated farm and that human habitation could not be far away.

But instead of the farmhouse, she soon found a wide, hard-packed road —a post road she dared hope—and vowed to follow it until she dropped. Just as the eastern sky lightened with the first rays of dawn, she glimpsed the lights of a town. Fired with new strength, she pushed on, discovering new lights around every turn. Then before her like a miracle she saw a *relais*, or inn where post chaises stopped, and upon inquiring of the innkeeper, found she had reached the outskirts of Calais.

In her comfortable room, Nicole could enjoy a hot bath and several hours of blessed sleep before the diligence for the south was due. What a pleasure it was to eat a slice of *pâté en croûte* and some very young veal in a superb Mornay sauce. She had almost forgotten the French genius for cooking. When she paid her bill and purchased her ticket, she was given, as change from one louis, a great fistful of paper *assignats*, which she regarded with considerable distrust.

Boarding the crowded coach in late afternoon, Nicole had to sit between an elderly tradesman and a middle-aged gentlewoman dressed in rich clothes. Unable to see out a window, she occupied her time, after exchanging a few pleasantries with her companions, by examining the new fashions. The three men on board, though they seemed to come from different walks of life, all wore long *pantalons* reaching to their boots instead of the familiar knee breeches and hose. The lady next to her, whom she guessed to be the wife of a magistrate or small landowner, and a young girl of much lower station, both had small bonnets with scoop brims and hairstyles free of the elaborate teasing and piling practiced for so long. Both women wore narrow unstiffened skirts, and Nicole smiled a little to remember that Marie Antoinette, whom the nation now professed to despise, had introduced that simple style in the last wicked days of Versailles.

Then Nicole noticed with alarm that all three men sported *cocardes* of red, white, and blue feathers, which she knew to be the insignia of the Revolution. And the girl opposite her wore a ribbon rosette of the same colors pinned to her shoulder. Could all of these people—from different regions and walks of life—believe enthusiastically in this dreadful revolt that only seemed inexplicable and tragic to Nicole? Pretending to want to peer out the window, she bent around until she could see that her wellborn neighbor also displayed a ribbon rosette on her cloak. Did some law require everyone to wear the colors? Perhaps she should purchase a rosette as soon as possible for safety—though the symbol would always be repugnant to her. Clearly, France had undergone changes in her absence that she could not comprehend.

Nicole listened eagerly to the conversations in the coach, and replied politely but guardedly when someone directed a question to her. Asked her home, she said she was from the Bordelais. She preferred to be truthful, and besides any native Frenchman could detect regional differences in speech. But when the gentlewoman asked her if she had been visiting relatives in Calais, some instinct told her to lie and say she had.

The men began a political discussion that Nicole wished to follow, but the gentlewoman took the opportunity to draw her into private conversation. "Perhaps I would know your relatives in Calais?" she inquired, after explaining that the town was her own home.

"Oh, I think not, madame," Nicole said.

"You do not wish to tell me their names?" the lady asked with some vexation.

Flustered, Nicole answered, "But you would not care to know them, madame. They are not a highborn family," she added, hoping to flatter the woman into silence.

"I thought perhaps they were English. . . ." she declared mysteriously.

"Oh, no," Nicole interjected hastily.

". . . because I see that you are wearing a dress of English worsted trimmed with a braid that I happen to know has not been made in France for many years."

Nicole nodded blankly, pretending indifference to any further conversation. The woman was too wise. Closing her eyes as if to sleep, Nicole hoped desperately she would lose interest in her.

But after a few minutes of silence, the woman leaned near her and spoke in a low, confidential tone. "As you are no doubt well aware, mademoiselle, the National Assembly, to which we all of course render our sincere allegiance, deems it a capital offense for any French citizen to flee to a foreign land. And if one of these *émigrés* dares to return to France, whether he be noble or commoner, male or female, innocent or guilty, he falls under automatic sentence of death."

Nicole was so astounded by this revelation that she could do no more than make a feeble nod. Could the woman's statement be true? But such a sentence seemed ridiculous! Not only had she committed no crime, but in fact she and her predecessors had always ruled Beaux-Clervaux with justice and compassion for the peasants, as anyone in the Bordelais would attest. And she had left France almost against her will. No, she could not believe that such a sentence would ever be imposed against her.

But still, she wanted to avoid at all costs any encounter with the authorities. Something about the new France filled her with distrust. Was this woman giving her a kind warning, or a cruel hint that she could turn her in at the next municipality? How much could she tell about Nicole? Was her sojourn in England as easy for anyone to detect? Did she perhaps have traces of sand on her cloak or shoes, despite her efforts to clean them? Even if this woman was not an informer, would there be others giving her the same close scrutiny?

An excellent supper in a country inn soothed Nicole's nerves. She was happy to see that no one on the staff wore the tricolor *cocarde*. No doubt she was simply exhausted from her dreadful voyage, and so had reacted to the gentlewoman's comments with ill humor. After all she was back home in France. In only three or four days she would reach Beaux-Clervaux, and ought to feel nothing but delight and satisfaction.

Most of the passengers were dozing, when an hour after supper the diligence was stopped by soldiers in a red and blue uniform that Nicole had never seen before. Without great concern, the occupants of the coach climbed down and lined up for an inspection that was evidently familiar to them. But Nicole was frozen with fear that the soldiers would ask her name and residence, and hastily made up some story to give them. To her great relief they quickly searched the men, passed the gentlewoman without a word, and excused herself and the other young girl after teasing them with an embarrassing poke or two.

But when they had been allowed to return to the coach, the passengers all began to fret and grumble, craning their necks to watch through the back window while the soldiers hauled luggage out of the large wicker hamper at the rear of the coach. Everyone agreed that these undisciplined provincial guards were no better than thieves, and only stopped the diligences to pilfer the baggage of the passengers.

Peeking out of the window, Nicole saw a soldier open one of her valises and hold up her heavy cloak, which carried the valuable rubies under its collar. How she would hate to lose her mother's beautiful heirloom! Her heart was in her throat until she saw him stuff it back into her satchel and turn his attention elsewhere.

The passengers seemed to be satisfied that the soldiers had stolen nothing after all. This detachment appeared to be well disciplined by its *brigadier*. Perhaps they really were looking for smuggled firearms and military deserters after all.

The coachman had already remounted the box when the *brigadier* pulled open the door of the coach, and demanded to know who was the owner of the two small valises held up by the soldier beside him. When Nicole readily identified herself, he announced that she was under arrest and ordered her to climb down and go with him.

12

Although embarrassed to stand before men in the shapeless shift that hardly reached to her ankles, perfectly aware as she was that the lace on the bottom of her drawers could be seen, Nicole was nevertheless relieved to be called before the regional commander. For a month she had been held in a former convent here in Rouen without any idea of the charges against her.

She prayed she would be allowed to sit down instead of remaining in front of a bright window so that the commander and his assistant could see in clear detail the outline of her figure through the thin fabric. But she had to admit that neither the stout, florid colonel nor the young lieutenant seemed interested in scrutinizing her. The colonel was leafing through a file of papers apparently about her, as the lieutenant carefully briefed him.

Rubbing his chin thoughtfully while he read, the older man finally looked up at her. For a moment he seemed to appreciate the sight. His eye traveled from her mass of golden hair, which she had not been given time to pin up properly, to her plump breasts and silhouetted hips and legs, and he smiled almost wistfully. But then he reached for a kerchief and mopped his damp purple face, shifting with considerable discomfort in the chair. How well Nicole knew the signs of chronic overindulgence in wine. No doubt he had preferred Burgundies to the Bordeaux wines, she thought with loyalty to her region.

"Gaillard?" he read. "You gave your name as Nicole Gaillard, daughter of a peasant in the Bordelais?"

"That is correct, *monsieur le colonel.*"

He shrugged indifferently. "We have no doubt you are lying. There is ample reason to believe you are in fact a noblewoman."

"Oh, no, colonel! I am hardly that—" She was trying to remember the exact accents of the peasants in her region. How much did the colonel know about her? Had he found the coins and jewels hidden in her clothes? Or had he guessed as easily as the woman in the diligence that she had just returned from England? Probably her heavy cloak had still been damp when they first examined it, damp with traces of sand. Was she about to be sentenced to death, executed in front of the firing squad that she knew claimed many lives every week here in Rouen.

During her month in the convent, Nicole had heard a hundred stories of the suffering of the nobility. For the last week she had had to listen to a comtesse sobbing every night about the murders of her family, before she herself was taken only yesterday morning to be shot. Nicole had become half-convinced as she endured the poor woman's wailing that she was facing a similar fate.

If only the colonel would reveal what he knew. Perhaps she should make disclosure of her true identity in the hope she would be exonerated by a trial in Bordeaux. Heaven knows no one there would speak a word against her. On the other hand, if the simple act of returning to France after emigrating was actually punished by death, she must keep her peace. She had encountered no returned *émigrées* in the convent and had no information abut their treatment. Who, after all, would be stupid enough to return—if she knew!

Licking his thumb, the colonel turned several sheets of paper. "Of course you will not be surprised to learn that we discovered in the seams and hems and collars of your clothes thousands of francs' worth of jewels. Diamonds, pearls, rubies, a valuable watch—" He held up a list and shook it at her. She could see there were more than a dozen items on it. So they had found almost everything. "Inevitably we conclude that such a fine collection of heirloom jewels would only belong to a woman of aristocratic birth."

Was that all? Would he not accuse her of being an *émigrée*? She had had a month to consider various stories. "Of course I am not an aristocrat, colonel," she began, smiling a little, pretending to be flattered that he could imagine such a thing. With a deep sigh as though resigned to confessing at last, she said in a country accent, "It isn't as though I really stole the jewels. She owed them to me—at least in part. The cruel woman had not paid me a sou of wages for more than three years! And there were other servants who had served even longer without pay. I took the gems when I found she was running away. She and her whole family crossed over the border, hoping to make their way to London. And no doubt they did, for she had powerful friends. I took the whole collection because I intended to share it with all the others she had made work for her with no more pay than a slave."

"So you claim you stole the valuables from your mistress, an *émigrée*?"

"Not stole, colonel, only seized what rightfully belonged to the poor people she had cheated!" Her voice had a militant ring.

"Yes, yes," he murmured, impatient with revolutionary rhetoric. "And what was the name of this employer?"

"The Marquise de Vaucroze."

"Does—did she reside here in Normandy?"

"No, colonel. I worked for her as *femme de chambre* at the Royal Palace of Versailles until the day it was pillaged by the Paris mob."

"How came you then to be riding in a coach from Calais to Amiens?"

"For many months the marquise hid in lodgings in Paris, and I remained with her. When at last she announced she was leaving for Spain, I refused to desert my native land," Nicole said piously. "She in turn refused to pay me, and so I took her jewels and ran away. Once I was on my own, I met—a man. He promised to . . ."

"He promised to marry you. But he did not. *Hélas*, it is a familiar story. Fortunately you managed to steal a few louis from him. . . ." The colonel shrugged philosophically, and gave her a reassuring smile. But soon he had to mop his brow again. Exhausted by such concentration, he handed the file back to his assistant and rose to leave the room.

Nicole was greatly relieved by his acceptance of her story, but he seemed to be shedding responsibility for her already. No doubt the efficient assistant did the real work for his ailing commander. And did the lieutenant believe her as well?

The tall, boyishly handsome man bent over to jot a few notes, then straightened the desk with precise movements, and looked up to meet her stare. "We will investigate your case thoroughly, mademoiselle. You may rest assured." His manner was so scrupulous that she could detect no bias at all. As he handed her over to a matron for her return to the convent, she noted with a little chagrin that he had not at any time allowed his eyes to travel down her figure.

But on the following afternoon, just as she had finished scrubbing the dinner pots, the same young officer ordered her brought before him in the convent refectory. Nicole was rather happy to be interviewed once again, for she longed to have an opportunity to judge the success of her story.

"Mademoiselle Gaillard, may I have the honor of introducing myself to you. My name is Lieutenant Roger Duchamp, and I beg to be allowed to escort you on a brief walk around the city—" He rushed through this stiff invitation nervously.

Nicole was astonished, but recovered to accept quickly. Of course he must have some ulterior motive, no doubt hoping to trick her into an admission of guilt. She would have to be on her guard. But in any case she would not dream of refusing, for she was dying to escape even for a short while from the dreary convent.

"Oh, wait, could I—?" she said impetuously, then grew shy. He was after all her jailer.

"Could you have one of your own dresses to wear in public? But of course! Forgive me for not anticipating such a natural wish!" He sounded genuinely distressed at his thoughtlessness.

After a word from the lieutenant, a matron produced one of the demure frocks made by Kate and a respectable supply of undergarments. Nicole hurried to her cell, where she dressed quickly, splashed water on her face, and arranged her hair in a soft bun. Even though she had no mirror, she felt satisfied that she looked presentable. What a delight it was to be dressed in real clothes again, to be neat and pretty—and to go out with a courteous officer for a stroll on a summer day!

Finding after polite inquiries that she had never visited Rouen, the lieutenant took her arm and led her down narrow streets toward the center of the town. His hand was in no way tight or restraining. For a brief moment, Nicole had an urge to try to run from him. Could she possibly escape down one of the little streets or across a crowded square? Turning to give him a shy smile, she realized that he was a large, muscular man—not as tall as Falkland, but heavier without being fat. Muscles bulged in his neck, shoulders, and arms, as though he had deliberately exercised to enlarge them. If she started to run he would grab her immediately. Then she accidentally bumped against his hip. He was wearing a pistol or perhaps even a sword. And there were frequently other soldiers in sight. The man was no fool. He would not be taking her out if there was any real chance she could escape from him.

Together they admired the elaborate Gothic traceries of the cathedral, which Nicole knew was one of the famous churches of France. Duchamp remarked that the tower in the flamboyant style on the left was called the Tower of Butter.

"Because of its yellow stone?"

"No, because it was constructed from the dispensations bought by the faithful to be allowed to eat butter during Lent."

Nicole puzzled over the lieutenant's curious accent. Was he from some distant region of France, or perhaps even a foreign country? She thought she could detect an effort to disguise his true origins. Sometimes his words seemed quite labored and unnatural.

Walking along a street so narrow a single coach could barely pass between the curbs and partly covered by the overhanging half-timbered houses, they came to a beautiful Renaissance mansion that actually spanned the street. Just above the archway was a large gilded clock that told the days of the week and the phases of the moon. Only a short distance beyond the mansion, Nicole saw a large Gothic building of extravagant decoration that was apparently not a church. Seeming reluctant to notice it, Duchamp finally said hastily that it was the Palais de Justice where the Tribunal sat. Nicole shuddered. So that was where her friends from the convent had been sentenced to death—and where she herself would stand trial.

In temporary embarrassment they walked on to the Old Market Square, where he offered her a chair at an outdoor café and ordered two glasses of calvados, a potent apple brandy native to Normandy.

"Do you know what famous event took place right here, not twenty feet from our table?" he asked. "In fact, you can see a marker set in the pavement just there."

"You don't mean—!" Nicole exclaimed with alarm. Every schoolchild knew that Joan of Arc had been burned at the stake in Rouen, and Duchamp confirmed that this was the exact spot. "It makes my flesh crawl!" she cried, with an expression of distress.

He looked upset. "I hope it does not prevent you from enjoying our—this little tour of the city," he said earnestly. "Perhaps then we should leave." His reaction was so fretful Nicole had to reassure him several times. Yes, he was earnest—and so serious, words Falkland had once applied to her. Now she could see that the traits could be a little comic, and somewhat trying. So that is how Falkland had seen her, she thought with pain.

To give the lieutenant his due, she had to admit she was having a delightful afternoon. Of course leaving prison even briefly was a joy, and the town was a veritable museum of medieval churches and houses. As the August sun and the calvados warmed her blood, Nicole began to appreciate his friendly smile and considerate ways. Undeniably he was a handsome man. Though strong and powerful, he also had a boyish air. "Perhaps it was the thick brown curly hair. At a distance he had looked too young to be an officer, but up close she could see that he had one or two gray hairs at his temples. Though at first she had thought he was no more than her own age, now she decided that he was probably twenty-six or a little more.

How curious that she would be sitting here in polite conversation with a man who had virtual power of life and death over her, yet whom she did not fear, and actually rather pitied for his awkward silences and painful shyness. From the intent way he studied her face when he thought she was not noticing and a dozen other little signs, she knew he was rapidly becoming infatuated with her.

Several times a week, Duchamp secured her release from the prison at midday and returned her safely before nightfall. They explored every part of Rouen, always ending at a café in the Old Market Square or on a quay along the Seine. When she lay at night on the hard pallet bed in her nun's cell, she always hoped that Roger, as she now called him, would be free to visit her again the next day.

What would the little nuns who had lived in this cell for so many years, even centuries, and whose spirits often seemed to Nicole to hover close by, say about her gallant suitor? Surely they would be jealous. She could only feel sympathy for them. They had never known the pleasure of running down the corridor to meet a handsome officer and escaping from these stone walls for an entire afternoon. What would they answer her if they could? That they had enjoyed spiritual delights she could not know—and remind her that she still faced a trial and possible death sentence?

Roger never mentioned her case, and on the single occasion when she had dared to ask him about it, he had apologized for his inability to tell her anything she did not already know. She guessed he feared any imputation of bias in her case, and would bend over backwards to be impartial. Even so, his very courtship gave her hope. Always so earnest and serious he was obviously in love with her, and he must expect to win her. Surely he would not allow himself to press his suit so sincerely—at such high cost to himself—if there was any chance of her being executed.

Roger was too shrewd, too intelligent for that. She had learned to have great respect for his abilities. He was precise, efficient, purposeful, hardworking, perhaps too humorless—yes, too serious. She was back to that. Earnest and serious. Falkland had said—sometimes she thought she could quote every word the duke had ever spoken to her—"No doubt we should choose someone as young, earnest, and *serieux* as you are yourself." Had she found herself an appropriate husband at last? Would the duke approve? No doubt he would be only too happy to marry her off!

Certainly Roger was attractive, intelligent, and considerate—should any girl hope for more in a husband? But certain strange traits disturbed her. Not only was his speech unnatural and sometimes rather pretentious, but she had found out he disliked revealing anything about his background, merely saying that he had been brought up not far outside of Paris, and that both his parents were dead. Then she had gradually discovered that he had very little formal schooling. While his penmanship was carefully formed, and he could discourse knowledgeably on military affairs including the difficult subject of artillery science, his general education was quite inadequate. When he took her to see the château where Joan of Arc had been imprisoned, she was amazed to find he had no knowledge whatsoever of that period of French history. Nor had he ever even heard of the famous playwright Corneille, who had been born locally and was made much of. Most surprising of all, Roger had not managed during their weeks of friendship to lose his apologetic, uncertain attitude.

When they were eating dinner in an inn one day, Roger motioned rather impatiently for the servingman to give him more broccoli, and Nicole realized with astonishment that he did not know the correct name for the vegetable.

"*Plus de choux brocolis, monsieur?*" the man asked with patronizing emphasis on the name, and Roger flushed. Nicole could hardly believe that anyone, rich or poor, could fail to know such a common name. One would hardly be surprised by ignorance of the word for blancmange or crayfish, but broccoli!

She expected Roger would pretend it had merely slipped his mind, but when the waiter had departed, he said honestly, "I fear I do not come from an elegant background."

Perhaps she should have hurried to add, "Nor do I," but the words stuck in her throat.

With surprising frankness, Roger confessed that, despite the impression of being a gentleman he had so carefully fostered, he was actually the son of poor peasants. His father had been no more than a woodcutter in the forest of a ruthless nobleman, a vicomte, and had had to feed his family by poaching game. His mother had died after her tenth baby, and Roger had spent his childhood helping his drunken father to steal a few hares and partridges from their incredibly wealthy master at the risk of the death penalty if they were caught. From a single book, Roger had taught himself to read and write when he was ten. He had never been to school. No one in his family had ever before been "lettered," as he put it. No one had ever helped him learn.

At fifteen he had gotten a job as stableboy to the vicomte, and had worked his way up through a series of promotions until at twenty he was *brosseur*, or batman, to the vicomte's younger son, who had a career in the military. The outbreak of the Revolution had given Roger his great opportunity. Quickly realizing the possibilities, he had studied military manuals furiously, wangled a position as *sergent-chef* left vacant in a political purge, and soon won himself a commission by virtue of his superior abilities.

In the days that followed, Nicole wondered why he was so embarrassed about his origins when he was supposed to believe she was no more than a peasant turned servant. Or did he believe it? Perhaps he never had. Only slowly losing his shame, he finally asked her to correct his speech and manners and to teach him the names of food and clothing known only to rich people, which she willingly did, always pretending to have learned from her mistress, the marquise. By means of great tact, Nicole tried to make the role of pupil bearable for him, proud and vain as she knew him to be, but she also learned that he was driven by a fierce ambition.

When he came to pick her up one afternoon in a hired *cabriolet* and drove through the pretty hills to the summit at Bonsecours, she expected that he would at last make some romantic declaration. He had so far spoken no words of love, had not so much as caressed her hand. Of course it was only further proof of his shyness, but for several weeks she had been rather annoyed that he could not even manage to peck her cheek with a kiss. Not that she longed for him to kiss her, she assured herself. But she just naturally hated to see anyone so tense and awkward that he could not accomplish a simple embrace!

Before them spread a magnificent view of the whole city of Rouen with its churches and château and busy river port, and beyond, the serpentine curves of the Seine winding to the Atlantic. Surprisingly, Roger seemed to have no thought of romance, and was instead bursting to tell her some news. Gripping her hands, he said in a sympathetic voice that her trial had been scheduled for a fortnight hence. "Brace yourself! Don't cry—" His excessive solicitude was annoying. She had anticipated the news too long to think of crying; it came almost as a relief. "You must not despair," he declared, "for I have everything arranged perfectly!"

"What can you mean?" she asked warily. She did not want to hear exaggerations.

"We—I have found out your real identity." He looked at her in mild reproof, like a schoolmaster admonishing a child for some misdemeanor, but Nicole only stared back coolly. "When we examined your jewelry, we saw that one gold ring bore the elaborate seal of a noble family. My *adjudant*, who is native to Normandy, remarked that it resembled the crest of the family of the Baron de Saint-Mathiez, now died out, which had once held the *manoir* in his district. I went to see their old house, a half day's ride from here. Half-timbered with a thatched roof, it was once handsome, but is now in ruins and only used by a farmer to shelter his cows." As he described the house, he looked sharply for any flicker of interest in her eyes. "When I applied to the curé of the parish, he told me a last daughter had gone as a bride to the Bordelais. Referring to his records he found that she had married a Robert de Clervaux and borne a female infant. He did not know the name of the child, but said it had been born twenty-one years ago this coming December—Christmas Eve, to be exact. Can you now refuse to admit that you were born on Christmas Eve, 1770, and that your true name is Nicole de Clervaux?"

"I have told you my name is Gaillard," she said softly.

"There is no need to be stubborn. I have already received an answer from the Comité Révolutionnaire of the Commune of Beaux-Clervaux." She started a little at the name of her home, but kept silent. "The parish records reveal that Lucienne de Clervaux, née Saint-Mathiez, gave birth on Christmas Eve, 1770, to an infant daughter who was christened Nicole."

She met his eyes defiantly, saying nothing, and he cried with sudden fervor, "Oh, my dear Nicole. I have already destroyed the letter! I would not collect information against you!"

"The Comité Révolutionnaire of Beaux-Clervaux! Can that district be in revolt?" she asked anxiously.

"Oh, Nicole"—he was squeezing her hands painfully—"you must believe that I would do nothing to hurt you. Already I have removed the seal ring from your jewels and falsified the inventory list. The *adjudant* who identified the crest has been told that a Saint-Mathiez married into the Vaucroze family. There is no evidence against you! Furthermore, a trooper in my brigade hails from the Vaucroze estates in the Nivernais. He will testify to the marquis's cruel and unjust treatment of his peasants. There is no doubt you will be acquitted of jewel theft, and probably even acclaimed for your confiscation of a noble's jewels." Evidently at last feeling worthy, he moved toward her on the carriage seat and whispered, "Can you ever care for me?"

"Of course," she murmured. "I owe you—many thanks." How flat and ungrateful it sounded.

He placed his hands on her arms, and hesitated as though summoning up his nerve to kiss her. Why didn't the man grab her and have it over with! "Nicole, will you tell me—?" Great concern was written on his face; what could possibly distress him so much? "Tell me—please assure me that you did not really run away with a man!"

"Did not run away—?"

"With a man to Calais. You were arrested en route from Calais to Amiens in a diligence. You told my colonel that you had been abandoned by—a lover."

"Oh, it was only a story! I was pretending to be a servant and a jewel thief." She tried to sound calm, but her brain was racing to find an alibi for her presence in Calais. Despite his apparent sincerity, she did not want to trust Roger with the knowledge that she had just returned from England.

But he had no thought of *émigrés* at the moment. "Please forgive me"—

he could not meet her eyes—"but it has eaten at me so, I have to know! Have you been—dishonored by a man?"

Dear heaven, what a question to have to answer! What should she say? Had the duke "dishonored" her? Probably the word was as good as any. But surely Roger had no right to ask—or perhaps he did. He was painfully in love with her, and probably dreamed of making her his wife. But Nicole knew she could never confess to this anguished suitor that she had yielded with the most profound pleasure to the uses of her cynical guardian. And that she had longed—no, burned for him ever since! "No, Roger, I have never been. . . ." She stammered a little, hating to tell a lie.

He took her reluctance for pure embarrassment, and gathered her clumsily in his arms. "Can you ever forgive me for asking? It's just that I—want to—that I care so very much! If only I were worthy to—to— But I swear to you one day that I will be!"

He finally pressed his lips on hers, his hands clutching her shoulders with little nervous squeezes. As she felt his breathing quicken, Nicole allowed herself to relax and enjoy the long kiss. But then he stopped and released her abruptly.

Her hands lingered on his shoulders a moment, and then she removed them, feeling foolish. Was that all he meant to do? But of course, he was a gentleman. A perfect gentleman. She realized suddenly exactly what the term meant, and wanted to laugh out loud. Roger the peasant was a perfect gentleman, and the Duke of Falkland was not. And oh, how she wished that she were sitting here in this little carriage with the bold and passionate duke, not Roger, beside her!

13

In the fortnight before her trial, Nicole worried less about the verdict than she did the problem of Roger. She had believed him when he assured her she would be exonerated. All along she had trusted that justice would be done, and now that Roger had seen fit to suppress the only evidence against her, she had little reason to be concerned.

But what should she do about her fervent suitor? His single kiss, while not unpleasant, had only reminded her how much she still desired Falkland. Heaven knows Roger was an attractive man. Not only was he courteous and considerate in the extreme, but she owed her very life to him, and she was racked with guilt that she would never be able to repay her debt as he deserved.

If only she could drive Falkland from her mind, her memory, her body! She tried to convince herself that what she felt for him was only sexual desire, not love; and that surely in time her longing for his arms and mouth and body would fade. But almost two years had passed since their night at Beaux-Clervaux, yet her memory of it was as vivid as if it had been last night.

She hated to believe she was capable of clinging to Roger out of fear for her own safety. Had she made herself pleasant company all these weeks only because she knew how much she needed him to see her through the trial? Most of all, she hated to believe that she felt some aversion because he came from humble stock. How deeply ingrained was her prejudice? After all, a new France was being formed. None of the old social rules would apply.

Always the duke's chance remark about a man as earnest and *serieux* as herself rang in her ears. Trying to imagine Falkland as nothing more than a responsible guardian—something of an intellectual feat, she found!—she strongly suspected that he would advise her to marry Roger. Was Roger not intelligent, energetic, ambitious, with excellent prospects! She must realize that her estates and their income were probably lost to her forever. If not Beaux-Clervaux, then where could she go after the trial? Certainly she would never return to the humiliation and frustration of Langmuir Castle —or worse, Falkland House. She must remain in France. What then? A life as a governess, schoolmistress—or nun! Far better a marriage to a fine man who was devoted to her. A man she could—perhaps—learn to love in time.

The great Gothic hall, which had once seen sessions of the Parlement of Normandy, today held only the rabble of the town. When Nicole was brought in, dressed in a gray dress of Kate's and manacled to a dozen other *prévenues*, the crowd rose to jeer and hurl eggs and vegetables. Amazed and frightened, she tried to jump back as an old woman spat directly at her and then pulled a pistol from the waistband of her skirt and brandished it. When the five judges, who could be seen by their clothes to be ordinary workingmen, entered and took their seats at the bench, the crowd saluted them with humorous and even obscene nicknames.

Now trembling, Nicole searched everywhere for Roger in the hall, and at last spotted him just inside the *barre*, deep in conversation with another officer as he surveyed the crowd. Even across the large room she could tell from his expression that he was very apprehensive.

Two noblewomen were tried first. One was accused of nothing more than being the mother of a son who had emigrated to Germany. She could offer no defense, and was promptly sentenced to death as the crowd gave a round of cheers. The second, an elderly woman, was said to have beaten and tortured many of her servants, a charge she denied vehemently. Commencing to call her own witnesses who would refute such an accusation, she suddenly collapsed in a faint, and the spectators so boisterously demanded a verdict of guilty that the judges sentenced her to death while she lay senseless at their feet.

At last the prisoner Gaillard was called. Nicole was unchained and led to the *banc des prévenus*, where she was formally accused of jewel theft. Under the questioning of the *accusateur public*, a baker dusty with flour but endowed with a ringing baritone voice, she was allowed to tell her story of service to the *émigrée* Marquise de Vaucroze. Then a soldier, one Lemaire, took the stand and described the cruelty and neglect suffered by peasants on the Vaucroze estates near Nevers. "This young girl," he declared, pointing at Nicole, "has performed a fine and noble act. All of the jewels she has stolen should be sold, and the proceeds distributed to the neediest of the Vaucroze tenants." At this proposal, the crowd burst into a loud acclamation.

Nicole thought she would faint with relief. This wild throng was actually cheering for her. Turning to look at Roger, she caught his eye and smiled broadly. But he responded with only a grave nod, and she became alarmed again. What did he know? Why wasn't he as jubilant as she was?

The *accusateur public* and Lemaire had been conferring together, cupping their hands to their ears to hear each other during the applause. When the noise subsided, the baker recalled Nicole to the *banc*, and asked, "Can you tell us the name of the former Vaucroze estate?"

"Why—the Château de Saint-Saulve." Fortunately, she had had time to remember the name after Roger had told her he had found a native of the estate. Only once, in a conversation at Versailles with the marquise's couturière, had she heard the property mentioned.

"Were you born there, Gaillard?"

"No, monsieur." Did one call a baker *monsieur* when he was your prosecutor in a revolutionary tribunal?

"You must address me by the new universal title of Citizen, which eliminates forever all offensive distinctions of rank. Then surely you visited Saint-Saulve many times in the company of your mistress in the—how many years did you serve her?"

"Three years, citizen."

"And did you not visit there many times, citizeness?" he repeated sharply.

She knew he would ask her to describe it. "No, citizen, I never attended her there."

"You never attended her there!" He echoed her statement for rhetorical effect. The crowd was hanging on every word. "Weren't you her *femme de chambre*?"

"She rarely went there herself. She hated to leave the excitement of the court."

"She rarely went . . . but sometimes? Sometimes she went?"

"Yes, citizen."

"And yet you never accompanied her?"

"No—" What possible excuse could she give? Improvising desperately, Nicole said, "She hated to travel with a retinue. She always said she could fly along so much faster in her little *berline-coupée*."

The prosecutor turned toward the crowd with a theatrical gesture of great patience, then whispered once again with Lemaire. The room was spellbound. At last facing her, the baker asked, "What was the name of the valet of the Marquis de Vaucroze, a man you must have known well at Versailles?"

Nicole squared her shoulders. She knew she had no chance, or perhaps only one. "It was—we simply called him Jean. I never knew his surname." She would gamble on the commonest of first names.

But before she had finished her sentence, Lemaire jumped to his feet. "The marquis's valet for twenty years was my cousin François Lemaire!" he shouted triumphantly.

The crowd exploded with wrath against Nicole, crying *"Noblesse! Noblesse!"* and shouting for her head. As zealots in the front rows pressed forward menacingly, Roger and a jailer hurried Nicole from the hall.

The matron had already reached the grille of the convent and unlocked it. Nicole could see a wagon filled with docile prisoners waiting at the curb. How many days would it take to reach Paris? Three, probably four, in this old farm wagon? And then execution? She was too dazed to comprehend fully the meaning of her departure.

She could only think how much she hated to leave without seeing Roger—without thanking him, without trying to repay him a little with a few words of affection, without being able to understand the real meaning of her plight by reading his expression. The call to board the wagon had come so unexpectedly, barely an hour after her trial, and even before she had had an opportunity to change out of her good gray dress. And now she would never see him again.

The driver was boosting her into the wagon, one hand on her bottom, when she heard Roger's voice shouting angrily. In a moment he had lifted her down again, and hurried her back in the convent to the portress's little room just beyond the grille.

Enormously relieved to see him, she reached out spontaneously with both her hands. She wanted to remember him as the handsome officer who had been her suitor. How fine he looked in his bright blue coat with gold epaulettes and black felt bicorne hat. He had been her good, generous friend.

Then she saw that his face was deeply flushed and his eyes were filled with tears. She had not expected such distress. So he knew her plight was hopeless. Perhaps she had half believed that Roger could save her, that with a word he might free her or at least keep her here in jail in Rouen. But of course he was just a little provincial lieutenant. How had she come to endow him in her mind with exalted powers?

As tears rolled down his face, he vowed in a tremulous voice, "I will not rest until I save you, dearest Nicole! I swear I will succeed! I love you, and I vow I will yet make you my wife!"

What should she respond to such a declaration, such a proposal, which she knew he was bold enough to make only in the face of her execution? The marriage would never happen. Did she still owe him a serious ananswer: I'm sorry, Roger, but I don't believe I would want to marry you if I were going to live? Or—I wish I did want to marry you because I respect you enormously, but what is good for us is not often what we want most in life?

With shaking hands, he took her face and kissed her lips gently. Strangely, his mouth could not convey the intensity of his expression. But she sensed how much he longed to hear her express her love. The man would never see her alive again, and so she said, "Dear Roger, please believe that I care so very much for you, and know that I thank you from the bottom of my heart. I owe you so much, and now can never repay you!"

At last he clasped her in his arms, her face pressed against his shoulder. In the hard, comforting embrace, she tried to absorb some of the strength she would need to see her through these last few days of her life.

From the beginning in the prison of La Force in Paris, Nicole saw many faces she recognized from Versailles: a lady-in-waiting to the queen, nobles who had trailed the king in his progresses, the riding master to the royal children, even a dancer from the court ballets. Most prisoners were titled, although many were clergy, the *prêtres réfractaires*, who had refused to take an oath to the Constitution; and there were foreigners judged enemies of the Republic, and others sentenced for inexplicable reasons—a poor seamstress from Lyons, the cook of the Comte d'Artois.

Although La Force had long served as a prison, there were now no regular felons, and conditions were far from unbearable. The great dungeons had central firepits that were supplied with plentiful wood, often the fences of parks and forests that had belonged to nobles and were now open to the public. The governor of the prison granted one blanket, a daily cup of water, and a bowl of gruel. But other amenities must be bought by the prisoners themselves by arrangement with the guards, who were only too happy to make a profit from the sale of hot and cold water, wine, food of all grades, clothing, private cells, and even servants. According to rumor, an occasional escape had been arranged for a munificent fee.

But Nicole had no money at all. At first she feared she could not survive on the single bowl of soup, but soon found that other prisoners, many well supplied with gold, were very generous to their penniless comrades. Hardly a meal passed but what she was offered a chop or omelette or apple and a mug of passable wine. Her only garment was the gray dress she had worn before the tribunal, but fortunately she could always borrow a prison sack to wear long enough to toss the dress into the tub of communal wash boiling over the firepit in her dungeon.

One afternoon, as she assisted a mother with her young children, she suddenly recognized with astonishment the smiling face of Simon de Brizac. After planting a kiss on her mouth, he exclaimed enthusiastically at finding a beautiful girl to brighten his "final days." Nicole was cordial enough, but resisted his efforts to embrace her, and merely laughed at his suggestion she would offer him a little pleasant "diversion."

"How well I remember the sight of your beautiful body, the satiny smoothness of your breasts—"

"Stop, Simon! Or I will run away and never speak to you again!"

"—but alas, our passion was so dramatically interrupted by the queen herself. I hope you have no doubt that Sybille betrayed me as well as you. She had quite whetted my appetite with a description of such a beautiful virgin, and told me of the curtained bed set in the wall of a charming hideaway. Of course she did not inform me the queen intended to dine there that night, and probably she knew as well that Falkland would be present. She was quite willing to sacrifice me to dispose of you," he laughed with a philosophical shrug. "Were you sent away immediately? I looked for you, but never found you again."

"Yes, I was sent home."

"And I was exiled also, to a garrison on a godforsaken rock in the Indian Ocean! Too bad we had to suffer such grave punishment when we had no chance to enjoy our crime! Better to hang for a sheep than a lamb, I always say. Soon, fortunately, the Revolution began, and I was able to make my way back."

"Surely you didn't join the side of the rebels!"

"No, but you might say that I profited from the confusion. Finally, I was arrested for smuggling some nobles across the Rhine into one of the German states. For pay of course—I'm no philanthropist! And you? How came you to La Force? Didn't I hear that Falkland took you with him to England?"

"Yes."

"And had his way with you, so I am told!" he exclaimed with vicarious pleasure.

"You never heard that from him!"

"Aha!" he chortled. "I tricked you! So you confirm he did the dastardly deed! You should know it's hardly Falkland's style to brag. But who could believe that he would fail to succeed with you. And I say bravo for him. He has only made it easier for the rest of us!"

"You are vulgar beyond belief!" she cried, and considered striking his face, but remembered too well what had happened the last time she tried to slap a man. Vehemently she began, "I warn you to stay away from me, and—"

Cunningly, he interrupted her, "I saw your esteemed guardian not one week ago. . . ." and she stopped her tirade instantly. "Then you *are* interested! I thought you might be. Would you like to know where?"

"Yes," she answered faintly.

"Not ten miles from the French border, just across the Rhine in Baden, where he was taking the waters in the company of an English beauty, a Mrs.—what was her name? Exquisite woman, really. Older than you. His taste seems to run to riper beauties. Actually, I hear she is a cast-off mistress of the Prince of Wales."

Nicole was listening with a sour expression, but could not control her curiosity. "What about Sybille? He took her to London and bought her a stylish house."

"Nothing has happened to Sybille. She flourishes, in fact. By no means has Falkland lost interest. Only recently, he flew into a rage when he happened on the Spanish ambassador replacing his cravat in her boudoir and threw the man downstairs. Broke the ambassadorial leg. It's been the talk of London."

Nicole tossed her head with contempt and turned as if to walk away. "He lives in a strange debauched world. Thank heaven I have no more interest in it," she said over her shoulder.

Simon stepped up behind her, placed his hands on her arms, and said into her ear, "Neither you nor I is long for this world. Pray let us enjoy our last few days together." When she tried to shake off his hands, he whispered, "How well I remember your hungry mouth, your writhing body—"

"Never, never will I let you touch me!"

"Then I must offer you something to pique your interest a little. No, don't pull away!"

"What an insult!" she cried. "Do you think you can buy me?"

"And so I will! With something better than gold. I can get a message through to Falkland to tell him you are in prison. He is still in Baden, and he cannot know of your death sentence. If he rescued Sybille, he can rescue you." Then laughing, he added, "Or are you afraid he might not want to? Did you try to tease the man to death, as you do with me?"

She turned to face Simon, in her amazement half embracing him. "A message to him—? But how?"

"He was to stay a month in Baden. Don't worry, I know I can reach him. All you have to do is visit my blanket bed tonight, there under the archway."

Shoving him away with unexpected strength, she swore, "Never, Simon! Believe me when I say I will never lie with you—to save my own neck or for any other reason!"

Despite her cold manner whenever he came near her, Simon seemed to enjoy the pursuit and bore no grudge for her emphatic rejections. Often he would sit nearby as she sewed or read to children, and sometimes brought his meals to eat beside her. As long as he did not touch her or speak lasciviously, she tolerated him, and in time began to relax and grow comfortable with him. After all, he was always amusing and knew more news and gossip than anyone else in La Force.

Not surprisingly, Nicole first heard of the new instrument of execution from Simon. One day as she stirred a pot of soup, he reached over and caressed her neck beneath the long wavy hair. "You must believe that chastity will save you from the guillotine. But you will learn soon enough that the blade cuts equally well through the flesh of the virtuous."

"The blade of the what?"

"The supposedly merciful new means of decapitation," he explained with relish. "Dr. Guillotin, a physician and member of the National Assembly, has succeeded in gaining official adoption of this efficient and humane means of chopping heads. Two upright posts support a weighted blade that, once released, falls with great speed to cut the neck beneath it; and presto! the superfluous cabbage drops into a basket, achieving a permanent cure for the victim's headaches, nearsightedness, baldness, insanity, or ringing in the ears. The good doctor Guillotin experimented for a year with corpses from the hospital of Bicêtre. Receiving no complaints whatsoever he persuaded the Assembly he had a faultless device. Only this week his first living client, a highwayman, forfeited his head to the new machine in the Place du Grève. And now our comrades from La Force will try it out today."

Whether expedited by the greater efficiency or increased popular interest, the number of executions grew with each passing week. And before a month had passed, Nicole, standing frozen as always during the reading of the list of the day's victims, heard the name Simon de Brizac.

Her heart raced as she looked around for him, and then she elbowed her way through the little crowd that had gathered around the warden. Already the condemned were being herded into a line and their moaning families driven back. But where was Simon? At last he sauntered blithely out of his dungeon. When he saw her, he broke into a broad grin with eyes bright and dimples flashing.

"At last you can't deny me a little loving," he laughed. "Make it good for it must last awhile!" She threw her arms around him and kissed him until she was breathless. He smiled appreciatively and pushed into her hands a knotted kerchief. She could feel the gold louis inside, fifty or more. "Had you seen fit to enjoy the nights with me, I would have spent these on a message to Falkland. But then perhaps you can still find him somewhere. I leave the gold with you—but you lose forever the pleasure of my bed!"

When the line of men and women was prodded to move, Nicole ran along beside Simon, trying to keep her arm around him or at least to touch his sleeve. Finally a guard pulled her off with such force that she fell to the floor. In her last glimpse of him, Simon was waving farewell jauntily to his friends on all sides.

For minutes she lay on the stones and sobbed as though her heart would break. An old woman stooped to comfort her, no doubt believing she had loved the condemned man. But she had never loved Simon, had in fact despised him until—when? Now suddenly she could not even remember his sins against her. Her heart was broken to see a young man so vital and resilient, so valiant and courageous, sent to the guillotine. Suddenly Simon had become an inspiration. She must manage to model her own walk to the guillotine on his unflinching bravery. Who would have dreamed that she would remember Simon de Brizac as a pillar of strength?

But when would her own execution ever come? Through how many readings had she stood paralyzed with fear waiting to hear her own name? Had Roger succeeded in removing her name from a list in some office somewhere? Was it possible that the officials who ruled, whoever they were, might not even know she was in La Force? But it was too much to hope for. Occasionally, she heard of someone among the prisoners who had been seemingly forgotten for a year or more before he was finally called. There was apparently no rhyme or reason.

But fortunately she had little free time to speculate. Upon her arrival she had begun to nurse the sick whenever the need arose, feeling somewhat qualified by her experience at the bedsides of Annie Maclure and her father. But soon she had met a priest, the Abbé Harbert—silver-haired and soft-spoken—who served as doctor to the prisoners, and who begged Nicole to put her youthful energies at his disposal full time.

While Harbert was not a trained physician, he had learned the arts of the surgeon—extracting teeth, lancing boils, letting blood, and setting bones—and the uses of the various herbs and drugs that he could buy from the jailers. So revered was this dedicated man, who was rumored to have refused release to stay and care for the prisoners, that almost every guard cooperated with him, and wealthy prisoners on their way to execution gave him what money they had left.

Harbert welcomed Nicole as a godsend, and she soon became his untiring slave. Early every morning she conferred with him, and received orders to attend the sick, or run errands, roll bandages, and wash linens. On rare occasions they were called upon to deliver babies, and one horrendous day they even amputated a leg. After a few births and many deaths, Nicole had acquired a good store of knowledge, and began to wonder if she would not prefer to become a nurse instead of a schoolmistress if, by some miracle, she should cheat the guillotine.

For the first time in her life, she knew the satisfaction of devoting herself totally to the needs of others. Amazed at the transformation in herself, she looked back with disbelief and shame on the distant days when she had been guilty of stubborn pride and worldly ambition. Had she once really cried herself to sleep because she was told she lacked the social position to marry the Prince of Soubise? Had she once flown into a tantrum because Falkland looked with love at the portrait of her own dead mother? Had she ever dared to consider even fleetingly a life as mistress to the husband of the Princess Royal? Princes and princesses, dukes, marquises, the Queen of France herself!—these titles had fascinated and intimidated her. What a little snob she had been! A cheap little snob. Where was all that wealth and power now? What meaning did it have inside the encrusted walls of this prison? Death was the great leveler. At least she had learned a little wisdom before she died, Nicole thought ruefully. Working beside Harbert, awed by his example, she tried to remold herself in his image. She often reflected that she had acquired some of the attitudes and ideals of a nun.

But for one difference! Nicole had to laugh aloud. She was regularly visited by dreams that no nun could—should—ever have. Nicole both hated and loved these racking reminders of her passionate night with Falkland. Would the man never leave her alone? No doubt only in the grave, but that soon enough!

Sometimes the dreams began unhappily. She might be seized by a faceless stranger and roughly hauled to his lair, or publicly humiliated by some stern schoolmaster or high-ranking officer or lord of the manor, who would chastise her relentlessly until she burst into tears. But more often the man would rush to her in loving excitement, running in through a garden door or galloping up on horseback, and would swing her high in his arms in jubilant greeting. But whether cruel or tender, he would soon grab her for a passionate embrace and they would clutch each other desperately until vague and intangible though it might be, they knew some marvelous completion. If at first he was shadowy and unknown—and once in the strange fluidity that dreams have he turned for a brief moment into Roger—she always learned at the end that the man who lay on her breast was the duke.

In the six months after Simon's death, Nicole continued to escape execution, although the leadership of the Revolution passed into the hands of extremists and the guillotine claimed ever greater numbers.

Even without Simon's talent for gossip, she learned readily enough of the distressing turn of events. A sou would buy a jug of water and the latest news from any guard. On a hot day in August the Paris mob had overrun the palace of the Tuileries where the royal family had long been held in a kind of house arrest. King Louis, Queen Marie Antoinette, their fourteen-year-old daughter, and their second son, the seven-year-old dauphin, heir to the throne since his older brother's death, had all escaped death, but were imprisoned now in the Temple, a medieval priory converted into a palace.

In September Paris seemed to go mad in an orgy of bloodletting. Many prisons were invaded by crazed mobs that seized famous prisoners, as well as others picked quite at random, and massacred them in the streets. Altogether, fifteen hundred people were butchered in five days. The most celebrated victim was the Princesse de Lamballe, a favorite of the queen with whom she was popularly believed to have had a lesbian affair. Now the intestines of the princesse were trailed through the streets as her head was carried on the end of a pike to taunt Marie Antoinette.

Before the month was out, the newly elected radical Convention declared the monarchy at an end and France officially a Republic. As though the gods were smiling on this new government, the army immediately turned back the Prussians at Valmy, not thirty leagues from Paris, after many months of unsuccessful defense. Soon other victories followed, some even on foreign soil. Brussels and Frankfurt fell to the French. A drunken spirit of overconfidence prevailed, giving birth to dreams of European conquest.

At any military news, Nicole wondered once again about Roger. She had not seen or heard from him during the year she had been at La Force. No doubt, she shrugged, he had forgotten all about her. Probably he had found some pretty girl, married her, and settled down happily in Rouen, worrying only about his next promotion. Or then perhaps he had been killed. How many bloody campaigns had been waged, and battles fought?

If her curiosity about Roger was an occasional pang, her longing for Falkland was a nagging ache to which she had long since grown accustomed. When Simon left her with fifty louis, she had considered trying to send him a message. She knew that one or another of the guards was willing to take a bribe. Of course Falkland was not still at Baden, but conceivably a letter might be gotten through to London. And what then? She had great difficulty imagining the spoiled, pleasure-loving duke becoming exercised enough on her behalf to risk his life in a rescue attempt.

No doubt she would still have tried, but that her increasing devotion to the abbé made her fear to lose the respect of the guards by whispering of some desperate escape. They would serve her, as the abbé's agent, far less well if they imagined she was plotting to slip out and abandon the selfless priest. And so, one by one, she spent the gold coins on medical supplies.

Christmas Eve, her twenty-second birthday, was a pathetic reminder for all at La Force of happier times gone by. No worse news could be imagined than the recent commencement of the king's trial for treason, one more piece of evidence of the power of the radicals in the government. Abbé Harbert said a special prayer for the king in the midnight mass, and a feeble attempt was made afterwards by some of the women prisoners to serve the traditional supper.

Then on the following morning, a gloomy Christmas Day, Nicole was astonished to find Roger standing in front of her, dressed in the gaudy full-dress uniform of a captain. With a gasp she threw herself into his arms, and even though she felt him jump a little with surprise, he lost no time in covering her face with kisses.

She could not help but sob, distressed as she was by the king's plight, as well as the unbearable suspense of her own imprisonment. Too late she realized that Roger assumed she had broken down out of fear and longing for him. "Oh, my dear Nicole, I am quite safe after all! I could not come before, you must believe me!" He related how, soon after her trial, he had secured for himself a transfer to a batallion fighting against the Prussians, and was soon involved in a perilous retreat, always deeper into France, until the miraculous turnabout at Valmy, where he had distinguished himself and won his promotion. She could tell he was inordinately proud of his new rank, and was delighted when she asked him to pivot so that she could admire his expensive new uniform from every angle.

When he pulled her urgently into a far corner, she thought for a moment that he wanted privacy for a few romantic words, but found he was engrossed by his efforts to secure her release. He had worked frantically for many months, he assured her. Now conditions were growing worse, as demonstrated by the recent daring assault upon the king himself. Though money could still buy a release, the prices were rising ever higher. While his new salary was an impressive sum, he said a little boastfully, it was far from enough to attain her freedom.

But she must not despair. He had expectations of sharing in the spoils of future victorious campaigns. Perhaps not the next. Perhaps not as a captain. But as soon as he could become a *chef de bataillon*, he would bring home from commissions on army contracts and confiscated enemy wealth the thousands of livres that were needed for her ransom. For now he must be content with greasing the palms of her warders. She should not be called soon to the guillotine. "Would that I could do more for you today!" he exclaimed with tears in his eyes.

Just before he departed, he remembered to present her with the proceeds, a very few francs, from his sale of her mother's seal ring that he had had secreted all along. "Of course it was worth much more, but the moneylender believed I had stolen it. Perhaps I should not have let it go for such a poor price, but I was afraid you would be in desperate need of coins." She hastened to assure him that she greatly appreciated his thoughtfulness. Before he could bear to leave her, she had to comfort him with soothing words and kisses. At last he pulled himself away and hurried out of the prison, afraid to turn and look back at her.

She could only heave a great sigh when he was gone, strangely depressed by his visit. But why, when he had just given her a ray of hope of being saved? Why, when she had found out he was alive and still loved her? Could the burden of responding to his love weigh on her so heavily?

But Nicole had little time to think about Roger. From Christmas Day onward, her companions talked of nothing else but the deteriorating trial of the king. It had gone on for more than a month when a vote was finally taken late in January. During an incredible twenty-four-hour session, all seven hundred deputies to the National Convention were polled by name. At last the news of the verdict reached the prisoners in La Force who were waiting in silent suspense. Louis XVI had been sentenced to die by a majority of one vote.

14

Amid the hysteria that followed the news of the king's death sentence, many of Nicole's fellow prisoners refused to believe that he would ever be touched. Royalty was almost as sacred as the deity. Surely no executioner would ever be found. What man could bear to cut the flesh of the king? Surely the most frenzied mob would balk at such an unholy act and rush forward to prevent the fall of the blade.

No doubt, even before the day of execution, righteous men, French or foreign, would rescue the king. What of Austria, where Marie Antoinette's own nephew ruled as emperor? What of the other great thrones of Europe—England, Spain, Sweden, Prussia, or Russia? No king would rest easy after the King of France had lost his head.

Rumors of escape plots and rescue schemes reached La Force almost hourly. Many stories were so fanciful as to have no possible basis in fact. But the persistence and abundance of the reports, many of plausible attempts, led even the most radical warders to believe rescue was likely.

Two nights after the fateful verdict, word arrived that an attack was underway at that very moment inside the Temple compound. Rushing to windows on the north side of La Force, prisoners claimed they could hear shots and even screams, though the Temple was almost a mile away. Subsequent reports were contradictory: A hundred men had attacked the compound. They were no more than a dozen in number and poorly armed. They were Austrian soldiers in full uniform. They were French peasants who could not support the death of the king. The raiders had cannons trained on the Temple Tower. They had breached the outer walls, but were struck down before reaching the Tower itself. They had succeeded in delivering the royal family to a waiting carriage. They had failed completely. The attackers, seventeen of them, were all dead inside the Temple walls.

Sustained only by a belief that God would not let the king be sacrificed, the La Force prisoners wrung their hands for an hour, waiting for conclusive news. At last there was the clatter of heavy boots beyond the dungeon portcullis and the sound of loud, peremptory voices. The apparatus was slowly wound up, and a soldier marched into the room with a limp body draped over his shoulder and dumped the unconscious man on the stones. Behind him, other soldiers carried litters bearing three badly wounded men.

"Only these four still live. The other blackguards are all dead, shot in their tracks before they reached the king. And these four wretches will not trouble you long," the soldier snarled as he nudged the head of one man with his boot to disclose a gaping wound.

Nicole and the abbé ran to the victims, and after a brief examination she gathered rags to stanch the flow of blood. All four men appeared critically wounded. As she bent over the victim with the fatal wound, she could feel neither pulse nor respiration. Kneeling beside him, the abbé began prayers for the man's soul.

Assisted by several other women, Nicole tightly packed the wounds of the remaining three victims. One had lost a great piece of his chest, and she knew he could not live long. Another, a huge blond fellow who looked more Swedish or German than French, had taken several musket balls in his shoulders and legs, but perhaps had a chance to survive. The last victim was half covered by his own blood, pouring from a wound on his head.

After a survey of the men Abbé Harbert negotiated with a guard to obtain a small empty cell with a fireplace, where the three could be nursed with some chance of success in the freezing January weather. Nicole hurried ahead to light the fire, sweep the floor, and ask for a layer of clean straw to be spread.

In these new quarters she worked half the night to comfort the man with the chest wound. Even with opium, his agony was so intense she did not wish to leave his side. Miraculously he remained conscious, and as the breath gurgled in his lungs, he tried to talk to her. At first his words sounded like gibberish, but then she made out, "We . . . could . . . not . . . We . . . could . . . not . . . save. . . ." For a second, she did not realize that he was speaking English. Still clutching her hand, he sank into unconsciousness, and when he released her at last, she knew he was dead.

Nicole was left with two charges whom she had so far barely taken time to examine. The blond man had fallen into a light sleep. Poking gently at his temporary dressings, she determined that bleeding had ceased, and decided not to awaken him to change his bandages.

At last she regarded the final patient, who lay all too still on his blanket bed. Frightened, she grasped his wrist to see if he was still alive. With some difficulty she found a rapid, thready pulse, and sighed thankfully. In the firelight she peered at his head wound, which had been stanched by a pad. It was a long cut near the hairline that had probably been made by a saber slice. Then she saw that a deep cut, also from a sword, had gone unnoticed on his left forearm, and wound it with a long strip of linen.

Both wounds had bled profusely, covering his face and half his torso with blood, but she suspected from the pattern of the stain that he also had some injury to his chest or abdomen. When she started to remove his blue nankeen jacket, she saw he made no response at all. There was no moaning or uncomfortable shifting of the body or even a flicker of the eyelids.

Unbuckling his wide leather belt, she started to pull down the blue and white striped trousers. When she noticed that the large yellow patches on his trousers had been sewn with loose running stitches, she knew the sansculotte outfit was only a masquerade. Probably he was English, like the dead man. Yes, something about him made her sure he was an Englishman, though she could not say exactly what. Actually, she could see almost nothing of his face, covered as it was. Even one side of his long dark hair was matted with dried blood.

Struggling a little, she lifted his body just enough to take off his white shirt. Still he did not move. At last she saw a small hole in his left side just above his waist. She guessed it was the entrance wound of a musket ball. Was the ball still inside? The wound had only bled a little, whereas the back of his shirt was soaked. Hopeful, she rolled his body a little and saw a large torn and oozing exit site near his spine. Fortunately the ball had gone clear through him, but the back wound was ragged and ugly and in a very dangerous location. She washed the two sites and bandaged them. Then trying to avert her eyes from his private organs, she slipped down his drawers only long enough to determine that he had no more injuries. Finally she covered him with two blankets, and set about washing his head and arms.

Happy to rise from her kneeling position and stretch her legs, she left the cell to fetch fresh water from the stoneware cistern, then stopped to collect more rags torn from the clothes of executed prisoners. Returning to the cell she found the dark-haired man exactly as she had left him. Yawning a little, she stopped for a moment to stare absently out the small barred window. The sky was pink with the first rays of the rising sun. Feeling exhausted, she almost decided to leave the chore of his bath till morning and catch some sleep. This poor Englishman, if that was what he was, would care little if his cleanup were delayed. But she knew the abbé would arise well before her and would undertake the task himself if she left it undone.

Dipping a rag in the cool water, she washed around the bandage that covered the forehead wound. The blood on his cheeks was thick and dry. Even when she scraped a little, his eyelids never moved. Finally she finished one cheek, and began to wash his chin. She could feel more than see his whiskers, the fire having died down in the last hour or so. Before she went to bed she must put on another piece of wood, for the January air was freezing. She ran the fingers of her free hand along his skin to feel the bristles, then realized she had done a rather strange, almost affectionate thing. Just as she told herself that the man had a nice face, a handsome face, the truth dawned on her. *Dear God, could it be?* Feverishly, she scrubbed his other cheek, then cautioned herself that she must be careful or she would wake him up. No, he would not wake up. He would never wake up! "Oh, my God, I can't believe it!" she cried aloud. She had found Falkland just in time to watch him die!

She did not know how long she lay slumped over him, possessively clutching his shoulder with one hand and caressing his cheek with the other. Then it occurred to her she must be hurting him, though he did not move or groan. For a moment she listened with fascination to his heartbeat. How strong it was, thumping loudly in her ear; too fast, perhaps, but unfaltering. She would not have thought a man about to die would have such a beat.

Fortified with this small hope, she sat up and stared at him. *Was there any doubt it was the duke? Was she having some kind of hallucination, had she finally lost her mind?* Hers would not be the first case of insanity at La Force. She jumped up and put more kindling on the fire, building up a bright blaze. Then in the new light she saw there could be no doubt at all. It was Falkland. She leaned forward to put a kiss on his lips, as her tears splashed on his face. If only he would live! It did not matter that he had humiliated and scorned her, that he would never be able to love her. She would have him here to take care of. Only she would tend him. He would belong to her alone.

Then her mind began to question his deep coma. The arm injury was minor. It would heal well, if only they could avoid a suppuration of the wound. Was the head injury the cause of his sleep? She pulled off the rag and felt the limits of the tear. It reached all the way across his forehead and up into his hair. He would have a fine scar if he lived, but she did not think the skull had been shattered. Then the musket ball through his body must have played great havoc. What dire thing had happened inside him?

Remembering at last to check her other patient, she lay down only a few inches from Falkland to try to sleep. She would be close enough to reach out for his wrist and feel his pulse from time to time during the night. But she dropped almost immediately into so deep a sleep that she did not awaken once.

"What a good, dedicated nurse you are to sleep beside your patients," the abbé commended her, when he saw her eyes finally open. For a few moments she could not remember where she was and looked around the square cell with its high vaulted ceiling and single unglazed window with iron bars and a scrap of burlap to keep out the wind. The fireplace, merely an arched recess in the stone wall, was small, and the fire had burned down to coals again.

At last coming to her senses, she could only lie still, sick with fear, while she watched the abbé examine Falkland. "The man has lost half his volume of blood," Harbert declared, shaking his head.

"Will he die?" she asked hoarsely.

"No doubt he is still bleeding internally, or he would have awakened before now. His head wound is not serious. There is nothing we can do, my child, but pray for the poor man."

"Then he will die soon?"

"I believe so. No doubt we will save only our great blond friend," he said, pointing at the other patient.

Nicole hovered over Falkland all day long, even bringing her dinner bowl to eat beside him. At last at nightfall she saw him roll his head a little, and she cried out with excitement. An hour later he groaned and shifted his arms. Even though he had not yet opened his eyes, she was enormously encouraged, and ran to tell Harbert the news.

"Will he live, *mon père*?"

"I do not know, dear child," the priest answered, eyeing her closely.

But by midnight, Falkland had progressed from his coma to a raging fever that had him thrashing violently. Nicole could do little more than pull off his blankets and apply cold compresses to his head, which he tried to hurl away. At last he stared directly into her face. His dark eyes burned, and she felt once again her old fear of him. Would he recognize her? She was almost afraid he would. Angry as he looked, she expected him to order her banished from his sight.

But the eyes did not know her. "Ferguson will saddle my horse. You must ring for him," he commanded, growing more angry when she did not move. "Send for him now! I cannot wait!" His voice had the tone of the imperious child's. Did he think he was a boy again back at Langmuir? Was Ferguson some Langmuir groom? Falkland was delirious all night long, but said no more recognizable words. There was no indication that he knew Nicole.

Consumed as she was by fear, for she knew few survived so hot a fever, her attention was drawn to the blond man, who had suddenly taken a turn for the worse. His wounds, from which he would otherwise have recovered easily, had become badly inflamed. As swelling, pain, and fever increased, the abbé despaired of him too. There was little treatment beyond herbs and compresses. Nicole paid a guard to send to an *herboriste*, then gave him tea of feverfew and poultices of fungi and chervil and melissa. A frantic morning of suffering passed before the blond man finally died.

When his body was finally carried from the cell, Nicole could sink to her knees beside Falkland and let her head fall for a moment on his shoulder. In this restful position she realized he had grown far quieter. Could he possibly be better? But there was something ominous about this stillness. Placing her hand on his forehead, she discovered his fever was just as hot, hotter even. Then suddenly he was racked by a great convulsive fit, and she jumped up and screamed for a guard to help her hold him down.

When Falkland was calm again and Nicole had collapsed against a wall, the guard asked with a little cluck of sympathy, "Then have you missed the news, citizeness?"

She looked up at him with irritation. What in the world could be as important as her own torment in this cell? Hating to be rude, she sighed and asked the man to tell her what he had heard.

"The king is dead. He went to the scaffold this morning at twenty-four minutes past ten."

The blow struck her as one more wound would have felt to Falkland. At first she could only stare at her worn leather shoes in the straw. Then it crossed her mind that the guard must take satisfaction in this tragedy, and she raised accusing eyes to his face. But he wore an expression of genuine grief, and she felt ashamed of her suspicion.

From the guards and the abbé she learned even without leaving Falkland's side that the king had marched to his death with great courage and dignity. The guillotine in the Place Louis XV, just renamed the Place de la Révolution, was surrounded by a huge number of troops and thousands of spectators. In fact the streets of Paris were so clogged by the curious that his carriage required two hours to travel less than two miles from the

Temple to the guillotine. Along the way there had been one more rescue attempt, which also failed.

When the blade fell, the crowd had roared its approval and cried, "*Vive la République!*" then cheered again when his head was held up by the hair and his heavy body dumped into a wicker basket. Many citizens called out eager bids as pieces of his clothing were auctioned from the steps of the scaffold; and after the troops had departed, hundreds pressed forward to dip their handkerchiefs in the blood of the King of France.

Nevertheless, Nicole was assured, most Parisians reacted with shock and shame, no matter how intense their revolutionary ardor. All his life King Louis had been liked by the common people. It was his wife who was popularly despised. Inside La Force there was deep mourning, and occasional cries of "*Vive le roi!*" In the mind of every prisoner, the crown had devolved upon the little boy who huddled with his mother in the Temple Tower. Seven-year-old Louis Charles was now King Louis XVII.

Totally exhausted that night, Nicole lay down beside Falkland. He had been unearthly still since his seizure. His body had endured too much; he could not go on. No doubt his heart would simply stop sometime during the night. She had not even the strength to cry. All she could do now was pray that he would die quickly without more suffering. How gray his face was, his eyes deeply sunken. It was the look of death. She had seen it now too many times. Death had reigned today. How natural that it should claim Falkland also. The king and Falkland, his good friend. The duke himself would no doubt have been pleased, if he could have known.

And her own death? Now she prayed for it. There could be no more life for her. No possible happiness. Night demons of terror and despair crowded in around her. When had she ever known true happiness? Even her own birth had cost the life of her beautiful mother, so much more worthy. Her father had lived in mourning ever after. No doubt he had secretly resented her, had had to force himself to act as a loving parent. With her brain throbbing, she fell asleep at last, her face not two feet from Falkland's.

Another dream? No, this was real. Someone had called her name. "Nicole!" There it was again. Only a whisper, but she was certain. Opening her eyes, she saw it was dawn. There was a faint rose light in the cell, enough for her to see the duke's face smiling at her. "Nicole. . . ." he said again, with an unmistakable thrill of pleasure in his voice. Then he closed his eyes and seemed to fall asleep.

She sprang to her knees and bent over him, impulsively placing her hands on his shoulders. He mumbled something, still smiling, but did not open his eyes. She pressed her hand on his cheek. His skin was much cooler and his color almost normal. With her ear on his chest, she could tell his heart was strong and his breathing regular. Miraculously, he had passed the crisis. She broke into tears at the realization he was going to live.

Not only would he live, but he had sounded delighted at her presence! In a daylong ecstasy that even the recollection of the king's death could not spoil, Nicole took advantage of Falkland's long sleep to soak in a hot tub set up behind curtains, wash her hair, and even buy herself for a few sous a new dress—new to her—a pretty green *mousseline de soie* that she remembered had first belonged to the Versailles ballerina, now long dead.

When Falkland finally awoke he was very weak, but opened his right palm, and she slipped her hand into his. For a long time she was speechless in her fear and awe of him, but when he gave her a broad smile she returned it tearfully. As she sat beside his blanket, her legs curled beneath her and resting her weight on her left hand, she was close enough to him that her knee almost touched his leg. She had parted her clean, shining hair in the middle and twisted it into a large, loose coil pinned to the back of her head. The new dress was a little frayed and faded, but she thought the soft willow green very flattering, and the white gauze scarf, borrowed from a rich noblewoman, was pinned daringly low.

"Of course I thought I was in heaven," he finally said in a weak voice, trying to laugh despite the pain in his side, "when I woke up this morning and found you sleeping beside me. Imagine my surprise to find that my not unblemished life had merited the highest possible reward!"

"And did you expect to find me already in heaven?" she asked lightly.

"Oh, my dear Nicole!" His face grew solemn, and he pressed her hand. "I had truly begun to believe that you were dead." He paused a few moments, whether to catch his breath or control his emotions she did not know. "I hope you appreciate my ability to forgive you for the cruel shock your flight gave us—gave me. Of course I drove north to Langmuir immediately. Littleton, Kate, and the children were inconsolable and blamed themselves for the desperation that had driven you away." He stopped a moment and watched her reaction closely.

But she would not let him coax her into a response. She had no intention of reproaching him now for sins, real or imaginary, she had so long ago forgotten. Nor did he seem to need a reason for her departure. She had a feeling that he understood. While he caught his breath, she merely smiled shyly at him.

"I searched the possessions you had left behind, and determined that you had taken few clothes, indicating you were uncertain of your means of transportation. As for your destination, I remembered your stubborn resistance to leaving Beaux-Clervaux, and guessed that you were making a foolhardy effort to return. I need hardly lecture you now on the folly of that decision! I also discovered—though I must confess I did check with a moneylender in Langmuir Haven to see if you had pawned it!—that you had taken along my topaz pendant, which I found flattering, considering your evident hatred of me at the time. And I remembered other more valuable jewels you had worn, that were also missing. Therefore we had to conclude that you were trying to enter a nation torn by civil war carrying a small fortune in jewelry. I wonder if you can possibly imagine my anguish!"

When he had to stop to rest again, Nicole, overcome by his unexpected distress at her flight, began to tell him the sad fate of her jewels, but he indicated with a wave that he already knew. "I traced you to Rouen," he said. "Disguised as a priest, I stood in the little nun's cell you had occupied!"

Amazed at this revelation she slowly drew from him the story of his search for her. First he had sent Timothy to Beaux-Clervaux, where he had waited a month. Knowing at last that she had never reached her probable destination, and fearing that she had either been murdered by highwaymen for her jewels or arrested as an *émigrée*, Falkland undertook to inquire through his agents of the authorities in northern and western France. At last he learned that a woman pretending to be a peasant from the Bordelais had been dramatically unmasked as an aristocrat before the Tribunal in Rouen. Although she had stubbornly refused to give her true name, an inquiry in Bordeaux had easily uncovered her identity as the Clervaux heiress, and so she was enrolled in a Paris prison where she awaited death.

Falkland himself, disguised now as a deputy to the National Assembly who was trying to trace a relative, had talked to a young lieutenant who seemed familiar with her case. The man was obviously Roger, although Nicole did not acknowledge her recognition of him. "The lieutenant told me you had been sent to the prison of Salpêtrière in Paris only one month before." Nicole was at first rather surprised that the efficient Roger would possess inaccurate information. Then she remembered that the farm wagon, groaning with thirty prisoners by the time it reached Paris, had discharged half its load at Salpêtrière before moving on to La Force.

Neither Falkland nor his agents could learn of her presence in the dozen prisons of Paris including Salpêtrière, La Force, Recollets, the Abbaye, the Carmes, the Châtelet, Luxembourg, St. Lazare, and even the impregnable Conciergerie. As it happened, he had visited La Force himself, but even though he had pretended to be a Jacobin official, he was told that no Nicole de Clervaux had ever been registered there. When the bulletins of the guillotine, usually accurate and complete, were known not to have carried her name, Falkland was mystified. But after the September Massacres, his agents picked up the tale of a beautiful young blond girl dragged from the confines of Salpêtrière and murdered by a mob, and he had almost abandoned himself to the belief that it was she.

Seeing how weak and exhausted he was, Nicole gave him only the briefest summary of her two years, saying that her service to Abbé Harbert must have caused the prison authorities to protect her. As she rose to leave for the night, having already decided she could no longer properly sleep beside him, Falkland reached feebly toward her face, and she bent and kissed him on the lips.

"Have you forgiven me for—everything?" he asked with some timidity.

Gently she answered, "My heart overflows that I have found you at last."

15

Falkland's recovery was steady. Nicole rejoiced when he could take a sip of water, a few spoonfuls of gruel, and finally a whole glass of some claret she had been able to buy. Nothing would rebuild his strength faster than good, full-bodied Bordeaux red, she told him, and he chuckled a little. When he began to accompany her efforts to bathe him with horseplay and erotic suggestions, she knew he was growing stronger.

Nevertheless, she kept the news of the king's death from him as long as possible, until he guessed the truth from her increasingly awkward evasions. After she told him the events of the execution as she had heard them, he turned his face away and lay still the rest of the day, staring at the blank wall, until she began to fear a serious relapse. That evening, in a desperate effort, she put on the décolleté green gown, fixed her hair in a pile of frivolous curls, and forced a lighthearted manner to see if she could lift him out of his depression. But he refused his food, and she saw that his lashes were wet with tears. Only after she began to beg him to think of his own recovery, did he take her hand in his and press it to his lips.

"I do not like to distress you. You have been an angel to me. But I cannot fail to accuse myself of negligence to the king. And to my own king, who ordered me to save his life. Somehow I should have collected a larger force or managed to smuggle heavy arms into Paris."

"You all but gave your life for King Louis!"

"I could have given him deliverance as well. He deserved no less!"

But when Nicole entered his cell the next morning she saw with relief that his face had brightened. He greeted her with a smile and made a little apology for his black mood. His voice sounded much stronger, and Nicole suddenly realized she must caution him to conceal his recovery from the guards. As soon as the authorities thought he was well enough to walk to the guillotine, he would surely be executed. He had been safe so far only because the most hardened revolutionaries would not relish the execution of an invalid who had to be carried up the scaffold steps. She suggested that she spread the story his back injury had left him permanently paralyzed. When he consented without argument, the horrible thought went through her mind that the diagnosis might in fact be true.

Forcing a happy expression, she slipped her hand behind his head gently to help him rise and drink a little medicinal wine. To her amazement he sat bolt upright, grabbed her with his good right arm, and gave her an enthusiastic kiss.

"You see what a good nurse you are! Your patient has made great strides." Cupping his hand over one breast, he demanded, "Where is that lovely dress you were wearing last night? How well I remember when Kate made you this gray fright. It was designed to stymie my eyes as well as my hands in their pursuit of your breasts. The neckline is as high as a postulant's, the material too stiff to allow my fingertips any mischief. Henceforth do me the favor of wearing only the green, and even then I shall have to teach you how to adjust its scarf!"

Involuntarily, she closed her eyes and shivered as the long-forgotten wave of pleasure flooded her body. She could hardly bear to pull his hand away from her breast.

"So you have needed this too," he whispered.

"No, stop! Not now!" She shook herself loose, blushing, flustered, finally jumping away.

" 'Not now'? At least that's some encouragement. Then later. Tonight. That's a promise!"

The rest of the day whenever she came near him, he grabbed her waist or arm to pull her forward for a kiss, or tried at least to touch her breast. She quickly learned the error of standing too close to him, for once he darted his hand up her skirts to the dangerously sensitive skin inside her thighs. When she attempted as a dutiful nurse to give him his daily bath, he laughed and wrestled, splashing water all over the cell; and finally, even though he could not persuade her to look directly at it, succeeded in planting her hand firmly on his swollen organ for a moment before, slippery with soap, she wriggled free.

At last he dozed a little, and she was thankful for the opportunity to soak in the tub until some other woman prisoner impatiently dislodged her. When she had dried her body with clean flannel rags, she put on the one tattered petticoat she had left, followed by the green dress as he had directed. Its original ballerina owner had been flatter in the bosom than she, and Nicole decided to break a few stitches in the bodice darts and seams to give her plump breasts ample room. She had no mirror, but lowering her chin to her collarbone, decided she had been a bit reckless. From above at least, the globe of each breast was completely visible even to the pink of her nipples. Shocked, she wrapped the gauze covering prudishly around her, crossed it in front and knotted it firmly behind her waist, then relented a little, and loosened it until the scarf settled comfortably on her shoulders.

When she finally reached his cell, having had to assist the abbé with a new patient in the dungeon, night had already fallen. She entered quietly, thinking—hoping, actually—that he might be asleep. But in the dark room she could see that Falkland lay smiling up at her, his head propped on a roll of blankets. Though there was an iron ring set in the stone wall to hold a torch, she had not used one since the worst nights of his illness. Now in the flickering fire light he watched her silently as they drank the wine she had brought. Sitting against the wall she gazed through the little window at the clear night sky, then turned at last to admire the shadowed contours of the duke's face—his high cheekbones, aquiline nose, and strong jaw. His brow was wrapped by a light bandage like a scarf.

"You look like a pirate," she said softly.

"Not inappropriately, for I plan to seize something very precious tonight. Though it is no real theft unless you have promised yourself to another man in the months since you left Langmuir."

"You know I haven't."

He sipped his wine in silence for a few moments, then said softly but commandingly, "Untie your fichu, Nicole."

After a little hesitation, she reached behind and opened the knot. The crossed pieces swung loose, and the covering slipped down her shoulders.

"Remove it entirely," he directed.

She pulled it forward and folded the big triangle in half, then in half again, stalling for time. Of course she should not have complied. There was a little tingling sensation in her breasts already, stimulation merely from his gaze.

"Put your arms down and sit still, my darling. Let me study you. It's been such a very long time!" The last plaintive note in his voice stayed her resistance. Shaking a little, she let him stare at her.

After long minutes, he said hoarsely, "Now take off your dress."

She stared down at her hands twisting the fabric of her skirt frantically, and finally admitted, "I can't do it!"

"Please, Nicole." When she did not move, he slowly rose, propping himself on one elbow as she winced, knowing how much the wounds must pain him. "Then I'll come do it for you!"

"Oh, you mustn't! You're too weak!"

"You'll soon find out how weak! The part of me that counts most has suffered nothing more than a good, invigorating rest."

"Please lie down," she said solicitously. "I'll—I'll do what you want."

Taking a deep breath, she reached behind and unhooked the dress, letting it fall slowly down her shoulders and arms, until her breasts were completely revealed. Let him look then! She was proud of her breasts. Round, full, high. She knew the nipples were erect.

"And now the rest of your clothes." His voice was impatient.

She rose to her knees. With her breasts jutting, she fought with the catch behind her waist until at last the green skirt fell to the floor. Without being told, she untied the petticoat, and dropped it too. Frozen for a minute or two, she finally hurried to avoid the abrupt command that she knew would come, unfastening her drawers and pushing them down.

At first too frightened to move, she remained on her knees and let him examine her as he would. Then scurrying like a hunted animal she retreated to the very edge of the fireplace, crouching down a little, instinctively putting a hand over the hair below her belly.

"No, face me. Sit up!"

She obeyed him, and sat for what seemed an eternity. He never took his eyes off her, and she wished she could see his expression more distinctly. Did he like what he saw? She prayed that he did. Suddenly she remembered standing naked at Versailles before her cheval mirror wondering if a husband would find her acceptable. Surely she would have perished of shock if she could have foreseen this moment. Now her flesh tingled all over her body. She had begun to ache a little somewhere deep inside.

"Come here. Kneel beside me," he ordered, and she obeyed as though hypnotized. Without touching her, he asked solemnly, "Do you love me, Nicole?"

"Yes," she whispered.

"Can you say, 'I love you, William'? I'm tired of being addressed by some pompous style—or no name at all. Even when I was delirious you called me 'Your Grace'!"

After only a brief moment of shyness, she said, "I love you, William."

Rising with surprising agility, he took her face in his hands, and looking directly into her eyes, told her, "And I love you, Nicole, with all my heart! Will you believe that always?" When she had nodded her head in a kind of daze, he touched her soft lips with his own and kissed her tenderly. Then he wrapped his arms around her, apparently ignoring any pain from the wounds on his forearm and back. She hugged him gingerly at first, careful not to hurt him or touch his bandages; then when he registered no discomfort at all, she embraced his shoulders without inhibition, her naked breasts pressing against his own bare chest. How long she had dreamed of this moment—or more correctly, never dared to dream it would ever come again. At last she held in her arms the man she truly loved who now said he loved her as well, the only man she would ever love, and she almost fainted with the pleasure of his embrace.

"I have yearned for you so long, Nicole. There has proven to be—no possible substitute for you—" he said haltingly, as though surprised by his own honesty. "No substitute for your beautiful hair and soft skin and delicious body, your warm, innocent, loving nature. God Almighty, how I have tried to forget you—and ended by only wanting you more!" He buried his face in the curve of her neck and shoulder, then impulsively kissed her throat and ear and shoulder and breasts. As though at last releasing his own hands, he frantically felt her buttocks and thighs, and squeezed her breasts until she cried out. "I am too excited, Nicole. You must forgive me. I will try to slow myself to give you time."

Kissing her mouth again, now probing with his tongue until he met her own willing one, he guided her down to the blankets, and only wincing once with pain, lay down beside her. Immediately his mouth found her breast. She began to move her hips with little writhing motions, then covered her open mouth with the back of one hand to suppress her moans of pleasure.

"You have just told me you love me," he said almost irritably. "What does that mean to you? Can't you allow yourself to relax and find the satisfaction that surely you must need after all these months. Must you be racked with guilt even now, when—when we may not have many nights together!"

She forced herself to take a deep breath and managed to smile up at him. "I can't understand what is right or wrong anymore—"

"Your body understands well enough! You must trust your instincts tonight," he answered firmly. Caressing her belly with a circular motion that made her shiver and writhe again, he at last drove his hand into the hair between her legs, making her jump a little, and then, as quickly, soothed her by stroking. "Ah, *chérie,* you are flowing for me already! What a wonderful, passionate nature you have! Give me no more protests. You are as ready as any woman ever was. No doubt you enjoyed exposing your naked body to a man's scrutiny for a few minutes."

"Oh, no! I was frightened and ashamed!"

"—and excited too!" Watching her face carefully, he pushed his fingers inside her. She could not help but gasp with the pleasure and tried to hold his hand in place when he seemed to remove it. But as her breathing quickened he forcefully removed his fingers. "Not yet, you hot wench! You'll have to wait awhile! *Mon Dieu*, however did you go without a man to satisfy your lusts all this time? Or perhaps you did not!"

"Oh, but I did! No man has been allowed to touch me!" she cried with distress.

Kissing her lips soothingly, he said, "Calm yourself. I believe you. I know how innocent your mind is, even while you have the body of a saucy little trollop! Of course it is that very combination I cannot resist!"

Pulling the blanket off his thighs, he guided her head so she had to look at his rampant organ. Instinctively she reached out toward it, then withdrew her hand shyly. "Pray do!" he cried, pushing her a little, and she reached again and caressed it as he had once taught her, forgetting nothing. "Kiss me there, Nicole," he ordered, and she hesitated for a moment, then obeyed. She was amazed at her own willingness, at the excitement it gave her, and his own incredible pleasure.

Then suddenly he pushed her head away, jumped up, and roughly seizing her thighs, plunged between them, entering her with great urgency. "Oh, *mon Dieu!*" she cried aloud. How long had she waited? His mere entrance gave her a long tremor of gratification.

There was no pain this time, only the pleasurable battering at her bursting center, again and again, with the strength of a man who had surely never been an invalid. Together they rode the wild course until they cried out in unison, and Nicole was aware only of a hot flood of pleasure through her, the pounding of her heart, and then the heavy weight of his exhausted body collapsed on hers.

Even though she had managed for the last three mornings to wake up and leave Falkland's cell before daybreak to return to her own blanket in the dungeon, she knew their uninhibited nights invited discovery by the abbé, who would be painfully disillusioned with her; or even worse, by a guard who would conclude from their lovemaking that Falkland was perfectly capable of climbing the steps of the scaffold. Each evening she promised herself she would resist William for his own safety; and then he would laugh at her worries and assure her their warders were far too lazy to check on a man they believed half dead, all the while he was exciting her until she forgot her prudent resolutions once again.

At last one morning, the abbé drew her urgently aside and questioned her beside the iron pot of porridge simmering on the firepit. "Your patient progresses particularly well, dear child, does he not?" Nicole knew immediately from his choice of words that he had guessed something of their relationship. Since when was Falkland "her" patient? Always before, the abbé had simply called him "the Englishman," and he knew from his own examinations how well the recovery went.

"Yes, *mon père*."

"But now we must take every precaution to conceal his good health from the authorities."

"Yes, of course." Was that why he was giving her this warning, simple concern for Falkland's safety? "I thought we should spread the story that he is completely paralyzed from the waist down."

"Perhaps." He rubbed his chin thoughtfully. "Possibly that would work. Though of course he is not paralyzed, is he?"

"No, *mon père*." She noticed his peculiar emphasis on the last few words.

"*Hélas*, dear Nicole, sometimes a patient becomes too attached to his faithful nurse, whom he credits with his very life; and the nurse herself, young and perhaps emotionally drained by the horrendous events of recent months, may take refuge in a relationship that—ah, how shall I put it—?"

At the sight of his reddening face, she suffered for him. "I believe I take your meaning—"

"I, as your confessor, and, I trust, your friend, have to caution you to— to guard at all costs against a state of mortal sin!"

Her eyes widened at the blunt language. What did he know? Dear heaven, he must have opened the door during one of their passionate interludes and seen—oh, no, she could not bear to think what the pure, good man might have witnessed. Blushing scarlet to the roots of her hair, she could not look the abbé in the face.

Suddenly sympathetic, the priest hurried to add, "But you have betrayed your emotions a hundred ways, child, from the day he arrived—"

Relieved, she at last could catch her breath. "Have I?"

"And then last night at midnight, when I was looking for you to help with Madame Fortin and failed to find you in your blanket, I feared the Englishman might have suffered a relapse. Venturing as far as his door, I was stopped by your laughter. Naturally I was relieved to discover he was well and—er, so very happy, but I could not help but imagine that certain —intimacies might well accompany such delight."

Deeply embarrassed, Nicole began to stammer an explanation. "Oh, *mon père*, I—I knew him well before—"

"I could tell you did, but it does not give you the right—"

"Oh, no, I never meant—I only wanted you to know that—that he is someone I have loved a very long time."

"Bless you, child, I am glad. But still you must think of your immortal soul—and his! Living as we do on the very brink of the grave, we must repent of all our sins and studiously avoid new temptations."

Before he left her, he added, "I first saw the Duke of Falkland when I was almoner to the Duc de Penthievre, and His Grace often came to Rambouillet for the hunt."

Not wishing to cloud their happiness with talk of sin and death, Nicole did not tell the duke of her conversation with the abbé. She would bear alone the guilt the abbé had raised. Surely God would make new rules for two lovers so sincere—and so soon to die—who harmed no one with their passion. But of course Harbert would vehemently deny it. For months she had all but worshipped the abbé. Only with severe pain did she decide to ignore his advice.

Of course William would give her reassurance if she needed it. Always so arrogant, he would laugh at the inconvenient judgments of a priest. Heaven knows, William had never been so sympathetic to her, so understanding. Conversation came to them now as freely as their intimate caresses.

Already he had admitted to her that, while he had become intrigued by her beauty and her uncanny resemblance to her mother from their first meeting in the Galerie des Glaces at Versailles, it was sometime during their happy afternoons at Beaux-Clervaux that he first was conscious of his love for her. "Yes!" he exclaimed in answer to her question. "Of course I meant to kiss you in the blackberry brambles, but you suddenly looked so distressed." He had been greatly vexed by his responsibility as her guardian to protect her virginity and to arrange a fine marriage for her. Such scruples had restrained him, until at last he could resist his impulses no longer on the night of the *Gerbaude*.

At home in England he had been more burdened by guilt than he would have dreamed possible, having lived for years "by the careless morals of certain circles," as he described them; and finally he realized his anxiety about her was only more evidence of his deep love. At Langmuir he would have restrained himself no longer but that he faced a dangerous mission to rescue "some old friends to whom I owed much."

"And so loving me, you went off to save the Marquise de Vaucroze!" Nicole blurted, then hated herself as soon as she had spoken the jealous words.

"Of course you feel that way," he said patiently. "I can only be honest with you, Nicole. Sybille was—if not a completely faithful mistress—at least an ardent one for many years, and a loyal friend. Of course I could not let her family and herself perish. I saved them and several others at the same time—the Rondelles and the orphaned children of the Princesse de la Praz."

"Oh, please don't explain to me!" she said contritely. "I have no right to question you."

"But I give you that right. I want to commit myself at last. I intend to pledge my fidelity to you. I will take no more mistresses. I want you to be both mistress—and wife!"

Silently mouthing the unexpected word, she could only stare at him in shock for a long minute. Frowning, he searched her face with puzzled eyes, and her heart leaped at the growing concern in his expression.

"For once you cannot read my mind!" she exclaimed.

"No," he answered with relief. "For a moment I believed you meant to reject my proposal."

"Perhaps I only need to hear it in no uncertain terms."

"Then, Nicole, will you do me the honor of becoming my wife?"

For an answer she threw her arms around him and buried her face against his neck. Yes, she would hold tight forever. She asked nothing more from life. She could go to the guillotine peacefully now, locked in his embrace.

"We can be married wherever you want," he continued. "Perhaps by Dr. Littleton in St. Cuthbert's—would you like that? Or, if you prefer, in London. St. James's is very fashionable presently, if you want to cut a figure in society."

Afraid to look at him, ashamed to ask the question because it seemed to call him a liar or a cad, she finally said, "Dr. Littleton himself told me you were obliged to marry one of the king's daughters."

"So he told you that! No wonder you ran away from Langmuir! The man should have kept his peace. It is true I thought once I could comply with the king's wish, but after I fell in love with you, I knew I could never carry it through. I would have done Princess Charlotte no favor. Thank God we had postponed a betrothal several times, perhaps both of us feeling a certain disinclination."

At last she lifted her head and looked at him as tears streamed down her face. "You know—you've always known since the first days at Versailles that I am in love with you—and of course I want to marry you—"

"Then why all the tears?" he asked anxiously.

"It is just that I cannot imagine how you can talk fantasies when one or the other of us will be dead in a day or a week. There is no chance we'll both escape this place alive!" How could he delude himself so drastically?

"But there is! I have plans, confederates who will help us. They only await my signal!"

She stared at him skeptically. How many times had she heard of escape plots at La Force?

"Then you don't believe me," he said with a little laugh. "But it is true. You will see." He sat quietly, studying her sad face. "Then if you won't believe me, we must be married here! Your Abbé Harbert can marry us now in this very cell in La Force!"

16

Repeating after the priest with a carefully controlled voice that still quivered very slightly, the duke said, "I, Guillaume, take thee, Nicole, for my lawful wife, until death do us part." He was standing beside her in his cell, holding her right hand with his own as they faced the abbé.

A large fire crackled on the hearth. Nicole had brought in an extra armload of wood today, the weather having turned fiercely cold. She had longed to send a guard to buy some Beaux-Clervaux claret to toast the occasion, then felt far too guilty about spending gold that should go for medicines on an expensive bottle of wine. There would be no refreshments for her tiny wedding party. What a far cry from the festivities that would have continued for days at Beaux-Clervaux or Langmuir Castle, she thought a little wistfully.

Nicole repeated the same vow after William, and then the priest intoned, "*Ego conjungo nos in matrimonium in nomine Patris, et Filii, et Spiritus Sancti. Amen.*"

The kindly old Comtesse Valérien, who with her husband was serving as a witness, slipped off her own gold wedding band and handed it to the duke, who put it on Nicole's finger. "With this ring I thee wed, and I plight unto thee my troth," he promised.

"May thy wife be as a fruitful vine on the sides of thy house. May thy children be as olive plants round about thy table. May the Lord send you help from the sanctuary, and defend you out of Zion. Alleluia." Harbert was reciting the service from memory. He possessed no vestments or even a missal here in prison.

At last the duke kissed his bride with a new expression that looked almost like reverence, then accepted congratulations all around. Harbert was delighted at his protégée's excellent match and deliverance from a state of sin, and gave her a warm kiss on the cheek. Once again he cautioned the little group that no indication, however slight, should be made outside this cell that a wedding—any wedding—had taken place. Every precaution was needed to protect "Guillaume" from the guards' suspicion that he was fit for execution. Even in front of the wholly trustworthy comte and comtesse no mention of his full name had been made. They might make some inadvertent slip to other prisoners or guards. The Duke of Falkland was well known as a ringleader of the royalist cause.

Only when the comtesse began to leave did Nicole remember to return her wedding ring to her. At first the frail old lady protested, "Oh, my dear, I hate to see you take it off now. It might be bad luck!" But Nicole insisted, and thanked her profusely for its use. Then the witnesses and priest left one at a time to avoid attracting attention to the cell.

As soon as they were left alone, the duke seized Nicole for a long kiss, then laughing at his own impatience, began to unhook the back of her dress. But she hung back rather sadly, looking down at the torn and faded silk and apologized a little glumly for such a wedding costume. To cheer her he promised, "I'll hire you the finest seamstress in London, as befits the beautiful Nicole Fraser, Duchess of Falkland!" She laughed with disbelief at the elegant designation as he continued, "Your Grace also bears the titles of Marchioness of Blackmayne, the Countess of Dermot, the Baroness Falkirk, and in the peerage of Scotland, the Baroness Fraser. Our eldest son will be the Marquess of Blackmayne. You are third in precedence among the peeresses of England, marching in processions behind only the Duchesses of Somerset and Norfolk, and of course the wives of the royal dukes, but ahead of all other duchesses, marchionesses, countesses, viscountesses, and baronesses. In person you are properly addressed as 'Your Grace' or 'Madam,' and—"

"Oh, stop, William. I can't remember all that! I'm just a little French girl from the country, no more."

"It is enough," he murmured as he slipped off her dress and lowered her to the straw, where after many whispered promises and lingering, then frenzied kisses on her breasts and belly and thighs, he finally entered her almost ceremoniously as her husband, as she trembled with the high emotion of the occasion.

For a week they secluded themselves in his cell, enjoying oblivion to any sort of danger. They were content together for long hours at a stretch, exploring and playing with each other's bodies, joking and teasing outrageously, perhaps even confessing a sin or two—although Nicole for her part had little to tell him but her erotic dreams, which he assured her were only natural and healthy.

One day when she lay naked in his arms after a session of love, she asked out of a clear sky, "Who was the exquisite English beauty you took to Baden?"

"I took where?" he asked lazily.

"To Baden almost a year ago. You were there for a month."

"How in the world did you know that?" he asked with surprise.

"Simon de Brizac saw you there. He was captured soon after, and brought here to La Force before he was executed."

"But you never told me this! So poor Simon had another chance at your lovely charms before he died. Did he enjoy himself with these boobies," he asked, rolling her breasts vigorously, "and this chamber of delights?" he added, poking her between her legs as she squealed with laughter. "Did he pleasure you as well as I do?"

"I never let him touch me! You must know that!"

"Oh, when did Brizac ever fail to part a woman's legs?" he asked teasingly, then added with a snort, "Even Sybille's."

"Oh, no! Not the marquise! How embarrassing!"

"What is embarrassing? To know that you have shared two men, instead of one?" he drawled.

"But Simon never had me. And I don't care if you won't believe it," she said saucily. "I'm afraid I have a rather different moral code from Sybille's. Besides, how could we, when there was no private cell available to us?"

"Well, in that case, I'll allow you were probably chaste," he said facetiously.

"Anyway you are only trying to change the subject. Who was the lovely lady in Baden? Simon said she was the rejected mistress of the Prince of Wales."

"And he was bloody well wrong. Mrs. Connaught has hardly been rejected. The Prince of Wales wished to take the waters in Baden incognito. I was merely a convenient cover for the presence of his lady. And perhaps you should know, Miss Impertinence, that my main reason for going to Baden was to direct the effort to save your slender neck from the guillotine!"

"So then I must apologize? Are you annoyed when I ask about your various love affairs?"

"No, only when you imagine something that never happened." He lay still for a long time, staring at cobwebs in the ceiling. "Like that wretched business with your mother."

"Oh, William, I don't think we need talk about that!"

"Perhaps we should. I mean, in case—I should die, I don't want you to go on the rest of your life imagining—certain things that never happened between us."

"Please don't say any more," she said, suddenly frightened to learn what she had longed to know for so long.

"No, I want you to hear the whole story. That summer at Beaux-Clervaux I was only a boy—tall, skinny, rather gawky, I believe. I had never been in love, and heaven knows had never enjoyed a woman's favors, except in my already well-developed imagination. For perhaps three months I had pursued my studies with your father, learning a great deal, but working by myself more than half the day because your father prized his hours alone with his books. Then Lucienne arrived from Normandy with a maiden aunt and several servants. From the first moment I thought her the most incredibly beautiful thing I had ever seen. But she was aloof, proud, aware of her future position as wife to the lord of a rich manor, and had not the slightest interest in me.

"Robert, surprisingly, made little time in his day for her, and often suggested that I conduct her on a tour of the countryside. I know she was terribly hurt by his seeming indifference and even boredom with her, a young girl who had no particular background in his fields of interest. He had a way of stifling a yawn and growing restless if he had been away from his books too long."

"Oh, I know," Nicole said with fond amusement. "But he meant no harm. He was shy, really."

"Perhaps, but Lucienne did not understand. For a month she dragged around after me with a long face. For my part, I knew from the beginning I had fallen in love with her, and tried to grab her for a kiss as soon as I got up my nerve, but she always resisted, treating me as a mere nuisance. When after a dozen attempts, she finally let me complete the kiss, I was so surprised I nearly bungled it. But soon she was willing to retreat with me inside a barn or *chaix* or under the veil of leaves of that great willow tree where I might hold her very tightly and kiss her lips, the palm of her hand, perhaps her neck—but nothing more.

"Probably she never really fell in love with me, a mere boy, but by the end of the summer I dared to carry her one twilight into the little *pavillon*. No, don't turn your face away, Nicole! I've decided after long thought that it will be better for you to know the truth. There, in the summerhouse, I finally got her to lie down beside me, and then—then nothing really happened! We were both too frightened, and she was torn by guilt. There was little more than a few long kisses and an intimate caress or two.

"Today it seems childishly innocent, but then, I—both of us, really—

were driven nearly wild by the memory of that romantic hour once we returned to the château, and I wrote her the indiscreet letters you read, begging her to return to the summerhouse for a whole night. Of course she never did. Of course she never even put a word on paper. She was far too wise for that."

"But she saved your letters, and you knew she had done it!"

"I gave her the *coffret* as a birthday gift. I begged her to keep my letters in the false bottom. I didn't know she had actually done it until that day in your presence."

"But why would she, unless—" Nicole began with a catch in her voice. "Did she ever tell you—she loved you?"

"No—uh, I can't remember—but I'm sure she never really loved me."

"Oh, *mon Dieu*, then she did say it! William, tell me the truth! You must tell me if you took her virginity!"

He held Nicole's face in his hands and looked directly into her eyes. "By all that is holy, by the love that exists between you and me, I swear to you that I never succeeded in making love to her. Not that I didn't try! Not that I didn't think I would die if I failed to win her! She may have spoken a few ill-considered words to me. The strange alchemy of sexual excitement often inspires people to say things they later regret and reject. But the truth is, she would never allow me to take the maidenhead she knew she must save for Robert."

Nicole lay face down on the straw for many minutes, hating him a little, hating the picture of Lucienne he had painted, mourning once again the loss of the mother she should have had. Finally she asked in a choked voice, "Did my poor father guess any of this?"

"I pray he did not," he answered somberly. "He could hardly have read my letters or seen us alone together. I can only say that at the very end, just before her precipitous announcement of their engagement, he had taken to passing the whole day with her. Perhaps she had finally won him with her charm, or perhaps he had sensed some sexual tension between us. I fervently hope it was the former. But perhaps our little affair brought them together. And harmoniously. Later, after she was dead, he remarked casually to me, quite without deliberate point, that his own marriage had been a year of unbroken happiness and delight."

Despite the pain of enduring this narrative, Nicole was glad he had told her the truth, as she was satisfied he had. Perhaps not the whole truth— not every little sexual liberty, but the basic truth. And his passion for her mother now seemed an adolescent infatuation, a first proof of his manhood, and her mother's involvement an excusable reaction to Robert's thoughtless treatment. At last Nicole could lose her morbid jealousy of the little affair.

Life in the prison was outwardly calm, although Nicole knew that executions, which had been stopped by the severe weather, had now resumed. And there were small but ominous events. Once a guard, whom she neither liked nor trusted, stopped her with a knowing smile on his face and asked how her special patient progressed. She replied quickly that he had taken a turn for the worse, then hurried away. She wondered about the insulting smirk, and had to hope—since it was preposterous that he could imagine her to have a sexual interest in a dying man—that the guard himself wanted to catch her alone in the cell of a helpless patient where he would be able to have his way with her.

One night, cooking dinner at the central firepit, she thought she heard in the crowd of prisoners around her someone pronounce the name Falkland. But when she tried to find out the speaker or even the topic, she could discover no clue whatsoever and feared to arouse curiosity. Perhaps, after all, she had only imagined she heard it. No doubt her nerves were overtaxed.

After a dreadful nightmare, so unexpected in that she dreamed it in the circle of William's protective arms, she awoke one morning with the premonition time was running out for them. In the days that followed she felt almost ready to resign herself to her fate. What, after all, was a minute or an hour or a year? A day in William's arms would be a lifetime enough, an hour with him infinitely more precious than a year without. From the example of the selfless abbé, from the experience of love itself, she had learned not to demand a list of pleasures and privileges from life like a greedy child. She assured herself that the unexpected treasure of her marriage and her few weeks with William were a greater gift than she could ever have imagined.

One morning as she was receiving some nursing orders from Harbert, she noticed in the dungeon a group of new prisoners. The abbé explained that the Girondist deputies, who had made up the current conservative party, had been seized in the National Convention yesterday and thrown into prison, some ten or twelve of them coming here to La Force. The leadership of France had passed, by this illegal method, to dictators—Marat, Danton, Robespierre and others—who would rule through a body called the Committee of Public Safety. She could tell from Harbert's face he believed it a dire development.

Though she knew that not all members of the Girondist party came from the Gironde, some of these new prisoners might well hail from her home region. She examined the group carefully while listening to the abbé, her eyes returning more than once to a tall, heavy man with an unruly shock of light brown hair cut short in the radical mode. Then when he turned toward her, she suppressed a little cry.

"But of course! You have recognized an acquaintance from the Bordelais," Harbert said with pleasure.

Some instinct told her to turn away quickly, but at the same moment the man saw Nicole and came running forward, calling her name. For a split second she could not think of his. Then she remembered. It was Arnaud Coppin.

Bursting with enthusiasm at finding her, Arnaud questioned her at length about herself. She gave him short but truthful answers until he asked, "Then you've never had an opportunity to marry?"

"No," she answered blandly.

"Nor I. Though many times I wondered about you in England, and if—"

She felt she could not endure romantic overtures from him. Fortunately, her sudden frigid stare stopped him short. After making a few inquiries about his family, she at last summoned all her courage and asked, "What has happened to my home—to Beaux-Clervaux?"

He amazed her by declaring that it was absolutely untouched, the peasants undisturbed, the grapes as healthy as ever, and Maître Poujade undeterred in his production of the finest wines.

"Then the Revolution has scarcely damaged it?" she cried, incredulous at the good news.

"Oh, there has been no damage! Reason has prevailed in the Department of the Gironde. You yourself would have to acclaim every change that has been made. Your château is now a hospital and orphanage under the direction of a former peasant, a Pascal Georgeault. I myself made the appointment."

"Pascal Georgeault! But I remember him well. Pascal is no more than a liar and a cheat! He dishonored my maid, and I had to force him to marry her, and—"

"Oh, I care nothing about his private life. He has served as an able administrator and trustee of your estate, and managed to turn out the votes at every election—"

"Trustee of my estate! You mean he is entrusted with the income that belongs to me? The man will steal me blind!"

"Ah, dear citizeness! You do not understand. The money is no longer yours. It is distributed to the peasants who live on the land wrongfully held for so long by the house of Clervaux."

Nicole turned on her heel and stalked away indignantly, taking care thereafter to avoid contact with him in the dungeon. But to her annoyance she discovered he did not intend to be avoided. Several times he slipped up unnoticed beside her with oily little apologies or compliments, and was quite undaunted when she would bang down her dish or utensil and hurry off. Did the man wish to be merely irritating or was he genuinely lovesick?

She told William of Arnaud's arrival and his news of Beaux-Clervaux, but the duke only observed that she was lucky the château had not been burned to the ground. Still she was strangely disturbed by the knowledge she could not escape daily contact with Coppin. To cheer her one day, William reached up from his reclining position, which he kept for safety's sake as much as possible, and gave her a light kiss on the lips. Both he and Nicole exclaimed simultaneously at the delicious contact, and he pulled her down to his side for a long kiss.

As she lay in his arms, his lips wandering from her mouth to her throat to the lowest point of her neckline, the heavy door creaked open and Arnaud Coppin stood before them. Nicole jumped to her feet and cried, "You have made a grave mistake, monsieur!" William remained on the blanket, but tugged at her hand to remind her to control her temper.

"But you spend so much time in this cell, citizeness! Naturally, I became very curious. . . ." Arnaud said apologetically. He was already backing toward the door quite sheepishly. ". . . even jealous. My little trespass is only meant as a compliment to your irresistible—"

In spite of her great indignation, Nicole was at a loss for the right words. She could hardly claim, behaving as they had been when Arnaud entered, that he had disturbed a gravely ill, dying, or even contagious patient. Sputtering a little, she cried over and over that he had no right to enter the cell. Advancing on him as one shoos chickens in a barnyard, she drove him through the open door. But suddenly he stopped and returned toward Falkland, looking with new interest at the duke. "Don't I know you? Weren't you once at Beaux-Clervaux? Yes, the Englishman, Nicole's guardian from England! What was that name? Some fancy title or other. Whatever can you be doing here in La Force?"

"Go! Leave us! Don't ever come back!" Nicole screamed at Arnaud, as Falkland raised a restraining hand toward her. With a shrug of pretended surprise at her wrath, Arnaud backed again through the door and closed it.

Stamping her foot, crying with vexation, Nicole would not listen to

William's calming words. "I don't trust that man. He will soon remember your name, or find it out. He will recall in a moment that I was at Versailles with you, and then the rest will be easy. Rumors say these Girondist deputies will be released any day and even restored to their seats in the Convention. The Comité will never dare to execute them. Or, if need be, Arnaud will try to trade his own release for the news of your presence here in La Force. In any case, he will give us no peace. He used to follow me witlessly at Beaux-Clervaux, and he will do the same here. If you have any chance of escape, William, you must go now!"

As a signal, Falkland waved a torch in the cell window at midnight. In a quarter hour he repeated the sign, and then again a quarter hour later. His agent, who had been watching La Force, could not fail to see it. By prearranged plan, two English spies dressed as turnkeys would enter his cell at dawn, and cover him as he made good his escape with Nicole in tow.

Falkland had dressed himself in his sansculotte costume which she had long ago washed and mended. Nicole crouched in the cell counting the minutes until dawn, more nervous than ever now rescue was at hand. She wore the green dress once again, and worried that she had no cloak to cover her in the cold dawn air, although William assured her his men would bring disguises for more than one person, believing that some of his men still lived. Already she had visited the side of the sleeping abbé and slipped the coins remaining from Roger's sale of her ring into one of his shoes beside his blanket. How she would have liked to bid farewell to Harbert and to the others who had been so kind to her at La Force! But she trusted William would soon have the opportunity to send gold to the abbé and to assist many others to escape.

Finally wrapping herself in a blanket to stop the shivering she knew was caused more by anxiety than by cold, she took a deep breath and admitted to herself she did not believe they would both escape safely. It was simply too good to be true. Perhaps now that she had so much to lose, she could only believe she would lose it immediately. How could she be fortunate enough to flee to a happy life in England when all the worthy souls around her were suffering so greatly?

She was always overwhelmed when she thought back over the last few weeks: the first moment she recognized William, his survival of the crisis of his illness, their lovemaking and marriage, and their ever-deepening love. Would this be the end, then, today? Would they be separated by death? Or would they die together and pass over into—? Her mind balked at the incomprehensibility of life after death.

She studied William carefully as he waited beside the cell window. She had seen him stand so little that she took pleasure in this final evidence he was well and strong. No doubt he felt a little wobbly, but she had no intention of asking him, for he clearly was not in a conversational mood.

Almost without being aware of her own intention, she tried to engrave on her memory exactly how he looked this morning. He was dressed in the blue and white striped trousers with comical yellow patches over the knees—Timothy had sewn them on hurriedly, William had told her—and the blue jacket. Both garments were too large for him now, for he had lost weight during his illness and had had little chance to regain it on prison food. At last he had stripped off his bandages, kept on so long to persuade the guards he still suffered. She could not see the long red line running the length of his left forearm, but the bright slash of pink near his hairline made her wince. How dreadful that his handsome face must be marred! She would rather bear the scar herself. Of course it would fade in time, and no doubt lend him a dashing air that would hardly damage his success with the ladies, she thought with a little lift of her eyebrows.

Last night she had cut his black hair into the collar-length radical style. His new appearance—like a brawling soldier of fortune or some republican cutthroat of uncertain nationality—would scarcely be appreciated in aristocratic circles in England, but his hair would grow out soon enough, and the short length was necessary for safety today. She had been willing to cut her own long mop knowing she must dress as a man, but William could not bear to see her do it. He said he was sure his men would bring caps. If not, he would hack her hair quickly while they all waited. In the meantime, she had braided it tightly and wound the plaits into a knot at the back of her neck.

As he examined the sky once again, she suddenly jumped up and threw her arms around him. He chuckled a little in his surprise, and then encircled her with a vigorous but hasty hug. Her lips sought his, and at last he let himself relax a little and return the long kiss, then made one of his little jokes about how hungry she was. Today he would keep a light tone to buoy their spirits. She knew he did not want to hear any somber words; but she, feeling the tears burning in her eyes, could not refrain from a shy expression of her love.

"I want to tell you—"

"Don't say it," he whispered and kissed her on the temple.

"Oh, God, if we should be separated—"

"We won't be."

"—then I would die!"

"No." He sighed deeply, and she felt for the first time how strained he was. "You must live on and remember always the joy we took in each other. If you can, you must escape to England and claim your rightful position as Duchess of Falkland. I have been afraid to write out any document attesting to our marriage, which would serve as your own death warrant if you were captured. But when you reach safe territory you must address yourself to King George in person or by letter and tell him that I wished him to recognize our marriage. He will believe you if you say I begged it in repayment of his boyhood debt to my father, which he tried so many times to settle. He will know what I meant and believe that I would not have imparted the otherwise secret information to you except for this solemn purpose. Many years ago my father saved the life of young George, then Prince of Wales, in a storm at sea, but would never allow the story to be repeated, out of his own great modesty."

When she had promised him, not once but twice for he anxiously pressed her again, that she would carry out this wish, he said with sudden optimism, "Don't be afraid, dear Nicole. I know we will survive to love again!" She smiled at him with new cheer, and then he set her firmly to one side. "We must listen now, *chérie*." Indicating some rays of pink in the sky, he said it must be well past four o'clock. The shift would change at dawn. His men would try to walk in with the new team of warders.

For the next hour they stood tensely beside the cell door which was left ajar, waiting for any sound of footsteps in the corridor. But as the sky grew gradually brighter, she felt her own heart sink. Was it possible his plan would fail? Had his men been unable to discover he was carried to La Force after the attack on the Temple? Did they await him outside some other prison? Or had they believed him dead all this time?

When she finally allowed her disappointed eyes to meet his, he said reassuringly, "Can you really believe that Timothy would abandon his post?"

"Then Timothy himself has been watching every midnight for a signal?"

"That was our arrangement."

"And if he doesn't come?"

"Then we must fear his death, and take matters into our own hands." But at that very moment they heard a noise outside the door. Peeking through the opening, Nicole saw that the man was one of their regular guards, a pleasant-enough fellow named Burnet.

"Call him into the room. Tell him your patient has finally died, and he is needed to help carry the body."

She did as she was told, and the man followed her back into the cell. As they entered, she saw that Falkland had quickly bunched up the blankets to look like a body, then managed to disappear. But as soon as Burnet reached the center of the room, the duke sprang from behind the door and knocked him unconscious. Working fast, they tore the bedding into long, narrow strips, then after trading the guard's uniform for Falkland's clothes, tied and gagged him securely before he came back to consciousness.

They had to wait only a few minutes to catch themselves another guard by the same method. This time they had no outfit to replace his own, and simply covered him with a blanket. Now Nicole was also dressed in a guard's uniform, her braided knot concealed by the red *bonnet*, or long stocking cap, the symbol of revolutionary militance that the second man had been wearing. She pulled it low on her forehead, and William rubbed a little dirt into her chin as a poor imitation of whiskers.

All day they had to wait, the four of them staring grimly across the cell at each other. She hated to watch the two warders futilely struggling against their bonds, and feared to meet their hostile eyes. Burnet especially had always treated her decently and had been extremely generous to Harbert. William and she hardly dared speak to each other for fear of conveying some information about their plans. Growing ever more hungry and restless, they could only sit and watch the little patch of sky for signs of the advancing hour.

In mid-morning Nicole heard a noise in the passageway and jumped up, expecting as she was that the abbé would come searching for her. Fortunately she intercepted him before he showed his face to the two guards. Pulling him well away from the cell, she told him that William's plan had gone awry and now they must wait until dusk, then urged him to stay away for fear of being thought an accomplice.

When she had finally convinced him he must not even bring them food, he said simply, "Godspeed to you both! I know He will help you for you have been an angel of mercy to the prisoners."

"God bless you, *mon père!*" She hugged him with all her strength. "William will send you medicines and gold as soon as he can. I know you do not wish to escape from this prison."

"Never, dear Nicole, for I know I am meant to serve here."

At last the light through the cell window began to fail, and William arose, tightened the bonds around his prisoners, led Nicole into the corridor, and bolted the door on the outside. Excited to be free at last, they darted down one blind passage after another before they finally found a staircase. William had been carried in unconscious and had never been out of his cell, while Nicole had indifferently made her way up these steps so many months before that she had little recollection of the plan of the lower floors.

Having successfully passed more than one guard without attracting attention, they took heart and speeded their steps, William leading the way so as to conceal Nicole's feminine features and small size. Then before them at the foot of another flight of stairs they saw a door wide open to the outside world, and could actually glimpse carriages and pedestrians in the rue St. Antoine.

They descended more cautiously now, certain they must pass some sentry at the portal. Then with astonishment they saw that the whole vestibule was filled with uniformed prison employees, lined up for some kind of inspection before they were being allowed to depart.

She looked at William anxiously, but he pointed to a path of traffic on the right side of the room where some men, for whatever reason, were bypassing the line. Without showing either hesitation or undue haste, the duke led the way into the crowded foyer, heading directly for the open door. Having to push by the waiting queue, they brushed against a dozen guards, some Nicole knew well, before they reached the threshold of the outside door.

William had one foot on the cobbles of the street when a doorkeeper, seated at a table partially blocking the exit, reached out and grabbed Nicole's arm. "Wait, *copain*, have you forgotten it's payday? Call back the other fellow," he directed. The man meant to be helpful, comradely.

She saw William stiffen with fear as he stopped and turned a little. Wondering if she dare try to disguise her voice and say they had already been paid, she decided instead to try to wrench her arm free and run for it. Giving William a great shove, she pushed him a foot or two into the street, but could not pull loose her arm from the guard. Instead the man's grip tightened instantly, and he cried out in alarm. Other men crowded around her, and someone whisked off her cap.

Knowing she was lost, she could only think of William's safety. Glimpsing his horrified face close behind one of her captors, she screamed out in English, "Flee, flee! Save yourself!" With a terrible expression of shock and despair, he finally jumped back and vanished behind a passing carriage.

17

Shivering with cold and aching in every joint, Nicole tried once again to bunch up the filthy straw and arrange her body in some comfortable position. Not only was the straw too sparse to cover the bruising stones on which she must sleep without benefit of blankets, but she was covered with the painful bites of the vermin that lived in it. Even if she had been able to find a little ease, she would still have been awakened every time someone stepped over her head or legs in the crowded corridor.

Here in this passageway, nicknamed the "rue de Paris," where the penniless prisoners were forced to live at the Conciergerie, she had rarely slept more than a half hour at a stretch in the month since she had been discovered at the door of La Force. She was clothed only in a cotton sack which, to her great embarrassment, barely even covered her knees, and was allowed no shoes or stockings. She had to survive on the single bowl of gruel a day given to prisoners and whatever water she could drink from the palms of her hands at the fountain in the Cour des Femmes, a courtyard where female prisoners were allowed to take the air. But she had had little appetite since she arrived and scarcely cared whether she ate or not. She knew she was losing weight, and touched the sharp points on her shoulders and hips and knees with a kind of fascination.

Suddenly an evil brass bell shattered the silent dawn. All around her, the sleeping prisoners moaned with fear as they stumbled to their feet and ran to hear the reading of the list of the day's *fourée*, or cartload for the guillotine. But Nicole did not move. She had survived too many readings. If they wanted her, they would come and find her.

The Conciergerie, called the "antechamber of death," was notorious as the prison of no return. Its inmates were admitted only to undergo a brief trial next door in the Palais de Justice, or if already sentenced, to await prompt execution. Perhaps because there was no hope, because terms were so short, the Conciergerie, unlike La Force, offered no spirit of fellowship, no charitable assistance of other prisoners; only cruelty by guards who were assisted by vicious dogs, and desperate competition among the *pailleux*, the strawdwellers or poor prisoners who could not pay for privileges.

Ironically, this evil place had once been the luxurious palace of the medieval Kings of France, and was situated in a beautiful location on the Ile de la Cité in the heart of Paris, facing the pretty quays of the right bank of the Seine. Sometimes at night in the rare moments of peace, Nicole could hear the whistles of boats and once even the passing song of a riverman.

In her misery she huddled in a corner of the "rue de Paris" by day, and lay at night in a kind of stupor, given over to waking dreams that William would break into the prison and save her. She knew he might have had to go back to England to raise enough men and arms, and of course he would not be able to disclose the real purpose of the mission, that the object of the rescue was his own wife. No, he would not dare reveal their marriage to anyone as long as she was in enemy hands. But soon he would be returning to deliver her from this hell. She knew he would come. She knew he would try. She had seen the desperation on his face at their separation.

Then sometimes she would wring her hands furiously until she almost broke her own thin fingers. Was she sustaining herself with an insane dream that could never happen? Had she gone crazy at last? She knew the Conciergerie had never been invaded, that no one had ever been plucked from it. But still she persisted in her belief that William would try, try as he had tried at the Temple, try and fail, perhaps, but still she devoutly believed she would see him here in the Conciergerie.

Then she began to have another obsession. Was it also fantasy to dream that she had become pregnant by William? For a month now she had waited daily for the evidence that would disprove that condition. In her few sternly skeptical moments, she told herself that her bad health and malnutrition had caused the cessation of her periods. From her experience as a nurse, she knew that very ill women often no longer had a monthly flow. She realized that her weak and undernourished body hardly seemed a likely site for new life to sprout. And possibly her waves of nausea were only caused by the sight of crawling insects and the taste of putrid food.

But in spite of all arguments, she began to daydream that she was truly pregnant with William's child. Her mind spun the entire story, every word, every detail. Usually she pictured the delivery at Langmuir Castle—it would be a day in early winter—in the State Bed where all the dukes had been born. No doubt William would prefer a son for his first child, so she imagined a boy infant named William Robert or sometimes Robert

William, or perhaps Andrew after William's father, or even George for the king, if William insisted. She had fewer ideas for girls' names, though sometimes she liked Isabella after his mother. She certainly did not want to name a child Nicole. It seemed such a bad-luck name, just at present; and she rather thought she did not want to call a daughter Lucienne—or did she? Perhaps simply Lucy. Would that be a grand enough name for the daughter of a duke? No doubt family tradition would have to be considered. Fortunately she could leave some of these weighty decisions to William.

Then suddenly after hours of these happy thoughts she would be overcome by a crying jag as she imagined the execution that would also snuff out the life of William's child. Or she would decide with certainty that she could not be pregnant after all, and weep more dejectedly than she had at the idea of her own death.

She had begun to force herself to eat as much as she could for the sake of the possible baby, and was always rather pleased with herself if she experienced a good wave of nausea after her bowl of gruel. Then one evening as she was wondering if she might actually lose the food she had just consumed, she saw Roger Duchamp elbowing his way toward her down the "rue."

Feeling both extremely queasy and frightfully embarrassed at her appearance, she could hardly manage to give him a greeting expressing her genuine pleasure, and backed away when he tried to embrace her. "Oh, Roger, you must not, for your own sake!" She laughed a little in her shame. "There are tiny—bugs, you know. You'll get them on your wonderful new uniform."

"Oh, my poor dear! However have you stood it here? *Grâce au ciel,* I have some money now, some real money, and I have already bought you a private room. Come with me! Now you can have a real bed and decent food, and—a little hot water too! Oh, Nicole, I have tried to buy your freedom, but they say I am far from rich enough. Perhaps I will succeed eventually. I am a *chef de bataillon* at last, but we have had few victories lately. Fortunately, we leave tonight to attack the Austrians at Mainz."

Steadying herself against the doorjamb, she could hardly believe her eyes as she examined her new quarters. Though little more than eight feet square, the room held a plain wooden bedstead with a mattress covered with what looked like a fresh tick, a folded blanket lying neatly across the bed, a small table, a high window with glass and a shutter—even a piece of faded carpet! She had never dreamed the Conciergerie possessed anything so fine. It was more like a servant's room in some country house than a prison cell.

Squeezing Roger's hands in gratitude, she began to weep pathetically. After he helped her hide a little cache of coins inside the mattress, he gave her a kiss on her lips and begged her to take heart, then left her to go to bed, for he could see she was weak and ill.

For several days she hardly rose from the bed, sleeping for long hours, then waking up only long enough to eat the platters of meat and potatoes and bread that were carried in to her. After a doubtful start, she came to enjoy the food and soon had a strong, even ravenous appetite. Though she seldom felt sick anymore, she was very pleased to discover, as the weeks passed, that the improved state of her health still had not brought a return of her periods. There could be little doubt she was pregnant with William's child.

Thrilled now and strangely content, she would lie and stare at the ceiling of the tiny chamber and think how much she owed to Roger. Not only had she put on a pound or two—she knew her breasts were enlarged and her waist had gotten a little thicker—but she had lost that numb, dazed feeling and the habit of solitary daydreaming. She owed Roger for the restoration of the health of her mind as well as her body—and for her baby's survival. Was Roger to be her hero after all? Would he—had he already—saved her from the guillotine? After he had left her, she had felt guilty about letting him kiss her lips. What had she been thinking of, a married, pregnant woman, permitting this man to believe he could rescue her and make her his wife? She must tell him the truth—or at least some portion of it—when he came back next time. It was only that she had been so weak and desperate—still was so desperate! Oh, where was William? Why had her husband done nothing to help her?

In the middle of a sweltering summer night, Nicole was awakened by a flurry of activity in the corridor outside her room. She lay still and listened to hurrying footsteps, a dozen strange voices talking loudly, then furtive conversations by prisoners in adjoining rooms. When she heard the name of the queen repeated again and again, she was overcome by curiosity and arose and peeked out her doorway. A neighbor, a Madame Gaudard, slipped across the hall and informed her in an awed voice that the queen had been admitted to await trial and was quartered not three cells away; in fact her doorway could be seen just there, with the guard standing beside it.

Henceforth prisoners talked about little else but the affairs of Marie Antoinette. Nothing, or almost nothing, she did was secret, for she had no door on her room and only a small screen to protect her modesty from the stream of curious prisoners and even the ordinary citizens who managed to enter the prison to gawk at her. Nicole refused to join in this vulgar and cruel parade, and averted her eyes when she had to pass the opening of the queen's little cell.

Although Marie Antoinette was only allowed to speak or be spoken to when absolutely necessary, every word she said, everything she did, was reported throughout the Conciergerie. Nicole heard immediately when the queen was sick in bed for a day; when she must watch her guards play backgammon, for she was allowed no other occupations, not sewing or writing or even reading; when she received a box of clothes from the Temple and therefore did not have to wear constantly her torn black dress; when her maid was finally permitted to buy her a hand mirror; when she suffered from insomnia and asked for a night light that was denied her; when she was discovered to be hiding a watch that had been given her as a child by her mother, the Empress Maria Theresa, and how she wept brokenheartedly when it was taken from her.

The prisoners gossiped constantly about her dramatically altered appearance. Her hair, what could be seen of it below her wide mobcap, had become entirely gray. Her body was emaciated, stooped, sickly; she suffered greatly from the cold and damp of her cell now that the fall months had arrived. Her eyes were said to be always red, some believed from a disease, others from the constant weeping for her children. Rumor had it that her son, eight-year-old Louis Charles, would soon be allowed to visit her. But then another set of rumors circulated that the child king, believed a great threat to the Republic, was kept in solitary confinement under the tightest security.

Strangely, in view of the harshness of some of the rules made for her, Marie Antoinette was allowed to see a steady stream of visitors. Nicole heard frequent reports of these visits, especially from her ever-curious neighbor, Madame Gaudard, to which she paid little attention. But one day at the description of some foreigner speaking to the queen, Nicole was aroused to exclaim, "When we are at war with half the countries in Europe, how can a foreigner be admitted to the cell of Marie Antoinette? What nationality was he?"

"I don't know. He had a pronounced accent. Perhaps he was Dutch or English," Madame Gaudard said.

"What did he look like?" William had no accent, but Timothy's French was, though fluent, poorly pronounced.

The woman told her he was short, fat, and bald; and Nicole heaved a sigh. Timothy was neither short nor bald. Still, her suspicion persisted that Falkland might send some agent to speak to the queen since entrance was so easy. Perhaps he would even come himself to give Marie Antoinette heart and drop some clue or other to a rescue plan. Surely he must be plotting to save the queen from her certain death. Did he know Nicole was so close by? Or did he believe her still a *pailleuse* living in the "rue de Paris," because he could know nothing of Roger and his gold. Would William someday walk into Marie Antoinette's cell without realizing his pregnant wife languished a few feet away?

More rumors flew of the approach of the queen's trial. The temper of the Revolution had darkened. As the Republican armies failed abroad, scattered rebellions broke out at home, and desperate repressions were practiced. Nicole was aware that executions were now being held daily, and knew that the phrase "Reign of Terror" had been coined to describe the cruelties of the Committee of Public Safety.

One morning a somber-faced Roger entered her cell. She sat up hastily and grabbed an old shawl to conceal her rounded belly, though the prison sack revealed little. But Roger had no interest in her appearance today, and without preliminaries, blurted out that her life was in grave danger.

"I have lived in fear of execution for two years," she answered stoically.

"But now you are only days, perhaps hours, away from the guillotine!" he cried, alarmed at her passivity. "You must be fully aware, Nicole. The Comité puts the queen on trial tomorrow. She is certain to be sentenced to death, for the mobs of Paris demand it. After her execution, they can only be appeased by more and more bloodletting. I have already been told today here in the Conciergerie that the price of this room has tripled and will go higher, yet my gold is nearly exhausted. Our campaign against Mainz was a failure, and I foresee no easy victories. There is but one chance: My commanding officer has every hope that he can secure your release if we are married now inside the Conciergerie."

Stunned, she could only exclaim, "Oh, Roger, I cannot marry you!"

"Cannot marry me?" he echoed in shock.

"No, never."

But he recovered quickly. "Perhaps you do not now feel love, when you have endured so much, but the fact remains a marriage to an officer of influence is your only hope. Even then the plan may not work. Nicole, I swear to you I am telling the truth!"

"Please believe me that I cannot marry you!"

"Even to save your own life?" he demanded shrilly.

"No."

"You can't mean it!" He had never dreamed she would refuse. Aching with sympathy for him, she longed to tell him some part of the truth, but could think of little that would not invite his revenge against Falkland or even their child. "But why not?" he finally asked in a low voice.

"Oh, Roger, I don't know how to explain! All I can say is that I—care for another man."

His jaw jutted, his eyes blazed with anger. "For how long?"

She shrugged, not daring to tell him the truth. Roger was too clever by far, and had the tenacity of a bulldog. He could find out her whole story if he tried. "A long time," she murmured.

"How long?" he demanded. But she merely shook her head. "Who is the man?"

Closing her eyes in an agony of guilt and fear, she finally said almost inaudibly, "I can't answer you," and prayed he would not force more questions on her.

"Why have you never told me this before?"

"Perhaps you think I have taken advantage of you, that I am guilty of deceit and even fraud. Oh, Roger, I never asked you to spend your money on me. God knows I would pay it back if I could!"

He peered at her intensely for a long time. Then slowly, the color returned to his face. "How long have you been in the Conciergerie?" he asked.

"Six months, almost seven." She kept accurate count because of the baby.

"And how long were you in La Force before that?" She hesitated, trying to remember exactly, but Roger answered his own question. "You were sentenced in Rouen on the twenty-fifth of September, 1791, a little more than two years ago. I remember well that you were delighted to spend your afternoons with me in Rouen before you went to trial, and how you threw yourself into my arms and kissed me with abandon when I visited you in La Force. Do you really expect me to believe that you have fallen in love with someone you met in prison in the last few months? With whom, pray tell—some jailer, some filthy, lice-infested *condamné!* Far from believing you guilty of deceit and fraud, I think you have suffered some sort of mental derangement. I think your poor distressed mind has invented a phantom lover!"

Perhaps Roger was right, Nicole thought wryly, then laughed aloud when her baby gave her a vigorous kick. The phantom lover had given her a real baby, and a healthy one! Still, how much longer could she cling to the delusion that William would save her, her baby, and the queen, as well? If it would, the miracle must happen soon, for Marie Antoinette's trial had started this morning. Roger's information had been accurate. Rolling over in this bed that he had paid for, she paused to enjoy the baby's energetic movements, then thought once again with sadness of her confrontation with Roger. Perhaps someday when William and she were finally removed to England, she could explain to her husband, and he would allow her to repay Roger the money he had spent.

Reports had it that the first day of the trial had taxed Marie Antoinette's fragile emotions to the limit and offered little sign of an eventual acquittal. Prosecutors had accused her of squandering public funds on luxuries such as Petit Trianon, of sending secret shipments of French gold to her relations in Austria, of persuading her husband to resist the Revolution, and finally in an outrageously vile invention, claimed that she had persuaded her eight-year-old son to perform incestuous acts with her. This preposterous charge was unequalled not only in its cruelty but its unlikelihood, for all who knew her had always admitted that the queen was an excellent mother. The prosecutor waved a confession actually signed by the child, a signature obtained, gossip had it tonight, only after the child had been heavily dosed with brandy.

For once her opponents had gone too far. Marie Antoinette, though at first struck dumb by the accusation, had quickly recovered her wits and had made a ringing appeal to all mothers of children there in the Chambre Dorée to know that such a charge did not even deserve an answer. After a moment of silence, the gallery, otherwise hostile to her, had given a rousing cheer. But it was only a small victory for the queen, and no one seriously expected she could hold the advantage throughout the trial.

Just as Nicole was about to fall asleep, a lone guard bearing a lantern entered her cell and beckoned for her to follow him. Badly startled, she jumped up and hastily wrapped her shawl around her nightgown, believing that the time of her own death had arrived. But executions had never been held at night. Was this a new refinement wrought by the vicious Comité?

Perhaps she should turn and flee from the man, run down the winding corridors of the Conciergerie, gain a few more minutes or hours of life. He was leading her to a different exit from the one where tumbrils usually waited. So the night executions would follow a new procedure. The man himself was new, unknown to her at least; even his uniform looked fresh.

Every time they turned a corner, he looked behind at her and merely gestured for her to follow him. Never once did he speak. Could the man be a deaf mute? He was tall, spare, fair-haired. Suddenly it occurred to her that he might not be French at all.

After climbing one staircase, winding around some upper floor, then descending another set of steps, he brought her to a heavy gate, which, though it was a solid piece of iron, still admitted a cool breeze around its edges. She had lost her sense of direction, but she guessed it opened onto the quay along the river.

He had half turned away when he commanded her in English, "Wait here!" then hurried off, leaving her in the dark and deserted anteroom. Astonished, unable to absorb immediately the full meaning of her situation, she instinctively pushed against the gate with all her might, but found she could hardly shake it. Obviously it was securely bolted on the outside. Would William soon unbolt it and take her in his arms? She hardly dared hope. Would he, or perhaps one of his men, be here in minutes—or hours —to rescue her at last? Would she soon feel William's lips on hers, make love to him, tell him of their child? Oh, dear heaven, had her dreams not been insane fantasies after all?

Wondering where the queen would be stationed—might Marie Antoinette even be brought to this very gate to wait alongside her?—Nicole stood for an hour or more without hearing a sound. At last she needed to sit down, but crouched against the gate, resting her ear on the cold iron so that she would not miss the lightest tap on the outside.

But there was no knock, no footsteps, call, cry, tug at the bolt, or signal of any kind all night long. Perhaps she fell asleep for a few minutes just before dawn, but she had little doubt that any vibration in the metal would have brought her instantly to full consciousness. Then as she saw the light of dawn creep around the perimeter of the gate, there came, immediately after some sound like the scraping of a boat against the quay, a great burst of gunfire. She jumped up involuntarily and cried out, and then heard other cries somewhere near her, just the other side of the gate. A single shot rang out, and then another fusillade, greater than the first. Most of the shots came from somewhere above her head, but more than once a musket ball hit the outside of the gate, and she finally stepped aside in fear and stood against the stone wall. Only a few more shots were heard, somewhere a man moaned—and then silence. Only silence. No sound except the pounding of her heart.

She had hardly dared breathe when at last she became aware of sounds inside the Conciergerie, commands barked to soldiers, boots pounding down the corridors. When no more shots rang out, she knew that Falkland's force had failed. Desperately, she wanted to look outside, and standing on tiptoe managed to haul herself up to peer through a grilled window. There only a few feet below her on the cobblestones of the narrow quai de l'Horloge, with the river lapping just beyond, lay some twenty bodies. Already two or three prison guards were picking up the abandoned weapons and preparing to carry off the corpses. Closest to her, now with a grotesquely contorted face, was the "guard" who had led her to the gate last night. Scrutinizing every body, she finally noticed a black-haired man who appeared particularly tall. He lay in a pool of blood, his face turned away from her toward the river.

Could it be William? she wondered in icy terror. The black hair was long enough to be caught in a ribbon at the back of the neck, but of course it had had time to grow out since she had cut it herself that night at La Force. Then with horrified eyes she made out the red scar that ran the length of his left forearm. There could be no doubt. She had bandaged that wound herself!

Just as the team of soldiers reached William's side and hauled up his lifeless body, she saw her own strained fingers give way and her hands slide down, down the rough stones, as she slumped into merciful oblivion.

18

Nicole felt nothing when the warders told her she would die that morning. For two days she had lain in bed staring at the water-stained ceiling unable to eat or sleep. How few needs she had now, how little interest she had in her own body, as though she had died along with William. Yet paradoxically her brain raced on ferociously, like a carriage out of control she had thought more than once. She could not put a stop to the punishing thoughts of what might have been if only she had hurried her steps in that vestibule at La Force, or if she had pulled the cap lower on her forehead, or if they had decided to flee the prison sooner instead of indulging themselves in endless lovemaking, or if she had not balked so scrupulously at going through a marriage ceremony with Roger in order to escape the Conciergerie—a cruel trick on Roger, of course, but it would have saved William's life, and her own, and their child's. But still, no doubt, William would have felt bound to rescue the queen and would have died anyway— or might he have gone to some other gate if he had not had to take Nicole too, and might—? Dear heaven, she could stand no more!

And now her execution would come at last. God knows it was time! So there was some order in the chaos of life after all. She would go now to join William. It was as it should be.

When one of the guards offered her pen and paper, she only shook her head. Who was there left to write? No doubt the servants and peasants at Beaux-Clervaux, or most of them, would only be relieved that they no longer need feel guilty to enjoy what was rightfully hers. Her mind lingered over Clémence and the Gaillards, but she had not the heart to try to tell them what they had meant to her so long ago. Should she write to Kate and Dr. Littleton—and say what? That William was dead, and that she who had briefly been his wife would now die with his baby in her womb? They would hear of the duke's death soon enough. Why deepen their sorrow with her sad story? Besides, there could be little chance that a letter would get through to England.

When the warder handed her a cotton sack to put on, she felt some return of her old spirit. Could they actually expect that she would change her clothes here in front of two men? Seeing her consternation, they finally turned half away, and she pulled off her nightgown, shivering in the cold October dawn.

Should she cry out for them to turn around and see her swollen belly? Should she throw herself on their mercy as a pregnant woman, and beg them to allow her to live a few more months until her baby could be born? In her long imprisonment she had heard of such appeals being made and sometimes granted, the mothers being executed a few days after the babies were born. But she had not the will to try. Unable to eat or sleep, she could not imagine that she would live long enough to give birth, or that any life on earth would be worth living, even if she could buy it for her child.

When they were satisfied that she had had time to cover herself, the guards approached again, and pulling the pins from her hair, began to hack it off across the back of her neck. As Nicole felt the painful tugs and heard the scissors chewing laboriously through the thick mass that had not been cut short since she was a small child, she felt tears running down her cheeks. How absurd that she could weep only for her hair on this last day!

The men roughly tied her hands behind her back and gave her a little shove into the corridor, as though she were no longer worthy of being addressed with words. She saw immediately the bloodless face of Madame Gaudard, whose only greeting to her was a nod of her head toward the opposite end of the corridor. Nicole turned to look and saw a little knot of men around the queen's door. "We are in good company today," Madame Gaudard said with a tremulous voice. "We will follow Her Majesty to the guillotine!"

In the Cour du Mai where two tumbrils, or manure carts, awaited them, Nicole first thought that the queen had not yet arrived. Surely that tiny, bent old woman with a few bits of white hair visible below her mobcap was not the beautiful queen. Nicole knew Marie Antoinette was only thirty-seven years old, but this woman looked closer to seventy. Then Nicole discerned the prominent Hapsburg lip, the only feature that had not changed—that and a certain aloof dignity, even majesty.

Unable to feel any self-pity, Nicole was nevertheless appalled at the prospect of the queen's execution. Standing only three feet from her, briefly isolated as the other half-dozen prisoners were loaded in the second tumbril, Nicole had an impulse to say something comforting to the ashen, forlorn woman. But what could she say? She could not bear to tell her the one bit of news she might have had real interest to hear, that Falkland was dead trying to save her; nor would she make the prideful announcement, "He married me—no one else—and I carry his child within me"; nor a vindictive, "I well remember when you scandalized the court by your adultery with the man I love!" Instead, Nicole leaned forward and said gently, *"Vive le roi, votre fils!"* Long live the king, your son! Although Marie Antoinette did not smile, she fixed her blue eyes for a moment on Nicole, and nodded with what seemed like sincere appreciation.

The queen was offered a little ladder and stepped into the first tumbril, where she rode alone with a priest. Nicole climbed into the second cart and took a seat facing forward, then willingly changed places to allow Madame Gaudard to divert herself during her last minutes on earth by watching the queen's every movement.

In the Cour, Nicole had heard Marie Antoinette express great alarm at the open cart in which she was to ride. The king had been allowed a coach, she said, and she feared she might be torn limb from limb by the mob like the Princesse de Lamballe and others. Now along the rue St. Honoré, Nicole anxiously watched the jeering spectators for signs of a sudden surge toward the carts, and was actually relieved when the little procession turned into the Place de la Révolution. Though the huge square was crowded with thousands of Parisians, it was lined with seemingly endless ranks of foot and mounted soldiers.

Engulfed by the mass of people, Nicole could not see the slender uprights and the shining blade of the guillotine until the horses stopped at the very bottom of the platform. Frozen with terror, trembling so that her knees hardly held her, she tried to climb down from the cart when the guard prodded her. She was pressed against a young woman who moaned pathetically, and Nicole unconsciously put a soothing hand on her shoulder, comforted herself for a brief moment by the contact. Then she followed the enraptured gaze of Madame Gaudard, who was a step ahead of her, and saw that Marie Antoinette was already mounting the steps of the scaffold.

The queen seemed to have found new strength, and now stood atop the platform with her old inimitable poise, spine straight and head high. Even the black-hooded executioner shrank back in awe, as subservient as any lackey at Versailles. With regal presence, the queen surveyed the crowd fearlessly, then turned deliberately to look at the palace of the Tuileries, the last home where she had enjoyed some measure of freedom and happiness. Taking her own time to drink in this sight, she finally turned toward the guillotine, at last ready to acknowledge its presence. Then she knelt eagerly, gratefully, actually springing forward to lay her neck in the lunette.

The executioner moved swiftly to carry out her obvious command. The huge crowd watched silently until the blade crashed down, then gave a deafening cheer—and a moment later another, no less thunderous, as the executioner held up the streaming head by a wisp of white hair.

Now Nicole was no longer trembling. She was fired with a new fervor to follow in the footsteps of the queen and stand as brave and strong upon the platform, to throw herself forward with the same courage to embrace death.

When Madame Gaudard hung back in terror, Nicole pushed ahead to grasp the rough handrail of the scaffold. At that moment a frightened horse just beside her neighed and skittered and finally reared, until his raised hooves threatened to strike her head. Indifferent to her own safety, Nicole had to be hauled out of danger by a pair of grenadiers, just as another mount moved up beside her to help control the nervous horse. She did not notice for several moments that she was completely cut off from the other prisoners. She did not notice that a carriage with covered windows had pulled up beside her. Slowly the door swung open. A hand reached out. At first she did not think to climb in.

Was it a dream or not? Perhaps she was already dead and gone to heaven where William awaited her with open arms. But this man in the carriage was not William! William was dead and she was still alive—alive here in this shaded cab, shaking violently in the embrace of Roger Duchamp.

He was pressing his lips feverishly against her forehead and cheeks and now her neck. Revolted, she pushed away timidly, then more forcefully. "Please, please, I am ill." She retreated to the opposite side of the carriage and lay her head against the padded wall, as much to escape his touch as from her own weakness.

But he was quite undaunted and patted her, murmuring sympathetically, as he launched into an account of his bold rescue. After days of clever scheming—which he detailed in an endless narrative, savoring the names of generals and other high officials she had never heard of—he had won the assignment to control the crowds at the queen's execution. His most trusted men had stood at the foot of the scaffold, provoking the horse and faking the little scuffle. Only the other condemned prisoners had witnessed Nicole's rescue, and with a chuckle Roger noted that already they had ceased to be a threat.

Though this little incident had gone surprisingly smoothly today, she could have no real security, he told her, until she was safely married to him. His brisk, confident manner indicated that he was going to gloss over her bewildering refusal at their last meeting. Of course, she would have thought better of it by now, and after this morning's incredible ordeal, there could be little need to raise the question again. He never put it as a formal proposal. Of course she would marry him. Here and now.

The black leather of the carriage felt smooth and beautiful to her fingertips. She found herself stroking it with great curiosity and pleasure, loving the feel of the fine material against her throbbing forehead. How long had it been since she had seen or touched anything new and fresh and lovely? She wondered for a minute how Roger could afford such an expensive vehicle, but then decided it was probably one of the perquisites of his rank. Of course he was a far different man now than the little lieutenant she had known in Rouen. Even his voice had the ring of authority.

When the coachman halted somewhere and opened the door beside her, Nicole seemed to be trying to pull herself back to reality. After peeking out at some official-looking building, she turned to Roger with a dazed expression on her face. He showed only a flicker of annoyance at her lack of concentration, then assumed a rather paternal manner. "It is the Mairie of the Fourth Arrondissement. We will be married here."

"Married!" He must be mad.

"Come, dear. You have had an unbelievable ordeal this morning. God knows I would have prevented it if I could. But what is past is past, and now you must struggle to pull yourself together."

"Roger, I can't marry you!" For a thousand reasons. She was married to someone else—no, she was no longer! Oh, God, how could she still forget? Then the baby kicked in her stomach. Surely Roger must have felt that jolt. Should she put his hand on her rounded belly? She looked down for a moment. The rough fabric bunched stiffly around her waist. He would not likely have detected the enlargement.

"Nicole, you must—there is no choice! Do you want to ride in another tumbril?" It sounded strangely like a threat. She would marry him now or go back to the guillotine. But surely Roger could not be guilty of such vicious coercion. She darted a look at him, and saw his face was contorted with genuine grief. Of course he had only chosen his words thoughtlessly. "Oh, Nicole, I can't go on without you! Don't deprive me of your love!"

She had believed herself already dead. Could she still live after all? Could she actually survive with Roger's help—eat good food again, drink fresh milk from the country, learn to sleep once more, and wait out the time until her baby would be born? She drew a tentative breath, and decided she felt stronger somehow. Perhaps it was Roger's vital personality or perhaps the sunny day she could see through the half-open door. Oh, dear God, could she live? Should she try to give her baby life?

"But not—" she cried, "—not like this!" She had felt the jagged ends of her hair and looked again at her sack, suddenly realizing that her feet were bare and her legs naked to the knee. Belatedly, she reached down to tug at the short skirt.

"Oh, poor dear!" Roger exclaimed with relief. So she had only been thinking of her appearance. "But I anticipated it!" he said brightly, and handed her a package wrapped in brown paper. Her fingers still shaking, he had to untie it for her and take out a blue cape, which he draped around her, pulling its generous hood up over her head. "There now, you're as pretty as a picture!" he assured her, and produced from another package some white cotton stockings and a pair of leather shoes. He turned his head away so that she could pull on the hose, rolling them just above each knee, and slip into the shoes, which proved a size or two too large.

At last she was able to descend from the carriage. Clomping along in her loose shoes, she took Roger's arm and hoped her appearance was not too curious. Fortunately the cloak fell to her feet, and if she held it closed, no one could see her guillotine sack or exposed legs.

To her relief, she attracted little attention inside the Mairie. When the clerk asked her name, she hesitated and turned to Roger. Was it safe to give her true name? But then of course her true name was the Duchess of Falkland! Efficiently, Roger stated that she was the Citizeness Nicole Clervaux and supplied her birthplace, father's name, mother's maiden name, and even the name of the parish where Lucienne had been born, which Nicole could not recall ever hearing before. What a remarkable man Roger was! Of course she was incredibly lucky to know him, to have been helped by him all these months. And to marry him? she wondered with an icy shudder.

As the magistrate read the brief vows composed for civil marriages when religious services had been outlawed, Nicole gave her one-word responses in so low a voice that Roger finally turned to her with a reproachful glance. In a moment their marriage was declared valid, and Roger took her in his arms for a fervent kiss that she passively endured. Poor Roger! She felt sincere regret and guilt that she could not love him as he deserved.

As he tried to embrace her in the carriage, they drove across the Pont Marie to the pretty island called St. Louis, just upstream from the Ile de la Cité, and stopped before a handsome house on the quai d'Orléans. When she managed to give it a polite smile, Roger said regretfully, "Alas, I could afford to take only the top floor."

"Then you live here?" she asked shyly.

"I have only just taken it for us!"

"For us?" she echoed.

"Yes."

"Then you knew I would marry you. . . ."

"I hoped and trusted," he said patiently.

"Then you planned all this, Roger?" She was just beginning to comprehend. "You laid all these careful plans as I was preparing to die. Did you actually arrange to have me taken to the guillotine this morning with the queen?"

"Good God, can't you understand! There was no other possible way to obtain your release, since you had refused to marry me inside the prison. Do you imagine that I could lead a raid against the Conciergerie!" Shaking his head, he added frankly, "Besides I had to shock you to your senses!"

But of course he was right. Now was hardly the time to wonder at his methods, to feel appalled by his ruthlessness. His plan had worked. That was all that needed to be said. He had indeed brought her to her senses and made her see that she could live and give her baby life.

Dutifully she followed him up the four flights of stairs. At last they entered a small, pretty flat consisting of a salon, kitchen, and bedchamber. He had hired a servant, he said, but had not been unwilling to give her a holiday to watch the queen's execution, he added with a certain emphasis that Nicole did not understand. He offered food and drink, and when she refused, pressed her with great concern. "How else do you expect to regain your strength?"

She sat stiffly at a round table in the kitchen, choking down a few bites of bread soaked in milk, and absently watched him stoke up the fire and fill a large kettle with water. As he brushed a few drops of liquid off his handsome uniform, she finally awoke from her daze and realized that she, not her husband, should be serving in the kitchen. But he kindly told her to keep her seat, and removing his coat, lugged several heavy containers of hot water into the bedroom. "I am filling you a tub, for I know how you must long for it," he said. When he beckoned, she obediently followed after him with a little chagrin. No one before had ever ordered her to take a bath.

After he carefully tested the temperature, twice adding buckets of cold water until he was satisfied it was just right, he gave her a beautiful new bar of scented soap, and considerately withdrew from the room. How many months had it been since she had sat in the bath at La Force? What an unbelievable luxury it would be to soak here in this lovely room. She hurriedly removed the cloak, sack, hose, and shoes, and lowered herself into the delightfully warm water. Like everything Roger arranged, it was perfectly done, and relaxed and restored her as nothing else could have.

For a long time she only sat and soaked, and then feeling a little more energetic, began to scoot around in a circle to admire the pretty chamber. Once it had probably served as a child's room or a nurse's, when this building had still been a fine mansion. Though small, it was rather charming with floral wallpaper and a tall french window, which Roger had left closed and shuttered for her bath. There was a tiny fireplace with a marble mantel, a huge carved *garde-robe* with a mirror on the door, a candelabrum with crystal drops and fresh candles. Then as she made her last turn, she saw the big brass bedstead that was so shiny she decided it must be new. Had Roger bought a new bed just for her—for them? As she noticed the white garment lying over the counterpane, her mind was suddenly overwhelmed by the truth that she had been suppressing all along. Of course Roger was expecting to sleep with her! Now—today! Perhaps she had assumed that he would believe her too sick, too weak. Or that he, always so considerate and solicitous, could be easily dissuaded. Roger would always be kind, Roger would only want to take care of her. She could stall him, postpone over and over again the act of submitting to him. And the need to tell him about the baby.

But now she saw it all: the bath offered without apology—of course the fastidious Roger would require her to be perfectly clean, the meaningful little pause when he said the servant would be gone all day, the garments on the bed that she now saw were not street clothes but a robe and white nightgown. It was part of his carefully laid plans that he should possess her immediately.

Panicky, she grabbed the soap and hurriedly scrubbed herself all over. Would she be able to put him off with gentle evasions—or even angry words? Or should she simply let him have his way with her, concealing her pregnancy by bunching the nightgown around her waist? Perhaps she should try to convince him that her belly was only swollen from starvation. She had seen the phenomenon more than once at the Conciergerie. But no deceit would gain her more than a few days or weeks at best.

Grabbing the soft towel he had thoughtfully provided, she stood up, patted her breasts until they were dry, then stepped out of the water and rubbed her stomach and hips and legs, finally touching the zone between her legs with great reluctance and guilt. Oh, *mon Dieu*, could she ever let another man—even the good Roger, her legal husband—know her there, when she belonged to William, when she carried his baby inside her?

Resolutely, she walked across the room, and stood naked before the looking glass on the *garde-robe*. As she saw herself at last, she felt a wave of dizzying disgust. Not only was her hair sticking out all over her head in jagged tufts, but her face and neck and arms and legs were incredibly thin. How many months had it been since she had looked in a mirror? Could it be as long ago as Langmuir Castle? Now her face was both sickly —reminding her a little of Annie's—and somehow younger than it had been, almost childish; while her arms and legs had lost their pretty roundness. Yet her breasts and abdomen—! She could hardly stand to look at them. Her breasts were enlarged, overripe; her stomach distended to twice its normal size. The truth of her condition screamed out. There was no way her pregnancy could be denied. As the tears streamed down her cheeks, she tried to comfort herself with the thought that at least Roger would not want to make love to such a scarecrow.

When he finally knocked, she rushed to pull on the new nightgown and knot the belt of the robe before admitting him. He smiled reassuringly and slipped his arm around her, then laughed a little and began to comb her hair. Her tears broke out once again as he tugged at the snarls. "I will trim it for you later," he said. How thoughtful Roger was! She smiled in appreciation at his handsome face, the rather wiry hair that conveyed the impression of vitality, the alert brown eyes, the expression that was a little less strained, a little older and wiser than in Rouen. So close, he could not fail to bend and kiss her. She had not wanted it, but let her lips yield softly. Encouraged, he suddenly put his hand inside her robe and seized one of her big breasts. Shocked and revolted, she jumped away from him.

"Poor innocent Nicole! You are my wife now. You must learn to permit me to enjoy your treasures." Deciding to bide his time, he led her by the hand to the window, and threw open the shutters and the glass doors so that they could step out onto a little iron balcony. "Come and see our view. There are few panoramas more beautiful. It is sure to cheer you!"

She followed him to the railing, from which hung pots of red geraniums, and gasped at the sight before her. Directly ahead was the *chevet*, or apse, of Notre Dame Cathedral, its spire reaching heavenward, the flying buttresses arching magnificently above the trees of a little apple orchard on the point of the Ile de la Cité that almost touched the quay beneath their balcony. Only a small arm of the Seine separated the two islands. On the left of their vista stretched a wider branch of the river, vanishing behind a large building spanning it, that Roger told her was actually part of the hospital called the Hôtel-Dieu. A few boats floated downstream between the quays draped with ivy or shaded by plane trees, and just below the balcony a solitary fisherman cast his line.

After exclaiming at the beautiful scene, Nicole asked almost involuntarily, "Where is the Conciergerie?"

"All the way across the Cité. You cannot see it from here, nor La Force. I will make you forget all that, Nicole!" Then he tried to kiss her again, but she pulled away.

"I am ill, Roger. I cannot do what you want—"

"Then you must come and lie down. Of course you should stay in bed. And I will do nothing—to tax you. You will see that love can be a great restorative. Then afterwards, I will let you sleep all afternoon. Tonight, if you are well enough, you can try on some of the new frocks I have bought you, and we can go out to a cafe."

"Oh, my God, Roger!" She began to choke with sobs. "I can't be a wife to you! And you won't want me when you know! I tried to tell you the truth in the Conciergerie, but you wouldn't believe me. I told you—I had loved a man. Now I must prove it to you. Give me your hand. Place it here on my body, and you will feel that I am great with child!"

She reached out as he stared at her blankly, his mouth hanging open, but when her fingers touched his skin he jerked his hand away. Undeterred she opened her robe, and pressing on the folds of the white linen, outlined her swollen belly. With imploring eyes, she waited for his reaction.

Paralyzed with shock, he refused to lower his gaze below her face. "You are lying! It can't be true! I knew you were—deranged!"

A little smile crossed her face. "The baby kicked me just now. Here, you can feel it."

But instead, Roger turned away to conceal his agony, then whirled around and began to tear violently at her robe and gown, trying to rip them, pulling the robe off and tugging the gown over her head until, choking, she had to cry out for him to stop.

He gave her no help in uncovering her face, and when she had finally pulled away the cloth and could see him again, she was horrified at the revulsion and hatred in his expression as he looked at her bare body.

"Who did this? Who is your lover?" he demanded through gritted teeth.

"No one who matters now." She was terrified he would discover that a notorious enemy of the Revolution had fathered the unborn child, and try to take some revenge against it.

"I will not rest until I find out," he said fiercely.

Desperately she cried, "He is dead now!"

To her relief, Roger looked somewhat appeased. "Dead? Executed at the Conciergerie?"

She tried to pass it off with a shrug, but he shook her until she sobbed, "No—yes—I don't know. Yes, he was executed at the Conciergerie!"

"You are lying! Tell me his name, or I will kill you!"

"Kill me then," she screamed. "I have long been ready to die!" When he let her go, she grew a little calmer. "Oh, Roger, there is no longer any reason to be jealous!" She must lie to protect her child. "I had only a very brief relationship with this man—I am ashamed to admit how brief it was and how little importance it held for him. Can't you accept that as true? Only my great shame prevents me from saying more."

Roger stood rigid, staring at her breasts and stomach and her triangle of hair with an expression of mingled grief and hatred, and then spat out, "You whore!" With all his strength, he struck the side of her head, sending her sprawling on the floor. She thought he intended to kick her, and when she could right herself raised her arms in front of her belly to protect it. But he suddenly turned and stalked out, slamming the door of the flat behind him.

19

"Do you want to buy a wig, citizeness?"

"A wig?"

"So you can go walking in the streets without danger," the servant, Violette, suggested sensibly. "You will become very tired of these small rooms before your hair grows out."

"Yes—of course," Nicole quickly agreed. So the woman had guessed from the outset that her hair had been shorn for the guillotine, and only kept still out of some sort of loyalty to Roger, for it was obvious from her chatter that she was a devout believer in the Revolution.

For three days, Violette had watched Nicole fret over her hair. On the morning after Roger's violent departure, the servant had returned somewhat tardily from her holiday to find her soaping it over a bucket in the kitchen, having just trimmed it as carefully as possible. Violette stared with fascination as she rinsed it clean and toweled it until it was fuzzy, and the maid soon lost her shyness and helped to comb it into every possible arrangement, until laughing together they both pronounced it hopeless.

All alone the preceding afternoon and evening, Nicole had lain in the big brass bed, alternately weeping with despair and listening for Roger's footsteps, certain that he could only intend to return her to the Conciergerie. At last at midnight, after she had finished a pitcher of milk, she had fallen asleep, thankful that she had enjoyed at least a few hours in a soft clean bed in a pretty room where she could see the lights of the city and hear the sounds of the river and the bells of the cathedral.

Roger had not reappeared until several hours after Violette arrived, and then only long enough to pack some uniforms and eat a plate of food. Nicole had sat frozen on a stool in the kitchen from the moment of his entry, but he had not acknowledged her presence until he arose to put on his coat. Dropping a small pouch on the table, he said gruffly, "Here is the money you will need"; and when she had only sat staring at him with frightened eyes, he snapped, "Come and take it. It is now your responsibility to manage it well." Then before she reached the table, he was gone once again.

Now as she was walking with the servant across the Pont Marie, Violette reached over and adjusted her blue cape. To her surprise, the maid seemed more concerned to conceal her large belly, which was all too apparent in the dress Roger had bought her, than her shorn hair. From the beginning, the maid had seemed to treat her with a strange mixture of deference and puzzlement, often muttering to herself when she studied her and shaking her head.

At the shop of the *perruquier*, or wigmaker, described as a cousin of Violette's, Nicole detected that she was receiving glances conveying the same respect and pity from everyone in the store. It was hardly the reaction she would have expected militant Parisians to have for an enemy of the people narrowly escaped from the guillotine.

Soon she was pleasantly distracted by the succession of blond and brunette wigs that the *perruquier* placed on her head, and she laughed aloud at a black model with puffs and curls half covering her forehead. Though there were more beautiful wigs, she finally settled on a simple style with a bun in back made of blond hair similar to her own, choosing it for its low price. She did not know how long Roger expected her to stretch the gold that he had left behind.

Tying up her package, the *perruquier* confided to her, "Of course I knew from the beginning that you would pick this model." Nicole raised her eyebrows in polite curiosity, and he bent down to her ear and whispered, as his wife and his cousin Violette nodded in knowing agreement, "It is what all the little nuns select!"

Nicole was so astonished that she almost blurted out a protest, then thought better of it and, though her cheeks turned bright red, kept her silence. An impulsive denial might have cost her a ride back to the Conciergerie. Walking home beside Violette, she recalled the nuns she had known in prison and their sufferings after all religious orders were abolished. The penniless women had had to starve, hidden in attics or cellars, or face abuse and even rape by mobs. In some towns they had been forced to marry complete strangers by officials anxious to stamp out the last vestiges of organized religion. No doubt Violette imagined some such pathetic story to explain Nicole's pregnancy.

"Then did my short hair give me away!" she finally asked the maid.

"Yes, citizeness. That and"—Violette laughed rather apologetically—"the fact that you don't know anything!"

"Don't know anything!"

"I mean, because you've been shut away so long, and sheltered from so many things."

"From what, pray tell!"

"Why, for one, you don't know a thing about the new calendar. You thought the shops would be closed today because it's Sunday, when we don't even have Sundays anymore, only Décadi, a holiday every tenth day. And I had to tell you this wasn't October, but Vendémiaire, the month of the vintage; although Brumaire, the month of fog, begins in two days. And you don't know about money, how high our prices are, how the *assignat* is worth so little that a loaf of bread costs five hundred paper francs. You had no idea food is so scarce that sometimes we have to stand all night in line to buy meat at a *boucherie*. And you knew nothing of these wigs, which are so popular now that hair is plentiful."

"Plentiful? What do you mean?"

"Why, the hair comes from guillotine victims—didn't you know?"

Nicole gasped and looked down in horror at the package, wanting to throw it in the river. How could she ever wear the wretched thing, made of hair cut from some sobbing woman in the Conciergerie or La Force, perhaps some poor creature she had known?

"And you didn't have no clothes," Violette continued, not noticing her shocked silence, "or jewelry, even though you are a lady from your speech, and"—she hated to speak so bluntly to a little nun—"you was so sheltered you didn't even know how to get rid of a baby you didn't want!"

"Oh, Violette, about that you are very wrong! I want this baby, have always wanted it, more than anything else in the world!"

One twilight in Frimaire, the month of sleet, Nicole, having rested on the bed all afternoon, finally called to Violette and asked with pretended casualness if she knew anything about delivering babies.

"Oh, no, mistress! I ain't never had one, nor seen one come. Ain't never wanted to! Are you getting close, then?" she asked anxiously. "You face looks all pinched and white. Let me run and get a midwife. Old Mère Carrel lives on the quai d'Anjou."

"But I'm afraid we can't afford her. Prices are so high now, and there is little gold left."

"Oh, never fear. She will wait for her pay until Citizen Duchamp comes home from his campaign."

"No, no." Nicole could only shake her head feebly. "We cannot ask him for more than he has already given us, and I have no other way of raising money." Then as another painful cramp seized her again, she waved Violette from the room.

Thank heaven the Committee of Public Safety had left behind the great bell Emmanuel at Notre Dame when it had taken the others to recast as cannons. Perhaps Emmanuel was simply too huge to remove. Violette had told her that it took eight men just to ring it. Comforted by the sound, Nicole had listened to it ring the hours all evening long. Some time ago she had counted eleven tolls. Now soon it would be midnight, or had she missed the peals as she thrashed and moaned in her increasing misery. Violette had been pacing the floor, relating every story she knew about disastrous deliveries to convince Nicole to send for help—someone, anyone, a neighbor, perhaps one of Violette's cousins? Finally half an hour ago, she had departed to fetch a woman she knew who had given birth to ten children and would make no charge for her advice.

Though Nicole had only consented to her departure to be free of the distressing stories, now her pains were so overwhelming that she was greatly relieved when she heard the outer door click open and footsteps cross the kitchen. "Oh, Violette, do hurry! If only your friend can—"

But instead she made out the figure of a uniformed man standing in the shadows. Frightened, she tried to sit up, but was gripped by a new spasm and fell back. When she was able to catch her breath at last, she could only stare helplessly up at Roger. He said nothing to her, but took a towel and gently mopped her brow. Although she could not tell him so, she was comforted to see that his face showed real kindness and sympathy.

While Nicole threw herself about, she was barely aware of sounds in the kitchen: Roger's voice issuing commands, hurried footsteps, banging doors, strange voices, and then a circle of women, all strangers, leaning over her. Someone, an old woman with a steady, authoritative voice, gave her directions that made sense, that offered her great relief; and after minutes (or was it hours?) of purposeful effort—at last she understood the word *labor*—she produced a pink and healthily screaming baby boy.

When the infant was washed and dressed in a white gown she had sewn herself, and placed tenderly in her arms by Violette, Nicole had to endure a few minutes of animated conversation by the crowd of women who gathered around her bed to toast the baby with glasses of wine.

"What will you name him, citizeness?"

"I will call him André." She had wanted desperately to name him Guillaume, or William, but feared to give Roger such a clue to his paternity, and picked instead the French version of Andrew, the name of William's father, a fact hopefully beyond Roger's power of discovery.

"To little André Duchamp, son of Citizen Colonel Duchamp," the midwife declared, raising her glass. "May he follow in his father's glorious footsteps." When someone offered her a glass so that she could join the toast, Nicole declined, pretending weakness. She could hardly drink such a salute. When the well-meaning but extremely fatiguing little group finally left her alone, she whispered to the baby that he was in fact Andrew Fraser, the tenth Duke of Falkland. Someday, when Beaux-Clervaux was hers again, she would have the finest clarets shipped to Langmuir Castle and there drink a proper toast: "To Andrew, Duke of Falkland. May he have a long and happy life, and may he follow in the glorious footsteps of his true and dearly beloved father!"

She crooned over her baby the next day, noting with great pleasure his resemblance to his father, especially the forehead and chin. Perhaps too the eyes were more like William's than her own, although little André's colorless fuzz seemed to promise light hair rather than William's dark mane.

In other times she would have sought a christening for the boy, but now when the ceremony was illegal and very dangerous, and watched as she was by the republican Violette, she could not accept the risk. Even if she had been able to win Violette over to her side, the maid would undoubtedly have wanted to attend and expected to hear the boy proclaimed André Duchamp, son of Roger. Nicole planned instead to postpone the service until Abbé Harbert would be released from prison, as surely he must be before many months. Then she would hurry to him and ask him to execute a certificate of her marriage to William and privately to christen her child as the son of his true father. Then someday when the war with England was over at last, she would slip away with her baby, cross the Channel, and claim the child's rightful title.

As she mooned and fussed over André, at last it crossed her mind to wonder about Roger, and she hastily asked Violette where he had spent the night. "I don't know, missy," she admitted, hating to distress Nicole at such a time. "I don't know what trouble the two of you has had, and it ain't hardly my business, but I can tell you truthfully how worried your husband was about you last night. He ordered me very sharp-like to run get a good midwife, and a real doctor if we needed. Money was no object, he said, and pressed pieces of gold into my hands right then. I think he only left the flat because he was afraid of suffering and screaming and the like. There are few men as can stand all that. No doubt he'll be back tonight to see the fine boy you have given him."

Violette was right. A solemn Roger appeared at nightfall, bearing a bouquet of flowers that he had handed awkwardly to Violette to put in a vase. When he approached Nicole's bed, she thanked him promptly and sincerely for hiring the midwife.

"Allow me to congratulate you on your safe delivery of a son," he said as stiffly and correctly as though he were addressing the wife of his commanding officer.

"You have always been so very generous, Roger. I know what a dreadful shock all this has been—"

But when he flushed and turned away, she suspended her peacemaking. Watching tensely as he walked toward the baby's cradle, she thought for a second he might express his hatred in some terrible act against the child, but then she saw his face take on a look of awe, and relaxed and told herself how foolish she had been.

"He will be handsome—and probably blond like yourself," he said. "His father then was fair also?"

"Yes," she lied.

"What have you named him?" His voice was strained.

"I have called him André."

"André? An excellent name," he said archly. "Since I know it was not your father's, or an adaptation of your own or your mother's, may I ask if it belonged to one of your grandparents?"

"No, it did not." When he smirked at her knowingly, she met his stare and said, "Think what you want, Roger. Believe, if you choose, that I named the child for his father. In truth, the man's name is not one I care to recall."

"The matter is of little concern to me," he said snappishly, but in spite of his manner she sensed he was relieved, believing her pretense of no longer loving the man. Encouraged, she took the opportunity to congratulate him on his new promotion.

"Yes, it is a great honor to be made a colonel at such a young age, an honor of which I must strive to make myself worthy," he said pompously, preening before the mirror. When she paid him several more compliments, which she knew he fed on, he finally turned to her with a self-satisfied smile.

On the following day, Roger told her he had just registered the birth of the child in the Mairie. When she gasped in surprise, he added quickly, "But it is required by law. Did you wish to have to do it yourself?"

"Under what name—?" She hardly dared ask.

"André Duchamp," he said with what sounded like a note of pride.

"Duchamp?" she repeated disbelievingly. "And yourself as the father?"

"Of course."

Shaking her head wearily, she said, "Roger, I will never know how to—thank you."

"You have assured me you care nothing for the baby's natural father. You have even claimed he is dead. In any case I am willing to try to make a fresh start. When I return from my new campaign, on which I must leave tonight, we can undertake to build a happy marriage." Then he bent down to give her lips a kiss meant to promise much.

Just before he left the room, he added, "The Registrar required a second name for the boy, so I selected Robert after your father." Smiling and nodding to acknowledge her thanks in advance, he did not wait for a response before he vanished through the door.

Of course she had adored her father, and might well have picked his name herself. But just the same, she would have liked to have a chance to make such a decision. Then with a little laugh she told herself she was probably lucky Roger had not decided to name the baby for himself.

During the spring months, Floréal, the month of blossoms, and Prairial, the month of pasture, Paris glutted itself on the daily bloodletting by the guillotine. Nicole read the ever-growing lists in the *Moniteur* with horror, often seeing some name she remembered from the Conciergerie or La Force. Then the insatiable Comité began to destroy its own, and Danton, once the most powerful man in France, was led to the scaffold. At last the impassioned, relentless Robespierre held the reins of power.

For months the churches of Paris had been prey to official and unofficial violence. The royal sepulchre at St. Denis had been opened, and the bones of Kings and Queens of France dead hundreds of years were desecrated. Notre Dame was vandalized, its treasures stolen, and all its statues except one decapitated and thrown into the Seine. Only the proud and beautiful Virgin holding her babe had been spared. The mobs of Paris had slaughtered a thousand women, innocent and guilty, including their own queen, but they could not bring themselves to touch the holy Virgin. Finally the government decreed a Festival of Reason in the cathedral in which an actress, costumed as the Goddess of Liberty and wearing the red *bonnet*, sat on a throne. Roses covered the altar, and a corps de ballet danced in the nave. Gossip had it that prostitutes plied their trade in the side chapels to complete the profanation.

Every park was a parade ground for the drilling of regular troops and militia, for many men were needed to suppress large uprisings in the provinces. Nicole watched from her windows as young pupils from the École Militaire marched on the quays along the river. In spite of herself she would sometimes stop her stroll so that little André could listen to children singing the *Marseillaise* or the *Ça ira*.

>*Ah! Ça ira! Ça ira! Ça ira!*
>*Les aristocrates à la lanterne,*
>*Ah! Ça ira! Ça ira! Ça ira!*
>*Les aristocrates on les pendra!*

"Ah, it will go! Take the aristocrats to the street lamps. We will hang them there!" The song was the rage of Paris, but she would thank heaven that André was too young yet to mouth the words, and then she would hurry on, only to be stopped in the next street perhaps by a serpentine of dancers performing the Carmagnole, the rollicking dance that had originated among workers in southern France.

While Nicole hated all things associated with the revolutionary cause, she feared to make her attitude known, even to Violette. Once while she sat on a bench in the Luxembourg Gardens with little André at her feet on the grass, she joined in a conversation with some mothers and others sitting around her, and when pressed to accept a pile of rags to tear for bandages for the army, could not refuse. Promising herself she would break away in a few minutes, she heard an elderly man begin to extoll the recent French victory over the British at Toulon. "At last we have made the English devils run! They are our oldest, our hereditary enemies, our despised foes throughout history," he ranted.

When someone proposed the Prussians or the Austrians for that distinction, the old man would not hear of it and abused the English for every crime from the murder of Joan of Arc to the current blockade of all French coasts that threatened to strangle the nation. Sputtering and choking alarmingly, he capped his argument, "Was not Falkland an Englishman! No man rescued more *noblesse* nor gave greater comfort to the despised king and queen. Did he not nearly save the king from the guillotine, then somehow rise from his own grave and make an incredible attempt"—she could tell from the man's tone that he admired the heroic feat in spite of himself—"to save the queen before he finally got the gory death that he deserved!"

Rising dizzily, dropping her bandages, Nicole put her hand to her forehead and then when she had steadied herself a little, bent down to pick up André and ran from the park. Somehow she must shut out all voices of hatred, all signs of the war. She vowed to keep to herself henceforth, so that she could pass her days peacefully and think only of her fat, happy baby and the beauty of the city in spring.

It was quite safe, she found, to wander along the quiet quays of the Ile St. Louis, then cross the little bridge to the Cité and the quai de la Corse, where she loved to show André the flower and bird markets. But sometimes she discovered with a little cry that she had gone too far and was within sight of the Conciergerie and the quai de l'Horloge where William had died. Then she must turn and run away.

And she would shudder if she allowed herself to walk past the damaged portals of Notre Dame. But quite by accident she came upon the peaceful beauty of the deserted cloisters of the cathedral, and often sat with André in the little overgrown garden that had once belonged to the canons. Or she would walk around the plundered palace of the archbishop, just behind the cathedral apse, and pass the afternoon in its abandoned apple orchard, which was so clearly visible from her own balcony.

It was in the little orchard one afternoon that she opened the latest copy of the *Moniteur* and turned first, inevitably, to the list of executions. With a groan she saw that at least thirty people had died the day before. As her eye traveled down the list, she stopped with horror at the names of the Comte and Comtesse Valérien. What monsters could have ordered the deaths of such frail souls! Were there no depths to which the Comité would not sink? Next they would be guillotining cripples or children!

Then she recalled with a twinge of fear that the old couple were the only witnesses to her marriage. She had hoped she would be able to obtain their signatures on the document the abbé would prepare for her, although she had anticipated that one or both of them might be dead of old age. Now there was just that much less chance of proving her marriage. If something should happen to the Abbé Harbert. . . .

Henceforth she could not wait each day to read the lists. By the beginning of Thermidor, the month of heat, the numbers had climbed to sixty a day, and she always felt a wave of sickness as she read, even when she recognized none of the names. Then one afternoon, the list began proudly with the name Philippe Rohan, Prince of Soubise. With an exclamation of horror, she thought back to that glittering evening in the Galerie des Glaces and Philippe's shy efforts at flirtation. How charming, how young and innocent. . . . But even more vivid in her memory was the mischief at the faro table between Falkland and the queen. Indeed, William had been irresistible to the ladies, she thought with a sad little laugh.

As her eye traveled carefully down the long list, she was relieved to find that she knew no one else, no, not one more. . . . But then she saw the last name. Last. Yes, it should be last. They were well advised to try to hide it. What possible justification, even in the most demented mind, could there be for the murder of the Abbé Harbert?

Nicole was devastated by the news, and took to her bed for the rest of the day. She grieved almost as she had for William in the Conciergerie, imagining the heart-rending scene when Harbert was finally called to the tumbril, wondering what she could possibly have done to help him, if somehow Roger might have arranged his release or at least his transfer to some prison outside Paris. How well she remembered Harbert's heroic dedication to the prisoners. Never had she known anyone with such powers of self-sacrifice.

And with a great sinking feeling she realized she had lost the only chance to prove her marriage with some vestige of legal evidence. William, the comte and comtesse, now Harbert—*all* dead; no one else had known of the ceremony, not even a guard had had the slightest clue. They had all been too careful.

What lay ahead of her now was the most dismaying prospect. Certainly if she had had only herself to consider, she would have lived out her life in obscurity here in France. Once she appeared in England with her claim of having married Falkland she would be exposed to virulent abuse as a loose woman, one more of many mistresses, one who had merely had the luck to conceive a child who resembled him. Now that the duke was safely dead she had come forth with a fanciful story about a marriage ceremony to steal his title and his wealth for herself and her—bastard.

How much easier it would be to remain here on this quiet quay with the undemanding Roger. But instead, she must respect William's command on that last long day of waiting in La Force to present a kind of password to the king. How much more insistent William would have been —would be now—if he had known that she already carried his son in her womb.

Again and again she reworked the plans in her mind. As soon as the war with England ended, and she and André could cross the Channel with some safety and dignity—there must be no more ordeals like that of the Portuguese fishing boat—she would present herself in London at the offices of Botwhistle, Feather, and Armacost, who would surely assist her with advice and money in her status as William's ward, if no other. With their help she would address herself to the king.

Everything depended on King George's acceptance of her story. She would be revealing to him a sworn secret that he would recognize William would never have disclosed except for the most solemn purpose. The duke's own father, wishing to give no appearance of currying favor with his monarch, had severely suppressed the story of saving the young prince's life.

What had been the original deed exactly? William had told her that his father had saved the boy's life on board ship—that was all. She imagined a violent storm during which Duke Andrew—as powerful as a bear and even taller and heavier than his own son, she had learned at Langmuir—had grabbed the prince just as a wave washed the deck and lashed the smaller man and himself to a mast. There they had ridden out the storm. The ship had been in some northern sea in winter. Yes, they were returning home from a Baltic port after a state visit to Berlin—but how could she have known that?

Was it only her fertile imagination? No, she was not just guessing. She had heard the story somewhere. But where? Not at Langmuir. The memory was too dim. The source could only be her own father. Of course he had talked every day of Duke Andrew when he was writing his long work about him.

Then Nicole woke up one night in the small hours and sat bolt upright. She was sure the "secret" was actually reported in her father's biography of Duke Andrew! As a girl of fifteen or sixteen she had had to prepare the manuscript for the printer in her careful copperplate script. How she had hated the endless job! Even though her father tried to persuade her she was receiving an excellent education in European history, she sometimes copied without good concentration, only praying she would not omit a word and have to do the whole page over again. It was not surprising that today her memory of the text was far from perfect.

Somehow she must get her hands on the six volumes, regretting now that she had left her own set for Robbie when she fled Langmuir. Early the next morning, she hurried to visit booksellers in the Latin Quarter, but was told at every shop that the work was out of print. Finally a dealer suggested that she try one of the *cabinets de lecture*, where she could pay by the hour for the use of the volumes.

In the little reading room near the church of Saint-Germain-des-Prés, she was frightened to find a group of sansculottes—unwashed, unshaven and red-bonneted—who were speaking jocularly of the guillotine and reading the most militant journals. She had apparently blundered into one of the radical clubs that had fueled the Revolution. At first she thought to run out, then noticed the large collection of books, and summoning up her courage, asked for the work by title and author.

"Why do you want to read about a villainous enemy of the French Republic?" demanded the fierce old woman who kept the shop, obviously believing the book about Duke William.

"But—my husband is—er, a writer for the *L'Ami du Peuple*," Nicole said, picking the name of Marat's famous journal, "and he has sent me to take notes for an attack he is writing on our notorious foe."

Expressing hearty approval, the old woman hurried to find the volumes, placed them on a table, and deferentially pulled out a chair. For half an hour, Nicole read with tears in her eyes as her father's beloved voice spoke to her once again. Then at last she found the dreaded passage. Her father had described in great detail the dramatic incident on the Baltic Sea.

Frightened to seem to weep over an enemy in these militant surroundings, yet reluctant to part once again with such poignant reminders of her father, she held her hand lovingly on the leather bindings for a few minutes, then when she could control her tears at last, paid the proprietor and hurried away.

Now she knew that William's device to win the king's support was valueless. Her father's work had sold well in its English edition. Perhaps the king himself had bought the six volumes or received them as a gift—perhaps even from William! She was surprised at the duke's failure to remember this crucial passage. But of course the work was extremely long. In any case she would be laughed at if she carried out his plan to win the support of the king. Clearly she had no choice now but to spend the rest of her life in France, raising her little boy as a French citizen: a boy named André Duchamp, son of Citizen Colonel Roger Duchamp.

Only a day later, Violette handed Nicole a letter from Roger, then hung over her as she read it. In his labored, painfully correct handwriting —she could not help comparing it to William's bold, extravagant scrawl—he informed her of his victories in Belgium against the Austrians where he had not only received great praise from his superiors, but had made a small fortune from payments of "appreciation" by war contractors. Of course she would be thrilled to hear, he stated confidently, that he had already arranged to buy the house in which their flat was located, and planned to restore it to its former beauty and grandeur. Nicole, for her part, must examine the lower flats as soon as their tenants quitted them, and using her natural feminine talents for decoration begin to make plans he would approve when he returned, as he expected to do in the near future, to Paris.

She passed on this information to the delighted Violette, then read the final lines on the letter to herself with what she had to admit was a little thrill of anticipation: "Dearest Nicole, time and distance have driven me nearly crazy with desire to consummate our marriage at last!"

The day had been extremely hot, and when Nicole said a fatigued good night to Violette, she watched sympathetically as the maid climbed to her tiny room just under the eaves. It would still be a furnace up there. She thanked heaven her own chamber could be properly shuttered all day long. Now she could throw open the doors and admit the gentle breeze which rose at last from the river. After kissing the sleeping baby, she slipped off her clothes without lighting a candle and put on a fresh nightgown made from the same soft, filmy batiste she put on André in summer. Standing in the open door to the balcony to let the breeze caress her body, she prayed no one could see her. But of course there were no windows facing hers. Deciding the quays were safely deserted, she boldly walked to the rail. Then slowly a boat bearing a lantern drifted down the Seine. She could just make out a man sitting on the gunwale, trailing his hand in the water. Did he turn his head toward her? Was he staring up at her? She jumped back a little, guiltily. But since there was no light behind her, she knew he could distinguish little more than a vague white shape.

The man would not be able to see her two swelling breasts, the nowslender waist, her ripe, rounded hips. William had observed more than once that she was excited by a man's eyes. Was it true? She blushed to realize that she might have derived a little wanton pleasure from the idea of the riverman's gaze.

She had been widowed more than nine months ago. Now her legal husband was on his way home expecting to assert his marital rights. As she climbed between the cool, starched sheets, she knew that in a week or a month Roger would lie here beside her. Could she actually let him make love to her when she still loved only William, and remembered the sensation of her true husband's mouth and hands and fingers as if they had excited her only yesterday?

What advice would William give her if he could? She could almost hear the mocking, satirical tone to his voice: "Obviously, madam, you have allowed yourself to go through a ceremony—*un mariage municipaliter* to be sure, but a marriage nonetheless—with poor Duchamp, you have let the world know you as his wife, and you have accepted his ample support for yourself and your child. Why not grant the poor beggar some small repayment for his pains? Or are you going to pretend hypocritically all your life that you can only feel sexual desire for one man?"

Of course William would ridicule all foolish sentimentality. And it was true she must adjust to the idea of spending a lifetime as Roger's wife. Gradually she convinced herself that it was no sin to imagine the sensations she would experience here in this bed. Soon lying beside her, Roger would shyly press his lips to hers, then growing bolder quickly, would grab her to him, actually hurting her as he kissed her hungrily. His arms would bind her close, and she would soon feel his swollen organ pushing against her nightgown just between her thighs.

Then suddenly he would stop, throw down the covers, and pull the gown off over her head. She fervently hoped he would want her naked, as William had. Her pride still suffered from Roger's look of revulsion when he had stared at her pregnant body. Now she wanted to show him that she was beautiful once again, her limbs fleshed out, her stomach no longer swollen. Made restless and eager by her own erotic thoughts, she believed she could hardly wait to abandon herself to the frantic hands that would knead her breasts and hips and buttocks, could hardly wait to feel him force apart her thighs, and then push greedily into her until he satisfied them both.

"He'll be a general someday soon, citizeness," Violette said, musing happily as she sat knitting in the kitchen.

"A general?" Nicole murmured.

"Your husband! I said your husband will be a general soon! Your head must be full of plans for the fine new mansion today. Since Citizeness Laroche has gone out to rent herself another flat, perhaps you would like her servant to show you the luxurious details of the first floor. There are marble floors and whole rooms of the carved boiseries of Louis XV, and a curving staircase of beautiful *ferronnerie*."

"No, no, Violette, I will not trespass in her apartment."

"Then come and see the basement flat of poor Eloy, the *charbonnier*. It is the old kitchen with a whole wall of brick ovens, and a sub-basement cut out of solid stone, containing a great wine cellar, a root cellar, and a deep ice pit so cool that the ice can last all summer long. His family would love to show us around, and afterwards perhaps you could give them a little tip."

"No, I will wait, thank you. The truth is I have little eagerness to plan a pretentious house. I have been happy here in this small flat—far happier than I ever dreamed."

Violette made a moue that asked what one could expect from a little goose who would seek to spend her whole life in a convent. "*Maîtresse*, the world is not such a bad place after all. You cannot hide away all your life. Put on your wig and come with me early tomorrow morning to buy yourself a new summer dress so you will be pretty for the citizen colonel when he comes home. Then we can go along together," she said slyly, "to watch the guillotine."

"The guillotine! Never, Violette, and I forbid you to go!"

"But citizeness, it is the execution of the devil Robespierre himself.

Never has there been such an occasion. It will mean the end of the Reign of Terror at last!"

Finally Nicole relented and the maid was allowed to attend, but Nicole refused to accompany her and hated to have to listen to the descriptions afterward of the jubilation matching that at the death of Marie Antoinette only nine months before. Violette related with relish how one member of the Comité, Couthon, was so grossly crippled—by syphilis, it was said—that he could hardly be fitted into the lunette at all. Robespierre was made to wait till last. Then, his head bandaged after a suicide attempt, he was forced to sprawl with appropriate symbolism in the blood of all the others who had preceded him.

Despite her aversion to the grisly proceedings, Nicole paid a sou for a newssheet offered to her the next day as she stood in a long line to buy fresh milk. Clearly the pendulum, having swung all too far, had now returned; and she was excited by the implications of Robespierre's death. After reading the comment on the execution, she looked at the bulletins from the battlefronts. Evidently, Belgium was entirely secured to the French. She half expected to find Roger's name, but then the reports were skimpy, and the paper only a poorly printed, fly-by-night sheet she had never seen before.

Just as she was about to offer it to some neighbor in the line, Nicole's eye fell on a small paragraph on the back. Under a caption that said simply, "Copied from the British Press," she read the following brief report: "His Majesty King George III has announced the betrothal of his daughter H.R.H. Princess Charlotte Augusta Matilda, the Princess Royal, to William Andrew James Fraser, Duke of Falkland."

20

Nicole stood paralyzed with amazement. What could the paragraph possibly mean? She read it again and again. Her eyes, her brain must be playing tricks on her. The name of the duke must be Sutherland or Rutland or Cumberland. But no, there it was, Falkland, with his proper first name, and the second name she recognized so well as his father's and her own son's.

Then as someone behind her in the line nudged her impatiently, she realized what must have happened. Of course some relative of William's had claimed the title, a cousin or even a second cousin. There was a new Duke of Falkland. Why had she never thought about it before? Just because William had had no children at his death did not mean the title would become dormant.

So then this cousin must coincidentally be named William Andrew. An unlikely coincidence, but there it was. How else could she possibly explain the paragraph? Then of course there was the further coincidence of the betrothal with the Princess Royal. Was the king equally partial to this duke, was the princess as infatuated as she undoubtedly had been with the dashing William? No, Nicole shook her head. These improbabilities were too overwhelming.

What then? The newssheet, admittedly haphazard, must have made a jumble of some old story. Perhaps to fill up space in a hurry, the editor had grabbed some old English publication that had probably said the betrothal was rumored or imminent. Yes, that must be it. Unlikely as it seemed, they had used an English paper at least—how old? Nine months. William had been dead nine months. Perhaps the English paper had in fact taken that long to reach Paris, and the writers of her newssheet had cared little about its age. Conceivably, a rumor of his betrothal could have circulated just before his death, because of course he could make no acknowledgment of his marriage out of fear for her. At last she accepted this theory, and took out a kerchief to wipe her brow. She must try at all costs to keep her sanity. She must not allow herself to seize on the only other possible explanation—that William was still alive.

But after another minute or two of racing thoughts, she gave up her place in the line, which represented a good hour of waiting, and ran to find a vendor from whom she could buy the *Moniteur*. Tearing it open feverishly, she could locate nothing about William. Then she thought to ask the man if he had kept any old issues, and after poking through some stacks, he offered her three back copies. Buying them all, she started home, turning the pages as she walked.

It was in the middle of the Pont Marie that she read in an editorial tirade, "At last we know that the blackguard Falkland did not die after all in his assault upon the Conciergerie, but has been recuperating in England these months where he is about to receive the highest reward for his insults to France. King George will give him his own daughter as bride, in a marriage that will clearly establish the ascendancy of this archenemy of the French nation."

She sat down on the edge of the bridge, teetering dizzily. How was it even possible? Had he merely pretended unconsciousness that dawn on the quay, and somehow overpowered the guards when they leaned to pick him up, overpowered them just at the moment Nicole had fallen in a faint? Had he then jumped in the Seine and swam away, later to be carried home to London by his agents, where he had obviously forgotten all about her. Staring down now at the swift current of the river, she longed to throw herself in. Of course their pathetic little marriage ceremony had never meant anything to him. He had lied to her, lied to obtain her easy compliance with his sexual demands. Perhaps he had half believed what he had said to her then. Perhaps not. His suggestion for her to approach the king had been pure trumpery. Of course he had not wanted to write out any letter attesting to their marriage. Perhaps he had never intended to save her at the Conciergerie, only the queen. Why else had he waited so long to force his way into the prison? Either he had always planned to or had resolved after he had returned to London to obey the king's wishes and marry Princess Charlotte.

But then Nicole cried aloud and pounded her forehead with her fist. How could she be so stupid! All the months she had thought he was dead, he had believed *she* was! Of course her own death had appeared on the official list, and that list, containing as it did the name of Queen Marie Antoinette, had been reprinted in every country in Europe!

Grand Dieu, then it was a miracle after all! Her child would have a father, and she would have a lifetime of love and happiness! William was alive and he loved her still! Yes, of course he did! Of course he had been devastated when he read, perhaps in some hiding place in Paris where he had been carried by accomplices to recover from his wounds, of her death on the guillotine. He had lain grieving for her, perhaps near death as in La Force, even as she was exchanging marriage vows with Roger or displaying her swollen belly to him or lying forlornly in his bed, despairing of the future.

But then home in England, still mourning, William had finally consented—hadn't it been rather early? no, she decided firmly—to wed the princess. And now the bigamous marriage could take place any day! Somehow Nicole must get word to William that she was still alive!

But how could she dream of getting a letter through the British blockade? And if the letter were stopped and read by French censors, her child's life and her own would be worthless once they were known as Falkland's family. But still she must try by some means to let him know she was still alive. She had no idea how soon the wedding might be expected. In France a betrothal sometimes preceded the actual marriage by many years. But surely with this bride nearing thirty there would be no such delay. What if the vows were spoken before Nicole could notify him? Then of course the marriage would have to be annulled. It could be, couldn't it? Even though there were, she knew, widespread fear and hatred of Catholics in England, and even legal restrictions against them? With a shudder, Nicole realized that the chances of repudiating a royal wedding, accompanied as it would be by public festivities—feasting, bonfires, balls, masques, and the like—were extremely slim. Instead some official decision would be made that the little prison ceremony had never had any validity, no doubt because it had been illegal in its own country, and William would have to abide by it.

She had almost forgotten about Roger when he burst upon her one morning attended by a crowd of aides-de-camp and orderlies. Within an hour he had summoned a dozen workmen to begin the remodeling of the house. Violette and she were kept hopping the rest of the day running his errands, moving possessions from one room to another, and trying to provide ample food and drink for his hungry retinue.

It was only at midnight, after she had helped the exhausted Violette wash the day's accumulation of pots and pans, that she climbed into the brass bed beside Roger. Dreading to face the one wifely duty she could not possibly perform now that she knew William was alive, she prayed that he was already asleep.

But in a moment he whispered, for fear of being overheard by his orderly sleeping in the kitchen just next door, "Roll over toward me, dearest."

She reluctantly obeyed and said, "I am so very tired, Roger."

He rose on one elbow to look at her admiringly in the moonlight, and traced his finger around the curve of her cheek and across her full lower lip. "I will not exhaust you, Nicole," he said. In a moment he began to open the little pearl buttons at the neck of her nightgown.

Nicole took a deep breath and told him, pretending great embarrassment, that she was prevented by a certain regular indisposition from performing the act he wished.

Even in the dark she could sense his irritation. "A pity," he finally murmured, but proceeded to open the rest of the buttons. As he reached inside to touch her breasts, she groaned inwardly, believing that he intended to ignore her warning. She lay submissively while he groped her breasts, teasing, even squeezing them painfully, almost as though he enjoyed the discomfort he knew she must be suffering. But then abruptly he fell back on the pillow and adjusted the covers until he was ready to sleep. "No doubt it is just as well," he said.

"Just as well?"

"At least I know you aren't pregnant again by some other man!"

In moments he was snoring peacefully, but Nicole could only lie and stare at the open shutters, wishing the bed were closer to the window, wishing she could feel a cool breeze and glimpse some beautiful scene to soothe her. She smarted from his insult, and excited as she was by his manipulations, could only long for William. *Mon Dieu,* how could she ever have lain here in this very spot and lusted—yes, it was the only honest word—for Roger? How ashamed she was! How could she ever have imagined that she desired Roger? She had simply transferred William's attributes to the absent, half-forgotten Roger. It was William she had longed for, for whom she would always burn. Now she knew she would feel no joy until she could see William again, lie with him and love him, whether or not he could claim her as his legal wife.

In the commotion of remodeling and moving, Nicole had to decide how best to write to England. For several days she had planned a letter to the duke's solicitors, Botwhistle, Feather, and Armacost, but then realized if it fell into Roger's hands he would wonder how her family came to have English, not French lawyers, and could thereby discover her original relationship with Falkland. At last she settled on a letter to Langmuir Haven to Dr. Littleton. She would express her fondness, which was genuine enough, for himself, Kate, and the children, and say simply that she feared they had heard an erroneous report of her death on the guillotine. She would only seem to be obeying a sentimental impulse to tell old friends she was still alive. After great indecision, she decided not to mention the existence of little André. There was just too much risk. Roger was too clever. He would expect that she would ache to notify the father of her child of his birth, and he could easily find out that Langmuir Castle was in fact the seat of the Duke of Falkland.

Still, there were a hundred dangers. She feared that the curious Violette or even Roger would find the scraps of drafts she had abandoned, or even the final letter itself before she put it on board the *malle-poste*. And of course the greatest danger of all was that it would never be delivered. The *receveur* here in Paris had expressed great doubt. The only hope would be to divert it through some neutral country, probably Piedmont. As she wandered home disconsolately, she told herself she might as well have thrown a bottle into the Seine.

Every night she gave Roger some excuse for not allowing him to make love to her. At last when he grew very quarrelsome she was forced to concoct a story and say that Mère Carrel was distressed about her health, and advised her at all costs to avoid congress with her husband.

"I will speak to the woman!" Roger cried in outrage.

Nicole turned pale, but could only allow herself to shrug, praying that he would not carry out the threat. Early the next morning, she ran to the midwife, described a list of imaginary symptoms, and received a packet of dried *estragon*, tarragon, which she steeped as tea and sipped conspicuously whenever Roger was watching.

But after several weeks of observation, Nicole realized that Roger was so absorbed with the progress of the mansion, so preoccupied with uncovering all the ancient beauty of the structure and with each new extravagant purchase of furniture or bric-a-brac, that his emotional life was entirely full. Often he would talk enthusiastically about a new *étagère* or *bombé* commode he had bought, or rant about some tradesman who had cheated him until he fell asleep without remembering to ask Nicole if her condition had finally improved.

Even though he had begun to complain of the drain on his purse of the endless requirements of the mansion, he nevertheless purchased an expensive new *calèche*, bought two bays to pull it, and hired a coachman. Then ignoring her protests, he insisted on taking her to an expensive dressmaker where he ordered her a dozen gowns, and as many hats next door at a modiste's. Awaiting the delivery of this finery, he called in a coiffeur and worked with the man until together, with very little consultation with Nicole, they arrived at just the right style for her now-shoulder-length hair. Then one day he picked out her dress himself and made her ride beside him in the new *calèche*, fussing over her hair or hat even as they drove along. When she noticed that he constantly turned his head to see if she inspired comment and admiration in passing carriages, she finally understood that to Roger she was one more beautiful object to be displayed in proof of his own superiority.

How strange it was to think back to the afternoons in Rouen when she had sat and listened to him express his high hopes for the Revolution. She had not been free to give vent to her own opinions and was in fact rather admiring of his logic and fervor. But now that he had some money and status, he seemed only to want to imitate the aristocrats of the Ancien Régime whom he had helped destroy. One day he came home from an antique dealer's overwhelmed by his find of a portrait of the Chevalier Godefroy, who, Roger had recently learned, had originally built their house in 1640. "We will hang him in the salon," he announced proudly, then asked, "Do you see any resemblance?" as he positioned himself beside the painting. When she admitted that she did, he directed her, only half joking, that if she were asked she must not deny his relationship to Godefroy. Later, shaking her head at Roger's absurd ambitions, she told herself in an effort to be charitable that the poverty of his childhood must have left him incurably fascinated with money and position.

But at last she was free of him for a while again when he had to return to the front. The remodeling was finished, and she could not deny he had done a superb job. For a peasant boy, he had acquired amazingly good taste, drawing on his recent experiences in foreign countries where he was often headquartered in palaces and entertained by local nobility. Only rarely now did he have to turn to Nicole for advice. In every sense, the house was his, not hers. Although she respected the good work he had done, and admired the newly varnished boiseries, the sheen of the freshly polished marble, and the fine furniture that wanted only an occasional carpet or settee to be complete, she could feel no pride of possession. Perhaps because she was not able to think of herself as Roger's wife, she could not allow herself to love the house. But also she had developed a distaste for such pretentious finery, which was only an unpleasant reminder of Versailles or Falkland House or even Beaux-Clervaux—all sites that held distressing memories for her.

Nevertheless she was obliged to carry out the instructions Roger had left her to hire more servants, properly equip the big basement kitchen, and furnish the bedchambers and other secondary rooms. He also left her with a rather insulting list of things she must not undertake, for he insisted upon making every major choice himself.

Roger's little tyrannies were hardly noticed by Nicole, however, obsessed as she was by the thought that the royal wedding would be taking place any day. Never had she read the news so carefully, spending every free moment combing different journals for the dreaded story. But as the months passed, and she found nothing about Falkland, her hopes began to build. Perhaps someday, after all. . . . She hardly dared dream, knowing that next morning when she bought a newssheet her hopes of a lawful union could be be dashed forever.

Instead of the duke's name, she often now read Roger's in connection with the successful French invasion of Holland. Only when he wished her to carry out some order did she receive a letter from him. Lately he had taken to having her exchange visits with the wives of other officers. In one letter he wrote, "Please call immediately on the wife of General Pujol at 32 quai de Montebello. Do not bother to write and instruct me that protocol dictates she, as the wife of the superior officer, must call first. I can assure you this illiterate peasant woman from the Auvergne will be only too delighted to receive a visit from Citizeness Duchamp de Clervaux, as I wish you to call yourself in future."

What petty snobbery! To invoke the Clervaux name and estates, especially when she no longer owned them, had in fact gone to prison for owning them, and now was the ostensible wife of a high officer in the revolutionary army was laughable. How vulgar Roger was capable of being! Could he actually be styling himself Colonel Duchamp de Clervaux? She winced to think his own men might laugh behind his back, but then reflected that conditions had changed, that many titled *émigrés* had recently returned to France, lived quite openly, and had even seized power in certain regions of the south. Could Roger, far away in Holland, be more aware of the temper of the times than she was?

At last the beautiful spring month of Prairial returned again. Little André was almost a year and a half, and scampered about so energetically that it took two nursemaids to keep him from falling off the quay. Still having read nothing about Falkland, Nicole nurtured her dreams, only occasionally wondering if she could have missed the report. But she was not surprised that she had received no response at all from her letter to Langmuir. Nothing at all.

One afternoon returning in the *calèche* from a call on an officer's wife, she dismissed the coachman in front of her house and decided to take a walk before going in. After three days of rain, the air was delightfully fresh, the sky a paint-box blue, and the apple trees just ahead of her covered with pinkish-white blossoms fragrant enough that she could smell them across the little channel of the Seine.

But she had not strolled ten paces before she was accosted by a lone beggar so dirty and ragged, yet strong and husky, that she was quite afraid of him. She dug in her purse hurriedly to find him a coin, and then ran on, thankful that a man of respectability was approaching on the otherwise deserted quay. But when the well-dressed man had passed, the beggar came near again, seeming to want to trap her at the edge of the quay. She started to run ahead when he finally called out, "Mistress Nicole, please don't be afraid!" She stopped frozen in her tracks, almost afraid to look around. How long had it been since she had heard English spoken— English with an unmistakable Northumbrian burr!

She wheeled slowly and peered at the man's face, which was well disguised by streaks of dirt and a bushy red-blond beard. But the smiling blue eyes had once been so familiar to her in the faces of the dear children in the Manse at Langmuir Haven. This ragged beggar was Timothy Maclure.

Crying out, she wanted to embrace him, but he stepped back in time and shook his head. "Would be a strange sight for yer neighbors, mistress! We must be varry careful."

"Oh, Timothy, I can't believe it! I just can't believe it is you! Then did they get my letter at Langmuir? Does Duke William know I'm still alive?"

"Aye, on both counts, mistress, and ye can rest assured that His Grace was mightily thrilled. But it is not safe for us to talk here below the neighbors' windows. Yer lovely face is far too bright! Will ye meet me in an hour inside that great church there?" he asked, pointing toward Notre Dame.

"Oh, yes, Timothy, but I can hardly wait that long to find out—" she began, but he had already hurried away.

So William was thrilled! "Mightily thrilled," Timothy had said. Oh, thank God! Then he could not be married, surely! But Nicole was a little disappointed William had not come himself. Perhaps he would be along soon. Perhaps even tonight!

She was so excited her hands shook as she hunted through her wardrobe. Suddenly it crossed her mind that William might actually meet her now in the cathedral. Of course! That must be the reason Timothy, who had been given the tedious assignment of watching for her return, needed an hour to go find the duke and tell him Nicole had finally appeared.

Nervously she chose a blue chiffon frock and a natural straw bonnet in the new poke shape, and well before the hour was up, ran across the bridge that connected the two islands. She hurried up the rue du Cloître-Notre-Dame to the *parvis*, or square, in front of the cathedral, but Timothy was nowhere in sight. Raising the watch pinned on her bosom, she saw that he—or William—could not be expected for a quarter of an hour.

Turning reluctantly to face the cathedral, she read the banner that said, "The French people recognize the Supreme Being and the immortality of the Soul," then raised her eyes and sadly observed along a high gallery that ran the width of the façade, twenty-eight empty niches that once had held large statues. Believing them Kings of France, when actually they had been meant to be the ancient Kings of Judah, the mob had pulled them down with nooses and thrown them in the river. Only the gargoyles, much higher, remained to look down at her. Wild beasts or birds with human faces, they represented little devils who were believed to have been chased from the sanctuary by the Virgin, then miraculously recruited to stand just outside throughout eternity as guardians of her cathedral.

Steeling herself to the sight of further desecration, Nicole walked into the cool interior, dappled with the blues and reds of the stained glass. The stone walls rose to an incredible height, the vaults of the ceiling vanishing in mysterious shadows that might well be heaven itself. Though the Christian altar had been removed, and a handful of people were performing some strange rite in a chapel furnished with bizarre symbols, she was greatly relieved to find that the structure was undamaged. As long as she stayed out of earshot of the little group she considered sacrilegious, she found the otherwise deserted cathedral deeply inspiring. For many minutes she gazed reverently at the great northern rose window, when finally she heard Timothy calling to her.

He drew her behind a pier where they would not likely be seen or overheard, and she saw that he had cleaned his face and changed into the garb of an honest workingman. Hoping her disappointment was not too apparent, she could not refrain from asking, "Duke William—? I—thought perhaps he would come—?"

"And he would have! Without any doubt, he was more disappointed than ye can be, when on the very eve of departure, he was called to Windsor Castle by the tragic return of the king's lunacy. Only such a catastrophe would have kept him away, ye may be sure. He had talked to me of little else since the receipt of your letter not a fortnight ago. The letter had been many months in transit, and had crossed a dozen borders. It happened I was in the Manse playing with my childer at the very moment the letter was brung in to the rector. When I heard a strange cry from his study, I ran in, thinking the old fellow was taken bad, but there he was, laughing and crying all at the same time, hopping about waving yer letter for me and Kate to see—"

"Yes, yes, and Duke William—when did he—?"

"Well, I weren't thinking too clear at first, but the Reverend Doctor told me I must get word to the duke right away. So, seeing as I was going down in a day or two anyhow, I sent to get old Hodge at his brother's farm, and we started back to London in the coach that very afternoon."

"Did you carry my letter to His Grace?"

"Aye."

"And when he read it—?"

"His Grace stood up suddenly, very pale—well, he had seen a ghost all right, hadn't he?—and said in a strange voice, 'I must go back now—tonight!'"

"Go back?"

"He had just been in Paris secretly, but more about that later."

"And it was right then that he got word from Windsor Castle of the king's illness?"

"Nay, it was later. He could not leave that first night, as it turned out, because the gold did not arrive."

"The gold? I don't understand."

"'Tis a long story, Mistress Nicole—I guess I should be calling you madam now that you are—" He shook his head to clear it, obviously embarrassed by his breach of etiquette.

"No—please, Timothy! I will feel much more comfortable if you address me as you always have!"

"'Tis a long story, mistress," he resumed with a smile of thanks, and began to tell her how the duke had spent a month in Paris only recently in disguise, seeking to render his last great service to the French crown by —here Timothy swore her to absolute secrecy—accomplishing the release of little King Louis XVII from the Temple.

"And did he succeed?" she asked with excitement.

"Aye, varry nearly, and he would now have returned himself to finish the job, but I am back in his stead, and have with me a trunkful of gold to do the deed. 'Tis a king's ransom, truly—a veritable king's ransom! Soon I'll be killing two birds with one stone—if you'll pardon the phrase, missy —by carrying both ye and His Majesty away to England!"

"Oh Timothy, there will be another passenger!" she exclaimed, her face alight with pleasure. "I dared not mention it in my letter, but I have borne His Grace a son, a little boy I have named Andrew, though here in France we must call him André." Then realizing that Timothy must already have gathered she lived here as Roger's wife, she hastened to add, "He was born on the second of December, 1793, exactly eight months after William and I were separated in the prison of La Force."

But there was no skepticism on Timothy's face. "Oh, mistress—madam, I should say! What a wonderful day for the duke! I know what a happy man he will be." Beaming, he kissed her hand twice, three times. She would have thrown her arms around him, so delighted was she to unburden herself at last of her news and to stand now on the very brink of a safe and happy return to England, but the poor fellow would only be disconcerted. He was obviously preparing to treat her with even more deference.

"Is he healthy, then; the little fellow, Andrew?"

"Oh, yes!"

"And almost a year and a half? Does he run about strong-like?"

"Almost too much!"

"And talk gude already?"

"Oh, yes," she said proudly.

"And does he favor His Grace?"

"Indeed, though his hair is lighter, almost like mine. Perhaps it will darken later."

"Did ye ken Duke Andrew had a fair head? So ye have named him well. 'Twas the Duchess Isabella as was black as a gypsy."

Nicole met Timothy every afternoon in Notre Dame for the next three days, when he would report his progress in reconnoitering the little king's prison, and his plans for their journey to Calais. He had succeeded in buying an old coach, not rickety, but far from stylish. "Duke William has warned me not to make the same mistake as others made in the famous flight to Varennes, when the royal family attempted to escape the country riding in the most elaborate equipage on the road!" Falkland's plan was for Nicole to pretend to be the wife of some merchant, a draper perhaps, comfortably fixed but far from rich. Because they could not assume the added risk of a nursemaid, she must appear to be a mother accustomed to caring for her own children. The little king would travel as her son, and he would be instructed to call her *Maman*. "In appearance, he will fit well into yer family, for he is fair-haired; though if I may say so, madam, ye hardly look old enough to have a ten-year-old child."

"I will wear my hair in some severe style, Timothy," she said, with a little laugh. No problem could distress Nicole; she had never walked so lightly in her life.

"We will have room for two valises, hardly more. Will you be so kind as to purchase several changes of clothing for the little king. No doubt he is thin, having been in prison so long, though I have not yet been allowed to see him." Then Timothy described the precautions they must take at inns where they would be obliged to stop for horses and to take their meals. Whenever possible, she and the children should dine in a private room, but when she could not avoid the other patrons, she must be very careful how she addressed the king, and what names her little boy might mouth. With his majesty's permission, she would speak to him without royal styles at any time.

"Perhaps we should rename him, perhaps call him by his second name, Charles. No, it is too obvious. Perhaps... Léon...."

"Excellent, madam. I will inform him. The child will be far too thrilled that he is free to raise any objections."

"Will we be allowed to sleep at the inns?"

"No, regrettably. To save time we will travel on at night. No doubt it will be a somewhat grueling trip, but the coach offers wide benches, one for the king and one for ye and yer baby, if you will consent to the arrangement."

"Of course. But you yourself, how can you endure the long, unbroken drive?"

"Another carriage will follow us inconspicuously, and offer relief drivers and some protection if we should be detected." After cautioning her that she must do nothing to arouse suspicion in her household, he bid her adieu. "If all my plans go well, madam, I will call at your door in a dark blue coach late tomorrow afternoon with the little king already inside."

Giving most of her servants a holiday, she fussed all the next morning over her valises, packing the clothes she had bought for the king and selecting those of her things and André's that she would require on the journey to London. As she poked through her clothes, she passed over without regret all the expensive dresses Roger had bought for her, just as she had abandoned the remnant of the Versailles dresses at Langmuir Castle. At the sight of the blond wig, she cringed once again and thought with relief that she need never look at it again. Come as she had to Roger's flat virtually naked from the Conciergerie, she had no keepsakes from a previous life. Her only sentimental selections would be some of the baby clothes she had made for André herself and a shawl that Violette had knitted him—the poor woman would be pleased when she found Nicole had taken it. Finally she packed a picnic basket with a *couronne* of bread, a wedge of cheese, some apples, and a bottle of wine, and pronounced herself ready to leave.

Once again she would have to depart without a proper farewell to kind friends, and regretted especially that she had had to speak firmly to Violette only yesterday, for quarreling once again with the other housemaids. And then there was Roger—! How could she ever thank him, how could she ever begin to repay him? Once in London she would sit down and write him a long letter of explanation and appreciation—with William's permission, of course—and see that some transfer of funds was made.

But in a moment her buoyant spirits returned. Not only would she soon know all the delights of William's company and see his pride in their beautiful child, but she would have the satisfaction of helping to save the little king. She herself would finally take part in one of William's heroic deeds; and besides, she could befriend the poor boy who had lost both his parents and suffered great indignities, if not actual personal discomfort.

Only for a few seconds did she sometimes still doubt her future with William. His ties to the royal family must be even closer than she had imagined if he was required to stand by during the king's illness. Announcing his marriage would no doubt be even more awkward now the king was deranged. But if William chose to live with her secretly for some time, she cared little. It would be enough just to be with him at last.

As for his believing her story that she had never allowed Roger to know her as a husband, she had a few nervous moments. Actually she expected William would be ready enough to shrug off the thought she had slept with Roger rather as he had tolerated Sybille's infidelities. And she knew he would hardly have lived like a monk during the months he had thought she was dead. But then, of course, it was different for a man. She dearly wanted him to believe in her chastity, as well as her honest word, and remembered with hope his remark about how innocent her mind was. But the second half of the sentence had been, "even while you have the body of a saucy little trollop." How he loved to tease her! Had he ever really believed she had not lain with poor Simon de Brizac? She remembered his distressing sally, "Did he enjoy himself in your chamber of delights?" With a sigh she realized she would probably have to endure many stinging jokes about the "saintly Frenchman who rescued girls from the guillotine but asked nothing for himself," and "the officer husband who slaughtered the enemy in battle but never once assaulted you in bed." He would shake his head, "So much for the famous French *virilité*," and so on and on.

By mid-afternoon she was standing at a window dressed to leave, while André played on the floor beside her. As soon as she heard the clatter of the coach, she would grab the valises that, along with the picnic basket and wraps for herself and the two children, she had hidden under the staircase. Perhaps Timothy would dart inside to help her with them, or she could load them herself if need be, then pop André into the cab, and they would be off. It would hardly take a minute from start to finish.

But as each hour passed and there was no sign of the blue carriage she began to fret. At dusk when some of her servants returned home, she wondered desperately what could have gone wrong, imagining all sorts of horrors: the trunk of gold seized but the king withheld, Timothy arrested, Timothy shot and lying bleeding somewhere.

And then at last she heard the wheels on the cobblestones and ran to open the front door. But as soon as Timothy saw her, he held up his hand as a signal to wait. Something had gone wrong. Jumping down from the box, he swung open the door with great anxiety on his face, and beckoned for her to look inside the coach.

As her eyes adjusted to the dim light, she made out a small, wraithlike creature almost covered by a linen bag that looked for all the world like a shroud and even seemed to smell of death. The child's chalky face with closed, sunken eyes showed no signs of life.

"Is he dead?" she whispered.

Timothy held a broken piece of mirror above the child's nostrils, and in a moment she saw some steam collect.

"Oh, thank God! Has he been asleep like this all the time?"

"Nay, his eyes was open when I entered into his cell. Oh, mistress, ye should have seen the filthy cubbyhole he had to live in! It is a wonder he is alive at all. I had to clean him a bit before I would even put him in this winding-sheet, which I then pulled up over his head, so that I seemed to be carrying out a dead body. Then when I laid him on the seat of the coach, he had a great fit of coughing and spat up blood."

"Timothy, we cannot go! It would be murder!"

"But what then, mistress? We may all be caught if we do not hurry on."

"He can stay here. My husband—the colonel is away. I will tell the servants that the boy is—a cousin—anything! The child of executed parents, which, God knows, is true enough!"

Though Timothy continued to protest, she would not hear of risking the boy's life on the arduous journey, and ordered him to carry the king up to a small third-floor bedroom. Then she urgently called Violette and told her that the sick child had been pronounced dead in the Hôtel-Dieu, but on the very edge of the ditch in the cemetery of the Madeleine de la Ville-l'Eveque where his guillotined parents had been thrown, this man, a gravedigger, she said pointing to Timothy, had heard a moan coming from the shrouded form. Discovering her name as next of kin on the death certificate, he had brought the child here. She had always loved her little cousin Léon dearly, and implored Violette to help her save his life.

To her relief the maid accepted the story without a question. Together they washed and dressed his thin body whose flesh was so waxy white it had seemed to have no blood circulating in it at all. The boy looked younger if anything than ten. Nicole would have guessed him at seven or eight. For a second it crossed her mind that some mistake had been made, that Timothy had been tricked. Of course the boy had reddish-blond hair, and perhaps some of the paleness of his skin could be attributed to heredity. But then Nicole made out the small but noble arch of his nose, and looking at him in profile almost exclaimed as she recognized the famous Bourbon feature. The child was undoubtedly his father's son.

Pretending to need to pay the gravedigger a suitable reward, Nicole slipped downstairs to placate the anxious Timothy. "At least there can be no mistake as to his identity," she began cheerfully.

"Madam, ye do not ken the dangerous situation I had to leave behind at the Temple Tower. Very likely, the officials I bribed have already run off to enjoy their new wealth and the deed has been discovered. The duke intended that the king's escape would go forever undetected, and they swore to conceal the fact at all costs, but the ecstasy on their faces at the sight of such incredible wealth persuaded me they would be capable of no such discretion. All the worse then that I was not able to buy the right sort of body."

"Right sort of body!" she exclaimed.

"Aye, madam. The duke had arranged with the commandant of the Temple that the king would be declared dead of natural causes. We was merely to supply them with a fresh corpse, a boy of the right age with fair hair. But when my body snatchers surveyed the current crop, so to speak, the best they could do was a beggar lad dead of starvation, fair-headed, but of a somewhat greater age. The truth is, missy, he must have been sixteen or seventeen, even though his body was very wasted, for I had to shave his fuzzy chin myself!"

"Oh, Timothy! Then the body will never fool the soldiers who discover it?"

"Never. So I would have chosen to get and run. 'Tis not too late, madam," he said beseechingly.

She wrung her hands for a few moments, then declared, "The duke would not want us to risk his life. In truth, I believe the boy will die soon anyway. Let us wait a few days. Here at least he can have a physician and a few medicines for whatever good they'll do him."

21

Not till the *Moniteur* article appeared did Timothy lose his grave expression. Then one morning a few days after the rescue, he flew to Nicole. " 'Tis a miracle, mistress!"

She tore open the paper and read the government announcement. The young pretender to the throne, as they described him, had died of natural causes in his quarters in the Temple—that was all. Had the officials really been duped? Would they actually bury Timothy's changeling, a street urchin, as the son of King Louis XVI and Queen Marie Antoinette? Surely they must be aware of the substitution, but were apparently only too happy to rid themselves of their embarrassing charge.

Timothy was inclined to relax and enjoy the greater security, but Nicole was only just awakening to her historic role and was awed by it. She now almost alone had the responsibility to save the King of France—if he could be saved—and to help him grow up and restore the monarchy and reverse the evil events of recent years. For the next weeks she hardly left his side, even though she had hired nurses and the whole household pitched in to save the boy. But despite his good care, and visits by more than one doctor, "Léon," as they all called him, made very little progress. He slept most of the time or lingered halfway between waking and sleeping in a strange trance. At no time did he talk or seem to understand what was said to him, and was too weak to roll over or raise his arms. Even when his eyes were open, he seldom bothered to follow his attendants as they moved about the room. The doctors said he suffered from a mental or emotional disturbance as well as the lung ailment that seemed likely to claim his life.

In a few days, Timothy left for London on a brief trip to report their altered plans to Duke William. At their last meeting in Notre Dame before his departure, Nicole took with her little André, so that Timothy could meet him at last and prepare to give a word picture to his father. Timothy eagerly took the little boy in his arms and won him over with a few jolly words. How good Timothy was with children, Nicole recalled from her days at Langmuir. As they parted, she asked him if he was willing to accept the risk of carrying a letter she had written to Duke William. She told him she had omitted all names and places, so there was nothing to identify any of them. Although she did not mention the fact, she had tactfully left the letter unsealed so that Timothy could privately read it to assure himself he was not carrying a document identifying him as the agent of the Duke of Falkland.

There was nothing in it he should not see. It was simply a loving letter that informed its recipient of the birth of his son, stated in somewhat vague words that the "current arrangement" in which the writer had to live was only a "pretense," and closed with a promise of undying devotion to her true husband.

Timothy kindly accepted the letter, and she added a dozen verbal messages for William: "Say I wanted so much to name the boy Guillaume, but did not dare. Ask His Grace if he is pleased with my choice. The boy has not been christened yet. We will do it early in England. Can you remember André's exact birth date? I was afraid to write it down. And tell him André is inches taller than other lads his age. And please say that I was standing just inside the iron gate at the Conciergerie but then fainted when I saw him lying wounded on the quay; and will you—"

But laughing aloud, Timothy finally begged for mercy. "My poor head is too crowded already, mistress! I'll never be able to remember it all."

"Give him all my love, dear Timothy!" she exclaimed as she pressed his hands in farewell.

One day at Léon's bedside, she groaned when a maid informed her that Roger had returned from his campaign. Slowly she rose, gazing anxiously at the sleeping boy. What in the world was she going to tell Roger? She had not expected him for several months and had believed she would be long gone by then. Suddenly he seemed a terrible threat to the little king. For one thing, Roger knew perfectly well she had no cousins. He had once questioned her closely about her living relatives.

But she hardly need have worried. Entering the library, she sensed even before she saw him that some important change had taken place. For one thing his retinue had grown threefold. Officers of many ranks crowded around the desk where he sat writing. When she saw that one of the aides bore the rank of colonel, she knew what must have happened. As the group parted for her, she saw from his heavy epaulettes and the gold-encrusted tricorne hat on the desk that Roger had been made a general.

Not only did he speak with a new calm authority to everyone, but his attitude to her was particularly ingratiating. She hastened to explain that Léon was actually a child she had known in La Force brought to her by a guard who had seen her on the street and had followed her home, to apprehend her she had feared at first, but as it turned out only to ask her to take the dying boy. She had told the servants he was her cousin merely because they must not know she had ever been in prison. But Roger only laughed at her fluster and praised her for her kindness to the boy. He had no interest in poking holes in her story, being far more absorbed by his own promotion, his successes in the recent campaign, and some mysterious plans he was making that seemed to include Nicole.

Urging her to join him on the settee when they were alone in the salon, he immediately embraced her as she sat down warily, and asked, "Is your —er, health improved?"

"No—no. It is—much the same," she stammered.

"I have spoken to a physician, and he has given me some medicines for you to take. And in addition he recommends travel as highly beneficial." Roger glowed at her as though concealing some marvelous secret.

"Travel! I can hardly go anywhere—!" she cried with alarm. What was Roger planning? She would die if she had to leave Paris now.

"My dear Nicole, I will simply not allow you to say no!"

Roger's coy refusal to tell her their destination and his endless talk about himself annoyed Nicole so much that she made little effort to be polite in the coach traveling south. At first she had paid no attention to their route, only noting as they left Paris by the Porte d'Orléans that at least she would not have to endure the sight of the ghost-ridden palace of Versailles. But when they passed through Angoulême and Poitiers, she could have little doubt Roger was taking her back to the Bordelais. Finally, at the first sight of the valley of the Gironde, she cried distraughtly, "Oh, tell me now, Roger! I can stand no more suspense!"

"Control yourself, dear Nicole. You are about to have a wonderful surprise."

For a minute she kept a stunned silence, guessing what he must have done. She could not accept his generosity. *Oh, dear God, not now!* Tears came to her eyes, filling them, running down her cheeks. At last she dug for a handkerchief, and failing to find one, had to accept Roger's, which he handed her in his calm, efficient way. "Then are we going to Beaux-Clervaux?"

"Yes."

"How is it possible?" she asked dully.

"My dear wife, can you express no gratitude when I have just bought back your inherited lands for a princely sum? The ringleaders of the thieves, a Georgeault and his cohorts, who could only mismanage the wineries, have now a fortune to squander. We shall see how long it takes them to return penniless and beg for their old jobs back."

Straining for every familiar sight, Nicole sat on the edge of the seat, one hand by the glass of the coach window. Farmhouses, châteaux seemed unchanged; the vines, as they should be now in Prairial, were in full leaf with small, hard, green grapes. She began to relax a little when she could see no signs of the Revolution. *Mon Dieu*, how beautiful the land was! More than five years had passed since she left reluctantly that night with William on the packet boat. How many things had happened! Happiness then despair at Langmuir, the flight to France, arrest, trial, prison, marriage to William, his supposed death, the close brush with the guillotine, the birth of André—the rescue of the king! The King of France lay at this very moment in her little bedroom, coughing, gasping, perhaps dying! And Roger! Roger had happened. And now just as she was ready to run to the arms of her real husband, Roger had ransomed Beaux-Clervaux!

At the first sight of her own land, she pressed against the window again. Yes, the vines were flourishing. There had been enough rain, but not too much. At last they climbed the long hill, and Nicole held her breath as the towers of the château gradually came into view. "Oh, Roger, I'm home! How can I ever thank you—oh, how can I ever tell you how much—?" She was crying with joy and squeezing his hands in gratitude. Beaming with satisfaction, Roger leaned forward to kiss her lips.

But when she threw open the carriage door and started to run across the grass, he called to her very sharply. "Madame! Return this minute! What are you thinking of, to leave your husband behind and rush ahead like an undisciplined child! There are eyes watching us this very minute." Obediently, she walked back to his side and took his arm, then marched beside him solemnly to the great studded door where he pounded with the iron knocker.

Nothing had changed, she assured herself. Sheep still nibbled the grass on the slopes of the hill, vines still climbed on the stones of the château. Then a puff of wind brought the faint odor of smoke. Not the pleasant smell of burning logs; it was the acrid, stale odor of something already burnt. Detecting it also, Roger pounded again more urgently.

Long minutes passed before Nicole recognized the sounds of someone working to lift the heavy bolt just inside. At last the wide door creaked open slowly, and Nicole cried out, "Oh, *mon Dieu*, Clémence!" and threw herself into the arms of her old cook, now completely white-headed.

They hugged and wept wordlessly, then at last Clémence managed to sob, "*Ma petite* Nicolette, we thought you were dead!"

"But you can see I'm not," Nicole said tenderly. "So now you must compose yourself! I'm home at last and—" Then the realization overwhelmed her that she could hardly be mistress of this château if she were living in England with William.

As Roger pulled Nicole along impatiently to explore the rooms, the cook grabbed at her sleeve with alarm. "No, madame! You must not look!"

"Not look? But why not?"

"They have destroyed everything. Just yesterday. Stole what they wanted and burned the rest—in the inner courtyard; it still smolders. The stone walls is black, and I thought for a while the east wing would catch. The devils was throwing clothes and chairs and mattresses down into the flames from upper windows. Then they drove off with wagons full of all the wine and silver."

Nicole dashed ahead of the others, through the now-empty Grand Salon and the dining hall, which held only the long table, no doubt too heavy for the vandals to carry, then stopped at a door opening on the courtyard. She gasped at the sight, then tottered as the stifling odor overwhelmed her. A great heap of half-burnt furniture, rugs, and draperies filled the whole *cour*, nearly covering the little fountain and spilling under the arches of the peristyle. The black patterns of flames and smoke marked the stone walls, and a wisp of smoke still rose from the center of the pile.

Frantically, Nicole ran into the courtyard and began to tug at the smoldering treasures. Under a heavy Turkey carpet, she discovered the priceless Gobelin tapestry that had hung in the Grand Salon, and called for Roger and Clémence to help her pull it out of the pile. But when she lifted off a layer of carpet, some embers below burst into new flames, and Roger was barely able to restrain her from beating at them with her hands.

"You are mad!" he cried. "You will set your clothing on fire, and scar yourself for life!"

"Oh, Roger, I don't care! I can't stand to see these precious things destroyed. You must help me!"

"We will send for some of the peasants to smother the fire and remove what can be salvaged." But when he asked Clémence to go for help, she told them there was no one left, no one able-bodied who was willing to work here any longer. Only Gaspard, who was old and feeble, now remained.

"But Maître Poujade and all the workers? Where are they?" Nicole cried. "I saw that the vines are healthy. The *taille*, the pruning, has been done this year. Someone has been working."

Dabbing her eyes, Clémence said that Poujade was dead. "He wouldn't take orders from Arnaud Coppin and Pascal, so they had him thrown in jail. Just to teach him a lesson, it was—they knew they couldn't get along without him. But Poujade was too proud for prison and it killed him. Hardly a week after he was locked up, they found him dead of his heart. His men is all scattered, many in the army, or driven off by Pascal's cruel and foolish treatment. And those as still have rebellion in their hearts refuse to work on this land they believe they deserve to own."

"But my hus—the Citizen General has paid them for their shares."

"Pascal and a few others took most of the money and ran. Good people like the Gaillards got only a handful of worthless paper."

"Oh, the Gaillards!" Nicole remembered with sudden pleasure. "Are they here? Are they well? Can't the boys come and help us? Surely they have not become militant revolutionaries!"

"No, they was always loyal to you and scoffed at Pascal. But Quentin was killed fighting in the Vendée, then Gabriel and Marc is away in the army somewhere. The old man is in bed from a bad beating he took from Pascal's men. Noémie married the Porcher boy, but he was killed at Valmy, so she lives at home again. They all want to see you down at the cottage, mademoiselle—I mean, madame."

"And the other *châtelains*, have they no men they can lend us?"

"But the *châtelains* is driven off. Only the Coppins remained, then after Arnaud was guillotined—"

"Arnaud guillotined!"

"Yes, madame. Many of the Girondist deputies was executed in the Terror, just after the queen; and soon his family's château was seized."

Nicole's depression deepened with each step as she toured the big stone house. She was drawn first almost magnetically to her mother's Petit Salon, but she cried aloud as soon as she entered the room. Not a single stick of furniture—the dowry pieces her mother had brought from Normandy—remained in the room. Gone was the delicate table between the pair of tall windows on which had sat the famous *coffret* that had held William's letters. Thank heaven she had impulsively packed the *coffret* that last day in a trunk that now safely reposed in the basement of Falkland House.

Nicole could not bear to look at the vile lavender, loud and pinkish, that the boiseries, once the palest green, had been enamelled. "Julie Georgeault wanted to make this her own drawing room, and chose this hue herself," Clémence said with contempt.

"My maid Julie! Living as the *grande châtelaine!* Was she happy, then, playing the impostor, trespassing in another's house?"

"I hardly think, madame. Pascal was a beast to her, and no servant would obey her orders."

"Not you then, Clémence? I'm not surprised," Nicole said with a little laugh.

"They lived here and I lived here, but I never cooked for them, and they never dared to ask."

"Was this house really a hospital or orphanage?"

"That was only a fraud, so Pascal could live here in grand style. There was never a patient or orphan came to the door."

Just as they turned to leave, Nicole glanced at the north wall containing the fireplace and saw the large portrait of her mother in the dark green gown. At first she exclaimed with relief, thinking the painting was undamaged, and then she saw the fine slit of a sword that ran the length of the figure.

"Pascal did it the first thing after he heard you was coming yourself. He thought it was your own picture, the likeness is so great. Don't weep now, mistress," she said, hugging Nicole. "It can be mended, I have no doubt."

Every other room had been similarly stripped and defaced, the culprits only leaving untouched what was too large or heavy to move: a great marquetry cabinet, *dressoirs* or sideboards, court cupboards, settles, armoires, fourposter beds. "My mother's little harpsichord?" Nicole cried, running into the picture gallery.

"Thrown into the flames."

"And the chapel?" she asked, her eyes wide with horror as she saw the door, knowing that the tombs of aristocrats had often been defiled.

"I locked it, mistress, then hid the key! They could not touch it, though they banged at the doors awhile."

Clémence took a huge iron key out of the folds of fabric that covered her ample figure and opened the wide door. Inside, their eyes very slowly became accustomed to the dim light. Why was it so dark? A little daylight was filtering in through the stained clerestory windows. Then Nicole realized that there was only one candle burning, a single votive light.

"For you, mistress," Clémence said. "I have kept it burning since you left five years ago."

"Dear Clémence, even when you thought I was dead?"

"For your soul, as had not had holy rites," the woman answered gloomily, reliving the past for a moment.

"Oh, Clémence, how you have suffered!" She hugged her lovingly. The poor woman had always tried to be a mother to her. "But now I am going to tell you something wonderful. I have a little son named André, who is a year and a half and very healthy and handsome, and you must light a candle for him and keep it burning every day until he can come and live here too. Will you do that? Promise me!"

"Of course, madame," she cried, with tears of joy. "And for your husband? Shall I light one for him also?"

"Yes, Clémence, for—my own—beloved husband. Burn one always," Nicole said with measured words.

The old woman's eyes bore into her, but she said nothing. As they exchanged stares, Clémence's eyes narrowed. Could it be possible? Was this pretentious general not her husband after all? At last she whispered, "*Monsieur le duc!*" But Nicole would only regard her unblinkingly in answer.

Then to avoid the old woman's scrutiny, she hurried down the aisle and stood between the brasses that marked her parents' tombs. Each had been polished recently and bore a fresh bouquet of *muguets,* lilies of the valley. "Bless you, dear Clémence," she murmured with tears in her eyes.

Dinner was served to Roger's discomfort in the great kitchen, which had not been ransacked. Nicole refused to ask Clémence to carry the food upstairs to the great hall even though Roger had salvaged two chairs that had only been charred by the fire. He admitted that he enjoyed Clémence's sweetbreads in *buerre noir, boeuf à la mode,* and apricots in frangipane; but never ceased cursing the thieves who had looted the wine cellars. Not a single drop of wine or cognac remained in the whole château, and Roger grimaced theatrically every time he took a sip of coffee to wash down his food.

Immediately after dinner, he tried to pull Nicole upstairs to her chamber, where Clémence had placed on her fourposter bed a mattress overlooked in some servant's room. But Nicole broke away stubbornly, knowing perfectly well what he intended. After all, he had dosed her with foul-tasting medicines for a week.

"No, Roger, I want to go for a walk. I can't let the day end without touring my lands."

"The lands you can thank me for!"

"Yes, of course. And I do!" Oh, dear heaven, how could she discourage his sexual advances, yet display a decent amount of gratitude for this overwhelming gift he had made her? "Come with me, then. We can take a constitutional together. I haven't even seen Jupiter yet!"

But she noticed instantly the look of horror on Clémence's face at the mention of the horse's name. "*Mon Dieu,* what is it!" she gasped.

"Pascal killed him, mistress! I couldn't tell you before. He knew he was your horse. Yesterday, he took out all the others, then locked Jupiter inside, and burned the stables to the ground. The screams of that noble horse is still ringing in my ears!"

Roger folded the sobbing Nicole in his arms and led her upstairs. She walked along beside him unthinkingly with her head on his shoulder. "Let me take care of you," he soothed. "When you lie down and feel my arms around you, you will relax at last. What dreadful luck that we have no cognac tonight. It has been a frightful shock for you, I'm sure—your childhood pet so cruelly destroyed!"

He lay her on the bed in her old room. "Poor little darling! You must stop crying now." He unbuckled his boots, removed them, and placed them squarely beside the bed, while she only stared at a worn quilt she had not seen since she was a child in the nursery. He lay down beside her, and in a moment had slipped his hand inside her low, ruffled neckline and taken possession of one breast as though it belonged to him.

"Oh, Roger, you must not!" The impossibility of her situation brought on a new torrent of tears.

"Of course you are upset. The doctor explained to me that young women after their first childbirth, dreading a return of the same pains, often refuse to allow their husbands their rightful privileges. A kind of hysteria has overtaken you and you imagine you suffer from an illness that does not really exist. But the good doctor has informed me about—certain techniques that will excite you beyond all resistance!"

"Roger, do not try! The doctor's theory is wrong. I have no intention of allowing you—" What could she say to convince him? How could she actually resist him? She knew how strong he was. As a boy of sixteen he had liked to challenge the wrestlers who performed at fairs in his town.

"Stand up now, dear." He was patient as though addressing a difficult child. "Take off your dress before you wrinkle it. Here, I will help you. Walk around to this side of the bed."

But she lay still stubbornly, and he took the opportunity to push the fabric of her dress and petticoats between her legs and feel her groin. As the shock went through her, she jumped up and moved away from him, uncertain what she should do. How could she drive him from her room? Probably the only other mattress left in the house was in Clémence's chamber. That was it. She would go and sleep with Clémence as she had when she was ill as a small child.

Hesitating a minute by the door, she wondered if he would run after her. Could she lose him in the winding hallways? But then suddenly he was beside her, his hand on hers on the door handle. "Come back! you won't escape me tonight. How you excite me by your attempts to flee! You are like a frightened young doe in the forest, afraid to let the stag mount her and plunge his virile member into her warm depths." Roger spoke the words deliberately to stimulate and humiliate her, to allow her to recognize herself as a dumb female beast that had no other hope than submission to the dominant male.

"Come back now." His voice was steady, soothing, confident. He led her across the room, her own room where no man, hardly even her own father, had ever set foot. But this man was her husband by the laws of France. He had restored her ancestral lands to her today. He had saved her life and cared for her and her child.

Standing beside her, Roger untied her sash and, folding it carefully, laid it on the foot of the bed, then unbuttoned the back of her dress and let it fall down over her shoulders, easing the tightly gathered sleeves down her arms. Obediently, she stepped out of the garment. Now her breasts were exposed, pushed up by her stays to an unnatural height and size, her nipples pointing boldly ahead.

He spun her around so that she faced him, and seating himself on the bed, pulled her between his legs so that he could gently kiss first one breast and then the other while he worked at the tangle of ribbons at the back of her corseted waist. Soon her petticoats fell, and at last he drew down her drawers with a cry of triumph.

Holding her out at arm's length, each large hand clamped at her waist on the tight pink fabric of her stays, he studied carefully with little grunts of appreciation her shoulders decorated by tendrils of golden hair fallen from her coiffure, then the tense, satiny breasts seeming to beg for his favors, her small cinched waist, and, spreading below, the white hips with their full blond triangle.

Releasing her waist, trusting that she would know she could not escape him, he symmetrically grazed each smooth hip and thigh with his hands, producing a tingling pleasure she tried desperately to block in her brain.

"Please, Roger," she implored in a whisper. She must remember William! She must remember her marriage vows given before Harbert—and God. "You mustn't touch me any more. If you—if you force me tonight, it will be rape!"

"No, dearest. I won't have to rape you, I'm sure. I sense already the naughty little lusts you try so hard to conceal out of shame and guilt. But you have already given yourself wickedly to one man, and soon you will be crying out for me to satisfy your burning needs."

He delicately caressed her hips and bottom, as he gloated at her losing battle to control her excitement. Then cupping one buttock, he teased open her thighs just enough to admit a stealthy hand, and she feared he had spoken the truth. He was her legal husband—she would submit to him! She must! She had no choice, in any case. He would pursue her all over this great empty, ravaged house.

Slowly, masterfully, his fingers inserted themselves into her throbbing inner folds, and for a moment too long she let herself enjoy his clever manipulations. Oh, now she could not resist him! How exquisite the sensations were!

Then as he slowly, teasingly withdrew his hand, he taunted her in an acid voice. "Aha! You are ready so early! Where has all the pretended modesty flown? I hope we won't have to hear such hypocrisy again!" He was hurrying to remove his trousers and did not see the shock and pain on her face. He reeled in his surprise as she let fly with all her strength and struck him across the face.

"You wretched bitch! I'll make you pay for that!" he yelled, and knocked her over on her back onto the bed. Slapping her, pinning one shoulder as though he would crush it, he tore off his pants and threw himself between her sprawling thighs. She could feel his male organ thrusting to push inside her. With one hand he opened her slippery passage just as she managed to wrest her hips an inch away.

Through gritted teeth she cursed at him. To think that he would penetrate her now and perhaps give her his child, just when she was days away from her rightful husband! To think that she might have to go to William's arms pregnant with Roger's child! She would rather die first. "I swear to you, Roger, on the tombs of both my parents, that if you enter me now, I will kill myself! Do you understand? By whatever means, now, tonight, I will end my life; for I cannot bear the thought of your body coming into mine!"

So fiercely had she spoken, so startling was her manner after the obedience she had always shown him, that his body went limp. Slowly, torn between aggression and resignation, he sat up and began to replace his clothing. Finally, in a hollow voice she almost did not recognize, he asked, "How can it be, Nicole? Why do you feel such great revulsion toward me?" Then she could tell from the motions of his body that he was sobbing silently.

22

Coolly, Roger gave Nicole permission to return alone to Paris. Much as she hated to leave Beaux-Clervaux, she trembled to think of any repetition of the dreadful scene in her bedchamber, so after a brief, tearful meeting with the Gaillards and a sad embrace for Clémence, she fled her beloved home, fully believing she would never see it again. She would soon dwell in England as the Duchess of Falkland, and Roger would probably live out his life as the master of Beaux-Clervaux. It would serve as compensation for his loss of her. At last fate had paid him for his generosity; rather more than amply, she thought with bitterness, her heart aching at the loss of her beautiful heritage.

Only when she hugged little André once again in the house on the quay did she manage a smile of pleasure. But as soon as she climbed to Léon's room, the news was bad once more. Violette told her his fever was higher, his coughing even more violent. As before, the doctor was unwilling to make a prediction.

As Nicole stepped into her own chamber to remove her traveling costume, she almost succumbed to tears. So she could not go to William yet! For a selfish moment she resented the child. Would she be trapped here forever while the little king lingered on in his misery?

Putting on an inconspicuous outfit, she ran across to Notre Dame, praying that Timothy had already returned from England. She needed a loving message—dare she dream of a letter?—from William to sustain her spirits. Her heart leaped when she saw the servant, cap in hand, waiting faithfully in the nave.

"Oh, Timothy, how you must have despaired of me! General Duchamp required my company on a journey while you were gone. Naturally I had no way of letting you know."

"I guessed it, madam, from my observations of yer house; either that or ye was ill, which I prayed was not the case. Then today I joyfully witnessed yer return from my perch across the river."

"Oh, please tell me about Duke William. Didn't he—did he send a letter to me?"

"Nay, madam, for he believed it far too dangerous. He even chastised me for the risk to yerself and the child of carrying yers, though I notice he read it eager enough. But now he has sent me with many messages to relay to ye."

"Pray do, for my heart aches to hear from him!"

"Now I must get everything in order," Timothy said and cleared his throat. "First of all, His Grace told me to declare his satisfaction with the fine name you have chosen for his boy—"

"And did he select a second name or names?"

"If so, he did not indicate them to myself, madam."

"And then—"

"And then, secondly, he thanks ye from the bottom of his heart for yer care of the little king, and said ye had surely done the proper thing to wait until the child was strong. For it would never do to put selfish pleasures ahead of the poor boy's life—them was his exact words. And he hopes ye will take like precautions in the future, but at the same time prays to see ye very soon. And finally—" He paused and blushed a rosy pink.

"And finally?" she prompted eagerly.

"And finally—but I am a bit embarrassed by this part, mum, and you must bear with me. He asked me to tell ye how dearly he treasures yerself and the boy and how he longs to—ahem, hold ye in his arms and tell ye o' his love himself!"

"Oh, Timothy, that was beautifully done! And you have made me so very happy."

"Thank ye, madam, I'm sure."

After Roger arrived home from Beaux-Clervaux, she avoided him as much as possible, but discovered to her surprise that he, while cold and abrupt, seemed just as eager as she was to prevent another painful scene. When they met at dinner, he put on a good front for the servants, discoursing about his attempts to hire men for the vineyards and begin the restoration of Beaux-Clervaux; or about his little political intrigues, ambitions, and frustrations in the army hierarchy. Ordinarily, Roger got exactly what he wanted; but one suppertime he went on bitterly about the success of that upstart General Buonaparte, a virtual foreigner who had only just changed his name to the more French-sounding Bonaparte, and who had managed to get himself named commander in chief of the armies by the Convention, a position Roger had dreamed of having.

When Roger was at home, Nicole was all too aware of the disgrace she was in his eyes, aware of the injustice she had seemed to do him, feeling an impostor—no better than her maid Julie—in his house. But then clue after clue gradually brought home to her the enormity of Roger's greedy obsession with Beaux-Clervaux, and she lost what feelings of guilt she had. He always spoke with a curious awe of the grandeur of the château, and had made vulgar plans to turn it into the sophisticated palace it never had been. Day after day she glimpsed him poring over the bulging ledgers of the wineries that for some reason he had seen fit to haul to Paris. What could he be doing? When she questioned him, he would tell her nothing. But she was shocked and annoyed and disgusted to find that he was having painted on the carriage and embossed on his stationery the handsome coat of arms with panther and swan and the motto, *J'ai du coeur*, that had belonged through the centuries to the Clervaux.

In the long fall and winter months, Léon endured one crisis after another, only seeming to grow weaker in between. Roger came and went, always preoccupied with his campaign in southern Germany or with the progress at Beaux-Clervaux, and only occasionally complaining about the boy whose illness had proved so long and costly.

Then at last with the return of spring, Léon seemed to turn a corner and grow stronger. For an entire week he went without a trace of fever. At last he could sit up and walk with support. Although he rarely spoke at all, and then only a single word or two to request a sip of water or a sweet, he seemed to understand most of what was said to him. One day, after she had determined no nurse or servant was in earshot, Nicole sat down beside his bed and told him of their plans for escape. No doubt it would be a difficult journey for him, she said, and he must be very brave, but at the end he would be free and happy at last in England. Not really expecting that he would ever use the word, she still felt obliged to ask him to address her as *Maman* and to remember that little André was supposed to be his brother.

Wrinkling his brow, trying hard to understand, he pronounced the single word, "*Maman?*"

"Yes, Léon, you must call me *Maman*, just while we travel in the carriage." And then from the strained look on his face as he groped for words that would not come, she realized he wanted to ask if his real mother would be waiting for him in England. As Nicole broke into tears, she slowly shook her head. "Your own beautiful *Maman* must wait for you in a far distant land, a land we will all visit someday, but where we cannot journey yet awhile."

At last Timothy and she were ready to depart. The same old blue coach, purchased so many long months ago, would be waiting at her door early tomorrow. Timothy had set the hour at ten in the morning. Nicole found the old valises and carried them into her room. Once again she must find clothes to fit the boys and steal food and wine from her own kitchen.

Unfortunately, she could not give the servants a holiday because Roger had invited many fellow officers and their wives to a large reception in the house tonight, which she was powerless to cancel. Not only was every servant working feverishly to obey his orders, but Nicole herself must put in an appearance at the party in stylish gown and appropriate coiffure.

She contemplated this lavish affair with the greatest annoyance. Why didn't she simply pretend she was ill? Then when she visualized the stream of wives who would visit her boudoir all evening long, she realized it would be easier if she carried out Roger's wishes and did nothing to attract special attention to herself. Sighing a little, she sat down at her dressing table and began to toy with her hair.

But as darkness fell and the orchestra struck up a tune downstairs in the salon, Nicole became so intoxicated by the nearness of her release from years of suffering and sacrifice that she could not resist making a true celebration of it. Impulsively she seized her most expensive gown, which Roger had ordered for her to wear to the Luxembourg Palace. Yes, it was just the right shade of lime green—the hue Sybille de Vaucroze had chosen to complement her golden hair and dark eyes years ago—and so sheer and naughty! Just the sort of extravagant gown that was in high style now in these days of reaction against the austerities of the Terror.

Peeling down to her flesh-colored stays and donning one of those strange new short petticoats of an ecru color, meant to give the impression of nudity under the gown, she pulled the green chiffon over her head and stared, not without shock, at herself in the mirror. Fashioned in what was supposed to be a Roman style with a high waistline just below her breasts, it had a columnar skirt barely loose enough to allow her to sit down, and was split all the way up one calf to show a glimpse of her knee.

Since the end of the Reign of Terror, the mood of the whole city had been one of reckless abandon, in an apparent effort to forget or deny the sufferings of the past, and styles in clothing had been the most obvious expression. Men displayed themselves in outlandish outfits, sometimes with hair dyed vivid reds or black. Female styles in particular had reached the limits of absurdity, one fad called the guillotine gown being a bright red shift with a jagged neckline. Some women greased their bodies to make their flimsy dresses cling seductively, and others were said to have actually died of exposure by stubbornly wearing sheer fabrics out into the freezing night. But for all ages and all walks of life, the narrow chemise with no more than one petticoat and often none at all was the dominant style, presenting a nearly bare bosom with the neckline dropped below the nipples or with such transparent cloth covering the breasts that nothing was left to the imagination.

At first Nicole had refused to have any part of the scandalous new clothes, but when she finally realized that to refuse a glimpse of her bosom excited more lingering stares than to grant it, she finally allowed Roger to order her this green gown. Its bodice was in fact conservative. Looking straight ahead into the mirror, she could see only the upper half of her plump breasts, forced upward by her painful stays, swelling above the scooped neckline. The green chiffon, two layers thick, reached to the center of each areola, so that only two half-moons of pink were readily visible. But to her own eyes, looking down, she seemed entirely naked, and only hoped she did not develop the nervous habit of tugging at her neckline all evening long.

She finally called in Violette to help with her coiffure, which they curled, piled high, and bound by parallel ribbons in the Roman style, allowing short, tousled curls to trail around her face and neck romantically. With a laugh of pleasure, Nicole approved her own reflection in the mirror. If she wasn't a sight of post-Revolutionary decadence! It was a costume as symbolic of its times as the silly milkmaid outfit had been on that last night at Versailles. What an appropriate way to bid farewell to the horrors of the last five years! Tomorrow she would journey to live in the solid, respectable, God-fearing nation of England.

Taking her place beside Roger in the receiving line, she could not help but be impressed by the brilliant party he had arranged. She would scarcely have recognized the house, decorated as it was with dozens of candelabra reflecting in great mirrors he had had installed just for the occasion, and huge bouquets of flowers. There were sumptuous buffets in every room, and liveried waiters pouring champagne. A ten-man orchestra had been hired, costumed in little white wigs reminiscent of the late Bourbons. Dear heaven, the whole party was nothing but an imitation of Versailles and the Ancien Régime. And what a price it must have cost Roger! Everywhere she looked she saw new crystal or silver or chairs, and a score of extra servants.

Glancing at his flushed face, she could see that Roger was already delighted with himself. In a ringing voice he introduced her to each guest as "my wife, Madame La Générale Duchamp de Clervaux," and she could tell from his expression after his eye had darted to her bosom and face and hair that he was proud of her appearance. His face took on a fresh glow of excitement when he welcomed some general of fame and prestige, and he would always match the length and warmth of his greeting to the importance of the guest.

Finally, just as Nicole was beginning to feel the pinch of her shoes, the butler announced the names of the General and Madame Bonaparte, and Roger sprang forward eagerly. Ever since Napoleon's spectacular conquest of Italy, Roger had decided he must ingratiate himself with the young general, even younger than himself, and had urged Nicole to curry favor with his wife Josephine. But Nicole would have none of Madame Bonaparte. Not only had Josephine shocked her by regaling a group with jokes and banter about her imprisonment in the Carmes, from which, Nicole knew, her first husband, Beauharnais, had been taken to the guillotine; but Josephine was well known to have given her favors freely to other men while her bridegroom was away in Italy.

But at least Roger's evening was complete, Nicole thought with a little derisive laugh. When Josephine murmured that she would be at home in the rue Chantereine on Thursday next, Roger poked Nicole and she responded, "Oh, thank you, madame; how very kind! I am delighted to accept," enjoying the joke of it all. On Thursday next, she fully expected to spend the entire day in the arms of her true husband in some great four-poster bed at Falkland House.

Roger commenced the dancing with Josephine, as the wife of the guest of honor, and then rather to Nicole's surprise, selected her for his next partner. Of course it was just for appearances, she thought, and then noticed that his eyes dropped frequently to her breasts, and his face had a shy, yearning look that she had not seen in ages. Not tonight of all nights, not another attempt at sexual conquest! But she would easily solve that problem by locking her bedroom door, and told him as much now with a little scowl.

Napoleon had not bestirred himself to take her as his partner during the opening dance. As the son of a penniless nobleman from the half-civilized island of Corsica, he was nearly as much a parvenu as Roger, but had none of Roger's eagerness to conceal his humble origins. Napoleon cared little what faux pas he committed and probably was not even aware that one of Roger's aides had had to jump forward and dance with Nicole. But now for no reason, as the orchestra struck up one of the new German waltzes, Bonaparte came toward her and bowed. Groaning a little inwardly because she expected that he would not know the new dance, she was relieved when he placed his right arm around her back in the half-embrace that the new dance required. She extended her own arms a bit stiffly at first, then happened to glance at her neckline and saw that it had slipped down distressingly. Better to dance closer to him than to give him such an excellent opportunity to study her breasts, she thought with panic, but then saw to his credit that he was not spying on her as Roger had.

They whirled about the salon, which had been cleared of its rugs and furniture, obeying the lilting rhythms of the waltz. Who would have expected that the blunt, impatient, self-absorbed Bonaparte would be a perfect dancer? She felt her blood racing with the excitement of the music, the champagne she had consumed perhaps too eagerly, and the attention of a circle of admiring guests. When the song ended, Napoleon continued to hold her gloved hand instead of departing with a bow, and she flushed a little at his favor. The next tune was even faster, and he gave her a half-smile of doubt at their own ability to keep the pace.

As they flew around the salon, Nicole caught a glimpse of some strange movement on the circular staircase, but had to wait for another complete revolution before she could satisfy her curiosity. Then when she got a clear view of the stairs once more, she stopped so abruptly that Bonaparte crashed into her.

Two men, dressed in the black uniforms and long white aprons of *infirmiers* or hospital attendants, were slowly guiding a stretcher bearing the sleepy Léon down the steps. One man, the nearer one, she instantly recognized as Timothy, newly shaved of his red beard. It was the other one, farther up the staircase, facing forward and looking directly at her, who fixed her attention. Forgetting Napoleon and the music and the roomful of guests, forgetting everything else in the world, she walked as though hypnotized to the foot of the stairs. Grasping the iron balustrade for support, she met with wide, puzzled eyes the fierce gaze of the tall man, half-disguised by a kerchief wrapped around his forehead. As she had sensed from her earliest glimpse, it was the Duke of Falkland.

Her first frantic words were drowned out by the orchestra. Finally, sympathetic guests who were beginning to crowd around her signaled the musicians to stop. Then she called out again to the duke, "I beg you to tell me the meaning of this!"

His eyes regarded her scornfully as he descended another step or two without answering. Why in the world was he angry with her? Had she somehow misunderstood Timothy's directions? Surely they had agreed to take the boy tomorrow morning at ten. Not the slightest hint had been given that William would appear to assist them. But of course Timothy might not have known. Perhaps William had suddenly found himself free to leave London and had had no time to send word ahead. But why were Timothy and he taking the child now in the middle of this reception? And why in the world was William staring down at her so furiously?

At last he spoke in his fluent French that now took on the accents of the Parisian working class. "Madame has long requested a bed in the Hôtel-Dieu for this consumptive patient."

It was a good enough explanation for the removal of the child. Of course she must trust him, trust that some emergency had arisen to change their plans. Her brain racing, she realized she could have mistaken the appointed time. Had Timothy possibly meant ten tonight, which must be approximately the present hour? Had he made a slip of the tongue or had she misunderstood him in her nervousness? Surely it was the only explanation for William's anger. He had come believing she would be dressed and ready to depart, and now concluded that she refused to go with him.

In an urgent voice, she told him, "You were expected tomorrow morning, and you have surprised me by arriving at an hour when—when I cannot possibly accompany—uh, Léon, as I earnestly wish to do!"

She was shattered when Falkland registered no surprise or even interest at this information. On the contrary his eyes moved from her face to her nearly naked bosom, and the muscles around his mouth seemed to twitch with contempt. Sheepishly, obediently, she pulled up her neckline, but his expression did not soften. There was no mistaking the hatred in his face. This was no act to fool their spectators—just the opposite, for he was dangerously departing from his guise of *infirmier*. She could only make the heartbreaking conclusion that he intended to leave her and André behind.

"I beg you to take the boy back upstairs! I—I promised to go with him tomorrow. He is far too frightened." All eyes traveled to Léon, who seemed only to be fighting to stay awake and gave no evidence of any worry whatsoever.

"It is impossible, madame," the duke said, with the pretended exasperation of a tradesman for an unreasonable patron. She saw his penetrating eyes move just to her left, and she turned to discover that Napoleon had been standing beside her all along. Just at that moment, Roger stepped up close to her right to lend moral support in what seemed like a dispute with a difficult employee of the Hôtel-Dieu. Falkland looked from Napoleon to Roger and back again, taking in their displays of gold braid and ribbons and medals with a curl of ironic amusement to his lips. Then he gestured impatiently for Timothy to take another step.

Nicole, her face streaming with tears, cried, "Oh, I beg you to delay till morning!" Then she tried to choke back her sobs, terrified she would betray the little king with her hysteria.

In sympathy, Roger wrapped his arm around her and said, "You are making a little tragedy out of this, dear Nicole. The poor boy obviously does not mind, and you can visit him first thing in the morning. Let him go now without another word."

Falkland allowed his eyes to linger scornfully on Roger, then spoke to her once again, staring directly into her eyes, "Alas, madame, you cannot ask us to wait. After all," he said slowly, with ill-concealed sarcasm, "you have had considerable opportunity—to make up your mind!"

They speeded their pace down the remaining steps and attempted to brush by Nicole without a pause. But she cried for them to wait in a voice that could not be denied. With all eyes upon her, she moved to Léon's side and kissed his forehead. The boy smiled up at her and seemed to try to form some word that would not come.

Then she raised her head and looked directly at William, who stood no more than a foot away. She could reach out and touch him if she chose. For a few seconds their eyes met, his cruel and accusing, while hers, brimming with tears, searched his face. She could hardly believe she was looking at the man she loved so well. What an incredible shock and thrill it was just to see him, and what an unthinkable loss it would now be when he walked away from her forever. How could she let him go!

And yet in a second he had passed her and was rapidly crossing the room. With Roger just beside her, with a whole roomful of witnesses, she could not lunge at William or scream out to him, "Don't leave me! I belong to you, only you! It does not matter if you love me or hate me. I must be near you just to live and breathe!" Only the little king's safety—and André's—prevented her from crying out her love for him—and sacrificing William's life and her own.

23

Nicole left Josephine's Thursday salon as early as possible, despising as she did the frivolous chatter, the extravagant new decor that was said to have bankrupted the young general, and the presence of at least two of the hostess's lovers—one, Barras, the most powerful member of the new Directory. And every man present examined the pretty women in the room as though they were available for the asking. The elegant salon was no better than a bordello, Nicole thought as she hurried away.

While her coachman drove back from Montmartre toward the Seine, she wondered if she would be drawn against her will into that debauched circle. Dejected as she now was, she feared she had little spirit left to resist Roger's determination to dog every step of the Bonapartes. Her imagination leaped ahead to see herself a thirtyish beauty like Josephine, toying with a covey of handsome young officers, teasing each to believe that he might be lucky enough to take the general's wife to bed that night. Never! Never would she sink so low, Nicole promised herself, groaning aloud.

On a sudden impulse, she told her coachman to cross to the Left Bank and stop before a shabby lodging house in the rue Huchette. She ignored his expression of concern for her when she told him to leave, saying she preferred to walk home after she had conducted her business.

These rooms above a bakery were the only address she had ever had for Timothy during the months he had stayed in Paris, and she doubted he had lived here at the last. Still, she was desperate for any information, any clue that would give her hope that William and Timothy were still somewhere in Paris.

The concierge, a sullen, suspicious woman, looked Nicole up and down before she replied, "A big foreigner with a red beard? And why would a lady like yourself want to know about such a fellow, madame?"

Nicole opened her handbag and handed the woman some paper money, but she scorned it and asked for a gold coin, which Nicole reluctantly produced.

"I don't know a foreigner, but there was a big man from Brittany with a red beard. Spoke bad French like all Bretons. Called himself Maclou."

"Yes, of course, Maclou; I had only forgotten the name," Nicole said.

"But what would you want with a man like that? Though he was a likable fellow, very jolly, he was a bit *louche*, shady, never having no regular job, yet living quite well all the same."

"He did some work for me, repair work; I'd like to hire him again."

"And what sort of work would that be?" the woman asked with a certain innuendo, obviously happy to imagine the worst. Had he been blackmailing this anxious young woman, or did he spy on her husband for her, or even perform abortions?

When Nicole gave her another coin, she supplied that he had not lived there for a year, had had no callers or particular friends in the building, and had left no forwarding address. When Nicole asked, she said he had taken all his meals in her kitchen, but had sometimes enjoyed a glass of wine just there in the café in the Place St. Michel.

After Nicole's inquiries at the café brought no more information, she walked sadly along to the quai de la Tournelle and the bit of stone wall under the plane trees where she had often seen Timothy sit and watch her house just across the river. What she wouldn't give now to find him here, fishing, smoking, or ambling along the quay to greet her with the warm smile she loved!

But she would no longer allow herself the luxury of tears. Some sort of control must be practiced if she was going to endure the rest of her life. Her heart was broken, and her life was over. But still she must go on—and she could survive only if she never, never allowed herself to think of William or even Timothy again.

No sooner had she given herself this good advice than she embarked on another sad study of her long love affair. What in the world had gone wrong? How could she have been so deluded about William? But of course she had not been, not really! She had feared all along that fate intended their love to end tragically. It was just that she could not believe he would reject his own son. Yes, that was the part she had not expected, the part that hurt most.

What a snort of annoyance William must have given when she came back from the dead so inconveniently! Of course she should have known— had actually known in her heart that something was wrong when he did not come himself to Paris. She had never really believed the story that his presence was indispensable to the English court simply because the king was ill.

No doubt William would have done nothing to acknowledge her letter to Dr. Littleton except that for the moment he needed her. He needed a woman to care for the little king who was motherless, frightened, and possibly ill. So he would string Nicole along with a few blandishments sent by the unsuspecting Timothy.

What would have happened if little Léon had been well enough to travel directly to England? William might have dallied with her for a few nights in London, then disposed of her with another exile to Langmuir or an arranged marriage to some squire in a distant country where they need never meet again. Or had Timothy been directed to break the news at Calais before she boarded the boat: They would continue on without her because the duke did not acknowledge the marriage after all. No, she thought not, for the duke would realize he could not trust the kindhearted Timothy with such a ruthless task.

Of course William had not known of the existence of his child when he had laid these plans. Then after Timothy had returned to London with her letter, hadn't William suffered some heartache or guilt at rejecting his fine, handsome son? Or had he stubbornly refused to believe the boy was his? Had Timothy—in a tragic slip of the tongue—given the wrong birth date for André, reporting February or some later month instead of December, so that the duke could not have fathered him after all?

But in any case events had finally confirmed what her instincts had told her so long ago at Versailles. The Duke of Falkland was a cynical libertine, a liar, a vicious opportunist—a man without a shred of honor.

And yet, as she moped across the bridge to the Île St. Louis, her mind returned as it had so many times in the last few days to William's strangely bitter sentence on the staircase: "After all, you have had considerable opportunity to make up your mind!" To make up her mind? What in the world had he meant?

Could he actually believe she refused to go to England and be his wife? After all, he had stared hard at Roger. Had there been jealousy in his eyes? Could he possibly believe she preferred Roger to him? But of course not, not if he had read her letter and listened with half an ear to the messages she had sent by way of Timothy!

Perhaps, just perhaps, William had loved her once, but had found himself unable to abide her long relationship with Roger. She was cheapened, tarnished, compromised in his eyes. He could no longer love and desire her as he once had, now she had given herself over and over to another man. Of course in his cynical way he could not imagine that she had lived chastely, never once allowing Roger to make love to her. And her poor little letter with its silly circumlocutions had only made matters worse. Who believes a woman when she goes out of her way to protest she has not slept with a man? She had been tragically mistaken about William's easy tolerance. When all was said and done, the great libertine was a puritan under the skin.

As for the child, there was simply too much doubt. Roger had been lurking about for years, and Nicole, even when she was prying into William's little love affairs, had never been candid enough to mention him. William had actually met Roger once face to face when he had gone to inquire about her in Rouen. Could he have remembered in that moment on the stairs? It hardly mattered, for he knew well enough that Roger had saved her from the guillotine—she had had to tell Timothy that in answer to his early question. Roger had cared enough to save her life. He could be the child's father as well as William. There was just too much room for doubt.

What wretched luck Falkland had chosen the night of the glittering party when she had been dressed in her tawdry half-nude gown and waltzing with England's most notorious enemy! She must have looked for all the world like a courtesan who had bartered her favors for a place in the highest levels of this wicked, debauched society. No wonder Falkland had felt contempt!

"If I may be allowed to make the observation—" Roger began, without looking up from his writing.

"Yes?" Nicole murmured politely. They were the picture of respectable domesticity this evening as Roger worked at his desk in the library, little André played on the rug, and she, attired in a high-necked, dark wool dress, tatted some lace to trim a petticoat. For once Roger had respected her wish to decline an invitation and stay home all evening. She seemed to take some comfort from this playacting at happy family life.

"Since poor Léon—ah, is no longer with us—" he said cautiously, checking her face to see that he was not upsetting her once again.

She sighed. She had told Roger that Léon had died in the Hôtel-Dieu only a day or two after his admission. Otherwise Roger would have thought it strange when she did not make frequent visits to the sick boy, and talk of bringing him home again.

"I can only believe, after noting your dark mood for a week, that what you need to fill your life is the care of another child."

She worked at the delicate pattern on the table in front of her without uttering a word, her eyebrows elevated more from resignation than surprise. Of course it was inevitable. Roger would expect to win eventually. It was his nature. He could not imagine she would not finally bend to his will. It was all a matter of finding the right time and place, the right mood. Perhaps he actually believed he had discovered the key to her nature, to any woman's. She could only accept her own sexual desire as a striving for motherhood.

At midnight after a light tap on the door, Roger entered her bedchamber in a surprising state of nervousness. Nicole gave him a wan smile, then another sigh. She no longer had the will to deny him his rights. She could no longer think of herself as Falkland's wife. Perhaps she never had been. It had never been a real marriage, even in the eyes of the church, if William had entered into it with deception in his heart. She had bathed and donned a pretty nightdress, with every intention of being as pleasant as possible during this ritual sacrifice.

With a hopeful, excited air, Roger brought forward a present from behind his back, apparently some kind of jewel box. Then she uttered a little cry of amazement. It was her mother's own rosewood case with the ivory inlay that Nicole had carried from Beaux-Clervaux to England and back to France, only to have it confiscated at her arrest in Rouen.

"Where in the world, Roger—! I can hardly believe my eyes!"

"I knew how thrilled you'd be. Only yesterday an officer, Lambelin, who has been under suspicion of theft for years, was finally arrested. He had been in Rouen when I was, with a rank then higher than mine. So today it occurred to me to search the items reclaimed from his residence, and there to my delight was your little case."

She opened the lid, saw that it was still half full, and lifted some chains and strands of beads with cries of pleasure.

"Unfortunately the scoundrel has sold all the precious stones. You'll find only the items of lesser value."

"Even so, I am terribly pleased! I never dreamed I would see any of these lovely old things again."

"Then I am well satisfied," he said in his smug way.

She picked up an empty setting of what had been a diamond ring, and tried to recall the other precious stones in the collection. Yes, the valuable ruby necklace was gone. And so were her father's handsome watch and all the heavy ropes of pearls. Then she remembered her mother's wedding ring and dug urgently in the box. "Did you take any kind of inventory?" She knew how methodical Roger was. He had probably ordered his poor adjutant to make five copies.

"No—I—what are you looking for?"

"My mother's wedding ring, first of all."

"Oh, that beautiful thing! I remember it well. One big central emerald—very valuable. No doubt he sold it long ago."

Something in his voice alerted her. He had no list, but he knew it was gone. The box did not appear to have been freshly inventoried; the necklaces and chains were too tangled. She rather had the feeling the box had been neglected somewhere for a long time. Someone had sold off the precious stones and forgotten about the rest, until—until it occurred to him it might make a useful bribe to buy his reluctant wife's cooperation in bed? Roger! Could Roger have actually stolen the box himself? Had he hidden these keepsakes from her all this time as he sold off her diamonds and rubies and pearls? But it could not possibly be true. Never before had she suspected him of such low deceit and cunning. And she remembered the name Lambelin, a man Roger had never liked. Surely Roger would not make up a story that she could check with very little difficulty. But then in a flash of insight she wondered if Roger might not be capable of planting the evidence on the officer himself.

Half rising she said, "I'm afraid I am unable after all. I feel rather ill suddenly. . . ."

"Dear Nicole, you can't refuse now!" he exclaimed shrilly.

She studied Roger's face, hoping to read the truth, but she could see only his consuming fear that she would reject him again, and slumped in defeat. *Mon Dieu*, she could not accuse the man of stealing her jewels. What if he were completely innocent?

At last he leaned across the bed and touched his lips to hers. He was selfish and tyrannical, perhaps even a cunning thief, and he had certainly tried to buy her tonight with a gift. Now that she was free to try to love Roger, she knew finally that he was impossible to love. Yet she must let him bed her, now and always—whenever he wished. It must be her punishment—for what?—for having enjoyed William too well?

He pulled the gown up over her breasts and head. Of course he had seen her naked before; why should she cower under his gaze? Far from seeming menacing, he looked almost frightened of this final success, and reached out with childish curiosity to touch one of her breasts.

His damp palms on her back held her upright as he took the nipple in his lips. She felt no stirring of excitement as he worked it awhile—only resentment and irritability. She wanted to strike out and hit him, force him by means of oaths and painful blows to leave her alone forever. Sensing this fury, he wrinkled his brow with surprise, then shrugged, and finally smiled with victory. She was his at last. She would not flee him this time, and he knew it. Sitting facing her fully clothed, he placed a hand on her shoulder and slowly pushed her flat on the bed in a gesture of conquest. She was his at last to enjoy as he wished.

Nicole could not suppress a little cry of humiliation—defeat, it was—and he answered it with a smirk. How she hated the man! When he stood up to remove his clothes, she closed her eyes and tried to shut him out of her mind. Nothing he did to her would matter. She would pretend it was only another bad dream, that he and his wicked, teasing hands did not really exist. Could the man possibly imagine that he could arouse her, lying now here beside her, that he could accomplish that impossible transformation? He seemed so assured and knowing as he manipulated her breasts, and grazed the delicate skin of her belly and thighs. No, of course he would never succeed in winning her cooperation, in making her writhe and moan for him and open her arms wide.

But the sick, aching need deep inside her must be stilled, satisfied by some means, and at last she clutched his naked body to her. They fit together comfortably, as well as any man and woman. And why not? she thought bitterly. It was lust not love that united them, simple animal lust.

Gloating now, grinning at his success, he would waste no more time with preliminaries. Pulling her thighs apart, he threw himself between them greedily. The bouncing of the mattress upset the jewel case beside her, spilling out the contents across the sheet, but at first she did not even glance at the jumble, distracted as she was by Roger's attack. But just as he forced his way inside her she caught sight of the fiery eye of the topaz that had been Falkland's gift. There it lay, reflecting the candlelight, burning with anger and scorn. She could hear William's ironic laughter ringing in her ears as she strained to find some satisfaction from Roger's hasty, shallow, inadequate foray.

Roger made love to her at regular intervals for the next several months, but she found little satisfaction and no greater affection for him. Quite the contrary, for she learned even more clearly of the dark side of Roger's nature, the sick, cruel streak that made him seek to pry from her shaming details about her first lover, like to fling gutter labels at her, and want to inflict punishment and even pain.

Punctually, he would inquire of her if she were pregnant, more aware of her own schedule than she was herself, and she soon realized how fervently he wanted a child of his own. For the first month or two of disappointment, he managed to control himself, but then later he would let fly some insult or other. "No doubt it is a divine punishment. . . ."

"What can you mean?" she asked, wary but unable to resist the bait.

"... for conceiving your first child as you did!"

The last night before Roger departed on what promised to be a long campaign, he came to her room earlier than usual, and she had only just lain down to read for a few minutes before removing her dress.

"So you are not ready for me?" he asked with apparent anger.

"No—I—" She had jumped up rather in surprise.

"Then please prepare. I shall enjoy the sight."

She stared at him with undisguised hatred for a moment, and was tempted to drive him from her room. But she had not the strength to endure another distasteful scene. Thank God the man left tomorrow.

Slowly she unbuttoned her dress, and pulled it over her head; then turning her back so that he could not see her breasts, she struggled to unhook her stays, knowing that he would not rise to assist her. Cheating him of the sight of her bare bottom, she pulled on her nightgown before she let down her petticoat and untied her drawers. William had been wrong, she thought suddenly. She did not enjoy undressing before a man. Not Roger now. Her senses were dulled. She wondered if whatever natural impulses she had once had had not been completely blocked by these months with Roger.

When she had smoothed down her gown and turned around to face him, he asked sneeringly, "Is that all? Are you quite ready to take me?"

"As ready as I ever am!" she snapped.

When he stepped toward her, she imagined from his fierce look that he meant to hit her, and she jumped back involuntarily. But he brushed by and pulled the little drawers one by one out of her bedside commode, dumping their contents on the bed. Then he riffled through the books and hairpins and little toys left behind by André that had been disgorged.

"What are you doing!" she cried angrily. "Have you gone crazy?"

Roger made no reply, but dashed into her dressing room and opened another dozen drawers and cupboards, picking up and examining every object he did not instantly recognize, sniffing bottles of rosewater and lavender water and perfume suspiciously.

"Stop! Tell me what you are searching for! Have you gone mad?"

"Oh, can't you guess?" he finally snarled. "I am simply trying to find what you have been using all these months to prevent conceiving my child!" And then he turned away contemptuously and slammed out of her room.

Roger left without a word of farewell to her the next morning. It was a widely known secret that Napoleon's vast force sailing from Toulon, with

Roger second in command, meant to invade Egypt. If they managed to survive the inevitable encounter with the British fleet on the Mediterranean, their campaign could last a year, or five years. Napoleon talked openly of his desire to follow in the footsteps of Alexander the Great and conquer Syria and Persia, and even India, which was fast becoming a source of great British wealth.

At last Nicole might draw a free breath and live some life of her own. She longed to recapture the peace and happiness of those early days when she had been alone with André and Violette in what Roger had long since referred to as their "garret." But now with an adventurous four-year-old child on her hands, a household of six servants to oversee, and insistent invitations from Madame Bonaparte and her circle, Nicole began to dream of slipping away to Beaux-Clervaux.

Only the fear of William's haunting presence stopped her. She imagined that she would encounter him in the Petit Salon standing before her mother's portrait or in the chapel or the *salle à manger*, extolling the wines at the head of the table. And upstairs, oh, Lord, how could she walk past the door of that sitting room where he had ripped her dress from her the night of the *Gerbaude*, then carried her into the bedchamber where he had sealed the fate of the rest of her life? How could she ever stand to see that room, that bed again?

But finally her longing for her beautiful home won out, and she closed down the Paris house and moved André and herself to Beaux-Clervaux for what might even be a stay of several years. Clémence could not stop weeping when she held the little boy in her arms at last, and pretended to discover a strong resemblance to Nicole and Lucienne and Robert, all three.

"But in actuality, Clémence, he closely resembles his father," Nicole said, when André had run off with the groom to help tend the horses.

"His father . . . ? Oh, yes . . . perhaps so. But of course it has been years since I saw. . . ." Then she cleared her throat and asked, "And General Duchamp—he is not with you today?"

"No, Clémence, he has gone with the army to Egypt. I hear that they may even march on to India." And meeting Clémence's twinkling eyes, she broke into a great smile and hugged the old cook, exclaiming, "So then we can pray that they will have themselves a marvelous long campaign on the other side of the world!"

Clémence could not be deterred from taking Nicole directly into the chapel, where she showed her three little candles that had been burning ever since her last brief visit. "For you and André, and for—for the duke!"

"Bless you, Clémence, but of course you need not burn them now, for we are here to stay."

"Not the duke. . . ."

Nicole averted her eyes and said with a catch in her throat, "The duke has finally made it clear to me that he does not recognize our marriage—even though it was conducted by a priest—and does not accept André as his child."

"Oh, *ma* Nicolette, I cannot believe it—"

"But it is true. And I must try to make myself abandon all my old dreams and put him from my mind. Please, no more candles, Clémence—at least not three!"

"But I must still pray for you and the child, for you are the only family I have."

Nicole was pleased to find, on a quick tour of the château, that Roger had made fewer alterations than she had feared. Only in one drawing room had fine natural wood paneling been covered by layers of rose damask, and the room filled with gilded rococo furniture, where there had once been old oak pieces of the provincial style. But though the courtyard had been cleaned, and fire damage had been repaired, the rooms were still largely empty. Nicole was a little mystified, remembering Roger's frequent tirades about what an expense Beaux-Clervaux had proved to be. But when she questioned Clémence, she learned that many things were on order and expected any day.

Then as Clémence accompanied Nicole to her room, the cook told her with a certain amount of trepidation that Julie Georgeault had been abandoned by Pascal and returned penniless to Beaux-Clervaux with three small children. Reluctantly, Clémence had allowed her to move into the ramshackle cottage beyond the pond meadow that had belonged to old Dodon, the mole-catcher. Nicole sighed, and replied that Clémence had done the right thing, and that Julie might stay as long as necessary, although, Nicole added, she hoped she would be able to avoid any sort of encounter with her.

Nicole knew that Roger had taken on Marc Gaillard, invalided out of the army with a leg wound, as master of the *chaix*. Roger had acted more out of desperation than anything else, for Marc was still young and inexperienced; but no other man seemed to have the knowledge of the local grapes, the ability to command the respect of the workers, and the honesty necessary to be trusted with large sums of money.

Messages had gone back and forth all afternoon between Clémence and Mère Gaillard, both women competing for the company of Nicole and André at supper. Finally a bargain was struck, and mother and son would eat the first few courses at Clémence's table, and then move on to the cottage for dessert with the Gaillards.

Nicole had always loved the tiny cottage, which had seemed to her in her lonely childhood like a wonderful playhouse staffed with eager companions. But now she was only struck by its small size, for it had a mere two rooms, and marveled that five children could have been raised here so happily. The creamy white Mermaid rose had climbed over half the house, and as she raised her head to wonder at its size, she saw a huge man standing on the roof where he was tossing about new bundles of thatch. At the sight of Nicole, he gave a great bellow of a greeting and leaped exuberantly off the roof to land directly at her feet.

"Oh, Marc, how you terrified me! What a wonderful thrill it is to see you again!"

Without a moment's hesitation, he picked her up, whirled her around, hugged her thoroughly, and then set her down and did the same for André.

"Oh, but I thought you were practically a cripple now!" she laughed, with great pleasure to see how amazingly strong and healthy and handsome he looked. He was a great ox of a man with massive shoulders and always an incongruously gentle expression on his face.

"Oh, I have me a game leg," he said, then demonstrated how he could bend his knee only by a jerk of his arm. "I was no better than a rusted tin soldier to them, so they sent me home; and I can tell you I am glad to be done with killing!"

She gave a warm embrace to Mère Gaillard, then entered the cottage a bit fearfully, anticipating that it would be sad and gloomy now that the old father had died, Noémie was married again, and Gabriel had left on the invasion of Switzerland. Only Marc and his mother lived here now. But soon there was laughter once again, and Nicole relaxed as she always had in this room, with loving friends who sought nothing from her. Not just friends, family really. In no time they re-established the old close bonds.

When Marc pointed to a hole in the roof and described his project of rethatching the cottage, Nicole exclaimed impatiently, "But why in the world haven't you moved into the fine old house you are entitled to as *maître?* I know it is large for the two of you, but you owe it to your mother to let her enjoy a lovely home after so many years in these cramped quarters."

"But, mistress, I thought perhaps you knew. General Duchamp has let the house of the *maître.*"

"Let it? You must be joking!"

"No. It now serves as a summer place for a merchant from Bordeaux."

"Then are you compensated for the loss of the house?"

"Ah, mistress, let us not spoil a pleasant evening with talk of business. . . ."

"Tell me the truth!"

"Alas, General Duchamp is now my employer. . . ." he said evasively.

In her exasperation, she switched to the familiar *tu*, you, of their childhood. "Do you refuse to give me the information I request? Do you actually believe I would sit by complacently while he cheated you out of half your pay? I can only be hurt and insulted by such a suggestion! What has happened to my old friend and companion and brother? Or are you really a revolutionary who believes all landowners belong in prison?" she added with a laugh.

"Oh, hush, Nicolette!" he cried, eager enough to switch to familiar forms of speech. "If I have not answered you, it has been to save you pain. The *chaix* have had—financial difficulties for some time. Your husband has not bothered you with certain matters, and no doubt that is just as well. . . ."

"But how can there be difficulties? I know that the last three vintages have been excellent. We have eagerly sampled everything you have sent us in Paris. You must be making huge profits. Of course the British blockade may have—"

"Let me assure you that the British find a way to buy their beloved clarets even in wartime."

"Then—?" When he still seemed unable to make up his mind to confide in her, she asked, "Did you know that General Duchamp will likely be gone for several years?"

"No. . . ." he answered slowly. "Then tomorrow shall we sit down and go over all my accounts?"

While Marc's arithmetic was beyond reproach, she found his clumsy handwriting so hard to read and his spelling so fanciful that sometimes she had to laugh when she finally deciphered a sentence. But Marc hardly noticed, so intent was he on leading her through the maze of numbers. At last she understood for herself and exclaimed, "Then he takes everything away, every sou of profit, and leaves you with no money at all to operate the *chaix*."

"Exactly. I have no way of paying a single man on the next *jour du terme*."

"But how does he imagine you will survive?"

"I am supposed to tell my men they must trust me awhile, and then when I can stretch it no farther, go beg for credit in Bordeaux."

"But where does he put the huge profits you have made the last two years?"

"I have no idea. They are not on deposit in your old bank in Bordeaux."

Together they worked each morning over records, trying to find some account they could collect, some creditor they could postpone awhile. Nicole enjoyed his companionship and often looked up to see his eyes on her. How devoted and kind Marc always was. One day, he led her without telling her why to a pasture behind his cottage, and pointed to a black Arabian horse.

"Oh, he is beautiful, Marc! He looks almost like—like—"

"—like Jupiter," he supplied. "In fact he was sired by Jupiter some two years ago, just before the fire. I have named him Apollon. Wasn't Apollo the son of Jupiter back in Greek times?"

"Oh, yes, and it is an excellent choice, for he has such a noble, graceful beauty."

"He is yours now, Nicol—madame. I have trained him for you. And when you will permit, I will teach little André to ride on some gentle pony."

In the next few weeks it became a common sight to see Nicole riding Apollon about the vineyards on tours of inspection, trailed by Marc on the big gray stallion he preferred over the smaller Arabians. They often picnicked with André on a bluff overlooking the Gironde, and everyone knew they could be found together working in the office of the *maître* every afternoon about five. Nicole found she was counting on Marc more and more to oversee some repair in the château, or to teach a skill or game to André, and in general to be a substitute father to the boy. Marc had a warm, playful manner that children loved, and André responded to him as he never had to the distant, unpredictable Roger. When Nicole would think ahead to some future time she always assumed Marc would be hovering helpfully nearby. However would she manage if he were not?

Nicole was surprised and upset when Clémence took her aside one day and lectured her about spending too much time with Marc. "It doesn't look right, mistress, what with the general away, and even if he weren't—"

"Oh, Clémence, who could possibly think ill of Marc, who is the most gentle, honest man, incapable of any wrongdoing?"

"But your partiality to him is so obvious! You are always singing his praises," the cook replied with some jealousy.

"Only because he deserves it!" Nicole exclaimed insensitively. "He is the kindest man I have ever known—and the most unselfish. Oh, Clémence, this is ridiculous! You know I think of Marc as a brother, and I always have. He was only a few months old when I was born, and we grew up side by side, as close as if we really had come from the same parents."

"Just so he remembers he's your brother," Clémence remarked drily. "From the look on his face when he is with you, the poor fellow has a bit of trouble."

One twilight Nicole put on her shawl and climbed down into the cold *chaix* looking for Marc, only to search every room without finding him, and started out on foot along the lane to his cottage. Near the pond meadow, she spotted him coming toward her with his funny limp, carrying two small, kicking boys under his arms like sacks of meal.

"Oh, Marc, what have you here? Are these your nephews? Has Noémie come home, or Jeanne?"

"No, mistress. These little rascals belong to Julie Georgeault. They got themselves trapped at the bottom of Bonjean's quarry this afternoon, and Julie called me to go over and pull them out." He gave them a short but stern lecture, swatted them both on their bottoms, and sent them running home.

"Julie Georgeault!" Nicole cried. "You never were a friend of hers before, Marc! Not when she was my maid. All the boys chased after Julie, but you never did back then. . . ." Nicole opened her eyes wide with shock as she realized that the Gaillards' house and Julie's little shack were separated only by a pasture. Then she saw with horror that a few fresh bundles of thatch were stacked beside the smaller cottage. "You're putting a new roof on her house too!" she exclaimed.

"But the rain has been pouring in, and the little children have often taken the grippe," he said defensively. "You wouldn't want them to suffer, mistress. . . ."

"Oh, Marc, you must watch out for Julie! You are such an innocent! You don't realize what she has in her head. Of course she wants to get her hands on you! You are so good and generous and so handsome"—Nicole gave him what she hoped was a sisterly smile—"and have an excellent job. Where else is Julie going to find such an easy mark as soft-hearted old Marc?" Nicole's voice was rising higher and higher. She was hardly aware in her excitement that they were walking along toward Marc's house.

Stepping inside his door, she laughed a little with him as she noticed the state of embarrassment her flattering outburst had caused. Of course she knew she was speaking indiscreetly, she told herself, trespassing in his private world, blurting out her thoughts too fast to consider every possible implication. But she was so terribly alarmed! Why hadn't she realized before what danger he was in? Why had she ever been foolish enough to let Julie remain here at Beaux-Clervaux?

"Poor Marc, you simply don't realize what would lie ahead of you. Did you know Pascal was back just for one night about a month ago? Clémence told me he was seen. Did you know that, Marc?" she demanded.

"No, mistress," he said with a curious half-smile.

The fire was crackling on the hearth and some *ragoût* with a wonderful aroma simmering in an iron kettle. Mère Gaillard must have just stepped outside for a moment. She was obviously in the midst of cooking supper.

"Surely you don't want to share Julie's favors with that scoundrel Pascal," Nicole said bluntly, causing Marc to blush a little. "Surely you don't intend to raise his brats for him, only to have him come back someday and take them away from you. Oh, Marc, Julie is no good! She was always a sneak and a schemer and an easy bit of baggage—" Nicole stopped suddenly when she noticed the blood had rushed to Marc's face. *Mon Dieu,* she must have gone too far! What a fool she had been! Marc actually loved Julie, unlikely as it seemed. And now Nicole had insulted her so gravely he would probably never speak to her again. She had uttered a few thoughtless words and lost Marc's friendship forever.

"Oh, Marc, I'm so terribly sorry! I simply didn't realize. Sometimes I say the most foolish things! Of course you are in love with her. Is that why you are so angry with me?" Then a new wave of indignation overwhelmed Nicole, and she said stubbornly, "But I can't help what I feel! Sometimes it is better to speak the truth. You would be making the most terrible mistake if you married her—well, of course she is already married— I mean, if you threw your life away on her, if you became her lover. You haven't already, have you? Have you? Oh, Marc, I would just die!" Hardly aware of it herself, she was pushing, almost pounding on his chest.

With a deep flush of emotion, Marc wrapped his arms around Nicole and gave her a fervent kiss. Then he said, "It is you I love and have always loved. How could you fail to know that? Oh, Nicole, if you could ever care for me, I would be the happiest man in the world. Just now I dared to believe. . . ." But already his eyes had clouded with doubt and his confidence was rapidly disappearing.

In her shock, Nicole could only think that she could not bear to hurt him. "But of course I do care," she said a bit uncertainly. Then she continued in perfect truth, "You make each day a joy. I need and trust and count on you. If I lost you, I don't know what I would do—"

And before she could finish the sentence he kissed her mouth again, and then her eyelids and blazing cheeks and her hairline just where the part began. The man was so huge, yet so tender, so careful to restrain himself and not crush her in his rugged arms. He was a gentle giant out of some fairy tale, she thought with loving amusement.

They jumped apart when they heard his mother's step on the path outside. Hastily, Nicole declined her offer of supper, and after allowing her eyes to linger a moment on Marc's, escaped from the cottage and ran back to the château as fast as she could.

24

Nicole fell asleep that night the moment her head hit the pillow, almost as though she had been drugged. But in the small hours of the morning, she awoke and tossed about, tormented by her conflicting reactions. On the one hand, she had a desperate fear of hurting Marc, and a premonition she had blundered into some new world where she did not belong. Yet, on the other hand, she was thrilled and flattered by his love, and yearned to make him satisfy all her lonely needs and hungers. Perhaps, she thought hopefully, she was entering on an exciting new chapter of her life.

Curling into a ball, she happily visualized the years ahead when she would grow old side by side with Marc, united as if by bonds of matrimony here at Beaux-Clervaux, which she would never leave no matter what commands Roger might try to give her; how Marc would serve as a real father and a fine example to André; and how, oh, yes, how she and Marc would indulge themselves in a few hours alone in some secret retreat, where he would caress and love and satisfy her as never before.

But then she groaned a little and, rolling over suddenly, buried her face in her pillow with guilt and despair. This was not what she had wanted for her life. She was too young yet to abandon hope. Much as she depended on Marc, and enjoyed his companionship, she knew she did not really love him. Not as she had loved—still did love William. Or could he teach her slowly to forget him? If the sex act with Marc proved as exciting as she dared suspect, perhaps—but then she groaned again. What had happened to her? How had she ever changed into a woman who lusted after a peasant, a barely literate peasant descended from a family that had been swineherds on the estate not so many years ago. Yes, she knew that bit of Gaillard family history. What would her father say if he could know she planned to spend the rest of her life as the mistress of Marc Gaillard? But of course such snobbery was supposed to be dead in this new democratic age. Swineherds were as good as counts and courtiers—and ambassadors.

Oh, *mon Dieu*, what would William himself say? She could still imagine his embrace just as vividly as if she had only slipped from his arms in the straw at La Force a few hours before. When would his memory ever dim? She suffered such mental torture she believed she should take another lover for that reason alone—not Roger, but a man who really loved her, a man in whom she could delight. But she could hear William's ironic laughter at her logic. "By all means, *ma petite*, allow your strapping peasant"—as he had called Marc that infamous night after the *Gerbaude*—"to pleasure you. He certainly gives the impression of just the sort of talent you require! But, be warned, my dear; you'll always have to struggle against your ingrained snobbery."

How she hated William! How she hated such lewd talk! But of course he was right about one thing: She was only a petty snob after all. If Marc were a *châtelain* by birth, she would be quite comfortable to settle down as his mistress. Or would she? When William was alive? When he was at this very moment—doing what? Romancing some London beauty; planning his royal wedding; dear heaven, not dallying once more with that relic, the Marquise de Vaucroze!

To Nicole's relief, Marc behaved as though nothing had happened when she went to his office the next day. Only when she looked at him with anxious eyes over the head of one of his employees did he give her a kind, reassuring smile. And when they were alone, he only talked about her luck that morning in managing to refuse delivery of a huge crystal chandelier Roger had ordered to replace the fine brass one in her father's library. In a scene requiring considerable dramatic talent, she had persuaded the outraged vendor that he must make her a refund of the large sum Roger had paid, except, of course, for a small percentage to compensate him for his inconvenience. And so at last Marc would have enough cash to meet his payroll, and the château would be spared such a calamity of taste. Marc congratulated her that she had managed to pull two millings out of one sack of grain, as the French saying had it.

It was not until he walked her home from the *chaix* one evening just after nightfall that he allowed himself to speak to her once again with the familiar *tu*. Then when he helped her down the stile behind the big barn, she dropped quite naturally into his open arms, and they pressed against each other for a long time. Nicole was still standing on the bottom step to be closer to his own height, and he laid her head against his neck and shoulder as he stroked her hair. She loved the comfort and strength of his hard body, and soon felt excitement welling within her. A little fearfully she wondered if Marc would act tonight. Where would he want to take her? Where could they go to be safe from any possible discovery? Strangely enough, she could think of few places on the great estate. Her mind recoiled from the *pavillon*, which she had carefully avoided since her return, and she sensed Marc's natural dignity would be offended if she tried to smuggle him into the château. Perhaps then he would simply take her to some bed of hay, and they would make love under the stars.

But even after he had kissed her a dozen times, he only walked her back to the château and sent her inside to stay. Though for the next fortnight he took a bit longer each evening to bid her goodnight, he never advanced beyond the boundaries he had set for himself. As Nicole thrashed about almost angrily in her bed alone, she knew that he was not soon going to abandon his own good resolutions. She had never known a man with such high principles. She knew he would not dream of insulting her with a single caress to her breasts, or, heaven forbid, her thighs! The one time her hip had accidentally grazed his swollen groin he had stepped away abruptly. He was as excited as she was by their innocent kisses and embraces, yet he remained determined to treat her like a little virgin. In her exasperation, she wondered how much longer she must wait to feel—to enjoy— But, oh, this was wickedness. Marc was right. They must not sin. Somehow they must go on together for months and years, and not sink to a state of adultery.

Then one night when he was doing nothing more than kiss her fingertips after she had fed him a sweet in the pantry, Clémence burst in on them and irately ordered Marc out of her house. He had a look of sheepish amusement on his face as he obeyed, and Nicole was laughing too until Clémence's tongue-lashing became too much to bear.

"Must you behave like a shameless hussy with this good man? Have you no sense of decency? I said nothing, to my great regret, when you were found naked in your own guardian's bed years ago. Did you think I didn't know? That we didn't miss you that morning? Julie came running down to the kitchen in alarm, and soon the whole household found out how you had celebrated the *Gerbaude*. I should have spoken out plainly then—and I blame myself most bitterly—to warn you to mend your morals, or you would come to no happiness! How right my instincts were! Your relationship with Falkland has ruined your life!"

"You can't speak this way to me, Clémence! I don't deserve such abuse. There was nothing I could have done to stop the duke that night after the *Gerbaude*. But of course, you're right, it has ruined my life—" She was weeping bitterly, and finally the old woman relented and hugged her.

"Oh, God, I am shattered to think the whole house knew, that Julie knew —that Marc might know—"

"And what is so precious about Marc? If you are foolish enough to imagine that you are in love with that hulking peasant—"

"Oh, but I am—I mean, I think I am. He is so very kind."

"Nonsense, you are in love with your wicked English duke and always will be! The look that was on your face whenever you was with him—I have never seen it before or since! You hardly regard old Marc with that same expression!"

"Oh, I was just a child then. Besides, I'll never see the duke again."

"You'll see him again. I know it in my bones."

"You are mad. How can you possibly say that?"

"I have prayed hard that he will recognize his wife and son."

"Oh, Clémence," Nicole moaned hopelessly. "It can never be."

"Someday, when the war is over. . . ."

Nicole only shook her head, then suddenly brightened. "Besides, Marc loves me. I honestly believe he will give me the only happiness I will ever have."

"Stop, I won't listen to that! You are married in the sight of God to another man, be he good or evil, and I will not have you committing sins here in your father's house." With burning eyes, she demanded, "Do you want to destroy this good man's life? Do you want to endanger his position on this estate? Marc, who has lowly origins, must establish himself as the master of these men, but you are only helping to earn him their ridicule as your plaything and shadow. Do you want the peasants of Beaux-Clervaux to despise you both, but him the more? And do you want to ruin Marc's happiness just as Falkland ruined yours? Don't you know Marc is such a good and faithful man that he will never allow himself to love another woman, never have a home and children of his own, unless you set him free?"

If it had arrived a week earlier she would have torn it in bits, but after Clémence's lecture—which she had to acknowledge as the truth—Nicole welcomed Roger's letter as a merciful solution. After a few words of cheap, obvious cajolery at the beginning, he ordered her to sail immediately to Egypt. Bonaparte had recently decreed that high-ranking officers might send for their wives, though not children, for—Roger emphasized— desert fevers were too severe. He expressed a need to "enjoy your companionship," and "try once again to produce a son." Clearly, he said, they had given the effort insufficient time. He said he regretted the unpleasant scene in her chamber that last night, and hoped she would accept his apology. But then, in closing, he sidled characteristically into a threat. Only with her beside him in Cairo, he said, would he be able to understand the financial needs of Beaux-Clervaux, which she had written to him describing so plaintively. She knew what he meant. Unless she went to Egypt, there would be no more funds for the *chaix*.

Her heart ached to leave André behind—for how long, she did not know—and to face the final parting with Marc. She had told him only that Roger was forcing her to go to Egypt in exchange for funds for the estate, and then had avoided him so carefully that he had become hurt and angry and then finally resigned. At last on the night before her departure, she had to go to him. Careful to slip out the kitchen door without Clémence's knowledge, she ran along in the dark, shivering a little in the thin muslin gown under a shawl Marc's mother had crocheted for her, hurrying down the hill past the kitchen garden and the barnyard, now empty of its daytime population of ducks, geese, chickens, goats, and pigs; past the new stables where Apollon must wait for her uncertain return; past the little mill and its pond and the pond meadow. And then, once again, she noticed with a stab of jealousy the light in Julie's cottage, located so close by Marc's.

As though she were only a lonely wayfarer, Nicole stood for a moment outside Marc's house and gazed sadly in the little square window framed by roses. He was sitting on a stool by the fire, leaning forward, his big arms resting on each knee, a pensive expression on his face. How young and handsome and vital he looked, how naturally he sprang to help his mother when she tried to unhook the heavy kettle. In reward she patted his shoulder absently. What a telling little scene it was, a happy moment in family life. And just what Marc would never know again, once his mother was dead, if Nicole persisted in her selfish domination of his life.

His mother spoke some word to him that Nicole could not hear, and suddenly she realized it would not do to stand here and seem to eavesdrop. When she pulled the door open an inch or two, Marc saw her in a moment and rushed outside, clasping her to him with relief born of his fear that she had meant to leave without saying good-bye. His mouth burned on hers so passionately she wondered if he had abandoned his resolutions at long last. She let herself follow his lead and return the hungry kisses until she believed she would lose her own control. If she did not pull away, they might soon be tumbling together here in the meadow.

When he touched his hand at last to the tingling skin of her breasts, she barely found the willpower to pull herself free. "Oh, Marc! I love to feel your caresses, but I cannot allow you to do what I know we both will later regret."

"Foolish girl! How can you dream I would ever regret making love to you? And how do you imagine I can endure your absence without some memory of—oh, Nicole, please reconsider this trip! We can manage without his money! It is unbelievable that you should have to sell yourself into slavery to Duchamp!"

"It isn't only the money. I let you believe that. I didn't know if I would have the courage to speak honestly to you." She pushed him away, hoping to stem the waves of desire she felt. "Marc, you must not wait for me to return!"

"Of course I will wait for you—forever!"

"No. You must not—and you must think of marrying someone else. It is your only chance for happiness."

"Don't be absurd," he laughed and pulled her tight against his chest again, tilting her mouth toward his.

But she pushed again more forcefully, and he released her with surprise. "I have to say something so painful it breaks my heart. I do not love you, Marc. I—I love another man!"

"No!" he cried. "I don't believe you! I will never believe you! You love me!" He grabbed her by the shoulders, shaking her painfully.

"Not the way I love the—other man, the man I am—committed to, the man who is the father of André. He is my real husband, and I can truly love only him!"

In the last hour before her departure, Nicole slipped into the chapel to lay bunches of roses on the two brass plaques. It was only on the way back out the door that she noticed the votive lights Clémence kept burning. There were three little candles flickering as though with wills of their own. For André and herself—and the duke! How stubborn Clémence was!

Then Nicole threw herself impetuously to her knees on the prie-dieu before the bank of candles, and prayed, "Oh, dear God, if only you would allow me to see William one more time!"

25

At her elbow, the admiral with his great bicorne hat and white feather cockade gallantly pointed out the Sicilian coast. "How fortunate that we have had an unusually smooth voyage, madame." And doubly fortunate, Nicole thought to herself, that they had not encountered the British fleet. Not yet. She knew that Admiral Brueys was far too polished to distress her with such a possibility, but the junior officers here on board *L'Orient* had made no secret of the great hazard.

"But how regrettable that you have had to pass the entire trip without the pleasure of feminine companionship!"

Nicole agreed she had been very surprised to find she was the only officer's wife, the only woman, on board—at least officially; though rumor had it that below decks many lower-class women, wives and camp followers, were traveling disguised as foot soldiers. "I know my husband believed other wives of officers would make the trip."

"And no doubt their husbands urged them, but they lacked your excellent combination of wifely devotion and adventurous spirit." Nicole suspected this courtly speech only concealed his disapproval of her foolhardy trip, and his belief that Roger was a blackguard and a fool to bid her cross the embattled Mediterranean to the burning deserts of Egypt. She had already detected Brueys's suave contempt for Roger.

When the admiral finally left her alone, she leaned on the railing of the quarterdeck and drank in the beauty of the summer day. Sicily was a rugged silhouette rising to a hazy apex that could well be Mount Etna; the ocean and sky were both a shimmering blue; a flock of white clouds ran a race with this squadron of tall ships, led by the three-deck, one-hundred-gun *L'Orient,* flagship of the French fleet.

How she had enjoyed the glimpses of Corsica and Sardinia and the Alps rising above the hills of Italy—in fact the whole voyage from the minute she had set foot on board at Toulon. Not even briefly had she felt seasick. Perhaps she might still turn into a fine traveler, and follow in her father's footsteps. She was excited to think that she would see at any moment, just there to starboard, the coast of Africa, and that she would stand on the soil of Egypt in little more than a week.

Guiltily, she realized how little she had missed Marc since her departure from Beaux-Clervaux. She might remember—feel, actually—his wild kisses on that last night, and then recall how she had been distraught to break his heart with those cruel words, and how in his typically selfless fashion, he had ended by comforting her tears and asking no pity for himself. But there was no doubt in her mind that she had done the right thing. Marc was free. And she? She could only return to the mockery of living as Roger's devoted wife.

But she would not fret today. The weather was far too delightful, with an exhilarating breeze cooling the rays of the summer sun that often beat all too hard. She had already found that her skin burned quickly, so today she had tied on her big leghorn hat with a white scarf. She did not want to present herself to Roger with a freckled face and red nose.

And then she smiled a little. Had this pleasant voyage so restored her that she could even think coquettishly of Roger? As she watched some seamen unfurl a sail, she marveled again at her mellow mood. Brueys had told her that Bonaparte and Roger had sailed on this very ship to Egypt. Suddenly she hoped that Roger would be free to meet her in Alexandria. Was there any chance they could find some happiness and pleasure together? He had once loved her well, she thought wistfully. Had he become selfish and cruel only when her unexplained fidelity to William drove him past all endurance? Now in Egypt she would have to try to give him a child, she would have to allow him to. . . . Suddenly she felt a stirring of desire for Roger, and laughed a little at herself. What a wicked woman she was to long for the caresses of her own legal husband! Quickly, she turned away from the curious stare of a midshipman who had seen her amusement. Why in the world was she in such a gay, optimistic mood? Why was she even dreaming fondly of Roger! Then the truth struck her like a cold splash of ocean spray. It was Marc who had made sex seem good and pure again, and cleansed her mind of the fear and disgust that Roger himself had taught her to know.

The little squadron anchored off Alexandria at twilight in the same location where Bonaparte had arrived with three hundred ships and disembarked to occupy the city. Nicole went ashore in a shallop and was led into what appeared to be nothing more than an old rock fort on a narrow peninsula. In the vermilion light of sunset, the silhouetted buildings of the town looked amazingly small and undistinguished. Where was the great marble metropolis of the Roman Empire? Why had they brought her ashore to sleep in this rough, remote fort of Kait Bey, which could only give her nightmares of La Force or the Conciergerie?

In the morning a punctilious colonel introduced himself as an aide to her husband, and urged her to board Bonaparte's own *berline*, which had just arrived to carry her to the Nile and Cairo. But she protested that she must first see the city of Alexandria. It little mattered that Roger had not bothered to come to meet her, but she would not be her father's daughter if she passed up this opportunity to see one of the most famous cities in the world.

"See Alexandria, madame? But you can see it all from this very spot!" the colonel exclaimed with amazement at such a wish.

Nicole explained patiently to the man, who must be only one more uneducated peasant risen to high rank, that Alexandria, founded by Alexander the Great, where Euclid had taught geometry and Cleopatra had dallied with Anthony, had not only contained one million inhabitants at its peak, but had possessed the greatest library of the ancient world and the incredible marble Pharos or lighthouse, four hundred feet tall and one of the marvels of all time.

"Alas, madame, the once-great city has shrunk to this mud town you see before you which has no more than four thousand inhabitants, mostly here along the Ras-el-Tin peninsula with a few more collected by the Rosetta Gate. These few houses no longer even fill the medieval Arab walls."

"But surely there are monuments surviving?"

"Only the single pillar of a Roman temple named for Pompey, and two obelisks called Cleopatra's Needles."

"But where are the graves of Cleopatra and of Alexander himself, whose body was brought down the Nile in a glass coffin to be buried in the city named for him? Where are the library and the giant Pharos?"

Carefully controlling his impatience, the colonel consulted a Turkish pasha within the fort, and then reported with a certain satisfaction that the tombs of Cleopatra and Alexander were both quite lost, as was the library. But the Pharos had stood on this very spot, and its stones had been used to build this fort of Kait Bey. She was presently standing inside all that remained of the fifth wonder of the ancient world!

And so Nicole had little reason to delay entering Napoleon's fine black carriage, embossed with the large gold insignia of the commander in chief and escorted by a detachment of two dozen troops. But as soon as the little procession left the coastal plain and its cooling sea wind, she was nearly prostrated by the heat. Never in her life had she suffered such a high temperature. She opened all the windows and tucked up her skirts, praying that no soldier on horseback would ride past the windows and look in. But the hot wind blowing sand and the glare of the sun made her even more uncomfortable, so she had to pull her shades and swelter inside a dark, sealed cab, only peeking out occasionally at the monotonous sand dunes.

The carriage stopped from time to time at villages where the soldiers would take water from the wells, sometimes having to draw their muskets to hold back the natives. If the inhabitants were not belligerent, Nicole would step down and stretch and try to exchange greetings with the men dressed in their white *galabiyehs*. How strange, she thought, that the women of the village only hovered at a distance, carefully covering their faces with a piece of fabric.

Sometimes the procession would pass a long, slow camel caravan, the stoic beasts carrying enormous bundles on their backs, and once she heard the soldiers cry out at a beautiful mirror-like lake as blue as the sky and decorated with a fringe of palm trees. As she blinked her eyes in disbelief, the colonel rode alongside and informed her that it was only a strange apparition that often appeared in the desert, and had sometimes tragically drawn their soldiers on to exhaustion in its pursuit. Such a vision had been named *le mirage*, he said, from the word for looking glass.

During the third day the procession did not stop once at a well, though the heat seemed worse than ever, and Nicole finally had to beg the colonel for a drink. He replied tersely that they were completely out of water but would soon reach an oasis. They traveled on for two hours before they finally stopped at what appeared to be only a dry riverbed containing a few palm trees. As she trudged across the sand skeptically, she made out the stone ring of a well and sprang forward. But in a moment, when the soldiers had drawn up a bucket, they cried out *"Empoisonné!"* This well too, like the others known to the French in the region, had been poisoned by the enemy Bedouins. Her procession had no choice but to press on in their misery. Already more than one horse had died, and several men were ill with heat exhaustion. With some difficulty, Nicole persuaded the colonel to allow the sick men to ride inside the *berline* with her.

But on the following day, when she believed she could endure little more, they passed as if by a miracle into a world of green vegetation and beheld almost immediately the wide brown expanse of the Nile. With incredible relief Nicole gulped from a canteen of water, and stumbled on board the narrow felucca, a graceful lateen-rigged boat, to begin the long voyage to Cairo.

Sped by the summer wind, the swift vessel maneuvered through the heavy traffic of three-masted xebecs, *dahabeahs* or house boats with sails, barges, and small *dgerms* on the chocolate-colored river. Nicole watched with interest the farms of wheat, rice, flax, or vegetables growing right to the river's edge, and enjoyed the strange music of the creaking *shadoof*, a kind of scoop with which farmers raised the Nile water to the level of the land, or the *sakieh*, a waterwheel turned by a blindfolded water buffalo.

Though she was well attended by an Egyptian servant who fed her meals of roast pigeon or turkey, guavas, figs, cucumbers, bread baked on stones in the hot sun, and coffee, she was always a little ill and could only sit listlessly on deck with a wet scarf across her face for some relief from the stifling heat.

But one day she jumped up with a cry of delight at the sight, in the purplish haze of the horizon, of three great pyramids. The first two were of a nearly equal size, and the third somewhat smaller and removed. Undoubtedly these were the Pyramids of Gizeh, and the felucca had reached the outskirts of Cairo itself. But in the same moment she detected a stench unlike any of the river odors she had become accustomed to. Then she began to see human bodies washed up on the banks of the river or floating no more than an arm's length from the boat. When she caught a glimpse of an Egyptian warrior decapitated by a single clean stroke, she covered her face with her hands. The odor was overwhelming—there must be hundreds! Obviously, it had been a great French victory. These men had been slain on Bonaparte's orders, on Roger's, to secure the conquest of Egypt.

When the felucca finally docked in the center of the city, the Nile was mercifully free of corpses. Hastily pulling herself together and trying to straighten her hair, Nicole climbed ashore to receive Roger's welcome. She was no pretty sight, she knew, sunbaked and ill, her dress clinging to her damp body. As fastidiously dressed as ever in the same heavy blue coat he wore in the temperate climates of Europe, Roger gave her a greeting she knew was staged more for his audience of aides than for herself—numerous pretty kisses to her hand followed by a wet kiss on the mouth, which might be banned by etiquette, but proved to all observers what an ardent husband he was.

Napoleon had graciously invited them to share the Elfi-Bey Palace with him, Roger told her enthusiastically, adding that of course this former home of the Mameluke beys, who had been driven south by the French, was large enough so that they need encounter Bonaparte only when especially invited to dine at his table. Roger only made joking answers when she asked why no other wives had traveled on *L'Orient*. "Cairo is full of Frenchwomen, if it is companionship you want—though you may not hanker to meet our common whores and wives of the meanest classes!"

"But I thought the wives of all high-ranking officers were being allowed to come."

With a little laugh, he bent to kiss her lips lightly and touch one breast. "Then we can only conclude that they were not so hungry as you for the— er, affection of their husbands, isn't that so?" Nicole was silent. How insulting he could be! She had almost forgotten. Somehow she must find the patience and self-control to submit to him tonight with some measure of good grace.

But after an excellent supper of French food at Napoleon's table in the company of five or six other officers, Roger rose conspicuously as they were all taking cognac in a parlor, and excused himself to the assembled group. He regretted that he must leave the palace on urgent business and would return at a late hour. Nicole was so astonished and confused, not knowing whether he had publicly insulted her or not, that she waited only a minute or two before she stood up, mumbled an apology, and ran to bed.

For the next week, whether they dined alone together or with Bonaparte, Roger went out every night after dessert and did not return. Not once had he come to Nicole's bed since her arrival or offered any explanation for not making love to her. In fact she had little opportunity to talk to him at all because the only time she saw him was at meals, when they were attended by a flock of orderlies and servants.

One night at bedtime in her chamber in the former harem of the palace, her Egyptian maid Ayyam assisted her as she tried on the handsome garments she had bought in the bazaar that day. Wearing a crimson silk dress with a tight Turkish *yelek*, or vest, Nicole added the heavy gold necklace she had found for only a few francs, and Ayyam exclaimed, "*Très belle! Madame est très belle!*"

Nicole thanked her and praised her rapidly improving French, then began to remove the beautiful things a little sadly.

"*Madame est très belle, mais elle n'a pas de mari!*" Ayyam said and shook her head pityingly. Madame had no husband, no real husband at all.

Nicole could hardly expect to conceal that fact from Ayyam, but merely shrugged as she put on her nightgown, then sat down again to let the maid brush her long hair. In the mirror she watched with a little amusement the intense look on Ayyam's face as she struggled with French to convey a plan to Nicole. If the mistress wished, Ayyam's own husband could follow General Duchamp and find out what woman he went to each night, for surely the man must have a mistress, and then some spell or curse could be put on the wicked creature to make the general return to his wife's bed where he belonged.

Nicole laughed heartily when she finally understood. "Oh, no, we will not use black magic! If some woman wants General Duchamp, she is quite welcome to him!"

Ayyam followed this thought skeptically, then asked, "But still you would like to find out what woman, no?"

Nicole pondered the question while Ayyam finished her hair. Then their eyes met in the mirror, and she answered slowly, surprised at her own daring, "Can you send him tomorrow night. . . ."

Every morning for the next week, Fawzi, Ayyam's husband, reported much the same story. He had followed Roger from the palace to the new outdoor café called Tivoli Gardens after its Parisian model, where all the French officers gathered. Roger would join some table of men he knew, order a brandy, and soon pick up one of the girls, French or Egyptian, plying their trade in the café. For another hour he would buy her drinks at the table, now grown boisterous as his friends, drinking heavily, were joined by women of their own, and then he would take the girl to a room in the bazaar where they would spend the rest of the night. Always Fawzi ended by assuring Nicole that the whore was not nearly as pretty as herself. He would stare with wide-eyed sympathy, no doubt expecting to see tears of jealousy as he backed out her door.

Nicole rehearsed in her mind a dozen biting speeches to put to Roger. Why in the world had he subjected her to a dangerous sea voyage and an incredible desert crossing only to avoid her so completely? What had happened to his wish to have a child? If not to use in bed, what perverse motive did he have for bringing her to Cairo? But still she had no opportunity to question him. Lately Napoleon had demanded their presence at every meal, placing Nicole at the end of the table as his hostess. Despite that little honor, Nicole had grown to detest the long dinners that began with the men paying her elaborate compliments and then ignoring her completely.

One night, Bonaparte, in the green coat with red facings of the Chasseurs, his *corps de garde*, lectured for a quarter of an hour about the superiority of Burgundy wines over those of Bordeaux, while Nicole could only sit and fidget in silence. It was not true, he declared, that Burgundy lost strength and flavor in traveling, and he required every guest at the table to praise the Montrachet they were drinking. How tactless the man could be! Of course he must know about her origins in the Bordelais, with

Roger forever bragging about his restoration of Beaux-Clervaux. But then, Napoleon's graceless small talk was the despair of Parisian society.

No wonder she let her mind wander so often during these tedious dinners. She had been paying little attention to some talk of foreign politics, but then sat bolt upright. She had just heard Napoleon say, "Thus provoked, Falkland in Naples responded by dispatching another flotilla through the Straits of Messina."

"The Duke of Falkland in Naples?" Nicole exclaimed in a sudden lull in the conversation, then regretted her imprudent words.

Napoleon courteously explained that the British efforts to defeat him in Egypt and protect their interests in the East were directed from Naples by Falkland, King George's most trusted adviser. Napoleon apparently felt a certain honor at meriting so worthy an opponent and enjoyed matching wits with Falkland, who had recently proved somewhat the stronger player. Not only did the duke have under his command the Mediterranean fleet of the brilliant Admiral Nelson, but had just wooed the Ottoman Turks away from their alliance with the French. Nevertheless, nothing could prevent the French from going on to India, Napoleon assured his guests without a sign of doubt.

After sipping his wine thoughtfully for a moment, he added in a wry tone, "And Falkland's network of spies sometimes reaches into the inner sanctum here in Cairo!" All the men at the table responded with knowing laughter.

Because of Napoleon's sudden departure with his entourage, Roger was left with Nicole and had little choice but to walk with her to their apartment, where he must collect his hat before going out. Apparently undismayed at being alone with her, he said sociably, "No doubt you wondered about the general's little joke at his own expense. He became enchanted here in Cairo not long ago with the young and beautiful Madame Fourès, but she professed to be happily married to her lieutenant husband. Napoleon took the earliest opportunity to send the lieutenant home to France, and as soon as he departed, found it surprisingly easy to entice the lady into his bed. But alas, Fourès's transport was captured by British ships in the Mediterranean. As might be expected all passengers were held as prisoners, but Lieutenant Fourès was rushed back to Alexandria by British corsair for no other reason than to confront his erring wife. It was Falkland's idea of an excellent joke on our commander in chief."

But Nicole only sniffed a little at the prank. Let the duke flaunt his power in Naples. His present supremacy had been bought at the price of her own ruined life—and her son's. She had no inclination to admire his witticisms.

Instead she asked Roger acidly, "Does every French officer in Egypt enjoy a mistress—or a succession of whores!"

Roger regarded her under elevated brows, but did not reply. As they entered their salon, she waved Ayyam away and attacked him again. "Why in heaven's name did you bring me to Egypt only to repudiate me? Not that I care, Roger! Not that I desire your company in bed, as you like to flatter yourself! But you have deprived my child of the care of his mother, and I have undergone great hardships to reach Cairo. I demand that you give me some explanation."

He stared at her with distaste and turned away to enter his dressing room, but she ran ahead to block the doorway. "Answer me now or I will apply to Bonaparte tomorrow for transportation home to France!"

"By all means do, but he will not grant it."

"And why not? He can hardly fail to have noticed that we are estranged, thanks to your vulgar display every night when you leave to visit your whores. No doubt he wonders why I have remained so long—"

"You poor fool! It was Napoleon who asked me to send for you. Why do you think no other women came? Not even Josephine herself was invited!"

"Whatever can you mean?" she exclaimed with alarm.

"The commander in chief decided that you should hostess his table here in Elfi-Bey, and perform certain—other functions," he said with a smirk.

"And you consented?" she cried so loudly that Ayyam looked in the room with concern, then withdrew at Nicole's impatient wave. "You consented to pander your wife to him!"

Suddenly sneering so contemptuously she hardly recognized him, he said, "What reason have I to cherish a wife who dropped a bastard in my bed in the first days of our marriage, and then, even when I was generous enough to register the brat as my own child, still used every possible ploy to deprive me of my marital rights, even as she moaned the name of some other man in her sleep; then belatedly granted me the favor of her passive body only after some lover had painfully jilted her?"

Nicole reeled under the assault, and then recovered and challenged him, "What reason indeed, now that you have used me and my family name to turn yourself into a pathetic imitation of an aristocrat! What reason now that you have stolen my mother's jewels! Yes, I see from your face that you did not believe I knew. What reason now that you have gained control of all my estates and are bleeding them dry of every drop of profit that you bank I know not where!"

26

What if—just what if her ship were captured on the Mediterranean by the British? Such a daydream was not impossible of realization. Nicole had little doubt she could persuade Bonaparte to send her home, even if there were some truth to Roger's story. If Napoleon made any overtures to her, she would resist him so tirelessly he would simply give up. She knew he hated to have his time wasted, and once he learned she was unresponsive, would quickly lose interest in the pursuit.

So she could dream of departing soon from Alexandria on a ship that might indeed fall into British hands. With each new day came more stories of Nelson's successes. What exactly would happen if her ship were boarded by the British? Should she ask to be taken immediately to the captain and identify herself—as who, pray tell? As the Duchess of Falkland? They would only think her a lunatic. On a French ship she would hardly be able to conceal the fact that she was married to Bonaparte's second in command. Should she ask to speak to Admiral Nelson himself—and tell him what? That she had been the ward of the Duke of Falkland and sought the protection of her guardian. Yes, that was best. Then Nelson would have to take her to Naples.

And the duke himself, how would he receive her, or would he be willing to see her at all? Would he let her languish in some *pensione* while his underlings stalled her with excuse after excuse, as in those first days at Versailles; or would he send her directly back to France to be rid of her as fast as possible, or even let her go with the rest of the French to one of those prison camps in Turkey where unspeakable atrocities were committed? But surely she would not suffer such a fate at Falkland's hands.

And when she had been ushered into some ornate drawing room in Naples to wait for the duke, how would he finally greet her? Would he be cold, pained, scornful, embarrassed by the unsubstantiated story of a child, anxious to be free at all costs of this tearful woman? Try as hard as she could, she could not imagine any happiness from a meeting with Falkland. Quite the opposite. No doubt she would be well advised to pray that her French vessel crossed the Mediterranean without incident.

But there was no doubt in her mind that she must convince Napoleon to let her leave on the first ship. And tonight, with Roger out of the city to subdue an uprising in Suez, she might have a chance to speak alone with him. Then to her shock she found she was quite alone with Napoleon at the dining table. During the first course, she blurted out nervously, in the middle of one of his monologues, that she wanted to go home immediately. He paused a moment with spoon in midair, nodded, and then picked up the thread of his conversation. He had looked both surprised and irritated, she decided, and congratulated herself at the end of the evening that her awkward little speech had prevented any attempt to seduce her.

But the next night and for a week after that, he continued to require her to dine tête-à-tête. When she reminded him of her desire to leave, as she frequently did, he always replied politely that he would advise her of the next departure from Alexandria. At no time did he try to touch her or refer to any kind of intimate relationship. But still, she told herself, he must have some immoral use for her in mind. Why else would he want to see her alone night after night? Her conversation was hardly brilliant, for he gave her almost no opportunity to speak at all. He talked incessantly—lectured really—just as he did before his admiring staff, about every subject from his reorganization of the local government to the height of the Nile at flood and his plan to engrave the names of all Frenchmen killed in Egypt on the sides of the Pyramids.

When the call came one night for yet another supper, she put on the crimson silk with the tight *yelek* and the heavy gold necklace more for her own amusement than any other reason. Bonaparte never noticed anything she wore, at least not favorably. Only once he had mentioned her gown to comment that its yellow color made her skin look sallow and hoped she had not taken some tropical disease.

His Mameluke valet, wearing an exotic costume, led her through a delicate trefoil arch into a great hall she had never seen before. It was lined on three sides by an arcade of lacy arches, with the high walls above decorated by carved arabesques and intricate mosaics, then superfluously covered by hanging carpets. On the tile floor was the largest rug she had ever seen, woven of blues and reds and golds more vivid than any ever employed in Europe by Aubusson or Gobelin. On a low divan before a fountain Nicole saw Napoleon, reclining in a bright silk *galabiyeh* and sipping lazily from a silver cup.

They both exclaimed at the other's novel costume and the coincidence of their masquerade, and at their cleverness and daring and the excitement of this fairy-tale palace. "Should we come to the East and taste none of its ancient luxuries and pleasures? Should we dine here every night in a civilization older than our own on French food and wines, as though we were still seated at our dining tables in Montmartre or the Île St. Louis?"

"By no means, *mon général*," she replied, marveling at the new warmth and charm of his personality.

Nicole seated herself on a neighboring divan with only a moment of hesitation—this piece of furniture was distressingly similar to a bed. But Napoleon had given no sign of amorous intent, and there must be six servants in the hall to serve them. She tried to relax and keep pace with the countless dishes that were placed on the low brass table between the divans. Somewhat hesitantly she tasted a lamb and okra stew, which Napoleon showed her how to scoop with the large disks of bread; then roast pigeons stuffed with wheat; *biram ruzz*, a mold of chicken and rice; beef and rice; rabbit and rice; eggplant stuffed with rice; and *tamiya*, a deep-fried fava bean cake.

When she was served a little glass of heavy red syrup, Napoleon asked her to guess what it was. She sniffed and tasted the liquid that proved almost too sugary to be palatable. It was familiar, but she could not be quite sure. "Is it pomegranate?"

"No, it is attar of roses."

She exclaimed with surprise and tried to take a mouthful, but the excessive sweetness was sickening, and they both laughed as she wrinkled her nose. How she would enjoy a good glass of wine to wash down this strange food!

As though he had read her mind, he said, "I have a surprise for you, madame!"

Her eyes brightened with pleasure. Imagine abrupt, preoccupied Napoleon planning surprises. He waved to a waiter who brought in a tray with several wine bottles. Even across the room she recognized the unique Bordeaux shape that as a child she had thought looked like proud men with high shoulders while Burgundy bottles were lazy old men with bellies. The waiter displayed a label for her to read, and she gasped with delight. It was a bottle of Beaux-Clervaux of 1789.

"Will you approve this year, madame, or would you prefer another? When I sent home for the bottles of your château, my order was filled with several different vintages."

"Oh, how extremely thoughtful of you! But 1789 was—an excellent summer. I remember it well. I worked in the harvest myself for several days. There were menacing clouds overhead, but we brought in the grapes without a drop of rain. It was a memorable year at Beaux-Clervaux—and for all of France," she said with only a trace of sadness in her voice.

"Then what would be more appropriate than to drink a toast to the historic events of that great year!" He had come to sit beside her on her divan on the pretext of reading the label. "To the Bastille! To the Revolution! To the tricolor and to France!" And so Nicole could not escape drinking this salute, with the wine of Beaux-Clervaux itself, to the Revolution she had always despised, proposed by the man who had already emerged as the heir of the mantle of its leadership.

"Nine years have passed, madame. Have they been as kind for yourself as for France?"

Nine years since she had first gone to Versailles and disgraced herself before the queen and fallen in love with Falkland and gone to bed with him at Beaux-Clervaux! And then Langmuir and Rouen and Roger and years in prison and a marriage ceremony in a prison cell and then William's anguished face as he lost himself in the traffic of the rue St. Antoine. Oh, God, that sight would haunt her forever. And then the queen at the guillotine and her poor head gushing blood and then that meaningless marriage to Roger and the birth of André and the little king racked with coughs gasping in her arms and then the final disaster—William on the stairs with hateful eyes burning into her, taking the poor king away and abandoning her and André forever.

And now this man, an upstart as ruthlessly ambitious as Roger—after all, everyone said Napoleon had taken the expensive mistress of Barras off his hands and married her, a woman six years older than himself, to win the command in Italy—rude, violent-tempered, coarse, vain, and power-hungry, derisively nicknamed the Little Corporal—this man had asked her such a question. She hated what he stood for, hardly liked him better than she did Roger though she knew he was vastly more brilliant, a genius in fact, and perhaps had certain good traits of character she was only just discovering.

Sitting close beside, his shrewd, solemn eyes upon her, he studied her face and hair and the red veil woven with gold and her heavy gold earrings and necklace, and said with surprising sensitivity, "You need not answer a question that pains you so greatly, madame."

She wanted no pity from Bonaparte. Or anyone. She turned half away from him so that he could not see the tears brimming in her eyes. Then she could stand it no longer and suddenly faced him squarely, looking at his face as she had never done before. His features were remarkably fine. Why had she never thought of him as a handsome man? Perhaps because he was so short and slight, hardly taller than herself in her little heels. A few locks of brown hair covered his wide, smooth brow—he was so incredibly young, only one year older than herself; his level eyebrows, seemingly meant only to question or scowl; his deep, dark, serious eyes that were surely his finest feature; his long, thin nose—too long perhaps, but still rather elegant, she thought; a small, almost prim mouth; and then the strong, determined chin that somehow gave unity and purpose to the whole. Yes, she admired, even liked his face. At this range it was difficult to resent and fear Napoleon. But still—still she must remember he intended only to seduce and dishonor her.

"I beg you to recall, monsieur, that I am a married woman. Perhaps it is easy to perceive that my life—my marriage has not been happy, but I swear to you that I am not a light woman who will break her vows. I pray you to accept my assurances and spare us both a distasteful scene." To add to her discomfort, the tears began to run down her cheeks. For some reason she was particularly unwilling to cry in front of Bonaparte.

But his face softened remarkably. This man, who was said to have often expressed contempt for women, seemed to feel sympathy and even a new respect for her. "Please believe, madame, that I will never—distress you with untoward advances. I give you my word of honor. And as for the pain I am causing you at this very moment, I offer my deepest apologies. . . ." He pulled out a white handkerchief and after a rather awkward jab toward her face, handed it to her so that she could dry her own tears.

"And now," he continued abruptly, happy to have passed the little crisis, "perhaps you will allow me to tell you of the discoveries of the scholars and scientists I have brought with me to Egypt."

"Now, at nine in the morning? Surely you must be mistaken," Nicole exclaimed to Napoleon's valet, whom Ayyam had just escorted into her chamber as she sat in bed taking breakfast. It was hardly possible that Napoleon could be requesting her company at this early hour. She felt as though she had just parted from him at her apartment door, where late last night he had bid her goodnight as platonically as if he were her own brother.

"I am quite certain, madame, that the commander in chief wishes you to join him at the earliest possible moment."

Should she refuse? Should she say she was ill? But Napoleon had done nothing more reprehensible than try to entertain and amuse her—or, more correctly, she thought with a little laugh, educate her—to the best of his ability. And he had given his word of honor that he would not make improper advances. Firmly setting aside any trace of guilt, she hurried to dress in some attractive and versatile frock. She had no idea what the day would hold. If only he could have been a little more considerate. She was hardly a soldier always at the ready. Still she was flattered. Yes, flattered and a little intrigued, she admitted to herself.

The open landau took her around to the main gate of the Citadel, where he had his offices. So Napoleon had been up hours ahead of her. She had often heard him brag that he could do nicely with four hours of sleep a night, and had never before believed him.

Here on the heights of Mokkatam, she could see across the Nile to the Pyramids located just where the lush green valley changed to desert. In the foreground was the whole city of Cairo with its sprawl of houses and palaces and domed mosques—said to be two hundred fifty in number, and she could believe it from the forest of minarets before her eyes. And this great medieval Citadel, with towers and ramparts of golden stone, had once been the most powerful fort in Islam, but now served the French as their headquarters.

At last Napoleon climbed into the carriage, kissed her hand impatiently as though he thought such a useless custom should be done away with, and declared without preliminaries, "But you have not been to Gizeh, you told me that last night!"

"To Gizeh! Then are we going to see the Pyramids and Sphinx?" she cried in delight.

"Of course. Did you believe I would let you leave the most fascinating country in the world with nothing more than a shopping spree in the bazaar?"

The streets of Cairo, narrow at best, seemed to be more crowded than any city she had ever seen. Napoleon's coachman and the single uniformed guard on the box had to call out constantly to clear a path through the mass of camels and donkeys and pedestrians. She was close enough to touch the men in their white *galabiyehs* and fezzes or turbans or Arab headdresses called *kuffiyyahs*, and in fact many beggars stuck their arms into the carriage with pleas of *"Baksheesh!"* money! The few women on the streets were always completely covered, except for their eyes, by the black *tob*. How curious, she remarked to Napoleon, that the two sexes would be so dramatically demarcated by their dress, the men in white and bright colors, the women all in black. "Surely it is a distressing symbolism. Why do they despise their women and punish them with rigid rules of confinement?" she demanded.

"Perhaps they are only seeking to protect beloved wives, treasuring them as would never occur to us!" he laughed, scoffing a little at her concern.

The Pyramids grew ever larger on the drive to Gizeh, but when the road finally ended, several leagues of desert still waited to be crossed. Napoleon enjoyed her consternation when he told her they must proceed the rest of the way on camelback. To convince her to try to mount the unfriendly beast, he demonstrated by positioning himself on the wide saddle, expertly hooked his right foot under his left leg, and preserved perfect dignity as the beast lumbered to its feet. Skeptically, Nicole followed the directions he called to her, found the saddle comfortable enough, but then cried out in fear, believing herself falling first backward and then forward as the beast rose, one long leg at a time. Not only did the camel scowl, snarl, spit, and exude a foul odor, but its walk was so rocking that she felt as sick as if she were being tossed in a small boat. No wonder they called camels the ships of the desert.

But when she finally stood at the base of Cheops, the largest Pyramid, Nicole realized that she could hardly have found a more enthusiastic or encyclopedic guide than Bonaparte. With a barrage of facts, dates, and measurements, he led her in a door on the north side and along a passage so low that they must crouch. This entrance, he explained, had been cut a thousand years ago by Arab grave robbers unable to find the real entrance, which had been carefully disguised. Guarding their heads, Napoleon and Nicole stumbled along into the funerary chamber where once the pharaoh, surrounded by his treasure, had waited for the voyage to the other world. But now the room was empty except for the stone sarcophagus, having been pilfered even of the mummy, and Napoleon could only point out the two air shafts, meant not for ventilation but to allow the pharaoh's soul to fly away.

At least 100,000 men had labored for twenty years to build this Pyramid, before any knowledge of the wheel, lever, block and tackle, tools of iron, or even the presence of the horse in Egypt. Apparently they had utilized enormous temporary ramps made of brick to reach clear to the top. The heaviest stones were dug nearby, but the fine limestone that had once provided a gleaming white surface had been floated down the Nile. Now almost all the casing had been pried off to build the monuments of Cairo, including the Citadel.

He led her into the other two Pyramids, and then they stood before the enigmatic Sphinx, the crouching lion with the head of a pharaoh. The face of the godlike creature was badly broken, its nose and beard completely missing, and Napoleon explained that a Mameluke sultan, regarding it as a heathen effigy, had trained his cannons on it in target practice.

Napoleon asked Nicole if she were willing to climb to the top of Cheops to see the unforgettable view, and without a moment's hesitation she agreed. Laboriously, they pulled themselves up the northeast corner, Bonaparte stooping to give her a hand over the stones, which were all three to four feet high, while she fought with her skirts, anxious to reveal as little leg as possible. He asked her repeatedly if she were dizzy or exhausted, and although she was both, she only shook her head, having no breath to spare, and forced herself up another block and then another. After a terrifying glance or two, she found she could not look down, and fixed her eyes on the stone she was climbing. At last, when she thought she could move no more, they reached the little platform at the very top and stood triumphantly four hundred and eighty feet above the ground.

For endless leagues the green belt of the Nile Valley stretched across the yellow ocher desert with edges as sharp as if they had been cut with a knife. To the south lay the procession of smaller pyramids and temples that followed the bank of the river, and to the east, the great city of Cairo half obscured by a purplish haze.

"It is a civilization that goes back five thousand years," he shouted into the wind. "It is the nation coveted and conquered by the ancient Assyrians and Persians and Alexander the Great and Augustus Caesar!"

"And Bonaparte!" she could not help but add, to give the man his due.

He looked at her with appreciation, and impulsively took her hand in his. It was a comradely gesture, Nicole decided. How much more flattering to feel he might really like her, when he had liked so few women, than that he simply wished to add her to his list of mistresses. And what an exhilarating experience to stand at this terrifying height and survey with the eyes of a conqueror this ancient land. It was the exhilaration of strength, of military might, of power—strangely akin to, yet vastly surpassing sexual conquest. Was there some profound truth here about the different dreams of men and women? At least, as she stood watching his face glow with desire—not to possess her as so many men had yearned—but for the conquest of nations, she understood something about the difference between Napoleon and other mortals.

And he was exhilarated too, for on the ride home, sitting unconventionally beside her on the *banc*, he talked more garrulously than ever, deluging her with the whole of Egyptian history. He would stop a second to laugh at his own excitement, and then rush on, hardly giving her a chance to make a comment or ask a question, until, when he had paused to catch his breath, she amazed him by supplying the pharaoh's name he had been searching for. Instead of resenting her little act of competition, he cried out with delight, "But of course I knew you were a clever girl!

Let me test how deep your knowledge really is. Tell me the name of the pharaoh who extended the Egyptian empire to its farthest limits."

"Thutmose III."

"Excellent. But apparently not difficult enough. Tell me what pharaoh tried and failed to build a canal between the Nile and the Red Sea."

"King Necho in the sixth century B.C."

He nodded with a little flush of surprise and pleasure, and sat contemplating her for a long time. "Who was my French predecessor who tried to conquer Egypt?"

"Saint Louis, King of France, on the Seventh Crusade was routed near the mouth of the Nile in 1250 and held for a huge ransom, which was duly paid. But that question was too easy! Ask me something harder."

"You are incredible!" he finally exclaimed. "An exquisite woman with a brain besides! I am overcome by the marvelous luck that has brought us together."

"Oh, I have simply had a lot of time to read since I arrived in Cairo." She had meant to sound modest, but winced when the words came out like a bid for romantic attention.

"Please don't demur. I am well aware you are the daughter of a famous scholar. I myself have read your father's great work."

"His great work—?" she repeated with some shock. Could Bonaparte have actually read the six volumes about Duke Andrew?

"His work about Julius Caesar. And I must say I would have enjoyed enormously the opportunity to dispute certain theses with him."

For the first time she beamed at Napoleon with real liking. How her father would have relished such a debate. And how he would have admired this man, acclaimed him a military genius, a man of destiny. She saw Napoleon through her father's eyes, and suddenly this chance of friendship seemed fateful. If everything else had been equal, wouldn't her father have selected this very man to be her husband? Was there still a possibility she might carve out some sort of happiness with him? But the mere thought made her agitated and afraid.

"Come with me to see Memphis!" he cried. "Surely you don't want to leave Egypt until you have seen the remains of the ancient capital city." With a sudden movement he grabbed her hands and touched them to his lips.

The gesture so embarrassed her she became aware for the first time how exposed they were in the open carriage now re-entering the densely packed streets of Cairo. Obviously, Napoleon had no fear of assassination in this newly conquered city, for he rode in full uniform in a carriage bearing various insignia of his rank. She glanced at the guard, now standing behind them, and saw a pistol strapped to his hip. Did he have muskets too? But with the crowd pressing ever tighter there could be little defense. And now as Napoleon held her hands so ardently, she read hostility on the faces of the Egyptians whose sense of decorum was outraged by such a public display.

"Then later when my army has conquered the south, we can go together to see Luxor and Karnak," he said, watching her face closely.

"Of course, when my husband can accompany us," she murmured, "I will be only too happy. . . ." She knew the answer had been weak, that she should have declared emphatically she would never go off alone with him to Memphis or any other spot on earth.

Napoleon studied her with a penetrating, almost hypnotic gaze, then smiled confidently, no doubt believing he understood her better than she did herself. At the gate of the Citadel, he brushed her lips with his own, and said, "Until tonight." Then he jumped down, and she closed her eyes with a sigh of resignation—and a little thrill of anticipation for the night ahead.

The landau moved on now slowly, at times forced to come to a complete halt in the thick crowd. Beggars harassed her, passersby seemed to stare as though any unveiled woman deserved lewd consideration. By the time she reached the entrance to the palace of Elfi-Bey, she wanted to scream for mercy. Was it guilt and fear of the evening's events, or some fatigue wrought by the hard climb in the sun that had destroyed her nerves?

At last the guard, in the green uniform of the Chasseurs, was raising his arm to help her down. Merely glancing to notice she had never seen him before, she allowed him to support her elbow as she alighted. Just then some beggars jumped before her, and she hesitated while the guard, close behind her, shooed them away. When finally her path was clear, the Chasseur said just at her ear in the English of a cockney Londoner, "Enjoying yerself mightily this afternoon, wasn't you, Duchess!"

But when she whirled around to face him, he had vanished into the crowd.

27

Had she dreamed it? "Who is that man? What is his name?" Nicole shouted to the coachman.

"I cannot say, madame! I never saw him before today."

An Englishman, a cockney, here in Cairo? Addressing her as Duchess! No one had ever called her Duchess—no one except William in those faraway days in the little cell at La Force, where just after their marriage he had teased her, sometimes in the Northumbrian dialect he imitated so well, with her elaborate new titles. But that had been some other lifetime, and no one else, not even Timothy, had ever called her Duchess. No one else knew she had married William—unless he had told.

Mon Dieu, was it possible William had made some acknowledgment of their marriage? The cockney's sarcastic remark had sounded for all the world like a recrimination to an errant wife who had been enjoying herself too much with another man. Was it possible the duke had sent this spy to watch her? Was it possible he was jealous of what looked like a budding affair with Napoleon? Nicole's heart pounded with the long-suppressed hope that William still loved her after all.

But then with a start, she realized the words could have been spoken in scorn and mockery. Falkland's army of agents might have learned somehow of her claim of having married the duke and held her in contempt. Very likely the man had ridden along on the landau to watch Napoleon, and then when the opportunity arose, could not resist a gibe at this woman who made the preposterous boast of a ducal title. Had William allowed the story to be told, allowed vulgar barracks jokes to be made about her? But she could not imagine his relating the story to anyone, casting as it did a dubious light on himself. Then Timothy? Had Timothy bragged of his rescue of the little king, and mentioned in passing, innocently enough, that the woman who sheltered the boy had claimed both a marriage and a child with Falkland? Had the story spread then, embellished in each retelling, until she was notorious?

One thing was certain. She must see nothing more of Napoleon. If a spy could wear the uniform of his elite guard with impunity, there could well be spies inside Elfi-Bey—French soldiers, Egyptian servants, even Ayyam herself! Nicole could not bear to have the story go back to William that she was dallying with Napoleon, hated to think he would hear about their day at the Pyramids and the excited chatter in the carriage and the little kiss at parting. Whether the duke still loved her or not, she did not want him to believe she had sunk to become just one more woman in Napoleon's bed. And if William loved her—oh, dear God, after so long. . . . She could only sit on the edge of her bed and tremble. But it was simply not possible. Life was never so kind.

"Tell him I suffer from the sun. Yes, the climb to the top of the Pyramid has proved too much for me." Nicole hurried Ayyam off to give her regrets for not dining with Napoleon, then climbed quickly into bed in case he should send some physician to treat her.

For several nights her stories of illness went unchallenged, and she grew comfortable and complacent in her self-imposed confinement in the harem of the palace. In any case, it was pleasant to have a long rest, and when she was not dreaming of William, she spent lazy days drinking in the atmosphere of the harem, reading the Arabian Nights—her mind being inclined just now to fairy tales with happy endings—and wondering if the girls had found happiness in these beautiful rooms as concubines of the sultan, or if they all had lived as precariously as Scheherazade.

Indifferently she told Ayyam one evening, "Make up the story yourself tonight. I have no more ideas left."

"Oh, madame, I could never think what to say to the commander in chief!" Ayyam cried with alarm.

"Then tell him I have—contracted some mysterious fever that I wish at all costs not to communicate to him." Nicole shrugged, laughing a little. Likely Bonaparte was no longer interested in her excuses anyway. He knew by now she had no intention of seeing him and would soon send her home. And then somehow on the Mediterranean, the British would intercept her ship. Oh, yes, it had to happen!

But never again, no matter how comfortable her life might be, would she know the luxury of a nightly bath in the wide pool in the harem. Once a score of concubines, guarded by tall eunuchs, had bathed here in this room entirely lined with carved pink alabaster in the warm water that flowed from a fountain made of gold and silver mosaic tiles and filled a pool where she could stand deep in the water or even swim a few strokes to one of the islands meant for reclining. The water was just the right temperature, just warmer than her body but not steamy and enervating; and the experience was always incredibly sensuous, even when she did not allow herself to stare at the empty throne-like seat where the sultan had come to admire the naked women and make his choice for the night.

And now with her hair pinned up on the top of her head, and Ayyam standing patiently beside the water, she soaked and splashed and swam a little, and then peeked idly into the tall brass ewers standing on the edge of the pool.

"They have oils and unguents and perfumes, madame," Ayyam said.

Nicole smelled some, and dabbed the musky fragrances behind her ears rather recklessly, and when she found a lovely light oil with the odor of jasmine, she began, standing just waist-high in the warm water, to massage it into her arms.

She hardly noticed the sudden shuffle of Ayyam's feet and a small noise, a click of the tongue. Nicole glanced up, and catching sight of the maid's look of surprise and chagrin, turned to follow her gaze. There in the pointed archway of the room stood Bonaparte.

"Please, monsieur! You cannot enter!" Nicole cried out.

Ayyam was strangely poised, resigned, and did not move or speak. Of course the commander in chief was just another sultan. Had she ever doubted it?

"Ayyam, my towel, this minute!" Nicole had instinctively covered her breasts with her hands, and then thought to duck into the water. What had he seen? Only her naked back? Or had she been standing in profile as she slowly rubbed the oil into her arms? And then there had surely been a full view for a second when she whirled around!

For his part Napoleon was flushed, even angry. Whatever he had expected, it was not to be met by a woman in a state of panic. His mouth open as if to speak, he stepped backwards, a bit off balance, and soon disappeared behind an alabaster screen.

Clutching the towel around her fearfully as she rose from the water, Nicole hissed at the maid, "See if he has gone, see if he has left the apartment!"

Ayyam scurried to look in an adjoining lounge, and then returned to report, "He is waiting for you just beyond the curtain!"

Frantically Nicole wiped the water from her body and put on the only garment available to her, a filmy silk peignoir that, fastening as it did with a single button at her bosom, she must hold tight in front of her. Both frightened and indignant, she hurried out to face him.

"I beg you to accept my apologies, madame," Napoleon said with an ostentatious bow. "I had no idea I was blundering into the famed bathing pavilion of the harem—though I must say it is a sight no student of the East should forego—and hardly expected to find you—er, in a state of undress." He blushed once again and then smiled at the happy memory, his eyes dropping to the damp garment that clung to her breasts and hips.

"I shall accept your apology at face value," she replied, "but I must demand that you depart immediately. I have said or done nothing to give you leave to trespass in my rooms. Quite the contrary!"

"And what of the message just handed to me?"

"The message of my regret?"

"Hardly regret! While I suspected it had suffered in the translation—for it was indeed too good to be true!—I could only interpret it as an invitation to visit you. To quote the exact words, 'Madame has a feverish wish to communicate with Your Excellency'!"

"Needless to say, that is hardly the message I sent! I told the maid to say I was ill and did not wish to see you at all. Please let me take this opportunity to ask you to cease all invitations to me in the future. And now," she demanded, "you must do me the courtesy of leaving immediately."

For once, Napoleon was not ashamed to defend a losing position. "You have hardly despised my company in the past—at our Turkish feast, at Gizeh, in the carriage! I believe you owe me some explanation."

"I owe you nothing! I have only one thing to say to you and it is that I do not want to be disturbed—insulted actually—by your attentions ever again!"

His jaw falling open in astonishment, Bonaparte turned sharply and stalked away.

Roger raged at her when he came home from Suez. "What perverse simplemindedness has led you to turn down the greatest opportunity we will ever have? And you have made a mortal enemy of him! Do you expect that he can ever forgive you—us? Only by sending you home immediately can I hope to salvage my own position, and preserve the career that has brought me such status and wealth."

Enormously relieved, praying nothing would happen to change his mind, Nicole threw herself into packing her trunks, and early the next morning ran out for a last shopping tour of the Khan el-Khalili bazaar with Ayyam to help carry the packages and assist with the bargaining. For

André she bought a toy camel made of real hide; a small red fez; a bridle with silver fittings for a pony; and a stone scarab or beetle, the symbol of the sun god, said to be three thousand years old. With a grimace, she turned down the withered hand of a mummy in a glass bottle, although no doubt it was the sort of thing an older boy would adore. For Clémence she bought a beautiful Coptic cross; for herself a silver ankh or crosslike symbol of eternal life, and on a sudden impulse, a picturesque evil eye of turquoise, said to have the power to drive off all enemies.

Just as she was examining some bolts of silk brocade, a French corporal slipped into the booth and addressed her furtively, "*Madame la générale*, if I may speak to you alone—if you will only step outside this stall for a moment."

"But why in the world—?"

"Please, madame, you will not regret it, I promise you." His manner was so agitated she believed he must have a message of the greatest importance, and followed him just beyond a partition of hanging carpets. "I am a guard in the dungeons of the Citadel, where we have many prisoners including French soldiers, deserters and the like."

"I hardly think this—"

"Wait, please. One man, who has been undergoing some days of torture, has cried out your name repeatedly in his agony."

"My name! Good Lord, who can he be?"

"If you will only pay a small gratuity. . . ." With a frown she handed him a few piastres. "He has refused to tell us his name, madame, but he has called over and over for 'Nicole,' and said, 'Mistress Nicole is here. She will help me.' It didn't take me long to discover that you were the lady he meant, there being so few French women of position in Cairo."

In her astonishment, Nicole guessed the poor man must be someone from Beaux-Clervaux who had recognized her on the street before he was arrested. "But of course I will try to help him. Why on earth is he being tortured?"

"He is being tortured because he is a spy, an English spy caught inside the Elfi-Bey Palace."

After hurried instructions to Ayyam to take the packages home, Nicole gave the man more money and bade him lead her to the dungeons as fast as possible.

Nothing at La Force or even the Conciergerie could have prepared her for this sweltering, fetid prison. From a narrow corridor she could look into cells so crowded that the half-naked men could only stand and cry pathetically for water, stretching their arms through the bars toward her as she passed. And then at the end of the passageway she heard curious inhuman screams and moans mingled with the creaking of some huge apparatus. After a glimpse of a wooden frame and wheel, she closed her eyes and covered her ears, stumbling on behind the corporal into a tiny cell just next door to the torture chamber where she was shown a man in rags, his arms and legs bleeding profusely, his head thrown back in an unnatural attitude suggesting death. Seizing the corporal's torch herself, she held it low, and turning the victim's face with her hand, saw that it was Timothy Maclure.

"In the name of God," she screamed, "you must halt that infernal machine, or I will call my husband and Bonaparte himself to witness this evil! Here, give the fiends these coins to desist, and bring me a lantern and some bandages and a basin of water. If this man still lives, I will care for him, and if you have killed him, then I must lay out his body. For he has been a dear friend for many years!"

Pressing her ear to Timothy's chest, she discovered with a cry of joy that his heart was still beating. But all the while she knelt beside him, washing and bandaging his wounds and whispering to him, he remained in a deep sleep. After several hours, when there was obviously nothing more she could do, she rose to leave for a few hours, paying the guards large sums to promise they would not put him on the rack again.

Much as she wished to attack both Bonaparte and Roger that evening on the subject of the inhuman conditions in the prison, she realized after she had regained her composure that she dare not reveal any acquaintance with Timothy. She would have to try to protect him herself with more payments of gold. As soon as Roger had gone out for the night, she secretly entered his dressing room and managed to steal a purseful of coins.

Early the next morning she drove back to the dungeons and found that Timothy had not only been carried into a small but private cell well removed from the torture chamber, but was awake and able to raise his head and shoulders as soon as he recognized her. "Oh, my dear mistress, I—" But no more words were discernible when he began to sob, groping blindly for her hands and squeezing them painfully in his extreme distress. Finally he gasped, "God has answered my prayer to see ye before I die!"

"Dear Timothy, you will not die! I will protect you. I have given gold to these men, and if need be, I will apply to Bonaparte himself to spare your life. Please don't weep. The worst is over now."

"Oh, dear mistress—" Then looking around, wide-eyed and frenzied, he whispered, "I should call ye Duchess! Oh, God, I swear I did not know he had really married ye in the sight of God! Ye never told me in so many words. I swear I did not know—until it was too late and the crime had been committed. Don't look so distressed, madam—Duchess, for I have already been punished by God. Punished enough! I only prayed to be allowed to explain to ye before I died, and set right the wrong I did you all!"

"What can you mean, Timothy? I think you are dazed or even a little delirious from your great suffering. Of course you always knew I was married to William. Don't you remember, I had to ask you myself to address me as you were accustomed, because I was embarrassed by the grand styles?"

"No, madam. I believed ye was married to Duchamp, and only meant to address ye as any married woman. I believed ye was really Duchamp's legal wife, though ye dreamed of leaving him and throwing yerself at the duke. It seemed no crime at all when I first told His Grace you was madly in love with Duchamp and had no wish to leave yer husband or ever see His Grace again, even though ye was proud and willing to help save the King of France. When the duke was so terrible upset and asked me so many times to repeat the exact words ye had used, I almost lost my resolution. But my mind was made up, and I did not falter. When he gave me a long letter to carry back to ye, I destroyed that as I had destroyed the letter ye sent to him."

Nicole had sat aghast through this recital, not knowing whether to think the man mad or to cry out in violent anger. At last she began slowly, "I can't believe what you are telling me. . . ."

"Well, 'tis true, and I have paid my penalty, God knows!"

"Then when William came to my house to collect Léon, he believed I had refused to go with him . . . ?"

"Aye. I had told ye one departure time, and then brought him early, during yer party, when I knew you would hardly be able to accompany us."

"But didn't he wonder why I was so terribly upset, why I begged him to wait till the morning?"

"He believed ye was crying out of shame to face him, and out of sadness at parting with the poor king."

"But what of André, his son? Even if Duke William hated me, he should have wanted—"

"Oh, but I had told him yer child had been fathered by Duchamp!"

"Oh, Timothy! It was an unholy treachery!" she cried in a hollow voice.

He answered with choking sobs, and she could only puzzle over the words he was trying to speak. Someone had died, he wailed over and over, but she could not make out the name.

"Who, Timothy? Tell me clearly!"

He finally took a deep breath and said, "My Robbie is dead! Oh, mistress, it was a judgment on me! It was God's punishment for the wrong I did His Grace and yerself and yer little boy!"

Timothy told her that Robbie had been on board a ship in the Mediterranean, the duke having bought him a commission in the navy—"He was nineteen, can ye believe it, madam?"—when he was taken ill at sea a month ago, and the captain kindly brought him to Naples. Both Timothy and the duke had been able to be present at his deathbed. "His Grace took on almost as bad as I did! By this death, Duchess, I knew that God Almighty meant to punish me. I bared my soul to His Grace, telling him of all my lies and trickery, and after some days of bitterness and brooding, he found it in his heart to forgive me. And now I can only pray that you will do the same!"

"But why would you want to destroy the lives of three people? I will never understand!"

"Oh, mistress, I believed yer child was only another bastard. Knowing how partial the duke was to ye, and how ye was a lady of good birth, I feared ye would manage to wheedle him into a marriage, or at least press a claim on him to legitimatize yer boy."

"But why would you care whether—?"

"Because I feared it would deprive Robbie, or even disinherit him altogether."

"Deprive Robbie—! I don't understand!"

"Deprive Robbie of his fair share! Or even all! I dreamed that if the duke should die without a legal heir, he would will everything to Robbie, loving him, admiring him, as he did. I dared to dream he would even leave him the title itself!"

"Timothy, do you mean Robbie was William's son?" she asked with profound shock.

"Gawblimy, mistress! Didn't ye know? Could ye even look at the boy and not recognize the duke had fathered him? Could ye live two years at Langmuir and not learn it? There was never any secret. Everybody knows for miles around!"

"But nobody ever told me . . . although perhaps. . . ." Suddenly she understood Annie's words on her deathbed, and remembered Kate's barbed remarks. How stupid she had been not to guess the truth, to see Robbie's resemblance to William and even to little André!

Dabbing his eyes, Timothy told how the duke had asked him to marry Annie, a young, pregnant shepherdess, and how he had readily agreed. "She was the most beautiful thing I ever seen, even six months gone—all dark auburn locks and skin as glowed like a pearl. Of course she had no feeling for me at first except gratitude, which she poured out till I was all too embarrassed and bade her stop. But in a few months, when she realized the duke meant to leave her alone for her own sake, the good Lord allowed her to feel real love for me, and we were blessed with trust and happiness until the day she died. Of course all the other bairn is my own, as any fool can tell with a single glance!" he laughed, happy for a moment in the recollection of his other children.

"But, Timothy, I don't understand how you could go ahead with your deceitful plan after you realized the duke and I were really married and our child legitimate?"

"But I never found out until it was too late, until Robbie was dead and I confessed to Duke William and then he told me the true magnitude of my crime."

"But didn't you read the letter I wrote Duke William before you destroyed it? It clearly stated he was my lawful husband."

"Not *lawful*, madam. 'True husband' was what ye called him. I took the words to have a sly purpose. Ye was an ambitious mistress seeking to coax yer lover into marriage, was what I thought. Neither the duke nor yerself ever told me ye was married in the sight of God, him because he feared to endanger ye if it got out, I now understand, and yerself because ye could not imagine I did not already know."

She sat beside him on the floor, staring down pensively at her folded hands. "How can I ever tell you the unhappiness you have wrought . . . ?" she murmured. "Oh, Timothy, I pray I can find it in my heart to forgive you." She took his hand and smiled at him sadly. "God knows you have already suffered so much. Your real crime was loving Robbie too well!" When she had managed a comforting smile, she said, "But surely you did not endanger your life to come to Egypt simply to beg my forgiveness."

"I came here at the express wish of your husband, Duke William, to take you to him in Naples. Then he will sail with you to Bordeaux to collect your child, and establish you as his wedded wife in London before he returns to conduct the war against Bonaparte."

After they had discussed these plans for a long while, she remembered to ask him what had happened to little Léon, about whom she had heard nothing since the night he left her house.

Timothy answered that the boy's health remained poor, often perilous. "But of course 'tis a miracle he is even alive, is it not, madam?" He was kept in a remote country house on the south Devon coast, chosen for its unusually mild climate, where visitors were not encouraged because they overstimulated the king and brought increased risk of assassination. His Grace generously paid the rent on the mansion, and maintained there as the boy's guardians his old friends, the Marquis and Marquise de Vaucroze—a happy arrangement for everyone, although *madame la marquise* was said to chafe at the extreme isolation of the site.

Nicole's brain whirled with schemes to rescue Timothy from the prison and to make their way from Cairo to the sea. She cursed herself for not bringing more jewelry with her from France, for now she could have used every single piece of gold. Each night she searched Roger's rooms, with less and less success, as he came to believe the servants were stealing from him. Finally she decided that she must take the risk of entering Bonaparte's own quarters in her search for objects of value. Perhaps Ayyam and Fawzi would serve as her lookouts for a share of the proceeds.

Again one morning, as she returned to the prison to see Timothy, she was met by a line of outstretched palms and had to sacrifice part of the gold she was hoarding. Proceeding on to Timothy's cell, she was surprised to find the door unlocked and ajar. Could they have taken him back to the torture chamber? Surely not, after all the money she had paid! But where else could he be? Her heart pounded as she ran to find the captain of the guard. He told her that he had been ordered late last night to let Timothy go. General Duchamp himself had come to the prison and given the command.

Driving back to the palace in a state of alarm, she realized that Roger could only have had the most sinister motives. Of course he must have found out about Timothy's relationship to herself. Why else would he interest himself enough to go to the prison in the middle of the night? What else did he know? She must be extremely careful now of everything she said and did.

But even before she had reached the harem in Elfi-Bey, she was met by a procession of soldiers and servants carrying out her luggage to a waiting coach. Her angry questions went unanswered, and Ayyam, running along beside the soldiers wringing her hands, could only tell her that these men had suddenly entered the harem and ordered her to throw every possession of Madame's into her trunks as fast as possible. "Oh, my poor mistress, you are being sent away against your will!"

Hardly knowing whether she should protest or acquiesce, Nicole thanked Ayyam for her devoted care and assured her she left eagerly; but when a burly soldier gripped her arm and pulled her toward the carriage, she resisted him angrily and managed to break away. Then out of nowhere, Roger stood across her path, blocking the archway to the street.

"Must you evict me so rudely that I cannot even fetch my hat and cloak! Not that I am sorry to depart, Roger—understand that!" she cried. She was torn by a desire, on the one hand, to unburden herself of the bitter hatred she felt for him, and fear, on the other, of his power to hurt Timothy or prevent her own escape. She must not let him goad her into some outburst, for he might well be inspired to revenge himself by keeping her captive.

With a wicked grin, he answered sarcastically, "But I am only hastening your departure out of mercy, before the commander in chief imprisons you for treason. Napoleon and I have followed your revealing conversations in the dungeon with the greatest interest!"

"What have you done with Timothy?" she asked numbly.

"Oh, you needn't worry, for he is quite safe. We are carrying him back to Naples, where just offshore he will be allowed to escape from our ship, thinking he has done so by his own ingenuity. Then he will disclose certain planted information to his master, the Duke of Falkland, whose devotion to you made such a touching story! I must not indulge myself in the luxury of telling you how you will be used to destroy your own lover—the man you call your—husband!" he spat venomously. "After all, there may still be British spies in our midst, and we would not want such a brilliant plan to go awry."

For a moment she stood frozen with terror, desperately wanting to pry some fact from him that could help William, wanting to discover there was no great danger after all, wanting even to implore him to change his mind. Dear God, he must not set some devious trap for William! But of course she was quite irrational. He could not hurt the duke. Falkland held the reins of power, not Roger. Nothing Roger could do could touch him. She must not lose her nerve.

Pulling herself up to her full height, trying not to look at him, she walked proudly to the steps of the carriage and climbed in. But when she tried to pull the door shut, he jumped forward and held it open while he poured forth a stream of lewd insults strangely mingled with pathetic entreaties to stay with him after all. Only after he saw that she was sobbing hysterically did he burst into crazed laughter and slam the door shut with all his strength.

28

A hundred feet above her head, the cannons of the fortress looked down on the small French frigate, on which she was the only passenger. These massive seawalls were known as the strongest fortifications in Europe, but the French tricolor flew now above Fort St. Angelo, at the mouth of the Grand Harbor of Valletta, capital city of the island of Malta.

Only last night the captain of her ship had told her he carried orders from Bonaparte himself to deliver her to the commandant of Malta. At sunrise this morning she had gone up on deck to await the sighting of the tiny island, and had clutched the rail with eager anticipation as the brown speck gradually grew larger and larger and she could finally see the great ramparts and the hilly city of terraced houses crowned by a palace and cathedral of mellow golden stones.

How delighted she would be to set foot on land again! The voyage from Alexandria had lasted twice as long as expected. Just out of port a violent storm had sheared off the mainmast, and for a week, while repairs were being made, the ship had stood off the coast of Africa baking in the sun. For Nicole each day was more suspenseful than the last, for she could not believe that the British navy would not capture the frigate. Disabled in the open sea in good sailing weather, it could hardly have been more exposed, yet no enemy ship came near. Surely the sea power of the British was greatly exaggerated—or Falkland had never intended to intercept her ship at all. Dear God, had Timothy lied to her again, spinning a fine tale so that she would risk her life to save him? Had she been his poor dupe once again? But perhaps the frigate had simply managed to slip across the Mediterranean undetected. She must not lose heart. Here on this small island, she would surely attract the attention of whatever spies the British might have, she told herself hopefully, as the ship dropped anchor in the crowded harbor.

Bonaparte had seized Malta only a few months ago on his way to Egypt from its traditional rulers, the Knights Hospitallers of St. John of Jerusalem. This monastic order had been founded to provide care for pilgrims during the Crusades, but in the next few centuries it came to be comprised of sons of the most noble families in Europe. After obtaining the island of Malta—for the rent payment of one falcon a year to the Emperor of the Holy Roman Empire—the order used this advantageous position to grow fabulously rich preying upon Turkish shipping. The brotherhood was sometimes called the Knights of the Seven Languages, or Langues, and each Langue—Aragon, Castile, Auvergne, Provence, France, Bavaria, and Italy—had its own luxurious *auberge* or hostel in Valletta. For centuries the different nationalities had lived in harmony; but early this year the French knights, torn by the unrest in their homeland, had conspired with Bonaparte to deliver the island to him. The reaction of the native Maltese, who had prospered under the Knights, had been violent. They fought their invaders so strenuously that Napoleon had had to leave behind six thousand much-needed troops to control the island.

Nicole was escorted to her new quarters in the baroque Palace of the Grand Masters, where she had a chance to explore the tapestry chamber, the throne room, the great collection of suits of armor, and even the library filled with ancient scrolls, before she was called to dine with the commandant, General Vaubois. During his impatient attempts at conversation, Nicole gathered that he regarded her as an annoying distraction in his struggle to keep order on the island. And apparently he had been given no explanation whatsoever of her presence, merely being instructed "to guard her with appropriate means."

"Alas, madame," he said irritably, "I can offer you no more safety than the rest of us enjoy. Revolt seethes at the very gates of this palace, and no Frenchman dare venture alone into the interior of the island." Nicole smiled a little to herself as she realized that Vaubois had interpreted his orders to mean she was a guest to be protected, not a prisoner to be confined.

The next morning, finding indeed that she was quite free to come and go, she ran down the long flights of steps to the harbor, desperately hoping to hire a fishing boat to carry her to Naples. But as soon as she tried to speak to any Maltese, she was answered by angry words in an incomprehensible language that sounded more like Arabic than anything else. Slowly she climbed back up to the palace. There seemed little chance of persuading anyone to help her, and probably she did not have enough gold left anyway. William was going to have to find her—if he would. There was nothing to do but wait.

One day, thinking innocently that she would enjoy a walk in the warm fall air, she idly selected a tangerine-colored frock with parasol to match. The dress was of high Parisian style, although her breasts were quite decently covered and only a pretty oval of shoulders and chest could be seen. For some reason there were few servants in the palace, and she had no maid at all to help her, but she rather enjoyed arranging her own hair in a knot on the top of her head, from which she made fall a cascade of little curls.

Strolling down a narrow street, she peeked into the open door of one of the severe narrow houses and saw a cool courtyard with tiny fountain and potted flowers, which she gazed at wistfully. But at the same moment a housewife ran out, yelling oaths she could not understand and hitting at her with her broom. Nicole was forced to jump away, stumbling in her surprise on the steps of the steep descent.

Then immediately a little group of Maltese gathered to pursue her down the steps, and their cries brought others out of their doors, until some fifty people blocked the street above her and another group cut her off below. Hardly able to believe her eyes, Nicole stood terrified like an animal at bay, instinctively holding her open parasol before her as a shield.

There was a sudden silence, and then a shout or two, and several men hurled stones at her, hitting her parasol and skirt and her bare shoulder. Fearing for her life, she suddenly recognized just across the narrow street the porch of a church. *Dear God, let the door be unlocked!* Tripping on the cobblestones, almost falling over a low step, she flung herself on the door, which miraculously pulled open.

Perhaps another stone or two hit her before she was safely inside, she could not be sure. As she stood panting for breath, her hand on her pounding heart, she could feel blood trickle down her cheek and she dabbed at it with a handkerchief. Her eyes had not yet become accustomed to the dark interior and she could see nothing.

"Hardly grateful for our civilizing presence, is they, mademoiselle?" said some female voice in French just at her elbow.

"*Ma foi!*" exclaimed Nicole, thinking she would die of heart failure. "How you frightened me!" Then she asked shyly, just beginning to make out a garishly dressed woman, "Did they chase you in here too?"

"Not a half hour ago, and I don't think I'll bother to venture forth till nightfall."

"But why are they so vengeful toward innocent women? I can understand that they might feel hostility for our soldiers who oppress them."

"Oh, they hate all French—the more with each passing day. Ain't Bonaparte stolen the gold treasures out of every one of their precious churches to take home to France? And our troops, having little discipline, makes too free with all their women. Only last week a young Maltese girl is said to have thrown herself to her death off the seawall rather than submit to the drunken attentions of a few of our heroic soldiers. You'd think the native folk would want to pin a medal on those of us as is here to take care of the —romantic needs of our troops, now wouldn't you, mademoiselle? But they don't. A puritanical lot, the Maltese is! The fact is they attacked you in the street because they thought you was a whore—like me!"

"Dear heaven!" Nicole gasped. "But why on earth? What did I do?"

"Well, for one reason, you is got up like the king's own tart! Take my advice and buy yourself one of the black *faldettas* the Maltese women wear if you want to go about the town undisturbed. And for another, that is the only kind of Frenchwoman that is here."

"But how terrible! Why didn't someone warn me before I went out alone?" Nicole cried, as she collapsed into a choir stall.

"*Ta ta ta*, you needn't take on so outraged! After all, we all know why you're here, and it ain't to open a nunnery!"

"Good grief, what can you mean!"

"Everyone knows you're Bonaparte's special baggage!"

"But it's not true!" Nicole cried.

"*Tiens!* The men that came from Cairo say it was common knowledge. And they say he comes here soon. That's why he has sent you on ahead to wait for him."

"Bonaparte coming here—! That's hardly likely when he wants nothing so much as to conquer India!" Nicole answered indignantly.

"India? Not now, my dear, not after his army has been defeated in Syria!"

"What do you mean? What have you heard?"

"The news was in on the last ship. His army was beaten before Acre, and then an outbreak of plague nearly finished off the rest of the troops. He will soon abandon Egypt and come here to put down this revolt so that he can say back home he has made at least one permanent conquest."

A kindly priest had finally helped both women escape out a back door, and Nicole ran back to the palace vowing that she would never again go forth in Valletta in French clothes. With some difficulty she persuaded a servant to buy the all-black Maltese attire for her, but when she spread out on her bed the dress and hose and cumbersome *faldetta*, a long black silk cape with a hood so stiffened it arched wide and deep over the woman's head, she only stared at them with distaste. Certainly these mourning weeds would do little to elevate her spirits!

Nicole had been thrown into a deep depression by the whore's disclosures. Could there be some truth to the story that Bonaparte had ordered her sent ahead to Malta for his own purposes. Now she remembered that she had heard something about reversals in Syria before she left Egypt, but had paid little attention. Had Roger known that Napoleon intended to hurry to Malta before Roger sent her away? Surely Bonaparte would be little inclined to waste time on such a reluctant woman, Nicole told herself. But then a new idea struck her. Could Roger have some fiendish plan to link her sexually with Bonaparte again in order to destroy William's love? For a few days she lay in her room unwilling even to go to the dining room, for she found Vaubois's occasional bold stares distressing now that she understood what was going through his mind. As always, the palace servants were rude and uncooperative, and she could hardly bear the thought of another trip into the town. She had not felt so friendless since her days in the Conciergerie. Yes, it was almost as bad, and there was no young officer with payments of gold to save her this time. Was she still foolish enough to dream that William meant to come? Once again she was waiting day in and day out—and nothing happened.

One morning she arose, told herself firmly that she must pull herself out of her despondency, and put on the black outfit with the intention of walking in the town. The whore had said such clothes would protect her, and she must try them, for otherwise she would surely go crazy locked up in this room.

But when she put on the plain black dress and the *faldetta* and looked at herself in the mirror, she had to laugh aloud. Her blond curls tumbling over this somber outfit only made her look ridiculous. No native Maltese woman had blond hair, and they wore only severe hairstyles that were a far cry from her frivolous coiffure, suggesting as it did all the sins of Paris.

She took off the *faldetta* and pulled back her hair in a single tight braid, then wound the braid at the back of her neck and pinned it. Still some ringlets escaped at her hairline, but she slicked them down with pomade, which also helped to darken her hair. When she put the *faldetta* back on, she decided she might at least be able to go about the city unnoticed.

She set out timorously, but within an hour was overwhelmed by the miracle her black clothes had worked. The Maltese had become friendly and kind, greeting her everywhere with smiles and bows. For a while she believed she was actually passing for a native, until she realized they were making an effort to talk to her in Italian and even occasionally in French.

After a few days of the same treatment, she knew they were not fooled as to her true nationality but simply took her, from her choice of their dress, to be a woman of virtue and goodwill.

One afternoon sitting on a terrace overlooking the harbor, she was observing, at their invitation, a group of Maltese women making the local lace with its unique wheat-kernel pattern. Everyone had watched with casual interest as a French bark slowly entered the harbor and dropped anchor. Now Nicole noticed that a boat had started ashore from the merchantman, but she paid little more attention until one of the women pointed to a small child among its passengers. Suddenly Nicole stood up. The little boy had tousled light brown hair, and he could hardly be more than five or six. Then she cried out, and calling delighted words they could not understand to her Maltese friends, ran down the steps to the water's edge.

She had barely glimpsed the child's face, and then only from a distance, but somehow she was sure. "André!" she cried, and the boy, just setting foot on the dock, turned toward her with a happy, expectant look on his face; but as she ran toward him, his expression clouded with fear. For a moment she could not imagine what had upset him, but then she laughed with relief, and pushed back the *faldetta*. He had not been able to recognize her. At last he called, *"Maman!"* and she picked him up and embraced him with great joy.

Weeping and laughing at the same time, Nicole could hardly stop hugging the boy, pausing only long enough to exclaim at how tall he had grown or how his hair had darkened or how he now had freckles on his light skin that looked so particularly Scottish. When she thought to question the captain of the merchantman, he could only tell her the boy's passage had been bought at Bordeaux by some unknown person, and that André had been put on board alone, soon becoming a great pet of all the passengers and crew. Though hardly satisfied by this sketchy information, she gaily squeezed André once again, and they climbed to the palace, where she selected for him the little room next to her own.

How much more fun it was to tour the palace and *auberges* and the whole town, seeing them now through the child's eyes. André, who had just passed his fifth birthday, loved the hall full of the knights' armor; the sailors with black hats and red sashes and the little gondola-like boats, called *dghaisas*, that had eyes painted on their bows; the limestone caves, some with human bones, beneath the city that were said to run the whole length of the island; the goats kept by everyone for milk because there were no cows on Malta; and the donkeys that pulled little carts. She even grew bold enough to take a picnic lunch and go into the countryside to visit a village *festa* with flags and firecrackers; or a prehistoric ruin that might have been inhabited by the Cyclopes, the race of giants with one eye in the center of their foreheads who were said to have first settled Malta; or the bay where Saint Paul had been shipwrecked seventeen hundred years before.

But as happy as she was made by André's presence, she had understood almost from the day of his arrival what Roger's plan must be. By sending the boy whom he now knew to be the duke's son to join her, he had baited the trap for Falkland. Perhaps with a story of the boy's grave illness or of danger from the revolt of the islanders, he would entice the duke to come to this fortress island.

She took to inquiring for any news of ships, French or British, on the Mediterranean, and often sat atop the ramparts, anxiously searching the horizon, while André might observe the fishermen or play astride a cannon. If William took the bait, Roger would try to destroy him with naval power or the batteries of Fort St. Angelo. Nicole shivered as she imagined seeing William's ship blown to bits before her eyes by these very cannons. But sometimes she trembled with a more ancient fear. How deluded she could well be! What real evidence did she have that William meant to come? How many times before had she futilely dreamed he would save her?

The same evening that a French brigantine had come into the harbor, General Vaubois sent a formal message asking her to grant him an audience at her earliest convenience. She sent back word that he might come immediately; and when he had entered her little salon, he bowed gravely and asked if the child could be taken away by servants.

"Pray relieve my anxiety as fast as possible, *mon général,* for you have quite distressed me!" she exclaimed as soon as André had left.

"*Chére madame,* it gives me great pain to have to inform you that your husband, General Roger Duchamp de Clervaux, has—been killed."

Nicole gasped, then sensing some strange reticence on the part of the general asked, "Killed? In battle, at Acre?"

"Alas, no. He fell victim to the attack of a band of—ah, robbers late one night in the bazaar in Cairo."

Nicole awoke at dawn to the sound of running feet in the corridors of the palace, where the servants were crying excited words that she could not understand. She slipped out of bed, put on a wrapper, and ran barefoot across the cold tile floor. In the hall she met a maid who pointed through a window at the silver-gray ocean. There silhouetted against the rising sun were a dozen tall ships with sails already furled, hove to and waiting on the calm sea.

"Who are they?" Nicole cried, but the maid only shook her head at her inability to speak French. "Who are they? Are they French or British?" Nicole called frantically at everyone she saw as she ran down the corridor, and finally grabbed hold of a manservant she knew could speak a little French. "Who is it? Is it Bonaparte?"

"*Mais non, madame!* It is the British! It is Admiral Nelson himself!" he exclaimed, joyful at the thought of liberation from the French.

Dear God, could it be William at last? If these were truly Nelson's ships, was William aboard, or were they merely combat vessels expecting to seize Malta in a violent battle? Why should William want to expose himself to the risk of death when he could stay safely behind in Naples? Of course he would have to consider the responsibilities he bore and could not expose himself capriciously to death. It was Nelson's job to conquer Malta. And in due course, after the British victory, she could apply to see her husband—if she had the nerve to announce such a relationship—in Naples.

For two days she hardly took her eyes off the ships, which were content to patrol the coast. In the town, every Maltese expressed joy at possible deliverance from the French, and excitement built as each maneuver of the ships was reported. The British were landing arms and supplies to rebels on the other side of Malta and the small neighboring islands, and were said to be waiting only for the Maltese to seize Fort St. Angelo before they entered the harbor. Or perhaps they were waiting for the cover of night, or reinforcements, or, some said, Bonaparte's own convoy from Egypt, which they would defeat at sea and then take Valletta without having to fire a shot.

But the second afternoon when Nicole walked out to watch the patrolling ships from the wide terrace of the palace, she clutched her light shawl around her in the biting northeasterly wind and finally had to retreat indoors. The weather had turned surprisingly cold and blustery for February in this subtropic land, and Nicole soon heard that a *gregale* was making up, the same ferocious winter wind that had shipwrecked Saint Paul's ship so long ago.

She could think only of the peril to the British as the winds beat harder throughout the day. By her own observations the ships had vanished; and when desperate curiosity drove her forth, clutching the *faldetta* tightly around her, creeping along the walls of buildings for fear of being knocked down by the gale, she learned from her Maltese friends that the location of the little fleet was unknown. Could they have taken refuge in some sheltered harbor in rebel territory? Or would they have tried to outrun the storm, and abandoned Malta? Or had they already suffered serious damage and even destruction? Many Maltese were crowding into churches to pray for the safety of their deliverers. Impulsively, Nicole entered the same little church that had given her sanctuary and fell to her knees with a prayer for the safety of the man who was her husband and the father of her child.

All the long night the *gregale* ripped at the city. Nicole lay awake listening to the dismal howling of the wind and the frightening sounds of breaking glass, flying tiles, and crashing trees. Was William riding out this storm somewhere nearby? Was he listening to the same screeching wind? She wished she could feel some special intuition, as those who loved deeply were said to be able to do. But searching her heart she could find only a forlorn dread. Perhaps it had been too long. Or perhaps their love was only her demented dream.

She dozed for an hour just before dawn, and then awoke with a start at the first rays of light. The wind had stopped. The air was still, and the reddish light of dawn already promised a warm, sunny day.

When she could see nothing from her bedroom window, she quickly slipped into one of the stark black dresses, brushed her loose hair a few strokes, grabbed a *faldetta* for warmth, and ran out on the terrace of the palace. There before her eyes were the twelve ships lined up just beyond the seawalls, maneuvering to enter the Grand Harbor. In minutes the flagship with some fifty broadside guns would be abreast of Fort St. Angelo.

Nicole exclaimed with joy at their safe return, then shuddered as soon as she realized the fort would surely open fire. Had the fleet survived the storm only to be destroyed now before her eyes? Of course the harbor fortifications were impregnable—they had been tested again and again through the centuries. The only hope was that the French cannons would hold their fire. The island was torn by rebellion, and General Vaubois would know he could not hold out long, but surely he would have to put up some resistance. To let Admiral Nelson sail into the Grand Harbor without firing a shot would be an ignominious surrender.

A dozen servants stood on the porch beside her, and she saw that every terrace of the city was lined with spectators, all watching breathlessly as the ships sailed boldly on. Was there some flurry of activity just below her in the fort? She clutched the parapet, bending over as far as she could. *Dear God, soldiers were loading the cannons and preparing to blow the ships sky high.* She put her hands over her ears and closed her eyes, thinking she would surely die when she heard the blast. But then a thunderous cheer burst from the whole of Valletta. Nicole opened her eyes and saw that the tricolor was being lowered on the staff of the fort, and the white flag of surrender run up.

The city went mad, and the jubilant Maltese began to push down the ramps to the water's edge. Hardly realizing what she was doing, Nicole ran into André's chamber, shook the sleeping boy until he woke up, and then with only a robe around his shoulders, carried him out into the crowded street. Vaguely, numbly, she imagined that she must try to get some word to Admiral Nelson. Of course William would not be on board. Now at last at the moment of reckoning, she was certain he would not have risked death in this daring challenge to the French.

Stumbling along, her back breaking with the heavy child, she was buried for a few minutes so deep in the mass of people that she feared for André's safety and her own. Then as they rounded a bend in the ramp, she was shoved against the railing of the terrace, and could see quite clearly that a boat had set out from Nelson's ship. Four sailors were working the oars, and two men rode as passengers. One officer wore a great bicorne hat heavily decorated with gold, and must surely be Admiral Nelson himself. The other passenger beside him was bareheaded. Nicole could see that he had black hair and was larger, taller, than the admiral.

Could it be William? Her heart raced with hope, even conviction. He had placed his hand above his eyes to shield them as he squinted into the crowd, as though hoping to recognize someone. If only he would lower his hand! The boat was coming closer. Oh, Lord, she knew that strong jaw, the finely sculpted nose, the long black hair tied at his neck. And then he removed his hand, and she saw the long scar across his forehead and the dark eyes she knew so well. *Mon Dieu,* it was truly William!

Feverishly, she pushed on down the ramp. If only she could get through this last tangled mass at the entrance of the dock. But in the minutes she had to wait, she was filled with a new kind of panic. How strange and unseemly, how appalling, she would look to this man—this total stranger—how untidy her hair, how unflattering the harsh garments. What in the world would William think of her—the Duchess of Falkland indeed!—trying to masquerade in black peasant garb with blond curls tumbling over her shoulders? And the child! He was only wearing his nightclothes, his hair uncombed. How she had wanted William to appreciate the boy's fine aristocratic features and close resemblance to himself. Surely she must go back to the palace and dress herself and André appropriately before she greeted the duke—received him—received him properly in her little gilt salon in the palace.

But there was no possible chance of retreat in this surging throng. She would be lucky not to be driven over the edge into the harbor. Almost against her own will, ice cold with fear, she slowly squeezed through the crowd until she could reach out and touch the ship's boat as it came against the dock.

And then as in a dream she raised her arm and cried his name, and the tall, dark man turned to look at her. She thought her heart would burst as she saw the expression of intense relief and joy on that face she loved so well.

Could it really be happening after all these years? He was leaping onto the dock and pushing toward her, and now she could feel his hard cheek against hers. *Oh, God, was it really happening, or was it only one more wishful dream?* He was clutching the child and herself to him now, desperately, and she was struggling to untangle her own arm in this cheering, shoving pack and wrap it around him. He was kissing the boy and saying some words she could not catch—yes, he was calling the poor confused, sleepy child, "My dear son, Andrew." And then William stared at her with his unforgettable dark eyes, and pressed his lips passionately on hers.